Wolf

Hunt

A Grayson Wolf Mystery # 2

Jack ⚡ Kolbë

Cover & graphics by Mangled Wolfang

BadDogBooks

ISBN- 9781093958492

DEDICATION

Stand and Fight!

Choose to live a life free from
encumbrances by family,
friends, neighbors and the
puritanical fascist bullies hiding
in plain sight attempting to
inculcate unearned guilt through
shaming and intimidating you to think
like them, act like them and
sink in collectivist sewers with them.

Stand and Fight!

CONTENTS

Chapter 1

Retired

"Good evening book lovers. I'm Carolyn Mayor welcoming you once again to another edition of Title Page Live, with the inside scoop on the latest and greatest books, authors and literary trends. Title Page Live is produced by Objective Arts Media, broadcast locally and globally via Sirius Radio.

"And what a special treat we have for you this week. For the second time this year I'm talking with Grayson Wolf, well-known author of over a dozen exposes about the underbelly of the world of business, politics and entertainment.

"Welcome back to the show, Wolf, and a Merry Christmas."

"Merry Christmas to you, Carolyn. Thank you for inviting me to your show; always a pleasure to appear on Title Page Live. I understand congratulations are in order—as of December first, your show is the most popular literary broadcast in North America."

"Over three million listeners and growing," Carolyn said. "That puts us in the top ten; in no small part due to interviewing the most exciting contemporary authors such as yourself. Which brings us to what is a most unexpected shift in literary direction for Grayson Wolf since we spoke back in the summer. You currently have two books, both bestsellers, neither of them your trademark fictional-nonfiction exposes. Has Grayson Wolf retired from hunting down the bad and exposing the ugly hidden away from the light of day? And if so, why?"

"The short answer is, yes. I'm done with mucking around the endless tons of mud and effluent produced by our not so esteemed corporate and political leaders. I've been up to my neck in social waste for over a decade and it's time to stop before I can't wash the stink off my skin and out of my head. Others are welcome to immerse themselves up to their necks in sludge if so inclined; plenty of it everywhere to keep dedicated muckrakers busy for years to come."

"Having seen too much of that muck you speak of in my own lifetime, I certainly can appreciate you wanting to step back from wading deeper into the social mire," Carolyn agreed. "I am, however, happy about you continuing to write, with great success, I might add. You've written two Tara Mason novels: *Underwater* and *Bulldozed*, both top sellers. How did these stories come about?"

"By mid-summer I knew that my muckraking career was over," Wolf said. "Thinking about what I would do next, I naturally thought about what I was good at doing, the obvious answer being writing. But writing what? I spent an evening ticking off a dozen possibilities— science fiction, fantasy and so forth—becoming increasingly frustrated. Then I remembered what my English professor told me when I asked him why I got a C- on a fictional work I submitted. He said, write about what you know."

"But your Tara Mason isn't any kind of muckraker," Carolyn said. "Quite the opposite, in fact."

"It's true that Tara Mason is not insinuating herself into people's lives and affairs like muckraker Grayson Wolf," Wolf agreed. "She is, however, an insurance claims investigator who, like Grayson Wolf, runs into all kinds of people in the course of her job, some of whom are not the most upstanding citizens and others who are downright nefarious."

"Tara Mason interacting with the good, bad and ugly, just like Grayson Wolf in his real life job," Carolyn replied. "Thus you are writing about what you know, and know an awful lot about."

"I've published two and finishing a third in the series," Wolf said. "I'm having a lot of fun writing and look forward to writing many more Mason novels."

"After your interview back in March, you published *Media's Useful Idiots—Pro-Regressives At Work*," Carolyn said. "That expose has made many in the news industry very unhappy. Exposing political biases and sweet-heart deals between media moguls and politicians has earned you some powerful enemies; millions of enlightened readers, too, of course. Do you think you'll ever dip your toe back into the murky pool of investigative nonfiction again?"

"One should never say never," Wolf replied. "I still have one more muckraking fictional non-fiction expose coming out, but I'm heavily invested in never."

"Would you share its title?"

"California's Soviet Valley: Growing The Anti-American Dream," Wolf said. "It's an expose about the increasing censorship and suppression of views contrary to the current politically correct orthodoxy of corporate leaders and the willingness of technology companies to accommodate dictatorships and undermining American values."

"I assume there will be names, deals and collusion exposed?" Carolyn said.

"The good, the bad, and I'm sad to say, a lot of the really ugly," Wolf replied.

"I know I'm speaking for millions of your fans when I say I'm looking forward to reading the last Grayson Wolf fictional non-fiction expose and sad, too," Carolyn said. "What if your retirement to writing fiction begins to wane?"

"If I need a break from fiction, there's lots to keep me busy at the Center for Individual Rights. As you know, Carolyn, I'm CIR's president and we're busier than ever with all the legal cases we're handling, not to mention the increasing interest in our work from around the country and internationally. As Ann Shirley, the protagonist of Anne of Green Gables said, there's lot of scope for the imagination working in the heart of CIR. I have lots of ideas about new and interesting characters for a dozen different kinds of fictional novels."

"Joan Galt, defender extraordinaire of individual rights," Carolyn quipped.

"I like it," Wolf said. "My kind of woman and my kind of hero."

"Tara Mason is a very positive role model," Carolyn said. "Do you see all your protagonists as solid as she is?"

"If you mean by solid that Tara is a woman who won't evade reality as she strives to make the right choices whether in her personal or professional life, then yes, that is the only type of protagonist I'm interested in offering to my readers," Wolf explained. "I hate anti-heroes. The libraries and entertainment channels are choked with a thousand versions of the flawed, predictable anti-hero; if that's what folks want to read about or watch on their TVs, so be it."

"Editors and publishers I've interviewed all tell me that the anti-hero books sell the most," Carolyn replied.

"The only editors and publishers I want handling my books have the same level of integrity and positive sense of life as my protagonists," Wolf retorted. "I've just emerged from wading in the muck after ten years. I have absolutely no interest of dipping any protagonist I write about into sewage so that he or she will stink up a story to satisfy the prurient inclinations of others. Been there, seen that. Not interested."

"Considering your personal trials and tribulations over the summer, I know our listeners can sympathize and appreciate your attitude," Carolyn said. "I'd love to invite you back to talk about those personal challenges, but you'll have to write a book first since that's the focus and purpose of this show: talking about what is written in books. Ever planning to write an autobiography, Wolf? If you do, I can assure you it would be a blockbuster!"

Wolf laughed. "Thanks for your confidence and having me on your show, Carolyn. If I decide to write one, you will be the first to know."

"All clear, Carolyn," a technician's voice sounded in the studio.

They removed their headsets and draped them over the microphones standing on the table in front of them. Carolyn invited Wolf for some refreshment in an adjoining room.

"It is a genuine pleasure to finally meet you in person, Wolf," Carolyn said, taking a sip of her drink. "What changed your mind about coming to the studio?"

"I happen to be in Boston and decided that talking with you face to face was better than our usual where in the world is Grayson Wolf schtick," he explained. "Besides, as I've said during the show, I'm out of the muckraking business so I'm not feeling like I've got to keep a very low profile."

"I suppose spending years surreptitiously immersed in—and rummaging through—the lives of the rich and famous, would have me looking over my shoulder every moment of the day and night," Carolyn said.

"The price of mucking around in people's lives," Wolf agreed. "I've never felt physically threatened by my expose targets, though.

Their form of payback tends toward some form of financial retribution or personal embarrassment."

"Some have sued you; all have failed," Carolyn said, grinning. "So far."

"There's always tomorrow," Wolf quipped. "However, any that do go after me had better be aware that I never reveal *everything* I've dug up on them."

"Nothing like keeping a spare Sword of Damocles in the closest to keep the rabble at bay," Carolyn laughed.

"Never tell 'em all you've got," Wolf agreed. "Never know when it's needed."

"I bet you're a hell of a gambler," Carolyn suggested.

Wolf shot her droll glance. "I never gamble. I play to win."

"I still think you should consider working on your autobiography," she said, changing the subject. "It would be a multi-million seller, Wolf."

"Autobiographies are for one's senior years, not thirty-six year-olds." Wolf barked a laugh. "Considering there are literally dozens of disgruntled and furious men and women seething in dark corners plotting revenge on Grayson Wolf, perhaps I should consider writing an autobiography sooner than later."

Carolyn was about to reply when an aide stuck her head thought the door informing her that a production planning meeting was starting and she was needed.

"No rest for the stunningly successful," she quipped. She gave Wolf a hug, adding, "Thanks again for coming in person...and please do stay safe out on the mean streets."

Wolf assured her he would not fail to keep an eye out for evildoers and made his way out of the studio, taking the elevator down to the lobby. He almost made it to the exit, when he spotted a woman rise from a bench along the wall and approach him.

Wolf stopped walking and turned to face her. He glanced at her hands, which, to his relief, where empty. She came to a halt a few feet away.

"You're Grayson Wolf," she stated.

"Yes." He held her eyes, but remained cognizant of her hands, which remained at her sides.

"My name is LeeAnn Hicks. I'm a surgeon employed by..." she hesitated looking around the lobby, then said, "I need to talk with you; could we go somewhere more private?"

"There's a quaint tavern at the end of the block," Wolf suggested.

"Okay," Hicks said.

Wolf led the way and the pair were sitting across from each other in a corner booth a few minutes later. A waiter took their drink order, Wolf including a fish and chips appetizer. Experience meeting with informants and whistleblowers had taught him that having both drink and food at hand helped one to relax.

"How may I help you, Doctor Hicks?" Wolf said, placing his glass back on the table.

She looked very nervous. Clearing her throat, she began.

"I'm a surgeon. I've been working at the Affirmative Transformation Treatment Center for a year. The medical facility is about eight miles west of here in Watertown."

Wolf gazed attentively at the woman, waiting for her to continue. He smiled encouragingly.

"I assume there is something not Kosher going on at this medical facility? Insurance fraud, perhaps?" Wolf said.

Hicks's eyes darted furtively around the room. "There are three surgeons working at Affirmative Trans. Since I started there in February, I've conducted eight surgeries and assisted in a dozen more. All told, the three of us have operated on two dozen patients. All but one of these surgeries was performed on women. All the women were in their early twenties; two were nineteen, one eighteen."

She stopped speaking. Wolf was unclear what specifically concerned the surgeon. He asked Hicks if she had witnessed some form of egregious malpractice or some other form of medical malfeasance.

"Of course, there's something very wrong," she replied, looking at Wolf as though he were dense. "Two dozen surgeries and all women but one?"

"I'm sorry to appear so clueless," Wolf said, "but how is the fact that most of your surgeries were performed on women a problem? What type of surgeries are these and were these women—and one man—forced to have these surgeries?"

Hicks must have realized she had not properly explained herself because her expression turned contrite.

"Oh, sorry. I'm just really nervous." Her gaze scanned the room. "Affirmative Transformation Treatment Centers perform sex change surgeries—mastectomies and so forth—and provide subsequent treatment, testosterone injections, counseling, and so forth."

Wolf stared at the surgeon with alarm. "Sex change ... and you said this facility performed over two dozen of these surgeries this year alone?"

"Yes. And we expect a significant increase next year," Hicks said. She leaned closer to Wolf, adding, "There are five more Affirmative Trans facilities in the country with another dozen being planned."

"With each one performing a couple dozen sex change surgeries," Wolf said, mentally adding up the total.

"And virtually every surgery performed on young women," Hicks said. "And the women coming in the clinic to explore this option are getting younger every day. We've got girls as young as thirteen dropping by to talk about changing their sex...and we are not discouraging them. The whole trend is a fad; there aren't thousands, mostly girls, waking up one morning feeling like they're the wrong sex. It's crazy."

"Doctor Hicks," Wolf began, "what exactly would you like me to do about adult women wishing to change their sex? It's not illegal and the service you and this medical facility is providing isn't illegal either. I'm unclear about what you want me to do about something that appears to be on the up and up. If you have a personal reservation about doing these sex change surgeries, then you will need to make a decision about continuing to work for this facility."

Her expression became hard. "Typical man; young impressionable women are screwing up their lives and it's just ho-hum, business as usual for the ladies."

"Excuse me, Doctor Hicks," Wolf countered, "but I'm not the one cutting on these women: you are. Attempting to evade whatever responsibility you feel about this issue by heaping unearned guilt on the nearest man will never motivate me—or any other man possessing a shred of self-esteem—to join you in whatever crusade you want to recruit me for."

Hicks looked aghast, clearly surprised by Wolf's vehement retort. She stood up.

"I guess it's true what I've heard: Grayson Wolf has retired from the fight for justice. This was a mistake. Good night."

She turned on her heels and rushed out of the tavern.

He thought about calling her back, but having unearned guilt hurled at his face by someone obviously feeling guilty about *her* own actions left him feeling indisposed to become involved in whatever Hicks was waxing on about.

And what exactly was she sufficiently steamed about to show up at the studio at a moments notice? Clearly it wasn't serious enough or she'd have done a better job communicating details of nefarious goings-on at the medical facility she worked at. It didn't surprise Wolf that a rising number of women were changing their sex; it was all the rage these days. Perhaps Doctor Hicks was upset at the notion of women electing to become men? Considering the ease male disparagement rolled off her tongue, the idea of women transforming into men might amount to little more than a threat to the doctor's identity politics whereby women are the victims and men the abusers.

At any rate, Wolf was not inclined to wade back into muddy social pools because a surgeon was upset at performing what she considered too many sex change procedures on women. Then insulting him for being a man when he didn't immediately wag his tail in compliance with her viewpoint.

Chapter 2

Barbarians at the Gate

Nineteen hundred miles west, in Aurora, Colorado, Colleen Silverstone was getting ready to call it a day when she got a call from security at the front entrance informing her that a cadre of FBI were waving a search warrant demanding to be admitted.

"Tell them I'll be down in four minutes," she said. "Call Legal and have them meet me at the gate."

Colleen emptied all the cash and gold coins from her wall safe into an attaché. Whatever was going on, she wasn't planning to have that cash and coin seized as part of some trumped-up charges. Next she initiated a Yellow Alert, every department uploading current work and standing by to delete all on-site data, a task requiring less than thirty seconds if she gave the signal. Lifting her money case, she walked casually to the front entrance of Silverstone Security and Investigative Services.

She slipped the case into a transfer passage adjacent to the secure entrance and shut the access door. Once free to leave—assuming the agents at her front door were not planning to detain her—she planned to surreptitiously retrieve the case from the outside and take off for parts unknown if the situation called for such a move. Having both represented and investigated many high profile figures in business and government, Colleen knew how the game was played. Someone high up in the federal government had decided that she needed to be reminded who was in really charge and it wasn't Colleen Silverstone.

"I'm glad you're here, boss," the head of security said when Colleen arrived at the main entrance. "The feds have been threatening to bash in the door if you didn't get here in another minute."

"Good luck with that," she quipped. "They'd need a lot more than battering rams to get into this building ... open the door, Jake."

"It's about time, Ms. Silverstone," a very annoyed looking FBI agent said walking up to her. "Another ten seconds and I'd arrest you for obstruction."

Colleen ignored him and said, "Please show me your identification." She handed the ID to Jake. "Call it in."

"You're stalling, Ms. Silverstone," the agent said.

"Any Tom, Dick or Harry can dress up to look like FBI," she retorted. "This is a secure facility and we have top clearance personnel working on top security projects. I have no intention of allowing anyone to walk in rummaging through files and servers without first confirming your papers and person."

"And I could just ignore you and go about my business," the agent said.

Colleen's expression darkened. "And that would be the last thing you would ever do, Mr. Healy."

"Are you threatening a federal office, Ms. Silverstone?"

"We have not confirmed that you and your crew are who you claim to be," she replied. "If you were foolish enough to ignore my instruction to stay put while my people confirm your identity, my security detail would take you and your crew out."

There was a rustling sound behind her. The agent's eyes grew large as he peered at half dozen heavily armed men and women aiming rifles at his direction.

"Like I said, Mr. Healy," Colleen continued, her tone casual, "this is a high security facility. Our corporate and governmental clients expect us to make absolutely sure that their data is secured against enemies foreign and domestic."

"He's clear, Ms. Silverstone," Jake said, coming over and handing the agent's identification back to him.

"Thanks Jake," she replied. Looking at Healy, she said, "Show me the search warrant."

He did and she read it—slowly—then handed it to her corporate lawyer who had joined her at the entrance. After peering at the document for a long while he said,

"This is nothing more than a fishing expedition. Justin Bellamy and the New World Fund is no longer a client of SSIS effective September the first of this year. We cancelled our relationship with Mr. Bellamy pursuant to his arraignment on criminal charges and he subsequently cancelled New World's contract with SSIS."

"I can't speak to any of that," Healy said. "I've got a warrant to search for anything connected to Bellamy and that's what my people are going to do."

"It's okay, John," Colleen said to the lawyer. "Everything we have on Bellamy and New World is in the archives. Follow me, Agent Healy."

Colleen led the small cadre of agents along several corridors coming up to a reinforced steel door. After entering a code, submitting to both an eye and full hand scan, the lock disengaged and she swung the door inward. She led them to a wall covered from floor to ceiling with small doors, unlocked one containing several drawers within.

"Bellamy's record," Colleen said, backing away. "A complete copy of all electronic data, reports, email and phone logs as well as hard copies of all key documents. New World Fund is the drawer directly below."

"We'll see about that," Healy said.

"No we won't," John said. "Your warrant limits your search to all things Bellamy, not let's see what's in the adjoining files."

Healy shot the lawyer a sour look. "I'm taking the entire contents for both Bellamy and the New World fund."

"Knock yourself out," Colleen said, looking bored.

Healy directed his team to empty the two drawers then peered into them afterwards assumingly making sure that nothing was accidentally left behind. Colleen was tempted to give the man a dust cloth to perform a proper cleaning but thought the better of it. Healy was obviously new to his role as team leader and ignorant of the security protocol at the entrance to her compound, something rather curious considering that had the agent tried to throw his authority around at the entrance and push his way into the lobby, he and his team would most likely have been shot. Whoever this puppet master behind the scenes was, he or she would most definitely have known how tight security was at SSIS, yet had sent a newbie agent into a potentially tragic situation. Why?

The agents secured the files and Colleen escorted them back to the front entrance.

"This is not over yet, Ms. Silverstone," Healy said, in what she supposed was his most authoritative tone.

Colleen was quite sure the agent was right about that. And just as certain that the man knew nothing more than being sent to retrieve everything connected to Bellamy and New World Fund. Like Healy, she had no idea what that reason was, but would know sooner or later. Most likely much sooner.

"This is what comes of taking on questionable clients like Bellamy," John Langston said, back in Colleen's office. "They're like eating cucumbers, they keep repeating, reminding you of the poor choice made when eating it in the first place."

"Come on John," Colleen said, laughing. "Don't hate the cuke. They're full of B vitamins and make for an effective afternoon pick-me-up."

"Be that as it may," the lawyer replied, "Bellamy's repeats are a real downer. Every time I think we're done with that crook some part of whatever he touched in the past comes back up again. The man is acid reflux."

"He is the definitive scumbag," Colleen agreed. "And like the best scumbags, sufficiently slimy and slippery to not only be out on bail but pull enough strings to keep delaying his trial."

"Maybe the feds are finally moving on him?" John suggested.

Colleen shot him a skeptical look. "By sending a junior field agent to collect our files on him? And sending him into harm's way by not briefing the man about our security protocol? It's a good thing the man's bluster didn't get the better of him because we'd be mopping bodily fluids off the entrance floor."

"I'm sure we are going to hear about pointing guns in their faces," John said.

"I don't think we will," Colleen replied, shaking her head.

John's brow wrinkled. "Because...?"

"Because the Denver office didn't send him and his team," Colleen said. "I think today's visit was off-book and that these agents came from out of state; DC most likely. I also believe Healy was instructed to assert his authority and act like his visit was a raid."

"My God, Colleen," John said, looking alarmed. "You're suggesting they wanted these agents to get shot by us?"

"Yes, I am. What other reason is there?" Colleen said. "The feds have a mountain of data on Bellamy and his pals. They throw this boy at us waving a search warrant to seize our files on the scumbag five months after he gets arrested? After I helped get him arrested? Think about it John: there is a rotten stench wafting in our direction."

John nodded thoughtfully. "And had there been a shooting in our lobby we'd be dumped into whatever rotten bucket these people have prepared for us. We'd be tied up in legal maneuvers for a long time—years maybe."

"Our security are not trigger-happy bozos," Colleen said. "Even if Healy's people had pulled their guns, they would have ordered them to stand down. But it would only take one nervous rookie on his team to take a shot...and from the look on their faces, every one of those agents were freshly minted from the Academy."

"Any clue who's behind this?"

"Considering the convoluted, incestuous snake pits people like Bellamy slither around in, most likely today's visit is only a preview of the main feature yet to come," Colleen ventured.

"Since the largest and deepest snake pit is Washington," John replied, "I'd say we need to keep our eyes peeled toward the east."

"Most certainly," Colleen agreed. "However, Washington is everywhere. I'll update our people about snakes coming from holes near and far and tell them to alert all our friends and contacts across the country."

"I'll leave you to it, then," John said, getting up from his seat. "I'll get back to my corner and get my legal team to prepare for snake bites."

Colleen thanked the counselor and saw him to the door. She was thinking of how she got herself involved in Grayson Wolf's investigation of a suspicious death in a local prison earlier in the spring when there was a knock on the door, opening some seconds afterwards.

"Got a minute, Colleen?" a pleasant looking woman said, poking her head in.

"Of course; come in, Kat," she said, walking toward her. "What's up? No trouble, I hope."

"All safe and secure," she replied. "Did you happen to hear the interview with Wolf the other day?"

"No. What's the latest?"

"Apparently he's done with investigative exposes," Kat said. "He's only writing fiction now; he's finishing the third Mason novel."

A smile crept across Colleen's lips. "You stay in contact with him?"

"No," Kat replied, firmly. "What about you? Talk with him since July?"

"No," she replied, giving Kat a knowing look. "Once we were done with the Collins case he went back to Virginia and I picked up where I left off."

"I am glad he came; my life needed interruption," Kat said, her gaze suggesting she was thinking of the past.

"How are things going with your fiancé?" Colleen asked, a teasing smile playing on her lips.

"Fantastic," she replied. "And it's all on account of Wolf pushing his way into my life and making me see I was hiding in my cubby down in SSIS's most heavily fortified sector. He's a lot of fun, Colleen."

"Except when he riles up bears that chase you through the woods or almost shoots you when you open a door," Colleen retorted.

"Or shoots a hitman before he could kill you," Kat said, a smug expression on her face.

"Who would never have targeted me if Wolf had never showed up on my front door in the first place," Colleen fired back.

Kat laughed. "Like I said, he's a lot of fun."

Colleen smiled and nodded. "Fine, he's a lot of fun ... In a decidedly annoying way."

Kat smiled and said, "We should invite him back next May for an anniversary party."

"How would David feel about having your old lover come back and schmooze with his old flame?" she taunted.

"He'd be excited and honored to meet the infamous Grayson Wolf, scourge of hypocrites, bane of evildoers and protector of the downtrodden." Kat assured her.

"You keep that up and I might just invite him. Then you'll be feelin' the heat for poking the bear," Colleen threatened. She cocked her head aggressively toward Kat. "Don't you have some work to do? I'm not paying you to be my court jester, Ms. Simmons—even if you are a famous painter."

Kat's grin grew larger. "I would, except my day is done."

Colleen glanced at a wall monitor behind her. "Five-thirty...feels like I just came to work an hour ago."

"It's called aging," Kat quipped. "Once you get to be your age, your metabolism slows down and time just seems to fly by."

"Excuse me?" Colleen retorted. "Last I checked, you're older than me. And neither of us is entering our dotage. Hanging out with Wolf has had a deleterious effect upon your mouth, so I'm nixing the idea of a Wolf redux."

Kat laughed. "Like I said, he's fun and he's—"

"Furry?" Colleen interjected, grinning.

"Actually he's quite devoid of fur," she replied, giving Colleen a knowing look. "I think you should give him a call."

"Prominent artist, gifted digital imaging proficient and a matchmaker, too," Colleen said, placing sarcastic emphasis on the latter description. "I can tell you with reasonable certainty that Colleen Silverstone and Grayson Wolf will never cross paths again. Wolves have fleas."

"Wolves also mate for life," Kat rejoined, an infuriating smile playing on her lips.

Colleen was just about to suggest that for a woman who was engaged to be married, Kat was talking a lot about a former boyfriend when there was a knock and the door opened.

"Excuse me, Colleen," a burly looking man said, standing in the doorway.

"What is it Cooper?"

When he didn't reply, she asked Kat to excuse them, the woman waving at the man and shutting the door behind her. Colleen threw a switch, doubly insuring her office was bug-proof.

"What's happened?"

"We've intercepted some chatter from the hill," Cooper said. "Your name was mentioned."

Colleen's thoughts flashed back to Agent Healy's comment about things not being over.

"What else do we know?" she asked, hoping Cooper had more to tell her. She was not happy about people on Capitol Hill tossing her name about.

"Only that they're Senate staffers," Cooper said. "I'll get the word out to our DC snoops to keep their ears to the ground; you might want to give a nudge to your Pentagon contacts."

"I'll wait on that," Colleen said, looking thoughtful. "Once my name is officially announced for whatever mud pies the DC luminaries want to toss at me, then I will contact my Pentagon friends. Don't want tip our hand that we have prior knowledge of planned activities."

"You mean as opposed to the DC sieve that leaks information from confidential Presidential meetings? Secure documents from the FBI to the Post and New York Times?" Cooper mocked.

"Thus my point about me not contacting anyone," Colleen said. She issued a frustrated hiss. "You, me and a whole lot more working for this company were soldiers. Perhaps I've grown unnecessarily cynical, but I'd think twice today about putting my life on the line to defend what is already a majority crying out for someone to rule them and the wastrels they vote into office pandering to them. Look how they protect scum like Bellamy."

When Cooper looked instinctively at the closed door, she couldn't help laughing. He shot her a sheepish look and said,

"Your office is one of the most bug-proof spaces in this structure, but old habits die hard. Besides, it's better to be doubly sure then to walk around feeling unsure."

"Okay Mr. Intelligence Man, what secrets did you wish to share with me?" Colleen teased.

"As you know, there are several of us working here that have the skills to make Chinese or Russian hackers cry like the babies they are," Cooper said, giving her a significant look.

"Not going to happen," Colleen said, decisively. "I will never potentially expose your team's stellar digital powers to uncover what the Washington posers have planned for me."

"I wouldn't be so nonchalant about this, Colleen," Cooper replied. "The feds show up at the front gate near closing time and we get chatter from DC mentioning your name. Something nasty is going on."

"There's always something nasty going on in swampland, Cooper," Colleen said. "If the plan is to call me for some governmental inquisition, it'll be a piece of cake. The Deep State rats operating under the cover of 'public service' have given the public a clear image of the rats operating under the cover of 'public service'. Look at the mess good 'ol James and his pals have made of the FBI. Their testimonies were some of the finest examples of overconfident, arrogant and self-righteous performances we've ever seen. If called, I'll smile a lot, speak profusely in swamp lingo and say absolutely nothing of significance."

"What if they hustle you in a basement and waterboard you?" Cooper quipped.

"You ever talk during your torture training, First Sergeant Adkins?" she challenged.

"Hell no."

"Right," Colleen said, giving him a knowing look. "Don't worry; whatever this is about I can handle it ... time to go home. Keep me abreast of any new chatter."

"Absolutely, boss. See you mañana, bright an early."

"Gracias amigo."

Cooper made it to the door when he turned and said, "Oh, by the way, it's snowing and coming down hard. Better leave sooner than later."

"Roger that."

Colleen gave him a snappy salute and he exited her office closing the door behind him. Looking over her shoulder she pondered her options: stay or go?

"Stay," she said to herself.

Rising from her seat, she walked to her desk, pressed a series of numbers on a keypad and watched as part of the wall at the rear of her office slid open, revealing a room. Her security firm was a twenty-four-seven operation, with a night crew on standby to respond to client communications and monitoring the numerous security systems and operations that SSIS was engaged in across the globe.

She sighed and walked into her home-away-from-home, the wall door sliding silently shut after her. Having her own bedroom suite in the building was just common sense and Colleen spend more time sleeping at her compound than she'd ever want to admit.

She changed her clothes, checked email, texts and sundry other communication mediums then made for the on-site restaurant to eat dinner. On the way out she glanced at a photograph of Grayson Wolf and her standing in the lobby of a local country club taken shortly before Wolf returned to Virginia, their mutual mission completed.

"What are you two smiling at?" she said, an involuntary smile touching her lips at the memory of their adventures last summer. She shook her head and went to eat dinner.

Chapter 3

Wolf Report

Grayson Wolf locked his penthouse door and took the elevator down four flights, completing the shortest commute to work of anyone in his circle of coworkers, friends and acquaintances. Having come back from Boston late last night, he slept past his usual rising time, arriving at the offices of the Center for Individual Rights an hour past opening.

"Late to work again," Robert Jano, CIR's head of Media and Communications said, as Wolf stepped through the entrance. "This is getting to be a habit, my man. Keep this up and folk might think you're retired."

"Very funny, RJ," Wolf retorted. "Keep talking like that and folks might get the impression you've got nothing better going on than listening to radio interviews on a weekend afternoon."

"Wolfie might be retired, but his bitch-slap is as potent as ever," RJ grinned.

"And don't you forget it, my man," Wolf replied, a droll expression glowing on his face.

"If you two are done playing pattycake, I'd love if you'd join me in my office," Diana Cruz, CIR Director said. "Before noon would be appreciated."

"Pattycake?" They both said in unison, looking amused.

She shot them a long suffering look and shook her head. "Come along boys."

"Boys?" Both mimicked, entering Diana's office.

"Okay, what kind of legal brouhaha have I stepped into this time," Wolf said, seeing Juan Mendez, head of CIR's legal team leaning against Diana's desk.

Juan grinned knowingly. Having worked at CIR for five years he would be intimately familiar with the many legal conundrums Wolf's exposes and antics had placed both Wolf and the firm in legal jeopardy.

"None, I am delighted to report," Juan said, shaking Wolf's hand. "Glad you're back; good interview, by the way."

"From that smile on your face," Wolf began, pointing a finger at him, "I'd venture the good part you are referring to is my public announcement that I am retiring from my career of making your life as head of our legal defense as exciting as possible."

"I won't deny it," Juan said, smiling happily. "It's good timing, too, with virtually every minute of our time consumed by our class action suits against half the colleges in the country. Good thing our case against the Rockfall County Police was settled recently or the class action would be a serious drain on our treasury."

"Three million should keep the effort fully funded until spring," Diana said. "And having the chief of police resign was a nice bonus."

"Not to mention President Wilson of Virginia Patriots College taking an extended leave of absence," Juan added.

"Nice of the two of them to coordinate their self-destruction," Diana said, a satisfied expression on her face. "Wilson allowing thugs on campus to harass and threaten students and when they fought back, she tried to have the *students* expelled. Chief of police Kelly pulling his officers off protection detail giving a green light for us to be attacked when we marched two hundred demonstrators to the college. Neither were the brightest bulbs in the package ... serves them right, the idiots."

"Not very forgiving, are you, Diana?" Wolf said, a droll smile playing on his lips.

"No, I'm not," she replied, sharply. "People like Wilson and Kelly have no business being in any position of authority ... I'm glad you're back and happy the interview went well. Most importantly, how did the meeting with our New England donors go?"

Wolf made a swaying motion with his hand. "Comme ci comme ça. It's the class action against universities. Most high rollers were supportive, a significant minority not so much. Bottom line: we're going to lose some money; upwards of twenty percent."

"Donors critical of our move have ties to various universities," Diana declared. "Your experience in Boston is our canary in the mine; we better prepare ourselves for a financial drop from our top donors across the country ... let me call Annika over; she needs to hear this now."

To everyone's surprise, Annika von Hauzen, CIR's Chief Financial Officer, made an appearance barely five seconds after Diana called her. Grinning at the look on their faces, she said,

"Heard Wolf had arrived and figured he'd be here. I was just outside the door when you called, Diana."

"Come in; Wolf has mixed news about our financial future," Diana replied.

"When is news about future ever not mixed?" Annika quipped. "And from the look on your face, Wolf, the report from Boston is a mixture that includes a definite chance of diminished financial returns."

"You'd make an effective weather girl," Wolf teased. "I'm guessing a twenty percent reduction from our New England friends. Diana extrapolates that figure to spread nationwide due to our assault against the ivory towers."

"I agree," Annika said. "Donations are down since October. Good thing we raked in more the first half of this year than we did for all of last year. The three million Juan negotiated with Rockfall County is keeping the coffers topped up."

"If we're lucky, we'll start seeing some settlements before the end of the upcoming year," Juan said. "We've gone after the lowest hanging fruit first: the two dozen universities exhibiting the most egregious disregard for the equal rights of all their students. Our case against Virginia Patriots College predates the other colleges and I think we might just get a settlement before New Year's. Considering the way Wilson and her hacks colluded with the police to obstruct the peace and security of our student groups, not to mention the right of the rest of the student body to express their views without being threatened and harassed, I expect a settlement soon."

Annika looked skeptical. "Do you really believe the VPC Board of Directors will settle for twenty million instead of going to court? I would think they'd rather go to trial where they can delay and expect the judge to decide on a lower settlement if found guilty."

"Would you want your dirty laundry exposed in a public trial?" Juan said. "A trial would delay the day of judgement, sure. They might even manage to pay half of what we're negotiating currently. But every student around the nation considering attending Virginia Patriots College will think twice about applying to a college where the administration tacitly sides with student thugs to enforce their politically correct policies. Twenty million is a small price to pay compared with a precipitous drop in tuition for years to come."

"I sincerely hope you're right, Juan," Annika said. "Our share will be six million. We'll need that kind of money to fund the legal frontal assault against the two dozen universities you have targeted, all of whom most likely will not roll over as easy as VPC."

"I don't expect them to," Juan agreed. "What I subscribe to is the Domino Theory." He stopped, presumably to allow the others to ponder his meaning.

"A blast from da past," Wolf quipped. "One nation after another coming under the control of Communism like falling dominos. You're expecting—hoping—that once the first college succumbs to your legal court press, the next one will teeter then fall, followed by the next, then the next until they all collapse in a heap."

"Pretty much the strategy," Juan confirmed.

"Hasn't the first domino started to fall already?" RJ asked.

"Virginia Patriots?" Juan replied. "Can't really count them as the first domino due to the seriously egregious conduct of the administration toward selected students. However, we do have some excellent candidates whose actions are reminiscent of the VPC administration that I expect to wobble and fall before next Christmas."

Wolf admired the man's ingenuity and acumen spotting the glaring legal gap college administrators had inadvertently opened wide by actively promoting a host of politically correct actions. Some of these collectivist premises such as safe spaces were largely benign drawing deserved ridicule. Other practices and policies weren't silly or superficial: suppression of expression by labeling it "hate" speech, racial and sexual preferences while impugning on the race and sex of those currently out of favor.

The biggest hole in the walls enclosing academia, however, was the implied contract by colleges' promotional literature and their de facto contract articulated in the student handbook. Every college handbook waxes on about ensuring an equal educational experience. Every college claims to offer students the freedom to explore ideas and express their opinions in a collegiate, supportive atmosphere and articulates expectations, rules of behavior and the consequences for breaking rules. It is such contractual guarantees that Juan is using to smash the legal veneer to expose the hypocritical core of college administrators' discriminatory (and illegal) policies and behaviors.

Juan had proposed that the Center for Individual Rights sue every college and university that has been violating the due process of their students and, like Virginia Patriots College, allowing a thuggish minority to deprive other students of an equal opportunity to fully participate in what these colleges contractually offer every student equally. Freedom to explore, he had pointed out, is not congruent with policies that punish some expression as "hate speech" effectively silencing students holding differing opinions, ideas and viewpoints. Juan claimed such policies and actions were nothing more than intimidation and Wolf agreed wholeheartedly.

He recalled Diana's free speech rally a mile from the gates of Virginia Patriots College pursuant to the attack on Students for Individual Rights by a cadre of thugs on campus. She called the place she rented for the event, Liberty Village, promising to call out and expose these "neo Red Guards or Brown Shirts—take your pick— prowling on our colleges, terrorizing students and cowering the faculty."

He smiled remembering her resolute stand, planning a march on the college with two hundred brave supporters, thinking how appropriate the modern George Washington was named Diana Cruz. Wolf also remembered the pelting of rocks and baton wielding mob trying to prevent the marchers from conducting a peaceful demonstration with police nowhere in sight.

"Three million for exposing two hundred marchers to violence is a bargain," Wolf said, aloud.

"Did I miss something?" Diana said, looking askance at him.

RJ laughed. "He was at a universe far, far away."

"Sorry," Wolf said, shrugging. "What were we talking about?"

"About the three million you're going to donate to CIR to make up for loss of revenue," RJ teased. "That's what happens when you fade out during high level meetings."

"You think we should have held out for more money?" Juan said, picking up on Wolf's comment.

"I'd never second guess you, Juan," Wolf replied. "Just thinking back at that march and the fun we had battling our way down that miracle mile trying not to get our heads bashed in or knees busted. Rockfall is a rural county; not much taxes filling their treasury. Three million and getting that looser police chief fired makes a potent reminder for proper policing in the future."

The assembled looked at Wolf in silence, perhaps recalling their own role in the march upon Virginia Patriots or maybe pondering future acts of direct action in defense of the fundamental rights countless others in the past had fought to preserve for their children. One thing Grayson Wolf was certain of in the ensuing silence: the struggle to defend the rights of individuals to life, liberty, property and pursuit of happiness was a never ending task that one dared not "retire" from if one hoped to avoid Ben Franklin's warning when asked what type of government the Delegates had created: 'A Republic...if you can keep it'.

"I'm glad you have one more exposé to publish, Wolf," Annika said, breaking the silence. "Considering the increasing concern folks running Silicon Valley have brought down upon their heads, your Soviet Valley is going to cause quite an uproar when people read about the nasty attitudes and views of the hoi-polloi some of these tech leaders are expressing behind closed doors. Not to mention their coziness with authoritarian politicians and nations."

All eyes turned toward Wolf. He was sure they had similar doubts and concerns about his planned retirement from his exciting— and stressful—career as America's preeminent scourge of the high and mighty that Carolyn Mayor expressed in her recent interview.

A knowing grin appeared on Wolf's face. "I know what you're thinking. Going underground and mucking around in people's dank corners is a major adrenalin rush and will I really want to deprive myself of my drug of choice? Like I told Carolyn and her three million listeners: I am done. Retired muckraker. I'll be thirty-six come January and made enough enemies to keep me looking over my shoulder for the rest of my life. Besides, I'll get plenty adrenalin jolts just hanging around with you guys."

"I remember when my dad retired a year back," RJ said, shooting Wolf a sly look. "Mom said he moped around the house all day making a nuisance of himself." He made a dramatic face, adding, "There was blood."

A titter arose. Clearly everyone in the room had a similar experience with a parent, sibling or a spouse.

"Tell you what," Wolf said, looking droll. "I get too antsy, mopey or dopey you can duct tape me to my chair and switch on Netflix for the rest of the day. Until I exhibit such symptoms, I'm still the president of this firm who is wondering why you folks don't have anything better to do than kvetch about your infamous leader?"

The prize for this comment was a combination of long suffering looks mixed with several Bronx cheers. Wolf pointed dramatically at the door, Diana noting with a grin that he was in her office, not his.

"I don't get no respect," he grumbled. "I'll be in my office moping if anyone wishes to see me."

Because Wolf's business took him away from CIR for long periods of time, his office was little more than a glorified closet. It did sport one lone window, an absolute requirement he had insisted upon in order to dispel any impression by visitors that the CIR president's office was a closet.

Wolf peered at the cramped accommodations as he entered the room. Now that he was retired from running around the country insinuating himself for months at a time into the lives of prominent corporate and political figures it was time for a space more aligned with what one would expect a president's office to look like.

He walked over to his desk—a total of three steps—and took a seat. Sitting there for a silent minute or two, Wolf began to chuckle at the distinct impression that he was in fact moping. True, he single handedly launched the Center for Individual Rights and was majority owner of the company (and co-owner of the Patrick Henry Building it was located in). And true, he'd been its president since the Center's inception. But his role centered on action, being out in the field doing investigative work and writing his findings in compelling novels that, though fictional in nature, were in fact, non-fictional accounts of people and their affairs. Sitting behind a desk completing administrative tasks and participating in social and business events and functions would require significant adjustment of personality and temperament.

Gazing around the room, Wolf wasn't all that certain that he wanted to make such adjustments. And having a larger, more impressive office would not even remotely provide a measure of compensation for trading a life of action for a passive existence of a corporate officer. Wolf imagined that nicer trappings might actually exacerbate his mixed feelings having surrendered his former life of Strum und Drang where he had to depend on his wits and make effective snap decisions in order to remain hidden in plain sight and achieve his objectives.

"Moping!" RJ cried, entering Wolf's office. "I definitely spot moping." He shut the door and pulled a chair up to the desk. It was a very short distance. "We've been bosom buddies for twenty years and you can't hide that mopey look on your face from me. You are out of sorts, my friend."

"You're right," Wolf admitted. "Sitting here in my office—"

"Closet." RJ interjected.

"Sitting in my closet," Wolf corrected, "the full reality of my retirement from active service, so to speak, is beginning to hit home, RJ. We've got top notch people like Diana and you running this operation and doing an amazing job. What exactly am I going to do besides sit in meetings, smile and nod and mope around getting into people's way? I'm not cut out for passive work; never have been."

"You could restart your professional gambling career," RJ suggested. "You were pretty good, as I recall." A grin lit up his face. "Until you started losing. But, hey, you could make a success at it this time."

Wolf's expression transformed into a scowl. "Anyone ever point out you're a real smart ass?"

"You have," RJ replied. "It's part of my ineffable charm, as you so often remind me." He slid his seat a couple inches closer to the desk, adding, "Wolfie, you are going to figure this out sooner than later. You always do. We both know your muckraking career had an expiration date and that it has arrived. Your love fiasco with Maddie last summer was a loud alarm about it being time to let that life go. You know it to be true." He intoned that last sentence trying to sound like Darth Vader.

"You're right, of course," Wolf said. "I've been feeling increasingly ambivalent over the past couple of years about my life not moving on to other important aspects; love being one of those important parts."

"Don't let yourself feel too adrift, bro," RJ smiled. "You're transitioning better than you might think. You've already made a big shift in your writing from being a hard-bitten exposé hack to a popular fiction novelist who's published two books within five months and completing a third. You're going to write a lot more and it's going to be great. As for your role around here, don't sweat it. You got me and a couple dozen coworkers who love you and will help you figure it out. And feel free to mope about, 'cause that's how you'll figure it all out. In the meanwhile, dinner is on me...and if you're feeling especially lonely, my invitation to join me in carnal bliss still stands."

"And exactly how would Zach feel about that, my good man?"

"He's open to a threesome if the third man is you, bro," RJ laughed, wiggling his eyebrows several times for emphasis.

"Good to have options," Wolf teased. "I'll keep it in mind. Thank for the pep talk, RJ; I appreciate it—and you."

His phone pinged, indicating a text. Wolf peered at the phone, looking surprised.

"What's up?" RJ said, seeing his change of expression.

Wolf looked up from the phone. "It's from Maddie..."

"You're kidding? What she want—accuse you of raping her again?"

Wolf shot him a sharp look. "That's not fair, RJ."

"Sorry. So what she want?"

"She's coming to Baltimore for a lawyer's convention and wants me to meet her in Baltimore this Saturday at one," Wolf said, adding quickly, "In the conference center's restaurant."

"And will you meet the femme fatale this Saturday at one in the conference center's restaurant?" RJ said, in a sinister tone.

"It's quite a talent you have for making her request sound like an invitation to engage in any number of sordid undertakings," Wolf replied. "And yes, I am going to meet Maddie for lunch. In the conference center's restaurant. At one. This Saturday."

Chapter 4

Wading Into The Swamp

Colleen's phone made a strangling sound. She didn't bother to check the caller ID—she knew who the call was from. She accepted the call and lifted the phone to her ear. She listened for a moment, then said,

"This Friday. You do realize today is Wednesday and I'm running an international security firm? ... there's no need for a subpoena; I will be there ... text me the particulars ... have a nice day, too." She terminated the call, adding, "Assholes."

Colleen informed her assistant to charter a flight to Washington, DC for Thursday morning and make reservations at her favorite hotel.

"Yes it's short notice," she said, in response to the aide's comment about confronting limited vacancy at the hotel. "Reserve a Penthouse or even the Presidential Suite if that's the only thing available. Let me know as soon as arrangements are made."

Colleen checked her schedule and shook her head. Thursday was crammed with staff meetings in the morning and client calls in the afternoon. She'd cancel the meetings and make the calls from the air and while traveling to the hotel and from her room. Friday morning included on-site meetings with several potential clients; she'd let her Associate Executive handle them, offering her sincere apologies for having to attend to an important personal matter.

Looking at her weekend, Colleen issued a sardonic sniff: she had no prior commitments. An uninvited thought struck her about making arrangements with someone living just outside the beltway in Tyson's Corner she had spent some time with back in the spring and early summer. She shoved such nonsense forcefully out of her head.

Having successfully rearranged her schedule for the next four days, Colleen's stomach made rumbling sounds and she remembered that she had not eaten breakfast, calling the kitchen to have a meal brought up to her office. She had just finished eating when her phone jingled. Seeing the caller's name, she answered it.

"Good morning Barry. What's up?"

"Hi Colleen," he said. "Thanks for taking my call."

A knowing expression formed on her face on account she often declined her stepfather's phone calls, opting for voice mail instead.

"I always try to answer your calls," she said. "Everything okay?"

"All good." After a moment of silence, he continued. "I hear you're coming to DC this Friday. I'm attending a conference in Baltimore this weekend...I was wondering if you'd consider meeting me Saturday...it's not too far from DC...I'd love to see you..."

Colleen closed her eyes for a moment. Her relationship with her stepfather had been deteriorating for some years, especially after the man was caught cheating on her mother resulting in subsequent divorce. She hadn't seen him all year and had hardly spoken with him since summer, when she helped Wolf arrest Kerry Bellamy and his father, Justin Bellamy, for rape and a host of additional crimes. Actively assisting in the arrest of her father's long-time friend and business associate along with the man's son might have also been a contributing factor increasing the alienation between father and daughter.

She sighed. "I can't make any promises. Text me the details."

"Great. Looking forward to seeing you, Colleen."

"I'll try to make it. Bye."

She ended the call, then sent a text to her department heads informing them of her change in plans for the next four days. A kitchen employee came by to pick up her breakfast dishes, Colleen following the young man out of her office. She approached the armored door to The Vault, the nickname to SISS's most secure information and communications complex, the builder who constructed it assuring Colleen that it could withstand the blast of a 500 pound bomb. Of course the rest of the building would be in ruins, but The Vault would remain intact. She conducted the required steps to gain entry.

"'morning, boss," Cooper said, seeing Colleen entering his domain. He made a grimace, adding, "So, you're off to see the evil swamp wizard."

"I have been summoned," she confirmed. "His aide didn't give any further details than show up Friday at nine a.m."

"Be sure to take your ruby slippers for making a quick exit if required," Cooper joked. He gazed at her sharply. "But this is not a social call, is it, scary boss lady."

"Scary," Colleen repeated. "Glad to see I haven't lost my mojo hobnobbing around with the likes of Grayson Wolf."

Cooper laughed. "Damn, girl; you *can* read minds! So, what can I do you for?" Seeing a guilty smile forming on her lips, he added, "So, this is about Wolf."

Colleen's eyes widened slightly. "Apparently you can read minds, too."

"Nah, just a damn good analyst," Cooper said, a self-satisfied grin lighting up his face. "You're flying in at Washington Dulles International, picked up by a team of crack SSIS agents who will drive you to your DC hotel down the Dulles toll road passing within a quarter mile of Wolf's Patrick Henry Building. Where he lives in that roomy penthouse on top with a great view and comes and goes on his two-seater 'copter."

"Cute, but no cigar," she replied. "Wolf was interviewed live in Boston last week. Why was he in Boston?"

"Stalking him are we now?" Cooper said, his grin widening.

"Sticking my finger in the air to get a reading of any change of temperature or wind direction," Colleen said, ignoring the taunt. "Wolf's in Boston, Senator Grisham summons me and Barry calls wanting to meet me in Baltimore this Saturday; he's at some kind of lawyer's convention. Three high-profile antagonists popup within days of each other elevates my paranoia."

Cooper puckered his lips looking thoughtful. "When you put it that way ... yeah, got my attention. Give me thirty seconds and the great and powerful Cooper will have the answers you seek."

The head of SSIS's intelligence center was a big man, taking only five strides to the nearest communications terminal fifteen feet away. His fingers flew over the keyboard, finding what he was looking for in less than twenty seconds.

"Wolf was in Boston meeting with CIR high-end donors."

"Just out of curiosity," Colleen said, "can you tell me something about what transpired in the meeting? I have a theory I'd like to test."

"Does a bear poop in the woods?" Cooper retorted, his fingers back on the keyboard. Results for Colleen's request took several times longer than his first search. "Not much there...the usual back and forth, promises made and so forth. However, there's some controversy in the donor ranks about CIR's class action against universities. Apparently more than a few are not happy campers. All I got."

"What you found confirms my theory," Colleen said. "CIR's donations are going to take a hit over going after colleges."

"Is this something you want me to follow up on, or monitor, boss?"

"Nah, just curious. Thanks, Cooper," she replied. "Keep an eye and ear on these new disturbances in the Force...I don't want to fly east and step off the plane into a wild brawl."

"Not to worry; I've got your back," Cooper assured her.

Colleen shot him a warm smile. Men routinely succumbed when confronted with it. The rest of her helped a lot, too. Cooper not so much, having a hottie of his own to snuggle up to.

"I know you do. Thanks, Cooper."

Colleen's plane arrived at Washington Dulles airport shortly before two the next day. A pair of SSIS security agents were waiting to transport the owner of their firm to the Jefferson Hotel, located a few block north of the White House and within a few minutes ride to the Capitol. Passing Tysons Corner, she looked to her right at the buildings rushing past, smiling at what Cooper would say if he knew she was thinking of who lived just a quarter mile from the road.

With Christmas just over two weeks away, hotels were booked solid, but her assistant did manage to secure the one remaining penthouse suite. "I could almost buy a condo for that amount" he had said, complaining about the outrageous price.

The men stopped at the entrance to the hotel, one taking Colleen's baggage, the other one escorting her inside, his eyes warily scanning the area for potential threats. Her reservation secured, they escorted their boss to her room, confirming times and duties for the following day and went on their way.

By the time Colleen had settled in it was approaching four, the penthouse windows darkening with the approaching twilight. She made arrangement to have dinner brought to her room and spent the rest of the evening going through her many correspondences, responding to email, texts and returning several pressing phone calls.

Running the most successful security firm in the country required its president to keep her eye on every aspect of its operations if she wanted SSIS to stay on top. Silverstone Security and Investigative Services included individual and corporate security, including cyber security, and a wide range of investigative options a client could choose from. Colleen's uncompromising character, reputation for absolute honesty, personal integrity and critical judgment was legion and infused into every part of her business. SSIS had a stellar reputation, a long waiting list of potential clients and was the envy of everyone else in the security business.

But even Colleen Silverstone can err when accepting a client. That had been the case when she agreed to provide security for Senator Terrance Grisham's daughter Carla and Justin Bellamy's son, Kerry, both students at Overland College located east of Castle Rock, Colorado. Her father had asked her as a favor and had agreed against her better judgment, her worst fears coming true last summer when Grayson Wolf began to investigate a rape and alleged prison suicide coming to her for help.

"C´est la vie," she said, aloud and got ready for bed.

Colleen entered the Capitol below the East Plaza passing through security screening without a hitch. Leaving her pistol in the safe back at her hotel room helped, too. She had a license to carry a weapon, but she wanted to get into the building without the delay announcing she was armed would assuredly cause. Her name was on the list and she was given a special pass allowing her to enter the Senate office wing.

Having been a visitor several times, she had no trouble finding Senator Grisham's offices. Entering, she approached the assistant who was busy talking on the phone and waited. He looked up, smiled and waved his hand in a circular motion assumingly signaling that the caller was going on and on. He interrupted the caller, telling him or her that an important visitor had arrived and that he had to end the call.

"Sorry about that, Ms. Silverstone," he said, rolling his eyes. He got up, adding, "The Senator is expecting you, please follow me." He led Colleen to a door at the far end, opening it after knocking.

"Thank you Colin," Colleen said, entering the inner office. Colin closed the door after her. "Good morning Senator."

Terrance Grisham was a third-term Senator from Illinois. He was in his mid-fifty's but appeared much younger on account the man was known to be very fastidious about his diet, exercise and his appearance. Divorced, he liked the ladies and knew his way around the social circuit, never dating one woman longer than it took him to get bored of her charms and proceed to the next juicy plumb hanging tantalizingly on the nearest branch. Grisham was the consummate politician, having literally spent his life in politics beginning as Student Government President at the local high school he attended in the suburbs of Chicago, a rising star in college and elected to the Illinoi State House within six months of graduating.

He eyed Colleen appreciatively. She felt her gag reflex kicking in.

"You asked for this meeting, Senator. How may I be of assistance?"

Her abruptness must have irritated him because his smile retreated precipitously.

"I never properly thanked you for, um, arranging for Karla to perform supervised community service in lieu of jail time," Grisham said.

He pointed at a seat. Colleen sat.

"Karla's security and safety was my responsibility," she said. "I simply did what was required."

This wasn't exactly true. Had she had her way, Overland College's "Queen Bitch" would have done hard time. Preferably breaking rocks in a quarry, far, far away. She waited for the Senator to continue, wondering what the real reason for her summons was.

"You're probably wondering why I asked you to come."

Like, duh, popped into her head, suppressing the urge to smile.

"You see, Ms. Silverstone, questions keep swirling about the reasons why Grayson Wolf would have asked you to assist him investigating a prison suicide," he said, looking concerned. "Which just happen to somehow involve my daughter and the children of other prominent families." He paused, peering at her. "There is talk about a Senate investigation of you and your company. People are concerned about unfriendly actors using leading investigative companies like yours to target them for some nefarious reason. This is why I wanted to speak with you right away."

Colleen projected the appropriate look of unease while absolutely certain that the concerned people Grisham was talking about was he and his nefarious associates. The Senator and his pals like Justin Bellamy were the central characters in Wolf's exposé *Screw You Suckers!* and though she had mixed feeling about Wolf featuring her stepfather as part of the supporting cast of looters she also knew he wasn't wrong.

Looking at Grisham's ingratiating, duplicitous face, she silently cursed the day she let Barry maneuver her into accepting these dirt bags as clients. Though upon reflection, perhaps she should be thankful to Barry for teaching her a most important lesson about the consequences of ignoring that subtle sour odor from the wine when toasting to a long and prosperous relationship.

Colleen had also learned other lessons from her service in the military and launching a security business in a competitive market. To wit, offense is the best defense.

"I want to thank you, Senator, for your consideration about my welfare," Colleen said, amiably. "What suggestions do you have about discouraging Senate hearings pursuant my dealings with Mr. Wolf? I would strongly caution your colleagues to reconsider; it's best not to poke the Wolf. We've all seen what he and his pack are capable of, wouldn't you agree, Senator?"

Unlike Grayson Wolf whose huffing and puffing did blow houses of ill repute down, Senator Grisham and his pals were all bark and wheezes. Their expertise lay in the realm of virtue signaling, posing and righteous indignation in the primary service of being re-elected and living large on their public service scam.

Grisham's expression might appear engaged and concerned—he was a successful politician after all—but Colleen could imagine all those well-oiled gears in his head spinning and meshing to produce the combination of meaningless words soon to issue forth. Deciding to throw some sand into the man's mental gears, she said,

"As a businesswoman, I feel strongly about offering value for value received. I appreciate you looking out for me, Senator. In exchange, I feel it only fair that I do likewise. You need to know that during my term working with Mr. Wolf last summer, I got the distinct impression that he knew more about Justin Bellamy's business and his associates than what is publicly known. I wish I could be more specific, but I thought you should know. I'm sure it will help you to convince your colleagues on your committee to think twice about convening hearings where the name Grayson Wolf is mentioned." Colleen paused, then added, "God only knows what that man is capable of revealing; he's got informants everywhere." She was quite sure that the latter comment would definitely cause the Senator's bowels to loosen significantly.

"You're quite right, Ms. Silverstone. Quite right," Grisham said, the wheels in his head assumingly spinning on overdrive.

Colleen bit off a sudden urge to laugh at the Senator's comment, it sounding much like a confirmation of loose bowels.

"I'm glad to have been of service, Senator," she replied. "If I think of anything else pursuant to my time with Mr. Wolf, I will contact you immediately. Is there anything else you wish to talk about?"

Colleen smiled amiably at the man, knowing with certainty that there was nothing further to discuss. He had summoned her with the expectation of intimidating her and she had issued a veiled threat in return. Stalemate.

"I think we're done for today and I do have another appointment." He rose from his chair, Colleen doing likewise. "I want to thank you again for looking out for Karla and for offering clarity about working with Mr. Wolf. I appreciate you dropping by; you and your family have a wonderful Christmas holiday."

"You do the same, Senator. Good bye."

They did not shake hands.

The Baltimore Conference Center is conveniently located just a short distance from I-95 and Colleen's escorts dropped her off at the main entrance by 12:30. She had spoken with Barry shortly before leaving her hotel, instructing her to come to Conference Room 201 located on the second floor.

The lawyer's convention appeared to be a well-attended affair judging from the throng milling in the lobby. Colleen spotted an escalator some distance ahead and proceeded to snake her way through the crowd. She was pleasantly surprised, and pleased, by the speed the escalator moved upward, most likely on account that the center hosted many events throughout the year and moving bodies about in an efficient and speedy manner was appreciated by participants.

Room 201 was a short distance from the landing and she reached it in short order. It was a modest sized space holding perhaps a dozen narrow tables with four chairs placed on the far side of each. It was a comfortable room decorated in shades of light grey and soft burgundy. It was also devoid of any occupant.

Colleen slid a chair out from under the nearest table and sat down, figuring Barry would come presently. After five minutes, she checked her phone for any text from him, but there was none. She waited a few minutes longer, then texted him. After another five minutes had passed and no return text appearing, she decided to call him, reaching only his voice mail. She waited a minute and called again. Voice mail.

"What the heck?" she said, aloud.

Colleen got up and went outside, standing at the entrance, peering down both sides of the corridor in hopes of spotting her stepfather. A steady stream of people passed by, but no Barry in sight. She decided to call him once more but still did not get a response. Frustrated, she left him a message saying she was leaving and to phone if he wanted to talk. She ended the call, slipped the phone back into its holster, snapped it shut and made for the escalator.

Grayson Wolf entered the lobby of the Conference Center and made his way through the crowd toward the restaurant at the far end. He was passing the escalator when he spotted a rather striking figure walking rapidly away from the staircase. Although it had been six months, Wolf recognized Colleen Silverstone immediately.

Making up his mind, he turned around and went after her. By the time he got to the exit, he saw her get in a vehicle and drive away. Wolf grabbed his phone, scrolled down his contact list and touched Colleen's name. The unit initiated the call, but she did not answer. He declined to leave a voice mail and walked back in the lobby making for the restaurant once again to meet Maddie for lunch.

Madeline Talbot was a lawyer who worked part-time for Silverstone and Associates, Barry Silverstone's law firm. She had also been a key informant providing Wolf critical information about New World Fund, Justin Bellamy's exceptionally successful financial firm who was closely tied to Silverstone's law firm which was heavily featured in Wolf's *Screw You Suckers!* expose. There had been an unfortunate accusation of sexual assault that Maddie had brought against Wolf back in July. There had also been exceptional circumstances for her claim which were all resolved at Wolf's trial back in August and the former lovers parted in friendly terms.

Wolf arrived at the restaurant's foyer and identified himself. The receptionist checked her list, confirming that he was expect by Ms. Talbot and instructed an attendant to take Wolf to her table.

Maddie was not there, but her coat hung over the back of a chair and a partially empty glass of wine sat on the table. The attendant pulled out the second chair from underneath the table and Wolf sat down. A waiter followed on the heels of the attendant asking what he would like to drink. Wolf ordered a Belgian ale and waited for Maddie's return, guessing she was in the restroom.

The ale arrived, but Maddie had not. Wolf took out his phone and pressed her number, the call going to voice mail. He smiled ruefully, thinking that most likely he'd not answer the phone either considering the circumstances. He took a swallow of ale and waited some more. When his second call went to voice mail again, he got up and walked toward the women's restroom. He described Maddie to several women exiting the facility, but none had seen her.

Becoming suspicious, Wolf opened the restroom's door, calling Maddie's name. No reply. He called her phone and heard a ringing coming from somewhere inside. Speaking loudly, he warned any women in the facility that he was coming in. He followed the ringing to one of the stalls and forced it open.

"Shit..."

Chapter 5

Person of Interest

"Call 911!" Wolf shouted, his voice echoing off the bathroom walls.

Maddie was partially on the toilet, her torso slumped against the side of the stall, her face white. Wolf hooked his hands under her arms and pulled her free of the stall, placing her gently on the floor.

"Call 911!" he ordered once more at a small knot of women standing some feet back.

He began to perform CPR, holding Maddie's nose while blowing air into her mouth, careful not to press too enthusiastically on her sternum as he worked to get her heart pumping blood.

He checked her carotid artery for a pulse. Nothing. Wolf continued to perform CPR hoping his effort would revive her. He heard some commotion behind him.

"Let us take over," someone said.

Wolf continued his rescue effort.

"Sir," a woman said, in a forceful tone, "we're emergency personnel. Let us take over—please."

Wolf stopped and looked up. "Sorry...please help; I can't get a pulse."

He got out of the way and the EMTs took over. Working rapidly they ripped open Maddie's dress, placing electrodes on her chest.

"Clear!"

The defibrillator made a high pitched sound followed by a discharge of an electrical current surging through Maddie's body. A medic checked her pulse. He adjusted the charge, Wolf sure it would by higher.

"Again... clear!"

After a third try, the medic working the defibrillator unit looked over at Wolf, shaking his head several times. Maddie could not be revived. They lifted her lifeless body onto the stretcher, covered her, placed straps around her then wheeled her out of the restroom.

Wolf started to followed them when he recalled seeing Maddie's purse on the floor in the stall. He retrieved it and exited the bathroom making his way back to the table where Maggie had left her coat. He stood there for a moment, feeling dazed at the events of the past half hour when his gaze fell on Maggie's partially drunk wineglass. Resisting the urge to pick it up, he was thinking of what to do when several police officers appeared next to him.

"Excuse me sir," the female one said. "Are you the person who found the victim in the women's bathroom?"

Wolf nodded. He pointed at the wineglass on the table.

"You need to check the contents of that wine. I think it was poisoned."

"How do you know that?" the male officer asked.

"Just speculating," Wolf replied. "It was on the table when I arrived."

"May I have your name and some identification if you would sir," the female officer said.

Wolf reached into his jacked producing a thin wallet that he opened and presented to her.

"Grayson Wolf, officer."

The officer's hand stopped in midair and stared at him. Recovering from her surprise, she took the wallet. Peering at the driver's license for a moment, she thanked Wolf and handed it back.

"Please have a seat Mr. Wolf at the adjacent table," the other officer said. "Metro detectives are on the way; should be here in a short while."

Wolf did at instructed and took a seat. He took out his phone and called Juan Mendez at CIR informing him of the situation.

"You know what to do," Juan cautioned.

"Sing like a bird?" Wolf joked.

"What every prosecutor loves to hear," Juan retorted. "I'll send someone up right away; call me where you'll be as soon as you know."

Wolf thanked him, ended the call and leaned back in his chair, thinking about the sequence of events upon entering the conference center. His thoughts were interrupted by the realization that he might be spending an inordinate time being questioned by police and waived at a waiter, ordering a sandwich.

His food arrived minutes before a pair of Baltimore detectives made their appearance at his table. Glancing up at the men, Wolf took a bite of his sandwich.

"Mr. Wolf, I'm detective Kowalski," he said. Nodding toward his partner he said, "Detective Davis."

"Good afternoon," Wolf said. He took another bite of his sandwich then took a drink from the bottle of Perrier he had ordered. "I know you want to talk with me...mind if I finish eating first?"

They told him to proceed and to remain at the table while they interviewed several of the women who had been present in the restroom during "the incident". Wolf thanked them and they proceeded to walk toward a small group of women sitting together away from the bulk of lunch guests guarded over by a pair of uniformed officers.

Wolf took a long draft of his drink, the image of seeing Colleen Silverstone walking through the lobby flashing through his mind. What was she doing here? She wasn't a lawyer and Wolf couldn't recall her firm doing much business in Baltimore, though SSIS interests and services were present in virtually every major city in the country. Most likely Colleen's presence on this particular day and time was just a coincidence, but Wolf had learned to be highly suspicious of coincidences having been blind sighted by a few of them over the years.

More importantly, why did Maddie ask him to meet her and why didn't she give him a clue when he had asked if everything was alright? Wolf issued an ironic snort. As anyone who has watched murder mysteries knows, when a character calls for a meeting with the protagonist and fails to reveal the details of the reason for the meeting, this character will become the victim of foul play.

Wolf was mulling things over when one of the detectives came by informing him to come with them to the station for questioning. Wolf asked which station they were taking him then called Juan to relay that information. Rising from his seat, he collected Maddie's purse and coat and looked at the detective expectantly. When the man didn't say anything, Wolf shrugged and started to walk toward the restaurant's exit. Perhaps the Baltimore police were accustomed to men carrying women's purses and wearing women's winter coats.

The trip to the nearest police station was a short three-block ride north of Baltimore's Inner Harbor. Walking through the station, every face turned toward the most famous muckraker in contemporary history, Wolf wondering if the stares were pursuant to his reputation or the fact he was still carrying Maddie's purse.

He was escorted to an interview room and seated on the far end of the table, the side furthest from the room's exit. Standard procedure for hardened suspects like himself, he mused. Detectives Kowalski and Davis took seat across from him, joined a moment later by a third man Wolf assumed would most likely be the big boss.

"I'm Captain Marks, Mr. Wolf," he said, leaning on the nearest wall.

Wolf smiled and waited for the questioning to commence.

"How do know the victim?" Kowalski asked.

Wolf held the detective's eyes. Having spent significant time in rooms like this one being questioned by every stripe of police authority operating in the US over the years, he knew that they knew most, if not all, the answers to the questions they were asking him. Wolf also knew that the wisest course in this situation was not to answer any questions. But what would be the fun in that?

"We were lovers," Wolf said. It was the truth, though that part of his relationship with Maddie was brief yet memorable considering the aftermath of their tryst.

"How long have you been intimately involved with Ms. Talbot?"

Wolf's brow wrinkled, giving the impression of giving the question serious consideration. "Eleven hours and twenty-seven minutes."

"Did you spend these eleven hours and twenty-seven minutes with Ms. Talbot beginning last evening at her hotel room?"

"No."

"When did you spend this time with her?"

"In New York City. Last July," Wolf said. He pointed at the file lying on the table next to the detective. "Just like it says on that report about my comings and goings, Detective Kowalski."

"Things did not end well with Ms. Talbot, did it, Mr. Wolf," Davis said, joining the game. "Did you have words at lunch today and things got out of control and you decided to get even with Ms. Talbot for falsely accusing you of rape? That what happened, Mr. Wolf?"

A grin appeared on Wolf's lips. "I'm not sure. Maybe one of the dozen surveillance cameras in the lobby and restaurant will attest to some part of your assertion, Detective Davis."

"Did you stop by New York coming back from visiting Boston?" Kowalski said.

That question surprised Wolf. He remembered his flight making a stop in Newark. They were fishing for something, but what? Time to tread carefully.

"No."

"Are you sure about that, Mr. Wolf?"

"Yes."

"What did you and Ms. Talbot talk about during lunch?" Davis said.

"We didn't have a conversation at lunch because Maddie—Ms. Talbot—was not at the table when I arrived."

"You went to look for her."

"Yes, after waiting a while and wondering where she was."

"You found her, had an argument and killed her before you realized what happened."

"You forgot the part where I followed her into the women's bathroom, argued loudly with her as half dozen women stood gaping at us, forced her to drink the poisoned wine that I so thoughtfully brought with me from the table, placed her in one of the toilet stalls when she started to pass out, rushed outside, came back in a few minutes later where I heroically performed CPR on her after feeling somewhat guilty about how we left things when we parted back in July. Got all that?"

"How do you know her wine was poisoned, Mr. Wolf," Captain Marks said, looking curiously at him.

"Simple deduction," Wolf replied. "When the waiter brought me to her table, Ma—Ms. Talbot wasn't there, but her coat was." He slid the purse and coat across the table toward the two detectives.

"There was a half empty glass of wine. When I found her in the stall and conducted CPR I did not notice any obvious marks on her body to indicate some kind of physical cause of, um, her condition. Ipso facto, someone adding poison in her wine being the most likely instrument of her death. Now, Captain, I think it's time to end this charade and take me back to the conference center where my car is parked."

"I can't do that yet," Marks replied. "We still have questions that need answering."

"Are you placing me under arrest?" Wolf said, looking amused.

"No, but you are a person of interest in this case and I can hold you up to twenty-four hours," Marks replied. He shot Wolf a droll look, adding, "Collect your purse and things and come with me."

Wolf collected Maggie's things and followed the captain who led him to his office. The officer pointed at a sofa in the corner.

"I'm quite certain you're not a flight risk or a danger to my people. Make yourself comfortable, Mr. Wolf. I'm hoping you should be outta here in a hour or two...I'll have someone bring you a bottle of water. Bathroom is down the hall on the right. Any questions?"

"Can you tell me about those other questions needed answers?" Wolf replied.

"Can't do," he said. "If that's all, I've got to get busy finding those answers. Oh, be sure to stay on your side of the desk. Don't touch anything."

Wolf gave him a scout's salute and took a seat on the sofa. The captain left the room, leaving the door wide open. Wolf eyed the man's desk in the hope of spotting something interesting and failing to do so, decided to go through the purse curious if he'd find some clue to the what happened to Maggie. He lifted the purse and his hand froze above the clasp. He thought it strange that the police never asked for her things as he schlepped them around in their custody. Maybe they figured he was her intimate friend and would take care of her things. Whatever the reason, he wasn't going to rummage through the purse or her coat pockets.

He got up and placed Maggie's belongings on a chair adjacent the desk and returned to the sofa, taking out his phone. After performing sundry communication tasks, he decided to stretch his legs a bit and started for the open doorway. At that moment, Susan Baker, a member of CIR's legal team entered.

"Hi Mr. Wolf. They told me I could find you here."

"Good thing you got here when you did," Wolf said, giving her a guilty look. "I was just about to make a break for it ... how are you, Susan?"

"Good," she said, chuckling at his comment. "The police liaison told me you were being detained as a person of interest. I'm glad to see they didn't put you in the holding tank."

"The captain didn't think I was a flight risk or sufficiently suspicious looking to lock me up," Wolf replied. "He promised to let me go as soon as he gets some questions answered."

"I hope you refused to answer any questions until I arrived," Baker said, looking dubious.

She obviously knew about Wolf's predilections while under interrogation by law enforcement personnel. When he gave her a sheepish grin, she knew the answer for certain.

"Well don't blame your highly competent legal team when they lock you away one day, Mr. Wolf," Baker warned, her smile lighting up her face.

"From your lips to Gods' ears," he quipped. "I've been hoping to write an expose about conditions and corruption in the prisons for years, but they refuse to lock me up."

She laughed. "Unless you wish to hang around longer than necessary, I'll go apply some heat and see if I can get you sprung sooner than later."

"Go for it," Wolf said.

He watched the young lawyer as she made her way through the bullpen, smiling at the way the men's eyes followed Baker after she passed by them. He realized he was enjoying watching her walk just as much and looked elsewhere, scanning the scene to see what he could see. Never know when something unexpected pops up pertinent to a current situation like today, or background for a future Tara Mason novel.

There being nothing he hadn't seen many times before when in a police station, Wolf visited the men's room after which he perused an adjacent bulletin board checking out the wanted posters and other sundry postings. He was making his way back to the captain's office when Baker intercepted him.

"You are clear to walk," she said, smiling.

Wolf shot her a droll look. "Just what type of heat did you apply to make that happen so fast?"

"Don't ask, don't tell," she quipped, laughing. "Ready?"

Seeing Marks approaching, he held up a finger.

"Thank you for the comfortable accommodation, captain," he said. "I've placed Ms. Talbot's belonging on a chair next to your desk. Perhaps you might find a clue about her death."

"I was hoping you were the proud owner of that purse," he said, looking resigned.

"I know where her parents live if you want me to take care of that task," Wolf said, looking sincere.

"Thanks, but we'll handle it," he replied.

"Captain," Wolf said, looking at the man suspiciously. "Why did your men let me carry a victim's property around with me and leave it in my possession? Not exactly protocol, is it?"

"Did we?" he replied, looking surprised. "I'll have to speak to the officers who picked you up and give them a stern dressing down. Maybe they thought you having been close to the victim you might spot something pertinent forensics might miss?"

"I haven't spoken with Maddie since the trial last summer," Wolf said. "And I have no clue why Maddie wanted to meet. I'm sure had I peeked into her things I wouldn't have gained any insight into who and why she was murdered." He shook Marks' hand. "If you find out, I'd very much appreciate you letting me know."

"And you'll let me know when you find something?" Marks said, looking knowingly at Wolf. "We're—law enforcement—are all aware of your investigate skills, Mr. Wolf. You'll let me know, won't you?"

"I've retired, haven't you heard?" Wolf quipped.

"Uh huh," the captain replied, giving him a wink. "You go and have yourself a merry little Christmas now, Mr. Wolf. And you too, counselor."

"The same to you and yours captain," Wolf said.

"Thank you captain," Baker said. "Have a merry one—and stay safe."

"Are you retired, Mr. Wolf?" Baker asked, driving him back to where his car was parked.

"I said I was," he replied.

Baker shot him a skeptical look. "Looks to me like what happened today might delay that wish."

"Wish?" Wolf challenged.

"As Justice Thomas used to tell me," Baker replied, "just because you think your done with a case, doesn't mean the case is done with you." When Wolf gave her a long-suffering look, she laughed and said, "You can try to burn a hole in my skull with your laser eyes, but it won't change the fact that Murphy has kicked you in the ass." Baker must have realized who she was speaking to because she apologized immediately.

"Never apologize for speaking the truth, Susan," Wolf said. "And I have to admit my ass is smarting from what happened today. But like I told the captain, I have no clue why Maddie wanted to see me. Whatever the reason, it probably involved some nasty business with some company that she wanted to pass on to me. Maddie was my informant before and I'd be a logical choice to share sensitive information with."

"Information sensitive enough to get her killed," Baker said. She pulled up to the entrance of the parking garage adjacent the conference center. "Here we are. I'll wait for you to exit."

"Not necessary, but thank you, Susan."

Wolf got out of the car and crossed over to the sidewalk. Baker's window rolled down.

"Please be careful, Mr. Wolf. Someone was desperate enough to kill Ms. Talbot. Whomever that is, might think you know something. Watch your back."

"I will, thanks," he said. "See you back at the fort."

Baker smiled and rolled up her window. She continued her vigil at the curb until he disappeared inside. Wolf saw her drive away and walked warily to the premium parking section located on the street level. He stopped twenty feet from his car and used the security app on his phone to check if anyone had tampered with any part of the vehicle, including placing anything on or under it. When your name is Grayson Wolf, paranoia becomes an old and trusted friend.

His electronic guardian giving him a green light, Wolf got in his car, immediately retrieving his weapon from the hidden tray appearing from under the dash. Knowing he would be prevented from entering the conference center, he reluctantly left the pistol in the car. Next he called RJ.

"I'm going to text you the number Maggie called me from," he said. "I need you to track down the Baltimore hotel she stayed in. I'm sitting in the car park next to the conference center and will wait for your call. Thanks, number one dude."

His phone rang a minute later, Wolf praising RJ's tracking abilities in glowing terms.

"Really," RJ retorted. "You speakin' like you just discovered my magical abilities. I am most seriously displeased, lowest dude on my list."

Wolf laughed. "Shut your pie hole and give me the goods."

"The Royal Sonesta, Room 181" RJ said. "Two blocks southeast from your location directly across the Inner Harbor."

"Thanks, RJ."

"I thought you retired, bro?" RJ said.

"Just because I say I'm retired, don't mean retirement is hearing me," he replied. "Don't worry, I'm just going to see what there is to see, which I expect to be nothing. If you don't hear from me in sixty minutes, call the coroner."

He terminated the call before RJ could cram any number of admonishments through the line. He backed the car out of the parking spot and drove the short distance to the Royal Sonesta Hotel, stopping near the entrance and walked to the elevator going up one floor. Room 181 was near the far end of the southern wing and he walked speedily along, slipping on a pair of latex gloves and taking out the keycard he found on Maggie when he was trying to revive her.

The door opened as expected and Wolf walked slowly into the room, pistol in hand. After searching through closets and drawers, he found only what one would expect to find, change of clothing, shoes, toiletries. Nothing out of the ordinary was missing.

Standing in the middle of the room, Wolf reflected upon the fact that Maggie was a lawyer. Who was attending a legal convention. Where was her briefcase? There wasn't one at the restaurant table and he didn't see one when he found Maggie in the bathroom. Whatever Maggie wanted to meet him about was is the missing briefcase.

Wolf shook his head.

"Damn," he said, looking disbelievingly toward the exit. "Looks like Murphy has kicked me in the ass once again."

Chapter 6

Insider Information

"They are not budging, Juan," Terrance Smith said, looking at his colleagues around the conference table. "Like every university we're going up against, Ivygreen College has a gaggle of lawyers whose primary job is to delay, obstruct, coopt or countersue any challenge or opposition to business as usual. I know we were hoping Ivygreen would be the first one to cave, but they've closed ranks."

The Center for Individual Right's head counsel shrugged. Juan Mendez had over two decades of corporate legal experience under his belt and he had known from the outset that launching a massive class action suing universities and colleges for failing to secure the equal right of every student to be secure on campus to express ideas and opinions would meet massive resistance.

"It's just a matter of time," Juan said. "The administrators running the ivory towers are its incestual offspring; bureaucratic hacks who spend the bulk of their time engaged in public relations or flying from one conference to another. They think they are safe and secure behind their paper wall propped up by an army of lawyers working on retainer, but we've got the fuel, the matches and the will to reduce them to worthless ashes."

"Fuel, matches and especially the legion of fire starters cost money, Juan," Annika said. "Even with the willingness of many sympathetic lawyers across the country to assist us gratis or at minimal retainer in exchange for a share of the award when our multi-billion dollar ship comes in, we're still facing costs running into the millions which will only increase once the trials begin in earnest. The three million from Rockfall County provides a small cushion for a short time, but you need to be prepared to scale down significantly by next summer if none of the colleges panic seeing smoke wafting in their direction from the paper wall burning. Sorry to be a party pooper, but that's the job I was hired for."

Monday's progress meeting having accomplished its function, Juan ended the session and his legal team started to disperse to their sundry offices and tasks. Then he remembered something.

"Susan—can you wait a moment? I've got something to ask you."

The lawyer stopped at the doorway and walked back into the room. "What do you need, Juan?"

"Have you seen or heard from Wolf?" he asked.

"Not since Saturday."

"How did he seem?" Juan said. "You know, emotionally. He liked Maddie."

"He seemed to take it as well as can be expected given the circumstances," Susan replied. "Being detained for questioning probably helped. Mr. Wolf appeared energized by the experience."

"He would be," Juan said, grinning. "Jousting with adversaries and authorities is his catnip. He never fails to rise to any challenge—thrives on it, in fact."

"True," Susan said. "I did remind him that he has retired from that life when I dropped him off at the parking garage."

Juan shot her a surprised look. "What did he say to that?"

"He smiled at me and deflected by saying that he had no clue about why Ms. Talbot was murdered," Susan explained. "But knowing Mr. Wolf, I told him that someone desperate enough to kill Ms. Talbot might also target him and to be careful ... you look worried; did something happen to him?"

"Not that I know about and hopefully not," Juan said. "It's just that he's very interested in our class action and didn't come to the meeting."

"You're thinking that perhaps he's put off retirement for a while?" Susan speculated.

"Knowing Grayson Wolf, I'm thinking there's no perhaps about it," Juan replied. "Especially walking—literally—into a murder."

"Now I am worried," Susan said.

"Let's find out what's what." Juan took out his phone and called RJ asking about Wolf. After a brief exchange he ended the call. "He's alive and kicking and definitely not retired, at least not from inquiring about Maddie. He's still in Baltimore dogging the cops."

"Good," Susan said, looking relieved. "Frankly I'd never make it going under cover and writing even an expose column less a novel or over a dozen like Mr. Wolf has. I don't know how he does it, year after year constantly having to look over his shoulders. And now he's probably going to do it again."

"Some people are just wired like that," Juan said. "They thrive in high risk environments. Soldiers going into battle time and time again, firefighters, the SEALS and a hundred more occupations and situation that men and women chose to accept and triumph over."

"Diana marching two hundred brave advocates of freedom through a mile of screaming, rock hurling thugs," Susan said.

"Or you and Terrance standing firm, challenging Virginia Patriot's campus police and getting yourselves locked up," Juan said.

"That's not anything close to what Mr. Wolf or Diana do," she replied, looking skeptical.

"It's only a matter of degree," Juan explained. "The fact that you chose to work at the nation's leading advocacy for individual rights and liberty tells me that push comes to shove, Susan Baker will stand and fight if and when the time comes. Am I wrong?"

A grin spread across her lips. "No...at least I hope not."

"I am absolutely certain that you won't back down when it counts," Juan said, smiling warmly at the young lawyer.

His phone buzzed, indicating an internal call. He signaled for Susan to wait a moment and answered it.

"Who? ... But if he wanted to speak with Wolf why call me? ... Really, that's interesting. Happy to talk with him; tell him to drop by ... I get that. Put me on hold and ask if he'd be willing to meet us at a place he designates."

"Do me a favor and call Terrance to come over," Juan said, looking at Susan and holding the phone at his ear. "I might have an interesting mission for you...hold on..." He listened to the assistant on the phone and thanked him. "Okay, meeting's at noon, man named Mbuso. I'll forward the text to your phones. Apparently Mr. Mbuso has something to tell us about financial finagling; didn't say where."

*   *   *   *

"Thank you for meeting with us, Mr. Mbuso," Terrance said. "My colleague, Susan Baker." They took a seat across from each other in the far corner of an eatery in the Pentagon City Mall. "I understand you have some information about college finances you wish to talk about."

Mbuso looked at both lawyers guardedly possibly weighing what, if anything, and how much of something he would share. When he sighed audibly, Terrance guessed he would tell them something.

"I am an accountant," he began, speaking with a slight British accent. "I work for a company named Universal Accounting; we have offices in a dozen states and here in Washington. My company performs independent audits and other financial services for colleges and universities." He paused for a moment, and in a lowered voice said, "I work with several universities including Ivygreen College."

Terrance's expression remained professionally attentive, but inside he was bursting with excitement. Glancing at Susan, he saw her eyes widen and lips tightening with expectation. Being an experienced CIR lawyer, he was accustomed to dealing with clandestine meetings and controversial situations and had learned to be patient. It was never helpful to rush an informant who most often was nervous or even frightened at the prospect of divulging information.

"I emigrated," Mbuso said, then stopped. "No, that is not accurate. I was driven out of my native land. I am a fugitive from an increasingly illiberal South Africa. I was a professor of economics at the University of South Africa where I taught for many years. Beginning in 2009 the ANC, that is the African National Congress, became increasingly corrupt, misusing funds for personal gain and the like. The party is also Marxist and leaning heavily communist.

"They have also become overtly racist, leading party functionaries making remarks about cleansing the nation of whites. As an economics professor teaching and traveling in Africa, I am a firsthand witness to the extensive economic damage Marxists and run-of-the-mill dictators have caused all across the continent. I strove to provide my students an accurate picture of what I saw firsthand and think deeply about economic issues in South Africa and their social and economic results." Mbuso paused, smiling sheepishly then continued. "Please accept my apologies for my long introduction, but I want you to fully understand."

"No need to apologize, sir," Terrance said.

"Please do continue," Susan said, smiling encouragingly. "I'm very interested in what you are saying; I know Terrance is too."

"You are very kind, thank you," Mbuso said, his bright white smile lighting up his dark visage. "Although my students were very appreciative of my class, local ANC party leaders were not. Because of my support for free trade and my criticism that the rise of governmental control over virtually every aspect of business—from the corporate board room to the street vendor—was strangling the economy and causing it to decline, they labeled me a tool of the white oppressors. They began a campaign to discredit me and pressure the university to fire me. When I published studies about the financial malfeasance of party members, the threats began. When I refused to stay silent, my house caught fire and I narrowly escaped. My options came down to a simple choice: become a fugitive or die. I came to America in 2013 hoping to teach at a college, but uninvited itinerant scholars need not apply. Being a former academic and economist, I secured employment with Universal Accounting by mid 2014."

Taking advantage of a pause, Susan said, "You are a man of high principle and you choose to act on your principles. You have seen something that offends you and contacted us."

"Yes," Mbuso said, nodding slowly. "I have become increasingly disturbed by the accounting practices of the universities I conduct audits for. I mentioned Ivygreen College initially because their accounting practices, especially by their Office of Scholarships and Endowment, appears to be the most, ah, *creative*. I also strongly suspect collusion by—no, let me speak about the colleges for now.

"Allow me to preface my concerns by voicing my bias against the ridiculous high cost of college. Student loan debt has exceeded consumer debt; it is not only a travesty, but a significant drag on the national economy and the future success and happiness of millions of young people. These debtors defer starting their lives because they are buried under one and one half trillion dollar debt and cannot afford to get on with their own American dream. A noteworthy cause of this malady is what I see when auditing the colleges."

* * * *

Diana peered at Dr. Mbuso's biography. "And you have verified that he is who he says he is."

"Yes," Terrance confirmed. "We've checked with our independent sources and Dr. Mbuso's story of persecution and attempted murder by arson is legitimate."

"As is his employment at Universal Accounting," Susan added.

Diana shot an expectant look at Juan, who had listened silently as the two junior counselors made their report to her. Having worked with the man for over five years he would know what her glance meant.

A grin formed on his lips and he said, "Dr. Mbuso is everything he says he is and more. The burning question, however, is he telling us the truth about financial improprieties at Ivygreen and the other colleges he audits?"

"You met with him for an hour," Diana said, looking at Susan and Terrance. "Based on your account, most of that time was spent him talking about the economic and political conditions and trends in South Africa and his concerns about similar trends here. What specifically did he tell you about the financial hanky-panky going on at these colleges?"

Terrance and Susan looked at each other. Susan spoke first.

"He didn't go into detail; he talked about how these colleges were misrepresenting their endowment campaigns and misusing the money being donated. When we asked if he had brought any financial records with him that would illustrate his claim, he said that calling us was a spur of the moment decision since he happened to be in town."

"That's convenient," Diana said, her tone tinged with sarcasm.

"Dr. Mbuso did promise to provide documentation in the near future," Terrance assured her.

"Assuming he's legit," Juan said, "it could be the leverage we need to flip Ivygreen or another college."

Although Diana very much wanted some way to kick in the gates of these walled educational bastions, she had specific parameters for the types of battering rams used. There would be no horse-trading, no backroom deals, no pay for play and no quid pro quo.

"If Mbuso is all he says he is," Diana began, "then he is coming to us because he believes we will take action on the information he is going to provide us. You agree?"

"Of course," Juan said. "With the media's leadership earning a reputation for screwing their own mothers for a one percent bump in clicks, whistleblowers know that only a select number of organizations can be trusted not to screw them, too. We are among that select few."

"If Dr. Mbuso hands you a three inch file crammed full with gory financial details that will bring down any number of college upper management," Diana continued. "What do you plan to do with them?"

Juan's eyebrows ticked up slightly. Diana knew the meaning of that subtle action, having become quite familiar with the man's physical and non-physical cues over the years. It was also one of the reason Juan regularly declined to play poker.

Juan shot her a droll look and said, "I'd tell Ivygreen's administration it's either agree to the terms of our class action suit or they personally crash and burn."

Both Terrance and Susan stared at their boss with open mouths. Diana and Juan laughed at their shocked expressions.

"You have chosen wisely," Juan joked. "CIR does not compromise—ever. We would never take incriminating evidence from Dr. Mbuso and use it as blackmail to get a college to roll over to our demands. Doing so even once would permanently damage our pristine reputation as an incorruptible independent voice. We'd be seen as just another wheeler & dealer for monetary or political gain."

"That's why Juan gets the big bucks," Diana teased. She smiled mischievously, adding, "How was the mall? Beautifully decked out for Christmas as always? Did you visit Santa?"

*　　*　　*　　*

"I can neither confirm or deny that someone matching my description might have entered the Royal Sonesta Hotel sometime within the previous forty-eight hours," Wolf said, to Captain Marks offering the officer what he hoped was a convincingly perplexed look.

Marks puckered his lips in a most, you are full of, it manner. "If you had to guess, what might this lookalike have found in Talbot's hotel room?"

"I'd imagine this person, whoever he was, would most likely have found exactly what your officers found when they searched her room," Wolf said.

"Are you certain he'd have found nothing?" Marks replied, looking suspicious. "Such a person might have discovered something important and perhaps wanting to be like Grayson Wolf, he might want to follow where that something led."

"Well, I do agree that a multitude of admirers are looking to pick up my mantle and go forth to battle evildoers now that I'm retired from my career as a superhero," Wolf grinned. "And I'm willing to bet that what my doubleganger discovered in Maggie's room was something *missing*."

"And what might that be?" Marks said, looking attentive.

"What every bonafide lawyer would have with them: a briefcase," Wolf replied. "There wasn't one in the stall where I found Maggie and I bet my shadow didn't find a briefcase in Maggie's room. I'd say that was significant."

"Any clue what was in it?" Marks asked. "What color was it? Any identifying markings?"

"Easy there, tiger," Wolf quipped. "You may recall I haven't seen Maggie since August, that I was meeting her at the restaurant and that she wasn't there when I arrived. I have no clue about contents, shape, color or markings of said briefcase. I am, however, pretty certain that she called for the meeting to give me the contents of the missing briefcase and that she was killed for what she knew."

"Okay, at least we have a motive, though a highly speculative one," Marks said.

"Have you found out what killed her?" Wolf asked.

Mark's eyebrows rose significantly. "You know I can't share information about an ongoing investigation."

"Captain," Wolf said, a hurt expression on his face. "I'm not some Joe off the street."

Marks barked a laugh. "That's exactly who you are. You walked into my office off the street."

"Look, I know Maddie was poisoned. Hypothetically, what might this poison have been? You can be sure that no mention of any guess will leak onto the streets."

"Still can't talk about an ongoing investigation," Mark's said, again. "But there's a rumor that whatever it was, it's fast acting. Ten, fifteen, minutes."

"That sounds like a nerve agent, but in her drink?" Wolf said.

"Absolutely, the liquid prevents it from evaporating and sickening half the guests in the restaurant," Marks said. When Wolf looked surprised, he added, "Ex-Army; toxicology specialist. Tons of bad shit out there."

"Anything on the surveillance recordings?" Wolf suggested. "Someone walking past Maggie's table or getting real close to the waiter carrying the drink?"

"What part about not allowed to discuss an ongoing investigation you not getting?" Marks replied, a crooked grin appearing on his face. "Assuming there is any surveillance record, I'd bet we'd find none of what you said on them."

"Then the poison was administered at or near the bar where the wine was poured," Wolf said. Studying the captain's face he guessed that his conjecture was correct. He also spotted something more...something not very encouraging. "Let's recap: Maggie Talbot was killed by an unknown assailant using a nerve agent that was placed in her drink somewhere near where the wine was dispensed and is lethal within fifteen minutes of ingesting it. Whatever surveillance record is available, none shows anyone getting close enough to the waiter to poison Maggie's wine. By now, your detectives have interviewed the staff and others who were in the area and have come up with bupkis. We have no suspect, no clue where and how the poison was administered and no witnesses who saw anything. That about sums it up, captain?"

Marks looked disgusted and shrugged helplessly. "Can't talk about an ongoing investigation, Mr. Wolf."

"So I've heard."

Wolf had spent all of Sunday and most of Monday prowling around the Conference Center talking with Maggie's colleagues attending the convention, everyone working at the restaurant, sundry employees at the Royal Sonesta Hotel and the last hour with Captain Marks, chief of Baltimore's Central District, all to no avail. Whoever killed Maggie was a professional who knew how to handle an extremely dangerous never agent. And whoever had sent such a highly skilled assassin had to be highly connected because whatever documents Maggie was carrying in her missing briefcase had to be devastatingly damaging to this person or persons.

Wolf decided further investigation was futile and started to head for home. He had just turned on I-395 heading for 95 south when his phone rang. It was RJ.

"Wazzzup bro?"

"Justin Bellamy's dead. Murdered in his highly secure condo."

Chapter 7

Suicide Mission

"RJ gave me the scoop about Justin Bellamy last night," Wolf said. Diana had called for a meeting of CIR's Executive Committee and the group had assembled in the Jefferson Conference Room. "Anything new about his sudden demise?"

Everyone in the room turned their eyes toward RJ.

"Why you 'all lookin' at me? I didn't kill the raping bastard."

"Maybe because you've been rooting for someone to take him out since they let him out on bail?" Brett Casings said, laughing.

"Just so we're clear, I'm firmly aligned with our mission of protecting individual rights," RJ said. "But I'm also not going to shed a tear when a scumbag like Bellamy can manipulate the system, get away with raping women along with his spawn and winds up biting the dust."

Wolf knew the reason for RJ's vehemence toward abusers of all kinds, having been the target of verbal and physical abuse during middle school for the crime of being gay. The two became fast friends when Wolf spotted RJ surrounded by a group of taunting boys on his way home from school one May afternoon. Taunting rapidly escalated to pushing and shoving, knocking the hapless RJ flat on his back, some boys kicking the prone victim.

Wolf rushed to his aid, thrusting his way through, his feet straddling RJ as he violently shoved the kickers away. RJ got up just as a melee ensued, fists and feet engaging in a free-for-all that left all combatants bruised and bloodied. Wolf was the better fighter, having a year's experience in Karate, his blows consistently landing with greater accuracy and force than that of his adversaries. That afternoon brawl ended further physical abuse of RJ by the local jerks and began a life-long friendship.

"And don't bother looking my way either," Wolf joked. "Captain Marks of the Baltimore Police has already checked whether I made an unscheduled stop over at Newark on my way back from Boston and has come up empty handed. Though I share RJ's disgust for Bellamy, I would much rather see that sicko rotting in jail than dead."

"Juan updated me about your impromptu investigation," Diana said, peering unhappily at him. "Susan was quite concerned about leaving you in Baltimore with a killer on the loose."

"There's always been a potential killer breathing down my neck," Wolf quipped. "I wasn't worried because whoever it was knew I didn't get whatever incriminating materials Maddie was intending to give me. Sure wish she'd have at least given me a clue what they were; we'd be tracking them down instead of sitting around speculating."

He hadn't mentioned seeing Colleen Silverstone at the conference center, certain that doing so would result in derailing the meeting as speculation about her being there would dominate the next hour.

"On that note, I'd like to move on to other business," Diana said. "You're up, Juan."

The senior counselor briefed the committee about the meeting with Mbuso, adding all the cautions raised during yesterday's report by Terrance and Susan. A lively discussion followed his presentation, the group debate centering on how Mbuso's revelations will complicate CIR's class action suit while simultaneously increasing the Center's work load potentially causing a loss of focus as well as burn-out.

"The reality is that our people are already working overtime," Jewel King pointed out. Jewel had been promoted as head of Human Resources back in the fall while continuing her responsibility taking care of scheduling and events. "We need to hire additional staff and we need to hire them soon—by January at the latest."

"Just in time when donations are scheduled to drop by twenty percent or more," Annika said.

"We are logging an average of five hours overtime per person per week," Jewel said. "We have forty-seven employees, not counting the Executive Team. That's almost a thousand hours overtime. How much are we paying for that overtime, Annika?"

The CFO sighed and said, "About fifty thousand a month; over half a million annually."

"Enough to hire ten employees," Jewel stated. "That's a no brainer from where I'm sitting. We control the entire sixth floor, so we have room to expand. More staff means more work being done and less stressed personnel working longer hours every week."

"I'm with Jewel," Teena Sanoe, head of security said. "I'd love to get at least one of those ten new hires to shore up our muscle 'cause we're even less popular with certain entrenched segments of our society than we were six months ago. I know that's shocking, but there it is."

"Which I consider to be the most accurate measure of our success there is," Wolf said. "Just wait until we smother a couple dozen ivory towers under Juan's class action blanket. I'm thinking half of those new hires Jewel is asking for should go to Teena."

No one laughed. Wolf's quip reflected the reality of the backlash that would ensue once universities began to crumble under CIR's legal assault. During Diana's free speech protest and march on Virginia Patriots College earlier in the year, not only was Teena's security detail beefed up, CIR became an armed camp as virtually every employee carried a weapon.

The committee voted on Diana's motion to hire eight new employees, which passed unanimously. Next order of business was how to employ whatever incriminating financial information about Ivygreen College and others Mbuso would provide. After the initial round-robin opening comments, Diana recognized RJ who took the floor.

"We're looking at this the wrong way: this is not a problem but a wonderful opportunity. The central theme of Juan's legal challenge is that these universities are practicing a form of bait and switch. The bait is a promise of equal opportunities, freedom to explore ideas, express opinions, all the while actively or passively taking action against ideas they disapprove of and punishing students who express them." He paused, scanning the room, clearly delighted by the expectant expressions on the faces of the group. He flashed an exaggerated grin and continued. "Enter Dr. Mbuso offering to hand us a financial cudgel with which to bash in their larcenous faces and we think this is somehow a problem? That recruitment malfeasance and financial malfeasance are separate animals instead of being litter mates from the same lying bitch?"

Wolf's smile lit up his face. Robert Jano was one of the most astute masters of communication who could organize a media campaign better than virtually anyone. Thank the fates RJ didn't work for some power lusting politician, lobbyist or shady corporation.

RJ's elucidation of the topic resulted in an upwelling of enthusiasm as ideas flew fast and furious, plans were outlined and congratulations offered to one and all. In the midst of this swirling excitement, Wolf's phone warbled, indicating an intercom caller. Looking at the screen, he saw it was from reception, CIR's first line of defense against practitioners of the dark arts hoping to bypass the caretakers of incoming communication.

He thanked the receptionist and accepted the incoming call, walking out of the room to get away from the vocal din.

"This is Wolf..."

"Mr. Wolf, this is Jeff Kramm."

He knew who the caller was, the receptionist having informed him. But it was still a shock to actually hear the man's voice.

"How may I help you, Mr. Kramm?" There was no warmth in his tone. Wolf hoped his reply didn't sound like a snarl ... well at least not too much like a snarl.

"I would like to speak with you at your earliest convenience," Kramm said. "I'm willing to come to a location of your choice, of course, but would prefer meeting at my home ... I sincerely hope you will agree to see me."

"May I ask the reason for this meeting?"

"My daughter's suicide."

Wolf's eyebrows ticked up in surprise. He had read about Stephanie's—or was it Steven's—suicide couple weeks back. It could be a trick; Kramm wasn't above using his child's death to lure him into a situation where the man could heap his vitriol about Grayson Wolf upon his head. Wolf chastised himself for such an unkind thought, though Kramm and his cohorts in the media were a contemptible lot.

Wolf issued an involuntary sniff at the thought that bad news and deaths, apparently, came in threes. Wolves being naturally curious, Wolf accepted Kramm's offer to meet, deciding that he'd walk into the man's home alone and unafraid. After all, it was everyone else who was afraid of the big, bad Grayson Wolf. And they had good reason to be if they were engaged in dubious or nefarious activities because this Wolf could and had blown down the mansions of the rich, the famous and the powerful.

Jeff Kramm's estate was a forty-minute drive north across the Potomac into Maryland then a few miles west skirting the river. Wolf lowered his window as he rolled up to the gate, stopping next to a security station sporting cameras and communicators. He looked directly at one of the lenses pointed in his direction and spoke his name. The gate rolled open and shut behind him as he drove up to the building's main entrance, parked and approached a set of impressive wooden doors, one of which opened as he neared. A man stepped out to greet him. Wolf opened his arms wide and said,

"I am armed."

"You will have to surrender your weapon, Mr. Wolf."

"Won't do that."

"Then I cannot permit you to enter."

"I understand," Wolf said, lowering his arms. "Please give Mr. Kramm my regrets." He turned and started to walk back to the car.

"Mr. Wolf," the guard called after him. "You may keep your weapon."

The operative led Wolf through the foyer, past several grand living and reception rooms into a less formal, wood-paneled hearth room complete with a blazing fire. Wolf noted the absence of any holiday decorations.

Jeff Kramm was standing next to his wife sitting in one of the comfortable arm chairs arranged near the fireplace. He thanked the escort.

"Good morning, Mr. Wolf." Kramm introduced his wife who smiled wanly in greeting. "Would you care for coffee, tea or other refreshment?"

"No, thank you," Wolf said. "Good morning; please accept my sincere condolences for the death of your, um, child."

An ironic smile touched Kramm's lips. "I prefer to remember her as our daughter not what she—" He stopped. "Please have a seat... I'm sure you must be curious why I asked to meet with you, especially in light of our past—and present—relationship."

A droll grin touched Wolf's lips. The man had a flair for understatement. Jeff Kramm was the owner of several prominent national newspapers including *The Washington Progressive*, its editor routinely attacking CIR generally and especially Wolf personally. Depending upon the week, or the weather, the paper featured one or the other or both as hapless tools of white supremacists, anti-immigration advocates, cheerleaders for rapacious capitalism, enemies of the poor and homeless and sundry other disparagements.

The Washington Progressive, along with virtually every other newspaper and media outle,t had been antagonistic toward Wolf and his organization as a matter of course for years coming to a fever pitch when Wolf published *Media's Useful Idiots: Undermining Liberty For Fun and Profit.* The expose prominently featured owners such as Kramm, living high on the hog, their papers and news outlets pandering to tribal instinct to keep readers' eyeballs on the pages of their (diminishing) print products and pump up online viewer clicks. Add clear political bias to the mix and the media was playing a central role in dragging the country down into a socialistic morass of one kind or another.

There was a justified reason for nicknaming *The Washington Progressive* the "Potomac Pravda," the latter having been the chief propaganda mouthpiece for Russia's communist dictatorship. Pravda is Russian for truth, an irony clearly evaded by a significant portion of America's media.

Wisely choosing not to step into that minefield, Wolf said, "You mentioned on the phone you wanted to discuss Stephanie's suicide."

Wolf saw Ms. Kramm's expression harden. A knot formed in his stomach at the possibility that his book might have been the trigger to drive their daughter to commit suicide.

"Yes," Kramm replied. "You are aware that our daughter changed her sex some years ago. She came home from college—she had just finished her sophomore year—informing us that she was a man trapped in a woman's body. She complained about feeling depressed and anxious for some time and had to change her sex. She was nineteen at the time."

"Stephanie was quite adamant," Ms. Kramm said. "She said she'd always felt like she was the wrong sex. I thought this peculiar since she was quite a girls girl throughout her childhood and dated boys in high school. She went to the senior prom, for goodness sake!

How could she wake up one morning and discover she was born the wrong sex after clearly being comfortable with whom she was for all those years?"

Wolf nodded sympathetically. He had a good idea what happened to their daughter: Rapid Onset Gender Dysphoria. It was all the rage these days afflicting mostly girls, which instinctually caused Wolf to consider the phenomena suspect. CIR had an employee who did have a sex change in his late teens and from the little he spoke of it, there was no doubt that he had been born the wrong sex. He was also quite clear about being grateful for the ability of the medical profession to change him from a woman to a man, emphatic that it changed his whole life.

"Stephanie was twenty-six," Wolf said. "Was there some traumatic event that caused her to end her life?"

"Not a tragedy," Kramm said. "Increasing and debilitating depression. Changing one's sex is not like getting a face lift or cosmetic dentistry. It's highly invasive, surgeries such as mastectomies, drugs that also make one sterile, hormone replacement therapy and then months or years of psychotherapy. She cut herself off from everyone and remained in her room. She didn't even leave her room to join us for dinner the last eight months. We did everything we could, bring in psychologists, medication for depression; nothing worked."

"Shortly before her death, Stephanie admitted she had made a terrible mistake," Ms. Kramm said. "She was angry at allowing herself to become convinced that she wasn't really a woman but a man striving to come out."

"That admission seemed to ease her pain; she even joined us at a few dinners. Carolyn and I started to feel like there was hope," Kramm said, looking at Wolf meaningfully. "Foolish of me. I should have suspected that her change of attitude signaled something even worse ... she died a week later."

Wolf listened and said nothing. Mostly he felt puzzled why Kramm asked him to come. It couldn't be just to lighten their emotional burden. He wondered if perhaps there was some question about it being a suicide, his thoughts flashing back to Colorado when he looked into another suicide that wasn't suicide. He decided to take the bull by the horns.

"Do you have any doubts about it being suicide?"

"None," Kramm said. "I'm sorry about being vague concerning why I asked you to come. I'd like to hire you to investigate the cause of this recent and disturbing trend. My daughter's situation and outcome is not an exception. I know several others in my circle of acquaintances struggling with similar issues and concerns. Stephanie's suicide is not the only one; there are others."

Wolf peered at the media mogul with incredulity. There was no indication in the man's expression that he was putting him on or baiting him with a hidden motive. He concluded the man was serious.

"I'm sorry, but I do not hire out my services," Wolf said. "I can't appear to have any real or imagined conflicts of interest."

"I understand," Kramm said. "Knowing your view of exchange of value for value and I didn't want to ask for your assistance without an offer of payment."

"Mr. Kramm," Wolf said. "You own several national newspapers. Why not have your staff investigate?"

Kramm shot Wolf an ironic look, his accompanying smile not a happy one. "Conflict of interest."

Wolf understood immediately. The head of the leading progressive newspapers directing his editors to investigate a keystone of the progressive agenda to achieve their fantasy of perfect sexual social equality would bring down a firestorm of condemnation upon Kramm and his papers. His position was a clear case of preventing the chicken furies from coming home to roost and creating a royal mess in his businesses and homes.

Wolf was not inclined to offer himself up as cover for Kramm's desire to assuage whatever guilt he and his wife felt pursuant to their daughter's suicide. For years, both had been prominent promoters of progressive ideas, including children's right to choose the gender they feel most comfortable with. He was about to decline, when he remembered the Kramm's had lost a child to suicide. Truth be told, there was something unsavory going on behind this nationwide momentum for changing one's gender and the cheerleaders who trumpeted it far, wide and loudly.

"You said Stephanie lived at home. I'd like to take a look around her room; get a better idea of your daughter."

Wolf's request sounded more like an order, but if they wanted him to look into the gender change craze, then he was going to set the terms—and the tone.

Kramm led Wolf to Stephanie's room, but did not enter. The place turned out to be an apartment suite complete with living area, bedroom, and large bathroom. It had all the amenities required for someone planning to hibernate for a long time. A mini-kitchenette with refrigerator, impressive entertainment center, comfortable sofa and several recliners. Though the rooms had been serviced, Wolf guessed that the suite was pretty much as it was when Stephanie last inhabited it, including the drawn curtains on the windows.

Wolf walked slowly and deliberatively though each room, his eyes scanning walls, floors, the type of videos stacked alongside the TV, sundry knick-knacks resting on furniture. He opened closets, fingering through clothing and inspecting the contents of drawers.

He sat on the bed, looking around, trying to get a feeling for what Stephanie must have seen every evening and morning from this vantage point. Like the living room, the curtains were drawn, blocking out the world outside. The walls were bare—no pictures, posters, or framed pieced of art created when she was still young and filled with life and dreams.

It was a depressing place and most certainly a depressing existence. Wolf felt genuinely sorry for the confused, angry young woman who spent three years cooped up in this living tomb. He got up to check the bathroom when he spotted a thin drawer nestled beneath the night table, its larger surface effectively concealing its presence. Sliding it open, he found some pens, notebook—its pages empty—and a brochure wedged in the back.

Dislodging it, Wolf looked at the glossy cover sporting the smiling faces of a man and a woman with the caption, "We switched and we're finally happy!" The bottom of the panel was imprinted with bright gold initials: ATTC. Flipping it over, Wolf discovered what the initials represented: Affirmative Transformation Treatment Centers, remembering where he had heard that name before. He returned the pens and notebook to the drawer, taking the brochure with him.

"Did Stephanie use this medical facility for her sex change procedure?" Wolf said, entering the hearth room holding the brochure toward the Kramms.

"Yes," Kramm said. "You found that in her room?" When Wolf nodded, he added, "I'm surprised she kept any reminder, especially not anywhere near her. Stephanie destroyed everything associated with ATTC and anything connected to gender reassignment. Burned reams of it in the bathtub; set the smoke alarms off for a week."

"Is there one in the DC area?" Wolf asked.

"I'm not sure," he replied. "Maybe today, but not four years ago. She attended college and had the operation there."

"What college was she attending?" Wolf asked.

"Ivygreen," Kramm said. "She never graduated ... It took months of recovery, therapy and further medical treatment. She missed the first semester of her junior year and never went back. She insisted on living on her own, but things got too much for her and she came home that summer. Like I said earlier, a sex change isn't remotely like getting a facelift."

"Ivygreen," Wolf repeated. Coincidences. Why did it have to be coincidences, he thought. If there was anything that set him off wading into the muck, it was coincidences. "Did you keep any of Stephanie's papers? List of friends? College papers? Yearbook? Contacts?"

Kramm's face lit up. "Have you decided to investigate?"

"I can't make any promises," Wolf replied. "As I'm sure you're aware, my people are rather occupied with several major projects and my inbox is stuffed and becoming more so." A smile touched his lips. "I've also retired from my old career, in case you haven't heard. I can tell you this: you are the second person who has approached me pursuant to gender change within a week. If I do find time to look into this, I promise I will let you know if I find anything."

"Can't ask for more than that. Thank you," Kramm said. "I do know this: if you do find the time and there is something hinky going on, you will uncover it." He stuck out his hand.

Wolf grinned and shook hands. "Of that you can be sure."

"I'm counting on it," Kramm said, his smile appearing genuine.

"Thank you, Mr. Wolf," Ms. Kramm said, rising from her seat. "You are a good man."

Hearing the sadness in her voice, Wolf's heart went out to the grieving mother. Having just experienced the death of a former friend, he had idea about the loss a parent would feel.

"I am very sorry about your daughter. If I do have the opportunity to look into this, I hope that I'll be able to offer both of you some measure of comfort by what I discover."

"If anyone can, it's you, Mr. Wolf," she said. A wan smile formed on her lips. "I've read all your books. So has Jeff. You're very brave. I also enjoy your new fiction novels."

"Thank you," Wolf said, smiling warmly. A thought struck him. "Mr. Kramm, is there anyone at one of your papers who might have written about gender issues in less than glowing terms?"

The media mogul shot him a humorous look. "If I didn't know who Grayson Wolf was, I'd think you were either impertinent or ignorant. No, I can't think of anyone...I'll call around and see if I can uncover such a turncoat within our midst."

"Viva the rational resistance," Wolf quipped, his grin showing lots of teeth. Beautiful teeth, to be sure. Dangerously sharp, too.

Kramm shot him a sardonic look.

"I'll walk you out, Mr. Wolf."

Chapter 8

Gender Studies

"I wish you'd stop doing your lone wolf thing running after tasty game to devour," Diana scolded. "I know you think I'm Wonder Woman who can keep all the balls we're juggling safely in the air, Wolf. But you're president of CIR and like it or not, you run the show. After it's all said and done, your decision is the only one that counts."

"Stop your bellyaching, Wonder Woman!" Wolf chided. "People overhearing you talk like that might think your powers are waning in your old age."

Diana shot him an evil glance. "You do realize you're within striking distance? Stop deflecting and inform me next time you get a call and disappear without notice. I'm serious, Wolf!"

"Okay den mother," he teased. "But, come on, Diana, it's only Montgomery County. Nothing happens in Montgomery County."

"You get a call from Jeff Kramm, one of America's media enemies of liberty prominently featured in your book, and walk blithely into his house," Diana said, her tone dripping with sarcasm. "And tell no one about you doing so."

"I was carrying," he said. "And he let me keep my weapon."

"You'll have to excuse me if I don't find this funny," she retorted. "Earlier this year you were run off the road and almost got killed. Days later, you were shot at while leaving a prison. A week later a bear almost made a meal out of you. And now you inform me about your little home visit to someone you really pissed off. No more going rouge, Wolf."

Wolf raised his hand above his head. "Alright, alright. From now on I'll keep you informed about all my travels and movements."

A humorous grin appeared. "You can skip the movements updates, thank you. So, what did the Kramm want?"

Wolf gave Diana an accurate account of his meeting with Kramm and his wife, omitting some key details. Reaching into his pocket, he took out a folded brochure and handed it to her. She looked at briefly.

"This is significant, why?" she asked.

"Because I met with a surgeon after my radio interview in Boston last week who works for these people and who expressed concern about the increasing number of sex change operations," Wolf explained. "*And* Kramm's daughter, Stephanie, who was attending college in Boston, had her sex change procedures done at that medical facility."

"*And?*" Diana said, looking expectantly at Wolf. She would know from long experience he always had more to reveal.

"*And*," Wolf said, grinning, "Stephanie Kramm was a student at Ivygreen College at the time she discovered that there was a man trapped in her female body that needed to brought forth."

"Ivygreen College," Diana repeated. "And what exactly is our esteemed Mr. Kramm asking you to do? And why isn't he doing it himself? He's got five newspapers and a cable network at his disposal." Seeing the look on Wolf's face, she added, "Unbelievable! He and his useless idiots peddle their collectivist crap twenty-four-seven for fun and profit and he want us to do the dirty work so as not to offend their permanently offended useful idiots and lose a few bucks! Are you smacked!"

"Yes to everything before the smacked part," Wolf said. "One word: Ivygreen. One more nail in their coffin. I can't point to anything rotten—yet—but it's there. We've already got them in our class action sights. If Mbuso's claims are legit, we'll have them by their financial throat. Add some kind of nasty sex change collusion and we might have enough explosive to level the entire college, or more than one college, Diana. And if what we uncover gives Stephanie's grieving parents some comfort, that's no skin off our noses, or money out of our pockets, or makes us their stooges."

Diana smiled in a helpless way. "What's the plan?"

"Start digging."

Brett Casings assured Wolf he'd get whatever data there was floating around in the Ethernet about the Watertown gender change facility to him in short order.

Jewel King made arrangements for a charter flight from Dulles to Boston, a car rental and reservations at the Hyatt Regency in Cambridge.

Wolf landed at Boston Logan by four that same afternoon, collected his rental and hung his clothes in the hotel closet before the stoke of five. After a relaxing shower, he checked his phone. As promised, Brett had a sizable chunk of information waiting for him about the Affirmative Transformation Treatment Centers, with a separate file about the one in Watertown. Knowing Wolf's preferences, Brett had provided summaries about the company nationally and the one at Watertown, including complaints, malpractice and other legal suits, articles critical of their practices, treatment and so forth.

Wolf slid from the driver's seat of his rental at ATTC's Watertown facility shortly after nine the next morning and entered the lobby. A receptionist sat behind a desk, her eyes looking down. Wolf was very familiar with that position and it never failed to provoke him to act accordingly.

He swept past the preoccupied employee and made for one of the doors marked, Medical Personnel Only.

"Hey! You can't go in there!"

Wolf stopped and turned. "Why not? You obviously don't care who comes or goes considering your nose was buried in your little hand friend the entire minute I was patiently waiting for you to come up for air."

At first surprised, her expression transformed into a confrontational one in a flash. "What do you want?"

"Getting your ass fired would be a start," Wolf fired back. "I'll settle for you calling Dr. Hicks and let her know her lawyer has arrived."

The receptionist's expression softened significantly. "Dr. Hicks is dead. Car accident last Sunday night."

Wolf held her eyes, thinking she was jerking his chain. Seeing her face fall further into something resembling distress he concluded she was telling the truth.

"Killed in a car accident last Sunday," Wolf said. "Thank you."

Wolf turned on his heels and made for the car.

"Car accident," he said, to himself sitting behind the wheel staring out the window thinking. "What a convenient coincidence." A sudden stab of paranoia caused him to press the Bluetooth unit resting on his ear. "Jeff Kramm," he said firmly. The phone repeated the name, which he confirmed. It connected on the third ring.

"You have reached Mr. Kramm's answering service, how may I help you?"

"Inform Mr. Kramm that Mr. Gray from Tysons Corner is calling him," Wolf said.

"One moment sir, I'll see if he's available."

The line went silent, followed shortly by a click.

"Mr. Wolf." It was Kramm's voice. "You have news already?"

"LeeAnn Hicks has died," Wolf said.

"Who is that?"

"Dr. Hick's was a surgeon at ATTC in Watertown," Wolf said.

"I don't recall Stephanie ever mentioning her," Kramm replied. "You say she died?"

"Car accident last Sunday," Wolf said. "Are you sure you don't have any connection to Hicks?"

"No I do not," Kramm shot back. "And I don't like what you are suggesting. I don't know this doctor, never heard her name. Please believe me."

His acute suspicions abating, Wolf took control of his emotions. "Sorry. Dr. Hicks is the person I mentioned who approached me about ATTC. I came to speak with her and she's dead."

"It's winter, Mr. Wolf," Kramm said, probably trying to sound helpful. "Lot more accidents in the winter. Just a coincidence, I'm sure."

"You might be right," Wolf said. "Sorry about getting testy."

"Forget it," Kramm said. "If I got upset every time someone was unhappy about me—or said harsh things about me in a book—I'd be in a permanent state of high dudgeon."

Wolf heard the subtle humor in his voice and couldn't help grinning. "Thanks for taking my call."

"Any time, Mr. Gray."

Wolf ended the call and made another to the local police station. He marveled at the ease he switched into private detective mode. Having recently been immersed in a protracted investigation of rape, murder, attempted murder of self, conspiracy to cover up the crimes and working with the foremost hardcore investigator in the country could account for that.

"Happens more than people know," Sergeant McCrea of the Watertown Police Department said. "Just because the roads look clear and dry, don't mean every part is. Snow melts in the day and washes over a section of road. Sun goes down, that water freezes and now we got black ice—hard to spot at night."

The policewoman was an avid reader, supporter of CIR and recognized Wolf the moment he walked into the station. She was excited about meeting him and happy to help anyway she could, hustling him into an office away from others.

"That what happened to Hicks?" Wolf said. "Hit black ice, slid off the road into the river and drowned?"

"'fraid so," McCrea confirmed. "Let me show you..." she pulled up a map showing a closeup of a section of road running parallel to the Charles River. "Hicks was traveling east on Charles River Road—we think about nine at night—came around this curve, hit that black ice skidded off the road. See how close the road is to the Charles; fifty feet at most. Nothing to stop her from going over the bank and hit the icy water."

"How high is the riverbank at that point?" Wolf asked.

"About five feet; less maybe," McCrea said. "But even that short fall can cause the average driver to become disoriented. It's dark, the driver's confused, ice cold water fills the cabin, impairs breathing and it doesn't take long for a person to drown. We get one or two cases like this every year. Drivers get careless, drive too fast and accidents happen. Shame."

"Thank you, sergeant," Wolf said. "I very much appreciate your time."

"You're more than welcome, Mr. Wolf," she said, smiling. "Happy to help anytime."

He shook her hand and stepped toward the door when he had a thought. "Would it be possible for me to take a look at Dr. Hick's car?"

"I don't think so. Sorry," she replied.

"I promise I won't touch anything," Wolf said, giving her a warm smile. "And I might just have a couple signed books available."

Her face lit up with humor. "Mr. Wolf, are you attempting to bribe an officer of the law?"

"I'd never consider bribing anyone, especially an officer of the law," Wolf replied, looking droll. "Just a token of my appreciation for service, office McCrae."

"Now that I think of it, I haven't looked at the car myself," she replied. "I don't know of any rule about not allowing a civvy to tag along. The car is in the impound lot; we'll drive over."

The ride was short and the keeper of the keys said nothing about Wolf entering the facility with McCrea.

"Here it is," she said.

The car was positioned under a covered portion of the lot, presumably to preserve evidence from being destroyed by the elements if the car stood in the open, unprotected.

"2016 Mercedes GLE Coupe," McCrea said. "Nice chunk of cash. Love how the silver paints seems to glow."

Wolf walked slowly around the vehicle, looking closely for any marks or dents that might suggest the car was knocked off the road. The only damage he could see was to the lower section which struck the bottom of the riverbank as the car careened over it as it plunged into the river.

"We've gone over the car already," McCrea said. "No tampering with the brakes, no flats, no evidence of being forced off the road. An accident; she came around the curve, hit ice and slid into the river."

Wolf took several steps back taking in the entire car. She was right: no signs of foul play. A bonafide coincidence after all.

"Looks like it," he agreed. McCree started to walk back, when, "Why are the windows open? It's freezing up here."

"Not unusual at all, Mr. Wolf," McCrea said. "Folk up here like fresh air. What you southern folk call freezing feels barely cool to us. We drive with our windows open quite frequently."

"Both windows?"

"Sometimes," she confirmed. "Improves circulation."

Wolf eyed the opening of the driver's side window then walked around to the passenger side and peered at that window's opening. A smiled appeared on his lips.

"Sergeant McCrea," Wolf began, "when you partially lower your front windows, how often do you manage to open both equally?"

She looked at the space between the partially lowered windows. She issued a grunt. "They're both opened about equally."

"I'd bet more than just, about equally," Wolf asserted.

"Are you suggesting that her car was hacked?" McCrea said.

"Let's find out." Wolf lifted his phone and called Brett.

"2016 Mercedes GLE Coupe," the computer tech said. "Mercedes are reputed to be hack proof..."

"But?" Wolf said. Nothing was immune from meddling.

"But," Brett said, "although there haven't been any victims of Mercedes hacks, there have been incidents of minor mischief, mostly involving the entertainment module. Remotely changing functions, stations and so forth—Wi-Fi. There is no direct connection from the infotainment module to any vital control such as brakes, accelerator, ignition and so forth."

"What about opening windows?" Wolf asked.

"Much more possible."

"Steering?"

"Much less possible," Brett said. "Controlling the steering, like in TV shows is out. However, briefly *interfering* with the steering is a go."

"Explain *interfering*." Wolf said.

"Make it difficult to turn the wheel, for instance," Brett said. "Perhaps even lock it up for a moment."

"I see...hold on for second..." Wolf walked back to the car and peered at the front wheels. "The car's wheels are pointed about ten degrees to the left. The road the driver was on was curved to the left. She hit ice and skidded off the road to the right into the river."

"You'd think she'd have steered into the skid," Brett said.

"Not if her steering didn't respond because it was momentarily frozen," Wolf said.

"It's a theory," Brett replied.

"But not a fact," Wolf answered. "Keep digging on Mercedes hacks and call me if you discover something. Thanks Brett."

"I'll call state forensics," McCrea said. "They've got far more resources and expertise than we do. I hear anything, I'll call you."

"Thanks sergeant," Wolf said. "I'll make sure you have a signed copy of my entire collection sent to you in the near future—as a gift of course."

The officer drove Wolf to his car where he called Brett again. "Is it feasible to connect a Wi-Fi kill switch in a car that cuts all electronic transmission?"

"Child's play," Brett laughed. "A little extreme even for your level of operational paranoia, though."

"Ask RJ for my car key then install one," Wolf said.

"Will do."

Terminating the call, Wolf decided to re-read the information about ATTC Brett had sent previously. If LeeAnn Hicks' accident was assisted remotely, perhaps rattling some chains was in order. Wolf started his car and drove back to the Affirmative Transformation Treatment Center.

"You heard correctly," Wolf said, to the receptionist who peered at him in disbelief. "Tell the director Grayson Wolf is here to speak with him. If he tells you he's too busy to see me, inform him that I will call for a press conference in the parking lot where I'll talk excessively about the murder of LeeAnn Hicks."

In short order, Wolf found himself in the swanky offices of Director Anthony Sipko.

"Marissa tells me that you think Dr. Hicks was murdered?" Sipko said, looking nervously at his visitor.

Typically when folks in positions of authority get fidgety, look worried or become evasive it's a classic sign that they're guilty of one thing or another. That wasn't necessarily the subject's case when meeting with Wolf since feeling intimidated that they might wind up in one of his exposes or on the front pages of CIR's website was a normal reaction.

Wolf ignored the question, saying instead, "In 2010 this facility performed four gender reassignment procedures. In 2014 that number tripled. This year the number of sex change procedures performed in your center was twenty-nine. Business is booming."

"There are thousands of men and women whose psychological gender is mismatched with their physical gender. We perform a vital service by properly aligning the physical and mental gender of these suffering individuals."

"Of these misaligned gendered numbering in the thousands," Wolf said, "what percentage are mismatched males wanting reassignment to females?"

"Male reassignment comprises a minority of our procedures," Sipko replied.

"Less than ten percent, according to published studies of all procedures performed by ATTC nationally," Wolf said. "Female reassignment makes up nine out of every ten procedures."

"Yes," Sipko confirmed. "There's nothing sinister in that. Many more women feel sexually mismatched."

"Feelings..." Wolf said, peering at the man. "What happens when these newly aligned humans begin to feel that their brave new sexual world doesn't fit them after all? Do they get a do over? A gender realignment refund, perhaps?"

"There is always a period of adjustment," Sipko said. "We provide counseling, medication and more."

Keeping his tone free from any hint of sarcasm, Wolf said,

"And if any of the thousands of psychological and gender mismatched want to return to their previous status, ATTC happily accommodates their feelings via gender reassignment once again. Free of charge, of course. Or perhaps many just feel like committing suicide."

Sipko stood up, his face hard. "I don't know what your game is, Mr. Wolf, but this meeting is over. Leave now."

Not so cowed after all.

"Funning thing about feelings, Director," Wolf said, rising from his seat. "They're often not the most reliable means by which to make decisions, especially decisions that involve mastectomies, life-long hormonal replacement therapy, shaving and transforming into one of those toxic males stalking our streets and saying hurtful things."

"Get out."

"One more question, Director," Wolf said. "What's the median age of women electing to be properly aligned?"

"Leave now, Mr. Wolf or I will have you removed."

Wolf opened the door, and said over his shoulder, "I'll be back."

He felt proud not sounding like Schwarzenegger, though he felt the moment had called for it. That's the problem with feelings. They're unpredictable, unreliable and most certainly should not be the deciding factor when making major (or minor) decisions about anything, especially anything of permanence.

Next stop was Ivygreen College, located in the gently rolling landscape of North Sudbury a dozen miles west of Watertown. Ivygreen fancied itself an Ivy League institution, a long succession of administrations working overtime to emulate the policies, politics and trends prominent in America's elite institutions of higher learning. Ivygreen College's promise to offer students a complete Ivy League experience, placed the college high on CIR's legal hit list, their efforts to ape their politically correct competitors having turned out to be too successful.

Although Wolf worked hard to keep his face out of the public arena—no photos on social media, book covers, no TV appearances—sundry images had leaked into the world over the years. Disguises, caps, baggy clothing, hoodies, occasional wigs and sundry accents were the order of the day, especially when visiting locations with crowds, such as colleges.

Being winter, Wolf donned a hoodie covered by a nondescript winter coat, the assemble allowing him to blend with the flow of Ivygreen students as he made his way to the Student Counseling Center in the Student Community building. Peering at the hundreds of brochures and flyers offering a myriad of counseling services, seminars, meetings and support groups, the uninitiated to the contemporary college campus would be justified believing they had entered a mental health institution by mistake.

It didn't take Wolf long to find what counseling service he was looking for, the gender services section prominently marked by a large poster showing a transformation of one gender into that of another. Wolf perused the literature, every single item proclaiming the advantages of gender reassignment and confirmation for those who have felt "uncomfortable" in their current gender assignment. Glowing testimonials of the amazing peace and tranquility reassignment had provided to transformed individuals were printed under the caption, "I finally feel normal!"

Wolf took one and walked into the counseling suite asking to speak with a counselor about his discomfort being a toxic male. He thought adding toxic might be a clue about him being facetious, but the receptionist said someone would be with him shortly.

"How may I help you, ah..." the counselor peered closely at him.

"Leslie," Wolf said. "It's really Grayson Wolf, but I've been feeling really uncomfortable about my gender, being toxic an all and it's time for a real change. I want to finally feel normal, like these people do." Wolf handed her the brochure he brought with him.

The counselor looked at Wolf with what appeared to be a mixture of puzzlement and apprehension.

"What can I do for you, Mr. Wolf?"

"Clarify your policy for students thinking about gender change," Wolf said. "Say I was a student and been thinking that becoming a woman would suit me better. What's your advice?"

"I'd ask how long you've felt like this and depending on your response, I would tell you to become more familiar with the procedure or refer you to a clinic."

"Where is the line that separates becoming more familiar and a referral?" Wolf asked. "I've been feeling like changing for a semester? Year? Since middle school?"

The counselor was looking increasingly uncomfortable. Being cornered in a small room by a universally considered dangerous wolf can have that effect.

"Scanning all the literature out in the entrance, most of them are provided by the Affirmative Transformation Treatment Centers. Is that where you refer students to? Or do you refer them to professional therapists who are more qualified to help students become clear about their sexual identity?"

"You'll need to discuss such details with the administration, Mr. Wolf."

"How many students has this center referred for gender reassignment?" Wolf said, pressing forward. "What is the number of women and men being counseled and referred? How many students returned to college after their procedure? How many committed suicide?"

A suggestion of panic appeared on her face. She blinked several times and said, "You need to speak with the administration." She reached for the phone.

"Have a nice day," Wolf said, and left her office.

He exited the building and strode toward the lot where he'd parked the car.

"That should get their attention," he said, starting the vehicle. He called Brett to inform him of his raid on the college, the tech assuring him that his digital dogs were out in force sniffing out and following whatever effluent flowed forth from the alarmed administrators rushing to cover exposed patches on their hind ends.

"And Brett," Wolf added, "Let Juan know."

Next he called RJ giving him an account of his brief foray into the hallowed halls of the Ivy League wannabe.

"You have any reliable members of your tribe with connections to Ivygreen?" he asked.

"I've got card-carrying members of my tribe imbedded in the highest—and lowest—places everywhere, bro," RJ replied.

"Of course you do," Wolf said. "Have them dig up whatever they can pursuant promoting gender reassignment and anything else connected with this dangerous fad."

"Easy there, Mr. Heterosexual Man," RJ fired back. "Plenty of genuine sexually mismatched folk out there. My people gonna be reluctant to help they think you're organizing some kind of crusade against change."

"You know very well this gender issue is just one more slice of the social justice mud pie being peddled by folks looking to maximize their popularity and power," Wolf replied. "It's just a matter of time before the ugly truth become public and then there'll be a backlash that very well might prevent folks truly sexually mismatched from making a positive change in their lives. Sell it, RJ."

Wolf ended the call and drove out of the parking lot. He was driving toward the main entrance when two campus police cars rushed passed him going the other way. He smiled thinking it would take a lot more to catch a rouge wolf than running to where he was moments before.

Driving back to his hotel in Cambridge, Wolf was musing about the two hornet nests he had riled up, certain that they were engaged in unethical behavior on several levels. However, he didn't think the investigation he had set in motion would uncover any criminal activity at the college counseling office. ATTC was a different matter, however. One of their doctors was murdered. Why?

Though Wolf's quest began as a way to ease the loss of a child for grieving parents by shaking loose whatever nastiness might come to light, the primary goal was to increase the pressure on Ivygreen and other colleges to settle the class action suit. Then he uncovered a murder. Wolf hoped the police could handle that one without his help.

The phone rang. He accepted it and said hello.

"Hello Wolf; Colleen Silverstone. I'm waiting for you at the Hyatt Regency. I'll be at the bar."

Chapter 9

Wolf Call

"Good afternoon Colleen," Wolf said, taking a seat next to her. "I see your stalking skills are sharp as ever."

She shot him a droll look. The bartender placed a Belgian Ale in front of him. Wolf took a long draught.

"Haven't had lunch," he said, placing the half empty glass down.

"A crab cake house special with a side order of Boston baked beans is on the way," she said.

He believed her. Colleen Silverstone was not known to joke, engage in idle banter or lead a man on. He did sleep with her once back in the spring. Emphasis being exclusively on the *sleep* part of that experience.

"Beans," he said. "You like to live dangerously."

"How was your visit to Ivygreen?" she said.

He grinned. It was her way of punishing him for the quip. My turn, he said to himself.

"How was your visit to the legal convention in Baltimore?"

Wolf was sure his remark caught her off guard because he failed to detect even the slightest twitch on her face. It occurred to him that such self-control could be used as a tell if he ever played poker with that gorgeous specimen of female architecture and brains.

"I'm sorry about Madeline."

That put the kibosh on further thoughts about female architecture and highlighted another important facet about Colleen:

admit facts. She knew she was at the Convention Center in Baltimore and accepted the fact that he had spotted her. What a refreshing and remarkable difference from dealing with mealy-mouthed hucksters scurrying hither and dither to evade the reality that their house of cards is going to fall down.

"When are you going to tell me why I have the pleasure of your company?" Wolf teased.

"I need you."

"I know," Wolf said, grinning.

Colleen swiveled on her stool to face him directly. She took a sip of her wine.

"To be more accurate," she said, "I am calling in my favor."

"I see." Wolf held her gaze. "You are calling upon my specialized abilities for a mission."

"I'm not. My stepfather is."

Wolf must have looked so incredulous that Colleen actually laughed.

"I've never know you to be a comedian," Wolf said. "But if you saying you're stepfather wants to see me, then you're doing a good impersonation of one."

"You know Justin Bellamy was murdered," she said. "Barry has been charged with his murder."

That was a surprise to be sure. Barry Silverstone and Justin Bellamy were, literally, thick as thieves. Silverstone's law firm had successfully defended the lying, cheating, raping, financial fund billionaire against all prosecutions: federal, state and local for decades. Though Wolf had no doubts about Colleen's stepfather being the definitive sleazy, money-grubbing, snake prominently featured in *Screw You Suckers!* murderer would not be among his long list of sordid pejoratives he'd attribute to the attorney.

"And you want me to help him?" Wolf said, astonished.

"He has asked me to ask you to help him," Colleen said. "I know how the two of you feel about each other. I'm calling in the favor you promised me."

"No."

Colleen's expression turned frosty. "No?"

"No need to surprise me with lunch and no need to call in a favor, Colleen," Wolf said. "Just call and I'll be there. Friends do that, you know."

"Yes, they do," she said, a smile touching her lips. "Friends also shouldn't assume that their friend requires playing a trump card to recruit their participation."

"Apology accepted," Wolf grinned.

"I know CIR, and by extension you, are up to your eyeballs in half dozen projects and Christmas is next week," Colleen said, her smile vanishing. "The situation is a little more complicated than Barry being the prime suspect. He's also a fugitive."

Wolf laughed. "Of course he is. Oh! You were meeting him at the Baltimore convention."

"Yes. I was in DC for a meeting and Barry asked to meet me, but he never showed," Colleen said. "He must have heard about Bellamy and ran."

"Was he with Bellamy prior to his murder?" Wolf asked.

"Barry met with him early Thursday afternoon before flying to Baltimore that evening," she confirmed. "He was alive and well when he left him in his condo."

"Colleen, Bellamy was murdered that Thursday night or Friday morning but the police didn't release anything about his death until Monday. How did your father know on Saturday and why run?"

"This is New York and Barry Silverstone we're talking about, Wolf. The Big Sieve where information leaks from every public institution by the ton and Barry's one of the most connected individuals in the city and state," Colleen said. "He knew seconds after the housekeeper found the body Saturday morning. Barry didn't run because he thought the cops were after him; he ran because he thought he'd be the next victim."

"That I can believe for sure," Wolf quipped. Colleen shot him a warning look. "Not apologizing for telling it like I see it. Frankly, I'm surprised someone hadn't taken Bellamy out years ago and by virtue of his close association, your stepfather, too."

"The same could be said about you," Colleen retorted. "Many consider you a most rabid wolf who they'd like to see put down, though I admit not for any reasons remotely similar to those wishing for the demise of Bellamy and friends."

"I'm not worried a bit," Wolf said, looking droll. "The certainty that the enemies of my enemy would wreak nationwide revenge upon them keeps them safely at bay."

"Overconfidence goeth before a fall," Colleen said.

"As much as I enjoy sexual banter," Wolf teased, "let's get down to business. What's on first?"

"A little house on the prairie," Colleen said.

"We're going to Minnesota?"

"We are going to aid and abet a fugitive," Colleen said. "Just want to be clear what you're stepping into."

Wolf shot her a clueless look. "Are we there yet?"

"This looks nothing like Minnesota," Wolf complained. "And there's not a square foot of prairie anywhere."

"Your parents must have loved taking you on trips," Collen said, issuing a sarcastic snort.

"I bet there's not even a little house wherever you're taking me," he replied, ignoring her.

Colleen was behind the wheel of a Toyota 4Runner Pro making her way deeper into the backwoods of Maine. The rear storage compartment was filled with fuel and supplies to last for weeks. She had not been kidding about the aiding and abetting part when she recruited Wolf.

Colleen had collected him the following morning at his hotel, proceeding to drive north on I-93 to Lancaster, New Hampshire were she dropped off her rental, walked half a mile to what appeared to be an abandoned garage where the fully stocked 4Runner was waiting for her. The next leg of their journey was east on Route 2 into Maine, north on Route 201 at Skowhegan and currently traveling on a narrow, poorly maintained country road in the middle of nowhere.

"I know you're one of the best and all, but what makes you think we're not being followed, tracked by an onboard transmitter or watched by satellite?" Wolf asked.

"Because I'm the best and I've got Cooper watching my back," she said. "Besides, Barry is a fugitive from New York state, not the federal government. Last I heard, New York doesn't have surveillance satellites. And my illustrious stepfather is connected up the wazoo, so he's got dozens running interference for him."

"Meanwhile, he's hiding out in some cave in Upper Slobovia," Wolf quipped.

"Never trust anyone," Colleen said. "Barry's inviolate rule."

"He trusts you."

"Only because he knows I believe him when he says he's innocent of Bellamy's murder," Colleen said. She slowed down and turned onto a single lane dirt road. "And that he fears for his own life, which I also believe to be true."

Looking at the narrow, bumpy lane ahead, Wolf issued a snort.

"It's Creede, Colorado, déjà vu all over again," he jibed. "Should have known when I got in this vehicle we'd be going off-roading. Hopefully this time no one will try to shoot at us when we get to Barry's hideout..." he paused and peered at the sky. "And that we make it out before it snows three feet."

"It's not going to snow three feet," Colleen said, the lane rising as it wound over a hill. "A foot, max. Besides, I'm from Colorado. This car and I can handle a couple feet easy."

"The little house on the prairie spiel, is it—" Wolf began, interrupted by a wheel hitting a rut jarring the car's occupants. "More and more like our Creede outing by the minute ... The little house quip, is it code to throw off unwanted snoops?"

"Works as code; but it's a joke," Colleen said. "When I was a kid he'd read to me. I enjoyed Wilder's "Little House" series and Barry would joke about visiting our little house on the prairie when we'd come to the cabin where we're going now. When he mentioned reading the Wilder book, I knew exactly where he was."

"What makes him think no one would know he owns property in nowhere Maine?" Wolf asked.

"Because he doesn't own any property in nowhere Maine," she replied. "The place belongs to a family friend of Barry's aunt who happens to be Canadian. She's in her eighties, hasn't visited the place in decades and probably forgot about it by now. Barry pays the pennies of property tax on it from a shell company owned by a shell company owned by some dude living in southern Spain. Only mom and I know about our little house on the prairie."

"Can't wait to see this magical place," Wolf said.

"Don't let your imagination run wild; it's just a small cabin," she said.

"Just looking forward to visiting the head," Wolf grinned.

The tight dirt road became rougher the deeper into the hills they drove, causing Wolf to issue an ongoing succession of comparisons between the current jaunt into the wilderness to the one they experienced in western Colorado last May. After waxing on about a particular nasty stretch of road, Colleen said,

"I have got to remember not to bring your motormouth with me on any trip lasting longer than thirty minutes."

"You knew I was a word slinger when you asked me to come along," Wolf retorted. "Besides, we can't all be the strong, silent, brooding, hot investigator."

Colleen shot him a slideway's glance. "Cute; don't get any ideas."

"Maybe I'll get lucky and you'll invite me to sleep with you again," Wolf taunted.

"I wouldn't hold your breath," she said, a faint smile on her lips. "The place sleeps ten."

The vehicle reached the summit of yet another hill when Colleen stopped. Spread out beneath them was a valley with a narrow lake to the west, it's ice and snow coating brilliantly reflecting the late afternoon sun. Even in the dead of winter it was a striking sight, Wolf thinking it would be majestic come spring.

"That's Baker Lake," Colleen said. "I'd go skinny dipping in the summer. Cold water even in late August."

Wolf laughed, knowing it was her way of teasing him after his sleep with me comment. And also knowing he'd try to imagine her skinny dipping. Which he did, and quite satisfactorily, too.

"How far to the prairie house?"

"Quarter mile ahead," she said, pointing north. "It's adjacent Baker's Creek." She released the brake and drove on.

The cabin was nestled behind a stand of pine, screening it from the lane. Colleen drove up the driveway and stopped near parallel rows of firewood stacked higher than the top of the car and four times its length, enough wood to keep the cabin's occupants toasty warm throughout the winter. A smaller stack of wood rested near the end of the house, protected from the elements by an overhang.

"Let's grab some of the supplies and go visit your favorite Silverstone," Colleen jibed.

Wolf was about to correct her about who was his favorite Silverstone, but let it slide. The time for suggestive banter was past. Besides, no matter how much *he* favored Colleen, she had demonstrated repeatedly that she was the real lone wolf and not disposed to cuddle up with him or anyone else, as far as he knew.

Wolf attributed her aloofness to the risks and requirements of the job, a career where, don't trust anyone, might very well be the iron rule for survival over the long term. Though he could relate being in a similar business, he mostly had to rely on his wits, whereas Colleen had to be prepared to back up her wits by drawing her weapon.

Wolf shut the hatch and lifted the bags of supplies when he spotted something on the far side of the woodpiles. Edging closer, he saw a boxy shaped object completely obscured by a camouflage covering hiding what Wolf guessed was Silverstone's means of transportation.

He turned back and hurried after Colleen, reaching the door at the same time. She knocked on the door, calling out Barry's name. The door opened momentarily, Silverstone standing back to let them in, shutting and securely bolting it after them.

"We still have more supplies to bring in, Barry," she said.

"Soon as you're ready, I'll open the door."

Paranoia, Wolf thought. A useful friend, but a nasty master.

"Mr. Silverstone," he said.

"Mr. Wolf," he replied.

Neither offered to shake hands.

"Coffee?"

"Bathroom."

Silverstone pointed to the far side of the main room. "End of the hallway."

"A man of few words." Colleen teased, as he walked past her.

He was sorely tempted to smack her on the ass, but wisely stayed his hand. He'd need both in good working order while roughing it in this remote corner of Maine.

Being located out in nowhere, Wolf wasn't sure what to expect, finding a composting toilet and sink offering a faucet that produced a thin stream of surprisingly, warm water. He dried his hands on the towel provided and returned to the main room, which was heated by a wood burning stove.

He joined the group and took a seat in one of the empty chairs by the table near the corner kitchen, directly across from Silverstone. A cup of steaming coffee was offered, Wolf adding a splash of a whitish liquid from a creamer that turned out to be soymilk. He took a sip; tasty enough, he concluded.

Gazing at the man, he said, "Whom do you suspect has set you up for Bellamy's murder and plotting to kill you next?"

"Besides half the people who read your book about me?" Silverstone quipped, looking at Wolf accusingly.

"Considering your propensity to represent the most egregious thieves and political manipulators, I'm surprised you think it's only half of *Screw You Suckers!* readers," Wolf shot back, his expression darkening.

"My propensity is only exceeded by the bullshit make-believe you weave throughout your so called nonfictional exposes filled with fictional dreck," Silverstone retorted, glaring at his nemesis.

"The only fictional dreck in *Screw You Suckers!* is the part about the type of payment the escorts received to entertain the Canadian suckers Bellamy fleeced in the oil sands fiasco," Wolf snapped, his lips twisting into a disdainful shape.

Silverstone's irate expression transformed into suspicious attentiveness. "Fictional? What are you talking about?"

Wolf shot him a scornful look. Like the man didn't know every dishonest fiber of his bosom buddy's predilections.

"I'm talking about the fiction women being paid for their services."

"It's not fiction," Silverstone said, looking adamant. "They *were* paid."

"Your sociopathic best friend screwed them like he screwed everyone else during his miserable existence," Wolf said. "Bellamy tipped off the cops; the women were paid in jail time. The man was a blight on life itself." Seeing genuine surprise in Silverstone's face, Wolf added, "Considering what you knew about Bellamy and his dealings, I wouldn't have put it past him to have you killed sooner or later. It's all about número uno; everyone else is expendable."

Glancing at Colleen, her face showed no reaction, though he did catch a glint in her eye. She had been an impassive observer throughout the exchange between him and her stepfather, Wolf quite certain she was keenly interested how Grayson Wolf would fare face-to-face with a man he had raked over the coals in one of his books.

Colleen looked at Barry and said, "Since Bellamy's dead, who might be next in line to want you dead?"

Wolf almost laughed. He was about to say those exact words.

"That's the trouble," Silverstone said, looking frustrated. "I don't have any prime suspects...except Wolf's readers."

"You asked for my help," Wolf said, grinning knowingly. "I would think I'm the last person in the world you'd want to see. After all, my readers would throw me a party and carry me around on their shoulders if I helped put you in prison."

"Under other circumstances I would agree with you," Silverstone said, giving him a humorous look. "But as incredible as this sounds, you are one of two people in the world I can trust implicitly."

"Let me stop you right there," Wolf countered. "I'm here because of Colleen. If in the course of assisting her to investigate I discover further nasty secrets and dealings connected to you I will not be bound to stay quiet. If you object, then this is as far as I go."

Silverstone shrugged. "Most likely you will stumble over some questionable dealings connected to me. Use them as you wish."

"Why include me?" Wolf said. "Your daughter is the foremost investigator in the country who owns the most successful investigative firm. My sleuthing experience isn't even in Colleen's ballpark not to mention that I don't have the backing of a couple hundred skilled field agents and top notch techs."

"Complimentary skills," he replied. "I saw what the two of you managed to accomplish in Colorado and you were only working together for a few days here and there. The sum of Wolf and Colleen is greater than each individually. Add the fact that I trust no one else, I can't think of anyone better anywhere than the two of you."

It wasn't an idle compliment. Wolf readily agreed with him that Colleen and he made a potent crime fighting duo. He still couldn't shake the feeling that Silverstone was playing him, using Wolf's own sense of justice, his firm commitment to his principles and personal integrity to deflect whatever form of karma was coming to bite the man in the ass.

Wolf rebelled at the idea that he was assisting Silverstone to stave off whatever justified punishment the man deserved. For decades he'd finagled the legal system, bribed politicians and profited handsomely from clients such as Bellamy who plundered and looted the society they lived in.

He was caught in an ugly contradiction: uphold the integrity of his principles to uncover the rapacious lowlife feeding off the ignorance and misery of their victims or assist said rapacious lowlife to evade the consequences of his actions.

When confronted by a contradiction, check your premises because one or more is wrong. Wolf had read that expression in various fictional and non-fictional works by Ayn Rand. It had always struck him as *the* litmus test for confronting situations that might, or would, compromise one's beliefs and integrity. It wasn't foolproof, of course. There is a strong inclination in humans to evade reality, believing such avoidance to be in their best self-interest. Until it proved otherwise, which it always does sooner or later.

Wolf certainly wasn't evading the reality confronting him. Reflecting on his conflict, he wondered if his assumption about *being* caught in a contradiction was wrong. He wasn't helping a charlatan, he was helping a friend to whom he owed a debt. He was clear that Silverstone was long overdue to reap the reward of the whirlwind he created, but that such justice occur within a courtroom, not via hitman. He had presented Silverstone with his condition that discovery of other transgressions in the man's life would be made public.

Wolf concluded he wasn't compromising his principles nor evading reality, only an emotion. He took a drink of his coffee.

"Before we go any further," Wolf said, lowering the cup on the table. "I want you to know that I'm helping Colleen, not you. If in the course of assisting her I find anything embarrassing, I will broadcast it worldwide. If I discover any evidence of criminal activity you're engaged in, I will personally deliver it to the police and cheer at your sentencing. You belong in jail, Mr. Silverstone and by asking Colleen to participate, you might just help me to put in one."

There was a long stretch of silence, followed by Colleen saying,

"Now that we know the ground rules, tell us what you know and suspect about who might want to kill Bellamy and now is after you." A wicked grin appeared on her face. "Keeping in mind, of course, that anything you say Wolf will use to put you behind bars."

Chapter 10

The Quest Begins

"Well good morning sunshine!" Wolf said, poking his head into Colleen's room. "I hope you're right about the Toyota handling two feet of snow because we've got over a foot accumulation and rising an inch per minute...we're gonna need to roll out of here ASAP or hunker down for days with daddy."

Colleen got out of bed, her skimpy underwear and tight T-shirt causing the surprised Wolf to retreat out of her room. She laughed at her little trick; Grayson Wolf might be persistent, uncompromising and definitely annoying at times, but he was also a gentleman.

She dressed, collected her gear and went downstairs. Her little house on the prairie wasn't large, it's four upstairs bedrooms barely ten by ten feet, but the few childhood memories she did have of her visits were good ones.

Breakfast was waiting for her on the table, her father and Wolf digging into their meal with obvious gusto. Glancing out the window facing her, the intensity of the snowfall effectively obscured her car. Wolf's quip about the speed of accumulation wasn't all that exaggerated.

"Good morning," she said, taking a seat. "We're going to have to eat and run, Barry, or we'll be stuck here."

"Why I had breakfast ready," he said. "I've made extra coffee to take with you. I've got extra water, sandwiches and protein bars at the door for you to take on the way out."

She looked at the man who had married her mother when Colleen was five and she could almost imagine being eight again, eating a hardy breakfast then escaping to the great outdoors sitting by the nearby creek watching foxes passing by, deer grazing and eagles circling lazily high in the sky.

"Did you want to ask me anything, Colleen?"

Barry's question interrupted her reverie and she returned to the present.

"No, just thinking about our next moves," she said. "The first one being to get moving on down the road."

"Leave everything," Silverstone said. "I'll take care of it ... Colleen, Wolf: thank you. And do please be careful..."

"I've been thinking about a possible suspect for Bellamy's murder," Wolf said, Colleen making good on her boast that a couple feet of snow is no obstacle to an experienced Colorado driver.

They had not spoken during the challenging miles traversing the deeply snow-covered, narrow access road back to the paved county road. The going wasn't any better, but at least the paved roadbed provided a smoother ride.

"Do tell," Colleen quipped when Wolf hesitated while she successfully negotiated a particularly impressive snow drift.

"Mr. Collins, James Collins's father," he said. "I know it's a long shot, but I spoke with him back in October when Bellamy slithered out on bail and the entire case against him started to fall apart. He was very upset; told me he'd kill the SOB himself if the system let him off."

"If we're looking at Colorado, might as well include Sara Lewis's father, too," Colleen said. "She was Bellamy and son's rape victim. Him getting out on bail and possibly walking, makes one hell of a motive, Wolf. I'll put Cooper on it. If any of these fathers left the state, he will find the particulars."

"I have no doubt about that," Wolf agreed. "My only reservation about either Lewis or Collins being the culprit is where Bellamy was killed and the how, which, according to my friend at BCPD, was not by gun, blade or garotte. Though I didn't have much contact with either man, if they set out to kill Bellamy it would most likely be by gun, not by whatever mysterious manner he was killed."

"Dimethyl sulfate," Colleen said, swerving the car around one drift, then a second immediately thereafter.

"What?" Wolf said, recovering from being tossed against the door.

"Dimethyl sulfate," she repeated. "He was killed by someone adding dimethyl sulfate to his humidifier."

"I know that DMSO can make people feel sick if they misuse it, but kill them by putting the substance into a humidifier?" Wolf said, skeptically.

"Not dimethyl sulfoxide," Colleen said, correcting him. "Dimethyl *sulfate*. Add a pair of oxygen atoms to DMSO and you got yourself a highly toxic chemical that if ingested in tiny amounts will cause convulsions, paralysis, coma, long term organ damage. As a vapor, it can kill. Placing it next to the heating element of a humidifier will release enough vapor to kill you—after paralyzing you first so that you're incapacitated."

"I can't imagine either Collins or Lewis choosing something that sophisticated to kill Bellamy," Wolf said. "Neither man worked with chemicals, though I can't speak for their previous work experience."

"You don't need to work in the field to know about toxic chemicals, Wolf," Colleen replied.

"Right," he said, issuing a sniff. "Just need to be familiar with Mr. Google. Definitely have your people check both out, though I'm reasonably certain neither is our perp."

It took them over three hours to reach I-95 switching to I-295 in Augusta. The interstates were partially cleared of snow and traffic was minimal, but top speed in the best sections was fifty. Conditions began to improve south of Boston allowing for higher speeds, but it was approaching nine o'clock when Colleen parked the car underneath a Manhattan hotel.

"Almost twelve hours," Wolf said, on the elevator. "Not complaining, mind you. We're in New York because of you. I would never had made it more than half a mile from the cabin ... if I decided to give it a shot, which I probably wouldn't have."

Colleen smiled at Wolf's tendency to understate his own skills and talents. Doing so was probably a requirement of having spent years submerging himself into service and menial occupations allowing him to effectively root around in the lives of notables he was investigating with near invisibility.

"Here we are," she said, a keycard appearing in her hand.

Wolf followed her into a spacious, attractive room. Colleen made for a door to the right, entering a bedroom. She placed her bag next to the closet and returned to the living area. Wolf, who had remained standing near the entrance, told her was going back down to registration to secure a room and would let her know where he'd be.

"Not necessary," Colleen said, gazing at him for a long moment. Seeing the question forming on Wolf's face, she issued a silent laugh.

"Where this a few decades ago, I might refer to you as a certain kind of tease," he said, scowling at her. "But having been burned once, I'm twice shy ... I'm assuming door number two on my left is where I will spend the night." He walked to the door, and said over his shoulder, "In case you change your mind, don't bother. I'm locking my door."

"Like I can't pick that lock in five seconds flat," Colleen teased.

Wolf stopped and gazed at her for a long moment. "You're really enjoying this, aren't you? Finally getting even with me for all my little suggestive remarks and looks back in Colorado, right? And don't even try to deny it—you know it to be true." He entered and forcefully shut the shut.

He had intoned the last part sounding like Darth Vader; a pretty good imitation, Colleen thought. Realizing she was still looking at his closed door and doing so with more interest than she wanted, she decided to order food from room service. It was late and she was tired from the long drive, but she was also hungry and sure that Wolf was too. Informed the food would be delivered in ten minutes, she headed for the shower confident she'd beat room service by five minute.

The night passed uneventfully, both Wolf and Colleen safe from intrusion by the other. Smirking at Wolf over breakfast, Colleen made a comment about her not picking the lock on his bedroom door, Wolf saying he didn't need to lock it since he knew that she knew she wasn't woman enough for him anyway.

"For a man who has written over a dozen nonfiction books, you sure can spin fictional tall tales with the best of 'em," Colleen said, her smile lighting up her face. "I do recall you sprinting from my bedroom the other morning after casting your eyes on my skimpy attire."

Wolf laughed. "Touché ... So, my dear Ms. Silverstone, what have you planned for us on this fine Sunday morning?"

"A visit to someone who knows Barry very well is in order," she said. "She's expecting us at our convenience."

"She?" Wolf said, looking intrigued. "Jilted lover? Mistress? A pro?"

"Mother," Colleen deadpanned. "She's the only lead we can speak with on a Sunday."

"Lead," Wolf said, looking droll. "Spoken like an authentic, hard-bitten gumshoe."

"Finish your breakfast, Wolfie."

The door swung open wide. "My long-lost daughter returns at last!"

"Good morning, mom," Colleen said, the women embracing each other.

Seeing Wolf at the door, she said, "And you brought a friend; come in, come in."

"Good morning, Ms. Silverstone; a pleasure to meet you," Wolf said. "Merry Christmas."

"Mom, this is—"

"I know very well who he is, darling," she said, cutting Colleen off. "Grayson Wolf: mountain-sized headache for Barry and his cadre of thieving, lying sons of bitches. It's an honor and tremendous pleasure to meet you in person." She proceeded to give him a big hug and kissed him on the cheek. "Please do not call me Ms. Silverstone; my friends call me Eileen and you are definitely a friend."

Wolf glanced at Colleen who shrugged her shoulders, a smile playing on lips. She had not warned him about her mother's antagonism toward Barry or her enthusiasm about Wolf. She liked to think the reason was to allow him to form his own impressions, but it was about the long habit of keeping her cards close to her chest. Privacy, confidentiality, secrets, discretion was her business and keeping one's mouth shut and fingers away from keyboards had made

Silverstone Security and Investigative Services the number one firm in the nation and a top international competitor.

"Please call me Wolf," he said. "To be honest, I didn't expect such an enthusiastic welcome, Eileen."

"Let's just say that everything you wrote about Barry was spot on," she said, a knowing look animating her face. "And you can be sure that you barely scratched the surface of that pus-filled boil. I divorced Barry when Colleen went to college," she said. "Would have done it years earlier, but unlike that cheating, detritus waste of a human being, I wanted a stable home life for my daughter so I stuck it out. The day Colleen went off to college I served that bastard divorce papers."

"Hell of a lead," Wolf said, to Colleen when Eileen went to the kitchen for refreshments.

"A very biased lead," she pointed out.

"A very motivated lead," Wolf replied.

Colleen said nothing, shooting him a skeptical look when Eileen walked back into the living room. She got up and helped her mom distribute the dishes and refreshments.

"Colleen domesticated," Wolf whispered, as she filled his glass with water.

She "accidentally" dribbled some water on his crotch, smiled apologetically and sat down.

"You heard about Bellamy," she said, to her mother.

"Happy days are here again," she replied, making a good riddance expression. "I knew he was a piece of shit, but after what he did to that girl in Colorado—and who knows how many more—he deserved what he got. If he did that to you, I'd kill him before he took three steps out of the courthouse door ... do you know who killed him? If you do, tell him I'll pay for his lawyer."

Colleen saw Wolf look at her in a way that suggested he was beginning to get a better understanding of herself. Her mother was second generation Irish but the intensity and immediacy of her fire hadn't been moderated by living in the United States. Colleen had inherited that fire, but had learned to temper and shape it into a highly concentrated form of energy. It's slow burning version she attributed to her Jamaican father and provided the fuel to achieve and maintain her dreams and goals. Then there was the neutron bomb version, the one inherited from her mother. She worked hard to contain that explosive self, though there had been occasions when Colleen unleashed was needed and justified.

"The police don't really know who killed Bellamy, but they do have a suspect, mom," Colleen said. "Barry."

She barked a loud laugh. "Barry? They think Barry killed that stinkbug? Hell, the man would turn pale when I pounded chicken breasts. Barry is a walking, talking outhouse dropping his filth far and wide like Pigpen, but he's not a killer or a fighter...the cops are barking up the wrong tree." A thought must have struck her because her expression darkened. "You're not here just to visit your poor mother for Christmas, are you? What is this about, Colleen—and don't give me any of your blarney about client confidentiality. Grayson Wolf and Colleen Silverstone in the same room is about as rare as a blizzard in Florida during July." A suggestive grin appeared and she added, "The two of you make an attractive couple; think on it...a mother knows these things."

"I—we—don't think Barry killed Bellamy either," Colleen said, ignoring Eileen. "Barry thinks whoever killed Bellamy is after him next. Wolf and I are looking into whom that might be. And to set the record straight, I am visiting you, mom."

Eileen grinned. "Of course you are, honey. But I don't have much I can tell you that might shed a light on who wants to do in Barry, though him being tight with Bellamy would be reason enough for the hundreds of *screwed suckers* out there." She shot Wolf a knowing look.

"Eileen," Wolf said, smiling. "Is there anything you can remember from the time you and Barry were still married? Something you might have overheard? Maybe he talked in his sleep? Someone he spoke to frequently or had a relationship with?"

"That was many years ago," she said. "I try to block out anything to do with Barry ... I can tell you this: whatever is going on here—the murder, Barry worried someone's out to kill him—whatever it is, I'd bet you dollars to doughnuts it's about money, or more specifically, stealing it, hiding it, transferring it."

"You still have friends in the financial community," Colleen said.

Eileen shot her a droll glance. "I'll put out some feelers...for you, honey, not that sack of shit."

"Mom, it's been almost twenty years," Colleen said, giving her a let-it-go look.

"No way," she laughed. "Thinking about that bastard fires up my motor every morning and keeps my mind sharp as a tack until bedtime."

"You worked in finance?" Wolf said, obviously surprised.

"Forensic accountant." Eileen clarified. "Trillions of dollars floating around New York that needs to be closely looked at. Banks, corporations, financial companies like New World Fund. I worked for several private accounting firms...just retired a few years ago."

"It must be expensive to live here, especially considering the location, overlooking Central Park," Wolf said.

Eileen swept her hand across the room. "The condo was part of the divorce settlement; I could never have afforded to buy this place then or now. Even so, it takes a high income to live here: taxes, condo fees, parking, doorman, upkeep, renovations of the commons— elevator, halls, roofing, windows, lighting—and tips, housecleaning, the list goes on and on." A wicked grin slid across her mouth. "Contrary to your oblique suggestion that I'm a gold-digging siren luring rich geeks into my lair, I happen to be a very good forensic accountant, lucky in my investments and fortunate in my selection of a brilliant, brave and beautiful daughter in need of a man who can stand up to her. I think you might just be that man, Wolf."

Colleen started to laugh seeing Wolf's embarrassed expression. The situation reminded her of the handful of times she had dared to bring a boy home, recalling that the real need was for a man who could stand up to her mother. Her, too, of course. But especially her mother.

"You and my mother would get along famously," Wolf replied, apparently regaining his balance. "I'd be sure to be far away if that meeting occurred, however. The power of potential squared can have unpredictable outcomes."

"Like running shysters like Bellamy out of town," Eileen said, chuckling. "Or taking over city hall."

"Something like that," Wolf agreed.

He shot an expectant look at Colleen. It was time to wrap things up.

"Mom, we need to go. I appreciate you contacting your friends, let me know what you find out. Nothing is too insignificant, so don't ignore anything, no matter how trivial or ridiculous; every rumor, too."

"Don't worry, I have a mind like a steel trap," Eileen said. "They tell me, I'll remember and share every syllable they utter ... you will see me before you leave for your next destination, yes?"

"I'll see you Christmas Eve and even Christmas Day, if you want to bring me to the party," Colleen said.

"Best Christmas present I could ask for," she replied, happily. "And what about you, Wolf? You coming with my lovely daughter?

"Thanks for the invitation, but I've got a mom and pa and a baby sister that would be bitterly disappointed if I failed to come home for Christmas," Wolf said.

"How about New Years?" Eileen said. "There's no better city to celebrate the New Year than New York."

"I'd love to; unfortunately I have a long-term standing commitment for New Year Eve," Wolf replied.

"I'm curious about your New Year's plans, if you don't mind me asking," Colleen said, leaving the building.

"Shocked, shocked I am that after hounding me for two years your agents didn't uncover all my deep, dark secrets," Wolf teased.

"I did not hound you," she retorted. "I investigated you."

"Pursuant to me exposing your stepfather's sleazy dealings with his sleazy clients in *Screw You Suckers!*" he said. "I guess blood is a bit thicker for Colleen Silverstone after all, even if that blood is tainted with a lifetime of ethically and morally questionable actions."

Colleen stepped in front of Wolf, the pair coming to an abrupt halt. Peering at his provocative grin an internal battle between her mother and her biological father was fighting for control. Wolf must have spotted that struggle because he abruptly apologized.

She turned on her heels and continued her trek to the subway, angry at herself for letting Wolf get to her. Having spent some time working closely with the man, she witnessed the effectiveness of his particular skill set to incite respondents to reveal useful or indicting information. Colleen had learned early in her life to control her emotions after becoming embroiled in school altercations that frequently resulted in bloody fists and faces. From high school onward, it was rare for Colleen to react emotionally to people or circumstances, but found herself particularly vulnerable to Wolf's comments. The mere whiff of vulnerability was inimical to Colleen's image of herself and she didn't like it one bit.

"In memory of my dog, Ruff," Wolf said, closing the door. "I visit his grave every New Year's Eve; have since I was sixteen."

"You spend New Year's Eve with your dog," Colleen said, disbelievingly. Though he could get under her skin like few others, the man was entertaining.

"In memory of saving my life and getting killed in the process." Wolf said. "Visiting him every New Years is my way of repaying a debt and a time to remember what's really important in life."

"You're serious." This was something new and unexpected about Wolf, considering her people had looked closely at him after he published the book that excoriated Barry. "What happened that night twenty years ago?"

"We got Ruff as a puppy when I was six," Wolf began. "At a year old he weighed a hundred pounds. We'd spend hours together, walks, exploring the woods, stuff like that. We'd play hide and seek, and he'd find me every time. One day I hid under a bed and played dead when he found me. Not responding, he took hold of my pants and dragged me out from under the bed. Ruff was one smart dog. After that we played that find and drag game often.

"Jump forward ten years. It was out driving with Ruff early on New Year's when I was broadsided by a drunk driver. I hit my head on the door from the impact. I have a vague memory of unbuckling my seatbelt and opening the door, but nothing after that until I became aware I was lying on the ground some distance away feeling a heavy weight on my torso. That weight was Ruff and he didn't move. Barely a dozen feet away the car was burning furiously and there was burning debris spread around me. Apparently Ruff dragged me out of the vehicle which had caught fire subsequently which resulted in an explosion. Ruff took the bulk of the blast and also hit by shrapnel. He died and so did the drunk who rammed into me. We buried Ruff in our yard and that's where I've spent every New Year's for the past twenty years."

Colleen peered at Wolf in wonder. Not only at the amazing story but because she gained some insight into why she was drawn to the man despite her misgivings.

"Did you sustain any serious injuries?" she asked.

"Mostly cuts from flying objects. I still have some burn scars on my right calf," Wolf said. "Had Ruff not been between me and the blast, things would have turned out quite differently, I'm sure."

"If things had been reversed, you would have dragged Ruff from the car." Colleen didn't know why she said that. Then she remembered how Wolf had saved her life by shouting a warning to get down while he shot up the car her assassin was driving past her.

"Absolutely," Wolf confirmed. "Hopefully we would have gotten much further from the car, too."

"Let's review what we know so far—which isn't much—and lay out a tentative plan on how to proceed," Colleen said, changing the subject.

"I agree, we don't know much," Wolf said. "Your, um, Barry has no clue who might be after him, assuming anyone is. The only reason he thinks he might be next is that whomever killed Bellamy might assume he knows whatever secret got Bellamy killed. Barry wasn't very forthcoming about some key possibilities, claiming client-attorney confidentiality."

"That's because he still represents New World and doing so would place him in legal jeopardy as you well know," Colleen said. She had no problem defending Barry when there was a legitimate case to be made. And no matter their adult relationship, the man had been the father in her life growing up.

"If New World is engaging in some form of criminal activity Barry will most likely be indicted," Wolf rejoined. "I would think that bending the client attorney rule in order to keep him from being killed ought to trump confidentiality. But I suppose hiding out in the backwoods of Maine with what looked like a year's worth of food while you and I beat the bushes to see who pops out would bolster the man's legal self-righteousness."

"God damn it, Wolf!" Colleen shot back. His penchant to cut right to the quick had caught her off guard. Restraining her anger, she said, "You are absolutely right. Barry does exactly what Barry wants to do, always has, always will. He didn't ask you to help, he asked me to ask you knowing that you would. So here's my promise to you: whatever I discoverer in the course of rummaging around in Barry's dark basement I will share with you. If what I find puts him in prison, so be it."

Wolf took several steps toward her. The sudden action caused her to stiffen as though preparing to repulse a physical assault. He must have sensed a warning in the change of her expression because he stopped moving.

"Easy now," Wolf joked, though he did appear to look a little self-conscious.

It dawned on Colleen that he must have been caught up in the moment and had an amorous purpose in mind. She smiled warmly but said,

"Let's not go there. I don't want to complicate things more than they already are."

Wolf grinned sheepishly and shrugged. "With Christmas Eve three days away I vote we put off hunting folks down," Wolf said. "Everyone is either gone for the holidays or on their way."

"Agreed," Colleen said. "Offices will most likely be open the next couple days and I'll set up meetings with some of the references Barry gave us for next week. I'm hoping my mother will get us some leads and I will go with her to her annual Christmas Day bash with her friends and acquaintances from the finance industry. Might pick up a few worthwhile morsels schmoozing with folks, most of whom tend to be partial to ingesting C_2H_5OH."

"You love shoving your chemicals in my face, don't you?" Wolf said. She gazed at him patiently and he continued, "It's ethyl alcohol. Happy?"

"What will you be doing down in balmy Virginia?" Colleen asked.

"Holiday parties at CIR of course," Wolf replied. "In-between guzzling drinks and downing finger foods, I'll be keeping my eye on developments in Maggie's murder, which has got to be connected to Bellamy's and the death of Hicks that we believe is murder by car hack. I will stay in touch with you every day. If something exciting pops up, we'll get right on it. Work for you?"

Colleen smiled and stepped well into Wolf's comfort zone. Holding his gaze for a long moment, she smiled provocatively and said,

"Works for me."

Chapter 11

New Year, New Deaths

"Eileen talks about you all the time," the matronly woman said. "She's very proud of you; says you operate a private investigation company." Leaning closer, she said in a low voice, "Investigating anyone at the party?"

"Not at all," Colleen said, smiling indulgingly. As expected the retired accountants enjoyed their Christmas Day bash and the liberal amounts of alcohol provided. "I heard what happened to my father's friend, Justin Bellamy. Terrible thing. I know he wasn't popular with everyone, but why would anyone want to kill him?"

"Justin made lots of his friends rich," she said. "But he made others poor. People who feel cheated out of their life savings might want to kill the thief."

"I'm sure you know that the police think my father killed him," Colleen said. "That makes no sense to me at all."

"It's absurd," she agreed. "Your father is a rich man and Justin had a hand in making him rich."

Colleen's mother had suggested several people she should approach at the celebration and Ms. Hennessy was one of the most informed of the lot. The accountant had worked in New York for over forty years, well connected and very knowledgeable about the world of finance and banking.

"If you were to speculate, who do you think might want to kill Mr. Bellamy and why?" Colleen asked. "Do you believe it was someone who lost a lot of money? If so, why now? Why not years ago?"

Ms. Hennessy drank the remainder of her beverage. "I was an investor in Justin's New World Fund for some years. Made four hundred percent on my investment, sold it and put it in Vanguard. Getting that kind of stellar returns in a few years is not out of the question, but I wasn't taking any chances so I sold New World." She made a regretful face. "But New World just kept sailing upward. I'd have double the retirement had I stayed in. Justin was either one of the most brilliant investors of all time...or he wasn't."

"And if he wasn't," Colleen said, interested what Hennessy would say, "What was he?"

"Someone who had found El Dorado," she quipped. "And since we all know that legendary golden city doesn't exists, then our exceptionally successful financial connoisseur has conjured his own El Dorado."

"The SEC, FBI and a few other federal regulatory agencies have been looking into New World Fund since its inception," Colleen said. "Everyone has suspicions and theories but can't find how Bellamy has managed to keep growing and beating everyone else year after year, especially the last dozen years. Maybe Justin Bellamy is what people say he is, or was: the most exceptionally gifted investment guru ever."

Hennessy issued a sarcastic snort. "And my cat is the reincarnated Queen of Sheba."

The half dozen retired accountants Colleen had spoken with that evening mirrored Hennessy's sentiment, all convinced that Bellamy and gang had bribed, blackmailed, threatened, conned, bought people in the know across a wide swath of industries to produce the sky-high annual rates of growth the New World Fund achieved.

"The gaping hole in their belief," Eileen said, after they arrived back at her condo later that night, "is that there are too many moving parts; too many people in too many industries that Bellamy allegedly bribed, bought off or supposedly coerced for insider information to pump up his fund's returns."

"I agree," Colleen said. "The SEC or FBI would have uncovered some of those insiders over the years. And there would have been one or more whistleblowers who suspected collusion by colleagues or their bosses. I've had my people dig into Bellamy and New World the last few weeks and they haven't come up with anything stinky either."

"And yet, Bellamy and the New World Fund reeks to the heavens," Eileen said. "Maybe he could read minds."

"Considering the man kept coming up smelling like roses from every investigation, him being able to read minds is more likely than rumors of Bellamy threatening to bankrupt emerging companies by massive shorts if they don't play ball," Colleen replied.

"He did short companies all the time and made a bundle every time," Eileen said. "But you're right: coercing insiders to play ball would leak out much sooner than later. Well, honey, my brain is fried and body is tired. The bastard is dead and we'll never know how he managed to make his firm the fastest growing, most profitable fund on Wall Street. Maybe Satan might have better luck getting it out of him as he burns in hell."

*　　　*　　　*　　　*

Wolf was driving home the morning after spending New Year's Day visiting his family and Ruff's grave, when his cell rang. Not recognizing the name he let the call go to voice mail, opting to listen to the caller's message. The feature had been one of Brett's ideas and a most useful option, allowing Wolf to take action if needed in real time instead of later when he listed to his messages. Deciding to take action sooner than later, he called back informing the person he'd be arriving at her location by eleven.

Wolf walked past the gauntlet of staring reporters to the copy editor's office at the far end of the newsroom. He had "worked" at *The Washington Progressive* twenty months ago as a janitor mucking around the trash, listening to gossip, employee grousing and placing listening devices. The paper was one of a dozen media organizations Wolf infiltrated, the result of his efforts published under the title, *Media's Useful Idiots: Undermining Liberty For Fun and Profit.*

"Good morning, Ms. Dean," Wolf said, entering her office. "How are you on this fine day?"

His nonchalant manner must have struck the copy editor funny because she issued a chuckle. Grayson Wolf sauntering past a couple dozen reporters and columnists as though he was out on a Sunday stroll must have been a new experience for the woman. He understood her reaction and smiled knowingly.

"Thank you coming; Mr. Kramm suggested I call you, " Dean said. "I didn't expect you to show up in the, um, lion's den, so to speak, however."

"Mr. Kramm did mention there was someone working for him that might call," Wolf said. "You have something to share about gender issues?"

Dean shot a glance at the open door. Wolf reached back and shut it.

"I've pulled my daughter, Jennifer, out of ninth grade to homeschooler her," she said. "She's been getting a lot pressure from various gender bender groups since she cut her hair last spring—she saw a picture of me at thirteen with really short hair and decided to cut hers. Her short hair caught the interest of lesbian and transgender groups—they're all the rage in school now—trying to get her to join, saying that cutting her hair was a sign she was in gender transition and so forth.

"Jennifer has always been interested in boys and suddenly she was wondering about her sexuality. It began to stress her out, affecting her school work and making her more irritable when she was at home. In November I got a call from her counselor telling me she's was going to provide stress counseling for Jennifer. I told her why Jennifer was stressed and suggested she counsel these groups to stop pressuring her. Then she asks me why I have a problem with offering "affirmative care" to students going through gender or sexual realignment. I told her that I'm the parent and that I do not want her to provide stress or affirmative care counseling to Jennifer, which she ignores, telling me she's going to talk to Jennifer and see what she wants. Now she's really pissing me off and I make an appointment with the Principal."

"Let me guess," Wolf said. "The principal tells you the school respects all gender proclivities of their students and supports their choice to determine their sexual orientation du jour whatever that may be."

"It's much worse than that," Dean said, getting worked up. "They're actively promoting gender exploration. Jennifer brought home a handful of brochures about gender reassignment counseling, surgery, gay and lesbian options. I've got one from Planned Parenthood offering testosterone to young women on informed consent without any medical or psychological evaluation.

Testosterone, for God's sake! They can't figure out how to effectively educate their students but they know what's best for their sex lives?"

"I suppose hearing about Mr. Kramm's daughter committing suicide was the last straw," Wolf said. "What do your coworkers think about your decision to homeschool?"

Dean shot him a sardonic look. "Mr. Wolf, you know where I work. This is ground zero for promoting the equality of everything for everyone everywhere. I don't discuss politics with anyone and never discuss personal matters. I've read Useful Idiots, so you probably know that most of us working at the Progressive pretty much keep our thoughts to ourselves. Safer that way."

Wolf knew exactly what the copy editor was referring to. Having a good understanding of history, the perfect society actively promoted by this paper and the rest of the media, in reality reduced social interaction down to its lowest common denominator. The individual disappeared under the weight of the people, the proletariat, das Folk, afraid of uttering any sound for fear their neighbor will rush to authorities and fabricate stories for little more than securing their apartment with its extra bedroom.

"Mr. Kramm said you wanted to hear my story," Dean said. "I hope I've been helpful with your inquiries."

"Yes, you have, thank you," Wolf said. "Would you be willing to talk to some of my people in the future?"

"Maybe," she replied. "It would depend upon what the purpose was; I don't want to become involved in one of your organization's fights."

"Ms. Dean," Wolf said, smiling knowingly at her, "you are already involved in our fight because the Center for Individual Rights fights to protect parental rights, too. But I understand your situation quite well. If you choose to speak with us in the future, we will respect any parameters you set."

Exiting the copy editor's office, Wolf noticed that the numbers of workers in the newsroom had swelled significantly, the word having spread throughout the building of his visit. He was tempted to wave at the masses as he walked toward he exit, but prudence stayed his hand. Never a good idea to poke over fifty bears simultaneously.

Though he was hungry, Wolf decided to make for home, driving through the city entering his penthouse suite thirty-seven minutes later. He didn't drive into Washington often and being the day after New Year's, traffic in the city was light on account of it being an extended holiday for federal workers.

Wolf had barely hung up his coat when his phone tapped out a sound indicating a call from RJ. The call turned out to be an iChat, RJ's grinning face taking up the screen. Looking past his face, Wolf saw that he was in fact standing outside his door.

"You have an uncanny way of knowing just when I come home," Wolf said, opening the door.

"It's called stalking, bro," RJ quipped.

"Don't you have better things to do than to hang on my coattails? Spending quality time with your main squeeze, for instance?" Wolf replied.

"Zach and I have spent sufficient quality time together, I can assure you," RJ said. "And we have plenty more of the same planned, which, by the way, is more than you can say since you have no honey to spend time with. And don't bother giving me any suggestive looks: we both know that brown sugar you hanging with isn't sharing any of her sweet particles with you just like she didn't back in Colorado last summer."

"If you're done waxing on about my love life, get to the reason why you're dogging me the second I get home," Wolf said, giving RJ a long-suffering look.

RJ grinned indulgingly. "Since you have confirmed that you and Colleen are not snuggling up together, where did you disappear to the weekend before Christmas? Inquiring minds want to know?"

"Working on a joint investigation," Wolf said. "Can't go into any details except to say it includes Bellamy's and Maddie's murders."

"And Colleen Silverstone is helping you. Why?"

"Need to know and at this moment you do not need to know," Wolf said.

"That's hurts, bro. Hurts me right here." RJ held a hand over his heart. "I'm your oldest and dearest gay friend and suddenly you keeping secrets from me?"

"I keep secrets from you all the time, oldest and dearest gay friend," Wolf said, shooting him a comical look. "Cut the crap and get to the point."

RJ laughed. "I've got news for you. I know it's news 'cause if you knew, you wouldn't be standing her talking to your oldest and dearest—"

"Where would I be?" Wolf interjected, cutting him off.

"You'd be in NYC asking why Joseph Ferrara was blown up in his home yesterday. Joseph Ferrara, founder of the Affirmative Transformation Treatment Centers. He provided the startup money and then managed its franchise system. He stepped down as Board Chair four years ago, but still owns four centers and a big chunk of ATTC stock."

"Someone bombed his home?" Wolf asked.

"Sure looks like it," RJ replied. "Cops not releasing details yet. But after that mysterious death of that ATTC surgeon up in Boston three weeks ago and now the father of ATTC gets blown to bits, well I'd call that highly suspicious. Better pack, bro. I've reserved you a seat on a three 'o'clock flight outta Reagan. I'll drop you off at the subway. You be lucky, maybe your brown sugar be waiting for you."

Colleen was waiting to pick him up at Kennedy International but it wasn't luck, just effective communications, though Wolf was surprised when she said she'd be his ride. The ride, however was an air taxi into Manhattan, Colleen saying that she wasn't crazy enough to fight her way through Friday evening traffic coming and going.

"Thanks for arranging all this," Wolf said, after arriving downtown. "To be honest, taking a copter would not have occurred to me, which is ironic since I own one. I guess I've traveled in the shadows for too many years to consider high end forms of transportation."

"And I've been traveling in the fast lane for too many years to consider sitting behind the wheel during a rush hour rolling backup," Colleen responded.

An Uber dropped them off at the hotel, Wolf putting his things away in the same bedroom he slept in before. Wolf paid for dinner and Colleen surprised him with tickets for Wicked, insisting that all work and no fun wasn't conducive to solving problems. By the time they got back to the hotel it was past midnight and Colleen bid him goodnight.

After breakfast the next morning, the first order of business was a visit to Joseph Ferrara's Brooklyn Heights home. Colleen had arranged a meeting with one of the city's foremost forensic fire investigators. There were many reasons, beyond personal ones, why Wolf enjoyed teaming up with Colleen not the least being her extensive network of contacts and influence to arrange things like meeting a fire inspector early Saturday morning.

The house was located a mile south of the Brooklyn Bridge. Approaching the structure, Wolf recalled RJ's quip about the place being bombed and seeing the extensive damage, was inclined to agree with his assumption. The place was essentially gutted; whatever part of the house the explosion didn't destroy, the subsequent blaze most certainly did.

"Damn," Wolf said, as Colleen parked the car at the curb.

Yellow crime scene tape encircled what remained of the home, though no police or fire personnel were present at the moment. As he and Colleen stepped out of the car, Wolf spotted a woman exiting a SUV parked across the road, who gazed in their direction. Colleen waved a hand and walked over to her, Wolf at her heels.

"Good morning Inspector Waring. Thank you for taking time to meet us here," Colleen said, shaking her hand. Glancing at Wolf, she added, "My associate, Grayson Wolf."

Waring looked surprised, a predictable reaction when meeting Wolf, especially unexpectantly. The immediate question then becomes, what fuels one's perception upon meeting him? Is he a hero or a foe?

"An honor to meet you, Mr. Wolf," Waring said, smiling warmly and shaking his hand.

Hero it is.

"Thank you," Wolf said. "Ms. Silverstone tells me you are New York's preeminent fire inspector."

"Sufficiently preeminent to determine that it was not a bomb that destroyed Mr. Ferrara's home," she replied.

"A gas leak?" Wolf asked.

"Methane was definitely the fuel that powered the explosion," Waring said. "Some random gas leak is highly problematic considering the house was built only five years ago. The source of ignition is also currently unknown."

"So the only thing we are certain about it that gas was involved," Wolf said.

"At the moment, yes," Waring confirmed. "My department will be digging carefully through the remains on Monday. If there is something to be found, we will find it, though the chance of any incriminating material having survived the blast and subsequent fire is slim to none."

"Are we sure that Ferrara was the victim?" Colleen asked.

"According to the coroner, yes," Waring said.

"Based on your experience with gas related explosions, any theories how someone might cause an explosion?" Colleen asked.

"Using gas as the fuel for arson does the job quickly and efficiently," Waring said. "A detonating device attached to a propane tank would easily burn down a house. We haven't found any evidence of such a method in our preliminary investigation. We do know that the source of the ignition was in or near the home's central heating housing. The challenge for the arsonist in this scenario is that he or she needs access to the home, have cut the gas line, allowing the gas to fill the house and have used some type of device to ignite the gas. Though the area where the central heating unit was located is totally destroyed by the blast, close examination of the gas line does not indicate that it was tampered with. Hopefully we will know more early next week and I'll get our findings to you."

"Could someone have rigged the equipment to cause a malfunction resulting in an explosion?" Wolf asked.

"Highly unlikely if not impossible," Waring replied. "Based on our records, the heating system was state of the art. What's left of the system we will go through with a fine-toothed comb. If someone did tamper with the unit, we'll find evidence of it; we always do."

Colleen thanked Waring and the inspector left. They stood gazing at the wreckage for a long moment.

"This was no gas leak, malfunction or coincidence," Wolf said. "This was murder."

"What's the motive?" Colleen said.

"Reprisal, payback, punishment," Wolf replied. "Justice."

"It may be about vengeance or punishment, but acting as judge, jury and executioner is never just," Colleen said.

"True dat," Wolf quipped. "But what if the circumstances don't offer a path to achieve justice? Say if a daughter commits suicide because she had made an impulsive choice that ruined her life because everyone around her encouraged and pressured her to proceed? Someone who had the financial means and possibly underworld connections to dispense justice to all concerned?"

"I thought you didn't suspect the newspaper publisher since he brought you in to inquire into his daughter's suicide?" Colleen said.

"Just looking at who has motive, money and connections."

"If I set out to get even with those who did me wrong I certainly wouldn't be talking about it to anyone, especially Grayson Wolf," Colleen said, grinning. "I'd move quickly, systematically and stealthily and they'd never know what hit them."

"Good to know," Wolf chuckled. "Maybe it's about power; the type of power that gives one a feeling that he could shoot someone on the street with impunity and walk away without repercussions."

"You might be on to something, Wolf," Colleen said, looking intrigued. "You publish Media's Useful Idiots excoriating Kramm and his colleagues. Later his daughter commits suicide, but his politics prevent him from taking direct action. He's angry, but what to do? Mulling things over, he gets a great idea: kill a bunch of birds with one stone. He invites you over as the grieving father. Lamenting about how his hands are tied and seeing the mother's tears, you agree to investigate. The entire time he's planning to kill the people he thinks are responsible for his daughter's sex change and suicide virtually in front of your eyes. Grayson Wolf, sucker extraordinaire. Getting even with everyone who has caused him pain or embarrassment. I definitely could imagine that scenario."

"So can I," Wolf said. "Think Cooper could peek into Kramm's life, phone and browser history and see if anything hinky pops up?"

"I can't make any promises, Wolf," Colleen replied. "Like your folks at CIR, my people are dealing with dozens of projects and hundreds of clients. To do a proper job searching through Kramm's affairs requires serious time and resources. And not everything about people is found in electronic records, as you of all people know very well."

"True dat," he replied.

She shot him a sardonic look. "Since when are you a New Orleans Saints fan? You say 'true dat' a lot."

"I don't follow sports," he said. "My sister's been working in New Orleans the past few months and she's been tossing that retort around the house during her Christmas visit. It's a catchy, pithy expression that says what it means."

"True dat," Colleen teased. "Also true, assuming our theory about Kramm is accurate, he might be saving you for his grand finale. You have got to watch your back at all times."

"Correction my dear Ms. Silverstone. *We* have got to watch our backs at all times because whoever killed Bellamy and Maddie might become very nervous about you and me snooping around and decide that we're too nosey for our own good."

"Now why didn't I think of that?" Colleen said, looking at him with a clueless expression.

A grin slid across Wolf's mouth. "I think some of my impudence is rubbing off on you. I like it. True dat."

Colleen rolled her eyes and made for the car. Worried that she might take off without him, he hurried after her, getting in the car and managing to shut the door before she pulled away from the curb.

Chapter 12

New World, New Hacks

"According to my sources," Brett said, "they've got a whole lotta nothin'."

Wolf was holding the phone between him and Colleen, the two sitting on the sofa in her hotel. They were communicating via iChat and could see that Brett was in his office at CIR.

"You do know that I'm not paying you overtime for pretending to be working on a Sunday afternoon," Wolf teased.

"No problemo; I'll just take some equipment as payment," he rejoined. He moved closer to camera, his face filling the phone's screen and continued. "I've been huddling with Cooper and his sources confirm that the NYPD's only suspect for Bellamy's murder is Mr. Silverstone and my Maryland sources confirm that the Baltimore Police have no leads whatsoever for Maddie's murder."

"Two weeks later and the police investigation hasn't uncovered anything new," Wolf said, frustrated.

"Let me say this about that, Wolfman. Whoever is behind these murders are some seriously dangerous bad asses. I know you got Ms. Silverstone covering your tush, but I'd recommend layering on more protection as you wade into deeper waters."

"I'll take that under advisement, Brett," Colleen said. "Don't worry too much about Wolf. He's assured me you're in his will."

Brett laughed. "Good to know; I'm looking forward to getting his colorful hand-knitted sock collection...I'll keep you updated the second anything new comes our way."

Wolf ended the call, placed the phone on the end table and slid his legs on the sofa, propping himself up on several pillows. Colleen did likewise on the other end, the pair facing each other over the length of the couch. Both appeared deep in thought.

"I'm thinking that we ought to visit your little prairie house and have a heart-to-heart with its occupant after we visit New World headquarters tomorrow," Wolf said, breaking the silence.

"He's not going to tell us anything more than he did before," Colleen said. "Besides, doing so might jeopardize revealing his location. We got away with seeing him the first time since the police had not publicly announced he was the prime suspect; now I'm sure they are monitoring my movements."

"I think Barry might be far more willing to ignore his bogus confidentiality position if he was found and brought in for arraignment," Wolf said. "Nothing like the prospect of possibly being next in line to be wacked to loosen the tongue." Seeing the look on Colleen's face he added, "I'm just saying. Currently both our security chiefs agree that it is you and I standing between Barry and his nemesis and we're in plain sight unlike our prime suspect. I think that adds some weight to my argument to prop him up next to us if he won't reveal some critical information that might help us unravel this conundrum."

"You have just described the key difference between the way you and I operate," Colleen said. "Grayson Wolf, for all intends and purposes, is essentially a hunter who stalks his prey, gathering vital and juicy information before he pounces and publishes. Colleen Silverstone is essentially a guardian of her client's vital and juicy information, working hard to keep unwanted wolves at bay. The repercussions of Grayson Wolf's predatory activities are borne largely by himself. The repercussions of Colleen Silverstone's failure to maintain the integrity of her client's trust are borne largely by her entire corporation, which by extension, includes every employee. Grayson Wolf is free to leap and bound here and there as his mood or scent of prey takes him. Colleen Silverstone must weigh and carefully consider any action that might impact her business."

"So you're saying we make the perfect couple: yin and yang, hot and cold, light and dark, male and female, brilliant and crazy, beautiful and ordinary," he replied, looking smugly at her. When she looked suspiciously at him, he said, "What? Hearing the truth spoken got your tongue?"

"I'm having issues with your progression," Colleen said. "You're hot, light, male, brilliant and beautiful. I'm cold, dark, female, crazy and ordinary?"

"Well, when you put it that way, it sounds about right," Wolf teased, his smile lighting up the room.

"You also forgot one more dyad," she said, her eyes narrowing slightly. "Happy-go-lucky and will kick your ass."

"Good cop and bad cop," Wolf laughed.

Colleen smiled and got up. "Show over and to bed."

Colleen glanced impatiently at her watch. The appointment with New World Fund's principals was scheduled for Monday morning at nine o'clock and it was edging toward 9:20. She shot a look at Wolf, who was tapping away on his laptop, working on his latest Tara Mason novel, something he'd been doing during their trip to and from Maine. It must be nice to be the president of a company where one only needed to agree with whatever decisions its Board made and spend the rest of the day writing stories.

Colleen chastised herself for her gross distortions and unkindly thoughts about Wolf's status. Reflecting on their adventures together last spring and their current collaboration, she had to admit that she had come to enjoy his company. She was wondering about the mixed feeling that arose pursuant to this revelation, when the receptionist appeared informing Colleen and Wolf to accompany her to the meeting.

They entered a beautifully appointed conference room seated across from half dozen New World corporate officers, each sporting an artificial smile.

"Good morning, Mr. Townsend," Colleen said, and introduced Wolf.

Smiles vanished, replaced by frowns. The sudden transformation struck her as hilarious and she had to restrain a strong desire to laugh, though she failed to prevent a full-toothed smile from issuing forth. She slid a document across the table toward the company president.

"Authorization from your attorney, Barry Silverstone, giving permission to Mr. Wolf and myself to discuss items pertaining to New World corporate legal matters," Colleen said. She slid a second document across the table. "Signed surety by Mr. Wolf and myself attesting to the confidentiality of all conversation and information presented during this meeting."

Townsend laughed, tossed both documents toward the head counselor and said,

"I wouldn't trust Mr. Wolf to keep anything we say here confidential if I wrapped him in signed and notarized confidentiality guarantees six inches thick and buried him in a solid steel pyramid the size of Manhattan."

"Do you really want me to respond to that, Bunny-Boo?" Wolf said.

Colleen's face spun toward Wolf sitting next to her. Bunny-Boo? What the hell was he referring to? Recovering from the surprise, she looked at Townsend, noticing that all eyes in the room were upon the very uncomfortable looking president, too.

He cleared his throat and said, keeping his eyes glued on Wolf, "Just a silly name given to me in boarding school. I had large ears and would jump a sudden loud noises."

After an extended stretch of silence, Wolf said, "I can guarantee you, Bunny-Boo, that we'll refrain from sudden loud noises so long as you and your people cooperate."

Taking his silence as agreement to Wolf's deal, Colleen fired a series of question at the group beginning with their speculation for the murder of Bellamy. She didn't expect to hear any major revelations, but was intrigued by the response of New World' UHI division manager, asking him to explain.

"The UHI division, that stands for the Unknown, Hidden and Ignored companies in the US and across the globe, is the atomic engine driving New World's fantastic growth over the past twenty years. This was Mr. Bellamy's brainchild and what he paid attention to: endlessly searching for these little known companies with great potential. He was great at discovering opportunities in established companies, too, but he was super at sniffing out pre-emerging superstars. Doesn't take a rocket scientist to figure out that killing the golden goose will hit the nest real hard. Short New World and kill Bellamy and you got yourself the money-making opportunity of a lifetime." The UHI manager looked sheepishly at the others, adding, "New World stock dropped over thirty percent immediately following Mr. Bellamy's death notice. That's pretty suspicious to me."

It was highly suspicious. All that was required was to track down the person or persons who profited the most the fastest. Satisfied that the men across the table had little more to add to unraveling Bellamy's death, Colleen thanked Townsend for agreeing to speak to them and left.

"How did you manage to discover Townsend's school nickname?" she asked, walking through the lobby toward the exit.

"You bought that story?" Wolf said, giving her a look. "Tsk, tsk, Ms. Silverstone."

Colleen took hold of his arm and hustled him toward the nearest wall. "You tsk me again, Wolfie, and I will administer pain. Talk."

"I love when you get physical," Wolf said, grinning. "Bunny-Boo is what Townsend's former mistress referred to his rabbit quick performance. No substitute for boots on the ground to dig for hidden gems."

"I happen to agree with you." Colleen said.

"I know you do; why your company is so successful: lots of boots on the ground," Wolf said. He shot her a droll look, adding, "You keep me pinned against the wall any longer people are going to wonder what we're doing over here."

"Keep dreaming." Colleen removed her forearm from his chest and started to walk toward the exit.

"It's not a farfetched theory," Wolf said, referring to the idea that Bellamy was killed as a way to short New World and cash in. "Maddie's murder might not be related to Bellamy's murder and be a bonafide coincidence."

Colleen stopped walking and stood facing him. "Bellamy gets gassed between a Thursday night and Friday morning and Maddie gets poisoned Saturday shortly before meeting you for lunch. Not a coincidence, Wolf?"

"If you are correct and the murders are connected," Wolf said, "then it is not likely that the murders have anything to do with shorting New World stock."

"Why not?" Colleen asked.

"Because of the missing attaché," Wolf said. "Maddie must have been carrying incriminating documents to give me. If it was just a matter of names shorting the stock or the name of Bellamy's killer, she would have mentioned that in her text."

"Why can't it be both?" Colleen said. "Stop Maddie from handing you incriminating documents that identify some criminal activity or insider trading activity and make a financial killing from the killing."

"What about the sequence of the killings?" Wolf asked. "If I knew X was going to turn over documents that will send me up the river, I go after X and kill X then think, hey! Why not kill Bellamy and cash in big while I'm in a killing mood. However, Bellamy was killed first, Maddie second."

"How about this version: I get the bright idea to kill Bellamy and cash in big," Colleen said. "I find out that Maddie has documents that can send me up the river and that she's going to Baltimore. I kill Bellamy, get on a plane to Baltimore, find Maddie, poison her drink, steal the attaché; happy days are here again ... what's so funny?"

"You do realize we're standing in the middle of the sidewalk like a pair of boulders as a heavy stream of humanity flow around us," Wolf said, smiling warmly.

She liked seeing that smile; it suggested interesting possibilities. Possibilities the hardworking owner of the nation's top security and investigative firm had little time for—or chose to have no time for.

Colleen gave him a droll look and said, "You do realize we're standing in the middle of a busy Manhattan sidewalk where the stream of humanity takes absolutely no notice of us."

"Maybe not but it's freezing, so how about we continue our conversation in a more hospitable environment?" Wolf rejoined, taking Colleen by the arm and moving with the flow toward the crosstown subway station.

"We have theories but no hard leads or suspects," Colleen said, enjoying the hot cup of cocoa Wolf ordered from room service. "And given that we're not moving forward and that I have pressing business to attend to back at Colorado, I'm taking a flight out this afternoon."

Wolf peered over the edge of his cup. "I'm going to miss you, Colleen, despite the fact that you can be a very scary woman to live with."

"Admit it: you like me to muscle you about," she replied, giving him a humorous look.

"It's not my preferred way to dance with a woman, but it'll have to do," he quipped.

"And, to be clear: we're not living together," Colleen said. She put down her cup, walked over and lifted Wolf's laptop from the sofa. Opening the unit, she clicked on his Skype application, entered a contact then made the video call. She handed Wolf a small plastic card.

"A copy of my key," she said. "You'll probably stay here for another day or two."

"And I'll stay here, why?" Wolf asked.

Her Skype call connected. Cooper's face appeared on the screen. She handed the laptop to Wolf.

"This is why."

"Good morning Wolf," Cooper said. "Colleen tells me you are freezing your hiney off up there."

Wolf shot a sardonic look at Colleen. "I'd rather be in Virginia basking in the upper forties, that's for sure. Colleen apparently thinks I'll be staying in New York and I believe you're going to tell me why."

"I've been looking into the death of your Mr. Ferrara," Cooper began. "Like lots of other zillionaires, Ferrara lived in a very, very smart house. Hot water faucets that were instantly hot. Rooms with independent temperature controls, lights that automatically turn on when you enter and off when you exit. Top security features including knowing how many people should be in the house at a particular time and where they should not be. Vehicle detection including flying objects such as drones. Toilets that wiped your butt when done—"

"Bullshit," Wolf scoffed, interrupting Cooper's litany of smart features.

"Close, but no cigar for you!" Cooper said, laughing at his little joke. "Your Mr. Ferrara's smart house also had a very smart central heating and cooling system that's an environmentalist's green dream. His smart climate system responded to small changes of external and internal temperature to efficiently conserve every sniff of gas and nanowatt of electricity. Super rich people are required to be models of Green compliance, you know."

"Now I know why Colleen said I'd be staying in New York: obviously listening to you expound on the thrills and chills of smart houses for the next couple of days," Wolf joked.

"Not days, just a couple minutes more," Cooper said, his toothy grin filling half the screen. "Did you know that a better than average hacker can fool a very, very smart house like the one Ferrara owned? Yes indeed. Being an above average computer nerd myself, I could find a door in the man's smart app, turn on the gas, keep the vent damper shut so that gas would build up in the lower level while he was resting peacefully in his bed two floors up. Then after an appropriate amount of time has passed I would send a signal for the igniting mechanism to fire a spark and, boom! Mischief permanently managed."

Wolf nodded thoughtfully. "Looks like I will be staying on in this deep freeze for a while longer after all. Thanks, Cooper."

"It's what I do, but the thanks for doing goes to the woman standing next to you," he replied. "Good luck...and I'd advise you to keep a sharp eye on all your smart appliances, too. That killer gets worried you're getting too close, he won't hesitate to outsmart your smart toys. And he will, so be sure to count on that as you proceed. Chao!"

Wolf shut the laptop and looked thoughtfully at Colleen.

"I've texted you Inspector Waring's contact info," she said.

"Thanks and thank you for Cooper and letting me stay," he said. A cute smile appeared and he added, "Though it won't be the same without you."

"I'm sure you'll survive the deprivation," Colleen said. "Let me second Cooper's warning: be careful, Wolf. This hacker has killed two people."

"Back atcha," Wolf quipped. "So has the killer you're looking for."

Colleen and Wolf shared an Uber, Wolf getting off at the fire department's administrative offices in southern Manhattan, Colleen continuing on to her flight at Kennedy International Airport. A receptionist led him to Waring's office, the fire inspector greeting him warmly. Wolf gave her a summary of what Cooper had told him about the definite possibility of a hacker causing the gas explosion from a remote location. To his surprise, Waring did not look at all skeptical upon concluding his account.

"Our records show that Mr. Ferrara had an Enviro-Tech super-efficient heating system installed a year ago," Waring explained. "The National Association of Fire Inspectors has warned about the Enviro-Tech's closed vent feature. Most furnaces have an open vent allowing exhaust gases to rise and escape out of the house. In these typical furnaces, even if the gas failed to ignite, the unburned gas would travel up the pipe and out on the roof. It wouldn't seep into the house causing an explosion from a spark or someone lighting a match. Besides, long before there was enough gas to create an explosion, people in the house would smell the gas, or more specifically, the Mercaptan gas added to the methane. Mercaptan has a pungent, rotten cabbage smell that's hard to miss. The Enviro-Tech super-efficient heating system's damper opens when the system initiates and shuts when the heating cycle is over. Closing off the vent prevents warm internal air from escaping up the vent and wasting energy. Our concern has always been the possibility of a malfunction preventing the damper from opening and filling the house with exhaust fumes."

"Now you can also be worried about hackers getting into the system and blowing up buildings for fun and profit," Wolf said. "And killing its occupants."

"I really hope you are wrong about that, Mr. Wolf," Waring said, shaking her head. "I will report this to the police and make a strong recommendation that their computer forensic people look into Mr. Ferrara's records. May I ask where you got this information from?"

"Ms. Silverstone's people," Wolf said. "If the police find anything, I'd appreciate it if you'd let me know as soon as you hear."

"Out of curiosity, are you investigating this incident for one of your novels?" Waring asked.

"Investigating, yes. For a novel, no," Wolf said, though it might wind up in a future Mason novel, he thought. "There is a strong possibility that Mr. Ferrara's death is connected to a second death a couple weeks back in Boston also possibly connected to computer hacking. That was one of the reasons I asked Ms. Silverstone to have her specialists check out the circumstances of the gas explosion at Mr. Ferrara's home."

"I see," Waring said. "I will definitely push the police to pursue the hacking angle and let you know if and when I hear back from them."

Wolf thanked the woman and caught a taxi back to the hotel. On the way he called and made an appointment with the head of security at the national headquarters of the Affirmative Transformation Treatment Centers the next morning. At the hotel he made dinner reservations at their restaurant, took a shower and got dressed.

He had over an hour until dinner, taking advantage of the time to check his messages. A text from Juan about meeting with lawyers representing Ivygreen College caught his attention. Apparently he and his team were in Boston preparing for talks tomorrow morning.

"Looks like the added pressure of financial misappropriations, and the rising stink about being a cheerleader for gender realignment has brought the college to the negotiating table," Wolf said, aloud. He texted back, "go get them!" and finished up reviewing and answering as needed the rest of his messages and emails. He was about to put his phone away when he got an idea and made a call.

"Miss me yet?" he said.

"Obviously you do," Colleen replied.

"Good flight?" Wolf said, ignoring her. "Bumpy ride? Not bumpy enough?"

"It was a Goldilocks flight," she retorted.

"Perfect balance of smooth and bumpy. The best kind of flight," Wolf said.

"Not over yet," Colleen said. "I'm twenty minutes from Denver and there is a stiff northern breeze, so bumpy is coming up soon ... how was your meeting with the lovely Susan?"

"As you'd expect when lovely women meet me face-to-face," Wolf said. "She's sleeping over. I'll send you a few hot pics to enjoy with your breakfast tomorrow morning."

"Looking forward to it," Colleen replied. "As much as I enjoy being entertained by your sexual fantasies, the captain has informed us to end all electronic communications. Take care of yourself, Wolfie."

The line went dead. Wolf peered aimlessly at the dozen app icons on the phone.

"Entertained by my sexual fantasies," he said, out loud. A smile appeared on his lips and he added, "The woman knows me much better than I thought."

Chapter 13

Honey Pot Ambush

Juan Mendez was running low on patience waiting for the Ivygreen College negotiating team to make a showing. The president of Ivygreen College had agreed to discuss the possibility of a deal in lieu of the college facing the full brunt of CIR's class action. The college administration was especially interested in avoiding the exposure of other unsavory practices, including revelations about misappropriation of legacy funds and being a prominent cheerleader for gender reassignment. The gender issue became an added pressure point when Wolf was asked to look into the suicide of a former Ivygreen student, his subsequent inquiry uncovering the murder-by-car-hack of the surgeon who had performed such procedures.

"Juan, I think we have a problem," Terrance Smith, assistant counselor said, looking out the window.

Susan Baker, the other member of the CIR legal team gazed out the window. A large crowd of students carrying signs had assembled outside the building.

"It's a protest," she said. "And judging from the slogans on their signs, it's aimed at us."

"And a bunch of them are entering the building," Terrance said. "The bastards have set us up."

"Jam the door!" Juan cried, rushing toward it.

Terrance was right behind him. Lifting one of the metal-framed chairs they shoved the top edge under the doorknob, wedging the chairs legs into the wooden floor as tightly as they could. Susan came over holding a heavy stapler in her hand. Unhinging the top portion of the unit, she got on her knees and began to wedge the thin base of the stapler under the door, using the top part as a hammer to wedge it tightly underneath.

"Damn girl," Terrance said, looking at Susan with surprise. "Impressive. Got anymore tricks up your sleeve?"

"I've got two brothers and we were a rowdy bunch," she said, grinning. "Any that come through that door and get in my face will see what else I'm capable of."

"I've called campus police and told them we are being threatened and to get here immediately," Juan said.

"Why do I have this feeling they've got more important things to attend to first?" Terrance said.

"Oh, they'll be here double quick," Juan assured them. A wicked grin appeared. "I told them we were armed and would not hesitate to defend ourselves against a mob of privileged students attacking three members of three different protected minorities. I've also alerted our folks back home."

Both Terrance and Susan laughed. Their amusement was short lived, however, when sounds of vigorous door pounding filled the room. Although the fury of the assault on the door increased, their improvised obstructions successfully prevented the barbarians from breaking in—for the moment. Then, to their collective relief, the wailing of police sirens filtered through the windows, followed thereafter by a significant reduction of banging on the door, soon abating altogether.

After a while the sound of orders to dispense were heard followed by a loud knock by someone claiming to be the chief of the campus police asking the occupants to open the door. Removing the chair was relatively easy; the stapler base under the door took more than a minute to un wedge.

Juan opened the door, and stood resolute in the entrance facing a cadre of police officers. One of them identified himself as the police chief demanding that he and anyone else in his group relinquish their guns immediately.

"What guns?" Juan said, looking surprised. "We are not carrying firearms, though there is that little matter of Massachusetts violating the Second Amendment, to wit, 'the right of the people to keep and bear Arms, shall not be infringed'. But we'll deal with that oversight in the future."

"I was told that a call was made from here by a person saying the group was armed and prepared to defend themselves against students attacking them," the Chief said.

"Armed is a general term with such meanings as, equipped, fortified or prepared," Juan clarified. "We were armed with chairs, heavy staplers and also prepared to use the flag poles in the corner to defend ourselves against these students playing at being Brown Shirts for a morning lark. My associates and I do thank you for your speedy response. Your officers are a fine example of proper campus policing."

There was a sound of voices in the hallway, followed by several officious looking men and women, one of which Juan identified as Ivygreen College president, Francis Sidwell. He stepped back from the entrance allowing the group to enter.

"I can't tell you how relieved I am to find all of you safe," Sidwell gushed. "I was surprised to hear that you were still here since I sent word that there was an emergency I needed to attend to."

Juan thought the man was conning him, but studying Sidwell's face he wasn't so sure. He'd met more than his share of college administrators and though most were good snake oil hawkers, conspiring to set a trap for visitors so that campus mobs can spew their venom upon them was rare. Though upon reflection, the Virginia Patriots College president colluded with county police to expose Diana and her free speech protesters to the fury of the nihilist thugs in Rockfall County.

"May I ask what the nature of the emergency was that caused you to cancel our meeting, Dr. Sidwell?" Juan asked.

"It has to do with Transitioning Gender counselor Heather Franken," he replied. "She was supposed to attend this meeting with your people, but she didn't come in today and no one could reach her."

"I don't understand? We could proceed without the counselor or bring a different counselor to the meeting."

"Oh, didn't I say?" Sidwell replied, looking befuddled. "It's horrible...I received word shortly after your arrival that Ms. Franken was struck by a speeding car walking across the parking lot shortly before the meeting. She is seriously injured and the doctors are not sure if she'll survive."

Juan was thinking where he had heard the counselor's name before when Susan said,

"Excuse me, President Sidwell. You said you sent someone to tell us that the meeting was cancelled, yet no one came. Do you recall whom you sent? An office assistant perhaps?"

The man thought for a moment then said, "A student aide, I believe. Why do you ask?"

"I find it curious that you sent a student to inform us that the meeting was cancelled and soon after a mob marches on this building," Susan replied. "Perhaps your student aide informed the leaders of this mob of our presence and leaving us to wait like sitting ducks for their impromptu protest. May I have the name of that student aide?"

"No you may not," Sidwell said, looking incensed. "It's bad enough your organization is attacking private and public universities for monetary gain, but I'm not having you go after a student based on little more than conjecture."

"You might wish to question this aide when your schedule permits, President Sidwell," Juan said. "If that mob would have succeeded to get through that door and harmed one of us, I can assure you that by the time we were done with you and your college, you wouldn't have a college left to run ... I'm sorry to hear about your counselor. However, my team is on a tight schedule having to meet with many other colleges for monetary gain and will need to meet with your people later today or early tomorrow. If your people can't accommodate my request, then our offer to negotiate a settlement prior to including Ivygreen in the class action proceedings is withdrawn."

Juan shot a look at Susan and Terrance and the trio trooped out of the room and exited the building. Once in the car, Juan turned to them asking if either one had heard the counselor's name before today.

"Franken, yeah," Terrance said. "I overheard Brett and RJ talking about this gender bender counselor Wolf had met while in Boston. Gotta be the same person."

"Call Wolf and tell him about her getting run over," Juan said, starting the car and driving through the parking garage.

"This have something to do with Stephanie Kramm's suicide?" Susan asked.

"Being the third victim related to the sex change issue Wolf is looking into, I'd venture a guess and say that Transitioning Gender counselor Heather Franken's accident in the parking lot is not a coincidence," Juan replied.

*   *   *   *

Earlier that morning Wolf was staring down several key administrative heads in one of the conference rooms of Affirmative Transformation Treatment Centers' national headquarters.

"We have nothing to hide and nothing to be ashamed of, Mr. Wolf," Vice President for Growth and Expansion Shelly Sanders said. "ATTC runs a much needed service for thousands of sexually mismatched human beings and our treatment centers employ only the most professional personnel. We are proud to be the leader in the field of gender reassignment surgery, therapies and counseling."

"According to your literature, you claim that the percentage of sexually mismatched individuals may exceed twenty percent of the population," Wolf said.

"That is correct," Sanders confirmed. "Several recent studies suggest that number to be even higher; perhaps a third of the population in the world."

Wolf looked at the group facing him, puckered his lips and nodded. "There are thirteen ATTC employees in this room. That would make about a quarter of you sexually mismatched. Would you please identify yourselves? I promise you I will not judge..." No one raised their hand. "Anyone in this group willing to own up to having gender confirmation surgery? Gender confirmation therapy? How about sex with a coworker?"

"That's quite enough of your nonsense, Mr. Wolf," ATTC attorney Carol Pressing said. "Besides the fact that your request is a violation of privacy, whether all, some or none of ATTC employees chose any gender related procedure is irrelevant to the mission of this firm."

"Oh I doubt that very much, Ms. Pressing," Wolf countered. "Every individual working for or with the Center for Individual Rights is aligned with our mission. It's a job requirement and it remains so throughout an employee's tenure. One may disagree on certain details but not on our mission if one wishes to remain at CIR."

"Are you seriously suggesting that every ATTC employee have undergone some form of gender procedure as a requirement of employment?" Sanders said, her tone sarcastic.

"I'm simply pointing out that of the five thousand or so employees of the three dozen ATTC facilities and offices, there are only five bonafide gender reassigned personnel. I don't claim to be a mathematical wiz, but five samples of your primary service out of the five thousand obviously not sexually mismatched or confused, comes to about, well, a tiny percentage of your people. And far, far, *far* short of your twenty percent and the third of the world's population predicted by those scholarly researchers ATTC paid for."

"Slander; please keep that up, Mr. Wolf," Pressing said, looking pleased. "You did agree to have this meeting recorded."

"Oh, yes, this is all on record…which you agreed to provide me a full and faithful copy thereof." Wolf paused long enough to see a suggestion of doubt appear on Pressing's face and continued. "Slander: noun; the action or crime of making a false spoken statement damaging one's reputation. When organizations get bigger and more powerful, a growing complacency sets in over the decades, rotting the system from the top down and inside out. This process has become increasingly evident in recent years, especially throughout higher education. The condition manifesting itself as a form of impudence and arrogance, administrators believing themselves insulated from the forces the rest of society is subject to, such as financial responsibility. Group think becomes rampant. I call it educational incest and it has borne many deformed, ugly and toxic ideas and practices. Private companies who have allied themselves with the worst practitioners of educational incest are going to get hit, too."

"What does this have to do with us?" Sanders asked.

"It has to do with the three professors of gender studies in three New England colleges ATTC paid to manufacture bullshit studies," Wolf said. "Studies you use as advertising fodder to boost uncertainty about the sexuality of impressionable children. Studies used to create hundreds of virtual support groups where one finds tons of glowing accounts of incredibly happy transgenderized and properly sexually aligned claimants. Endless social media posts that further increase doubt, worry and concern in impressionable minds of insecure adolescents and pre-adolescents." Wolf pointed at Bob

Channing, ATTC security chief and said, "Are you getting all this on the record?" He felt his phone buzz and read the text message.

"This meeting is over," Sanders said, taking advantage of his pause. "You are everything your detractors say about you, Mr. Wolf."

"Thank you for that compliment; having announced my retirement, I was a little worried that doing so might dilute that reputation. But before Mr. Channing's security detail tosses me out on your sidewalk, you better be aware that a count of suicides related to ATTC gender reassignment surgeries is being made. And I'm sure that the number will far exceeds that one, one thousand of a percent of your employees who have changed their sex ... oh, and let's not forget that highly inconvenient fact that over ninety percent of gender confusion and hoopla afflicts the female of the species. And perhaps most disconcerting and embarrassing to the benighted of our social media addled culture, is that the very large majority of sexually befuddled females come from the most progressive families." Wolf got up from his seat and started for the door, stopped and said, "And one more thing: there's a serial killer taking out people working for ATTC: your founder, Joseph Ferrara, a surgeon working at your center in Watertown and just minutes ago, Heather Franken, gender counselor at Ivygreen College. I'd watch my back—all of you."

Wolf made his escape and hurried out of the building making it to the sidewalk intact. His goal had been to upset the smug complacency evident in ATTC's operations by tossing a sizable monkey wrench into the administrative gearbox, confident that he had achieve that objective. The parting shot about a serial killer most certainly got everyone's attention but the news about Franken definitely resulted in shocked expressions. It had been a shock to him, too, when he read Terrance's text shortly before being dismissed by Sanders.

Waving down a taxi, Wolf called Juan to inform him that he was on his way to Boston. Next, he called the concierge desk at the hotel instructing them to have a rental delivered. Then he called Brett at CIR to update him about the situation, and instructing him to review the list of all confirmed suicides connected to ATTC and expand the search nationally. Then he called Colleen to apprise her of events and ask if she would allow Cooper to assist Brett with the national search of any suicide connected to gender reassignment surgery. Just prior to being delivered at the hotel's front entrance, Wolf called Diana, explaining where he was going. She reminded him to be extra careful.

"If this killer knows you are looking for him, he will know how good your sniffer is and may very well decide to eliminate you before you become a real threat," Diana cautioned. "Actually you're facing a double threat because you're also looking for Maddie's killer and by extension, probably Bellamy's, too. Ask Colleen to provide bodyguards, Wolf."

The taxi stopped at the curb. "We'll see; don't worry Diana. Gotta go, taxi driver giving me ugly looks!"

Wolf winked at the driver and handed him a generous tip. The man gave him a warm smile in return and drove off. Thirty minutes later Wolf was driving north on FDR Drive, crossed the East River and merged on I-278 on the way to I-95 and on to Boston.

*   *   *   *

When Colleen terminated Wolf's call, she notified Cooper instructing him to work with Brett at CIR. Cooper confirmed the directive then asked to meet her in The Vault.

"We need to discuss new information coming to light about Wally Gator. She's quickly becoming our most problematic client."

"I always knew Wally Gator would turn out to become a real liability," Colleen said. "I'll be right down."

The Vault was the bomb-proof communications center buried twenty feet below the building. But Colleen wasn't going to discuss any client. Wally Gator was code for we have a major problem.

Colleen sealed the door after entering Cooper's office. The paranoid security maven placed a finger on his lips signaling no talking as he completed his sweep for electronic listening devices. Colleen was absolutely certain that none would be found, but appreciated Cooper's diligence.

"Remember our federal busybody invasion before Christmas?" Cooper said, lowering the sensor unit on his desk.

"Of course," Colleen said, grinning at his version of the FBI initials. "It was the highlight of my day."

"One or more left some poop behind," Cooper said. "I was doing random scans throughout the building yesterday and this morning. I stopped by your office but you were out. On a lark I swept the place and to my surprise I found a little turd sandwiched between the Internet cable connected to the port at the bottom of the wall that goes up to your computer. Here's a pic..." He held his phone toward her. "See that cylindrical bulge between the cables, that's the bug. It's multifunctional: it can listen to conversation and rummage through your computer. Better hope they don't find those hot nude photos you and Wolf took during your down time together."

"You sure mention Wolf a lot; keep it up and people might get the impression you have a thing for the man," Colleen teased. "Back to the stinkbug in my office; do you really think the FBI planted it?"

"If you talking about the same FBI that conspired to prevent the election of our current President, then yes, and by yes, I mean I *know* it to be true," Cooper said. "Records of comings and goings from your office show that the *only* people that had been in your office without you being present were the FBI when they searched for whatever bullshit they were looking to find. Perfect opportunity to place the bug; take them all of ten seconds. Make that thirty seconds if it was one of the fuck-ups doing the job. May I ask what they're after?"

"Subtract the illegal surveillance bug and I'd say their visit had to do with hassling me for getting involved with Wolf and all that followed," Colleen said. "Add the bug back into the picture and what we've got is something that has nothing to do with the FBI raid." When Cooper shot her a most cynical look, she added, "I agree that certain segments of the FBI's upper management have engaged in illegal activities and belong in jail. But the rank and file are, on the whole, hardworking, honorable men and women. Whoever gave the order to place a bug in my office has done us a great favor because now we now *know* whatever is going on is far more important than being punished for slapping the wrist of a Senator's daughter for being a bad girl."

"How do you want me proceed?" Cooper asked.

"We leave the bug and use it to our advantage when the time is right," Colleen replied.

"You've got to remember to watch what you and anyone that comes in your office says," he warned. "With your permission, I'll monitor all traffic going through your line. With luck, I might be able to trace their signal back to their location, though I'm sure they've got it going to a remote location and ricocheting across the country. I've also started to check all electronic connections throughout the building. Never know; the little roach who pooped in your office might have gone on a little side trip and placed a couple more droppings here and there. I'll keep you updated about anything new and if we get a break and track 'em. They can run, but they can't hide. Eventually we'll get a break."

Colleen thanked Cooper, conveying her genuine gratitude for the man's tireless efforts to keep SSIS safe and secure. Heading for the cafeteria, she filled a mug with coffee and sat at a corner table mulling things over.

Going over the sequence of events in her head, the FBI raid started the progression first week of December. Next came Cooper's report about chatter out of DC mentioning her name, followed within days by a summons from Senator Grisham to make an appearance at his office forthwith. That same Friday afternoon Barry called asking to meet her at the Baltimore Convention Center Saturday at noon. Barry fails to show. The following week news of Justin Bellamy's murder, followed by a call from Barry to meet in Maine and wants Wolf. They go and investigate Bellamy's murder and come up emptyhanded. The trail has gone cold but Cooper's discovery heats things up significantly.

Perps just can't help themselves, Colleen thought. Fear of discovery never fails to motive them to take actions above and beyond necessary, which end up ensuring their discovery and eventual capture. Can't leave well enough alone; can't keep things simple. Cooper is right: they can run but they can't hide for long. We will find them and we will take them down.

Chapter 14

Piercing the Paper Wall

When Juan announced Grayson Wolf would be joining the CIR negotiating team, the self-assured expressions on the faces of Ivygreen College's representatives retreated notably. His recent announcement of retiring from writing incendiary exposes notwithstanding, a wary cynicism would be the order of the day. If administrators feared that Wolf's personal presence might produce a future book featuring Ivygreen in an unflattering light and excoriating them personally, such fears were rationally justified.

Wolf hadn't planned to join his legal team in their effort to convince the college administration to negotiate a separate class action settlement, having come to Boston to inquire into the suspicious accident that had landed Heather Franken in the local hospital's critical care ward. Juan felt his mere presence would push discussion toward a successful outcome and Wolf agreed to sit in. It was an easy decision to make since the college's leadership promoting gender identity and reassignment options was most certainly connected to Franken's "accident" in the school's parking lot.

CIR's legal trio, Juan, Terrance and Susan, sat together facing the Ivygreen negotiating team across the table, that outnumbered them by a factor of five. Wolf sat near the end of the table smiling insipidly at the throng shooting him surreptitious looks. He held an iPad strategically positioned to convey he was accessing a throve of possibly damaging personal and organizational information. His team might be outnumbered, but Grayson Wolf had the enemy flanked.

Introduction were made followed by Juan officially opening negotiations by noting the current number of aggrieved Ivygreen students and graduates who had joined the class action suit initiated by the Center for Individual Rights.

"This is nothing but attempted legal extortion," one of the college lawyers said. "Your two hundred twenty complainants are a joke. As anyone who has spent a day on any college campus knows, student complaints are as common as dirt."

"Unless the dirt they are complaining about is highly toxic to their physical, intellectual and emotional welfare and safety, counselor," Juan countered.

"And there is significant quantities of toxic waste being dumped on Ivygreen's grounds," Susan said. "Beginning with Ivygreen's administration ignoring and actively undermining the guaranteed equal educational experience to explore ideas and express different opinions as outlined in your promotional literature and student handbook."

"I object to the suggestion that we do not uphold the right of every student to experience the many wonderful opportunities Ivygreen has to offer," President Sidwell said.

"We do not deny that the college upholds the right of students to explore opportunities," Terrance said. "Our two hundred twenty complainants aren't suing the college over missed social or personal opportunities. They are suing because Ivygreen College actively stifles opinions contrary to its politically correct ideology by labeling such opinions as hate speech while tacitly permitting students to enforce campus orthodoxy through various means."

"That is patently untrue," Sidwell protested. "Every student is expected to adhere to behavior befitting an Ivygreen student."

"Apparently behavior befitting an Ivygreen student includes shouting down students who express views they disagree with in and out of classrooms without facing any serious consequences," Susan said. "Or the administration turning a blind eye to routine virtual assaults in the form of shaming and name calling on Ivygreen's social media platform."

"We can do this all morning," Terrance said, taking the verbal baton from Susan. "We have reams of documented complaints of the administration dragging its feet pursuant to failure to discipline students who have physically intimidated other students who dared to stand up for their beliefs and views."

"Our class action suit documents years of unequal treatment of students expressing opinions contrary to the college's political and cultural views," Susan said, continuing the tag-team performance. "Unequal enforcement of campus rules. Unequal treatment of students referred to the Dean of Students for disciplinary action. Considering the systematic discrimination practiced by this school, Ivygreen's motto, Conatus, Summo Christo decus, Veritas, should be changed to, Nisi Aliquam Omnibus Impar."

"That's Latin for Unequal For All But Some," Wolf said, causing all eyes to turn toward him. Sitting on the periphery and silent the entire time, folks had forgotten about his presence. "And just wait until the national news picks up the story about your gender bender counselor getting run over in the parking lot of the college leading the sex change parade. It will be national news because Heather Franken is the third victim within two weeks by an unknown killer. This person appears to be avenging the increasing number of suicides by confused and impressionable young women who were persuaded to undergo sex reorientation and realized they had made a tragic mistake."

"And we haven't even mentioned the controversy percolating beneath the campus green about mismanagement and misuse of endowment funds," Juan said.

A dead silence ensued. Several faces scattered throughout the Ivygreen side turned visibly pale.

"I think we have their full attention now," Wolf said, glancing over at his legal team.

"Let us hope that your opening gambit was just for show, counselor," Juan said, referring to the attorney's comment about the class action being legal extortion. "If we can't come to some reasonable settlement, tell us now so we can restart our invitation for more of your students and graduates to come forward. Considering the propensity of students to bitch and moan as anyone who has spent a day on any college campus knows, we'll be back with a couple thousand complainants next week. Our twenty-five million settlement offer will turn into two hundred fifty million."

"We'll need to discuss this and get back to you by the end of the week," the college lawyer said.

"No, we'll settle this now," Sidwell said. "Fifteen million."

"Twenty three million," Juan countered.

"Twenty," Sidwell said.

"Twenty two. Final offer, Dr. Sidwell."

"Francis, we should discuss this first," a second college lawyer said.

"I'm in full agreement with Perkins, Dr. Sidwell," a third member of the college legal team said.

Sidwell seemed to waver for a moment, then said, looking pointedly at Juan, "Twenty two million. And I want a closed settlement, no coming back for more."

"Agreed," Juan said. "However, if Ivygreen continues its current discriminatory practices, I won't turn down clients who want to sue your college for new transgressions."

"Understood," Sidwell said. "I'll have the papers drawn up and ready by noon tomorrow."

Wolf and the lawyers retreated from the room and crowded into Juan's SUV. Susan spoke first.

"Our agreement with the plaintiffs was a twenty-eighty split. Minus our share which comes to four million, four hundred thousand, that leaves seventeen point six million. Divided between two hundred twenty plaintiffs, each will receive eighty thousand dollars."

"About a year's tuition at Ivygreen," Wolf said, issuing a snort. "Or a twenty thousand annual scholarship, assuming one finishes in four years, which is becoming a rare feat these days."

"Until they show us the money, we had better not count our millions yet," Juan said. "The good Dr. Sidwell is not known for his decisive actions."

"I think we'll see the money," Wolf said. "Having some experience seeing people sweat at the possibility of their nasty dealings becoming public, rushing to make a twenty two million payment to keep things tightly locked away is a no brainer. Especially when it's not even your own twenty two million. We'll have the money wired to our account by end of the week."

"Most importantly, we have ripped off the first layer of the paper wall," Terrance said, a self-satisfied grin on his face.

"A very thin layer," Juan said. "But it's a start."

Wolf congratulated the group, promising that he would definitely join them tomorrow evening to celebrate the signing of the settlement. He said goodbye, and exited the vehicle. Time to do what he came here to do.

The Ivygreen campus police station was located at the north end of the campus, on the far side of one of the college's athletic fields. To Progressive bastions of learning such as Ivygreen and its ideological sister colleges dotting the New England landscape, terms like police and progressive mixed as well as oil and water. Placing the police station at the far edge of the college's realm was one way to achieve an out of sight, out of mind awareness of its existence.

The cadet at the reception counter led Wolf to the campus police chief who received him with a no nonsense expression and a firm handshake. Having done his homework about the police chief, meeting him in person confirmed Wolf's positive impression and he explained his reason for coming.

"A serial killer going after people involved in this sex change business," the Chief said, frowning. "A surgeon doing the procedure over at Watertown and now one of our counselors. Maybe this killer had a sex change and it's not working out for him, so he's getting even with the people that were involved?"

"That's quite possible," Wolf said, peeved he hadn't thought of it first. "My people are gathering a list of suicides pursuant to having a sex change procedure in hopes of identifying viable suspects who are family members and close friends of the deceased. We'll compile a list of individuals who had a sex change performed by ATTC next."

"That'll probably be hundreds of names," the Chief said.

"If the killer is a person who had a sex change, I think we're looking for someone who was a female, though that doesn't reduce the number by much," Wolf said.

"Why do you assume it's a woman?" the Chief asked.

"Being a male includes having more testosterone," Wolf said. "Females choosing to become males receive testosterone which comes with body hair and an increase of aggressive feelings. With gender reorientation having achieved fad status, especially among young women, we're seeing an increase in aggressive behavior, including assaults, smashing things up, screaming at people. And we see an uptick in terminal aggression upon oneself: suicide."

"Such hormone treatment must be under the supervision of a medical doctor," the Chief mused. "Maybe some who exhibit this type of aggression are skipping their appointments that monitor blood testosterone levels?"

"You would think such potentially dangerous manipulation of sexual hormones would be required to be performed under the supervision of a doctor," Wolf said. "Right now a young woman can walk into the local Planned Parenthood office and receive testosterone on nothing more than 'informed consent'. No prior psychological assessment required. Almost a hundred colleges, including Ivygreen, which is a leader in sex change promotion, and almost every Ivy League college, provide cross-sex hormone replacement therapy and surgery as part of their health insurance ... your daughter goes to college and comes back as a man. A daughter who now realizes that she has made a tragic mistake, that she is permanently sterile and seriously pissed off about it. All that testosterone coursing through her veins pumps up her/his rage and he decides to take out all the people who smiled as they helped to permanently screw up her/his life. Or maybe decides to end this misery once and for all."

The police chief peered thoughtfully at Wolf for a long moment. He nodded and said, his tone tinged with anger,

"I can understand why you're looking at family and friends of these sex change suicides. What can I do to help?"

"I'd love to take a look at any surveillance video you have of the accident," Wolf said.

There was video and the Chief walked him over to the communications room instructing one of the tech officers to assist Wolf in any way. Wolf thanked the Chief and promised to keep him informed of any developments toward finding the killer.

The technician cued the video and pointed at Franken as she walked between some parked cars into access road. She was part way across the drive when a dark SUV sped toward her, striking Franken before she could react and dodge out of the way, hurling her body forward and to the right, at least twenty feet. The SUV sped past the prone woman and out of the frame. Had she not been thrown partially sideways, the speeding vehicle would have run over her.

"I'm surprised she wasn't killed immediately," the technician said, shaking his head. "The onboard computer record clocked the SUV going over forty."

Wolf asked the technician if he could go through the footage on his own, the officer happily agreeing, saying he had other tasks to attend to. Wolf rewound the recording several hours hoping he might spot someone lurking or placing something in or near the scene of the accident, but found nothing suspicious. He watched the accident scene several more times, but nothing unusual stood out.

"Wait a minute," Wolf said, aloud. He called the technician over and showed him what he spotted at the lower corner of the frame. "What's happening there?"

"That's another accident; there were several," the technician replied. "It happened further back, out of view. We attributed these fender benders to people trying to get out of the way of that SUV coming toward them."

Wolf asked and received permission to transfer ten minutes of the pertinent section of the accident recording to Brett at CIR and Cooper at Colleen's headquarters, asking them to scour the recording for any clue. He also secured a copy of the police report including the statements made by the two other drivers who had been involved in the accidents while assumingly trying to avoid the oncoming speeding SUV that had struck Heather Franken.

Wolf thanked the technical officer and drove over to the parking lot to check out the scene of the accident and look around to see if there was anything suspicious to find. There wasn't of course and Wolf drove to Waterown to meet with police sergeant McCrea.

"Nice to see you again Mr. Wolf," the officer said. "I got your note about the strong possibility that Mr. Ferrara's death was done via hacking into his heating system."

"Thank you for sharing the state police report that confirms that the opening in the windows in LeeAnn Hick's car were virtually identical," Wolf said. "It just seemed highly improbable that she could have lowered each window separately that evenly. I've tried doing it in my car half dozen times and I never get closer than an inch or so and I'm looking at both windows as I'm doing it sitting in a parked car."

"Now we have a third victim," McCrea said. "I've had a chance to read the police report and I'm one hundred percent with you on the hacking theory for all these accidents. The driver of the SUV that hit the counselor can't account for what happened, thinking that he must have accidentally stepped on the accelerator instead of the brake. Everything happened so fast and couldn't stop the vehicle until he was almost at the end of the parking lot. Each driver of the other two cars say that their vehicle lurched forward, that they pressed on the brakes but cars kept moving. Both decided to turn the wheel and strike parked cars to avoid hitting other pedestrians. Way too many similarities to be coincidences."

"The question now becomes, how did the hacker know precisely where his victims where when he, or she, hacked the cars to turn them into lethal weapons?" Wolf asked. "The attack on Franken was on campus in broad daylight, so the killer could have been close by to see the victim and initiate the attack. Hicks was driving in the evening...how would the killer have known that she'd be there and disable her car at the right spot to cause the car to skid off the road and into the icy river?"

"If he had a reading on her GPS, then he'd know where she was," McCrea said. "Though civilian GPS tracking isn't that accurate; there's a time/position delay."

"I'm hoping my techs can spot something when they comb through the surveillance video," Wolf said. "Whomever this hacker is, he's very good and I think he's only begun his reign of vengeance."

"Reign of vengeance?" McCrea said, looking skeptical.

"The thinking is that this killer is a family member or a friend to one of the sex change related suicides," Wolf explained. "He's on a mission to deliver vengeance upon the people and organizations he holds responsible for the death of their friend or family member."

"Well ain't that just hunky-dory," McCrea quipped. "We've got a highly technologically skilled killer going after the gender reassignment community and we've got a major sex change surgery center right here in my neighborhood."

"Your department should warn the folks at the Watertown Affirmative Transformation Treatment Center about being a possible target," Wolf said.

"I'll recommend that to the Captain," McCrea agreed. "Though knowing that might cause greater distress than not knowing about it. How do you protect yourself against a hacker who can leak gas into your home and blow it up from a thousand miles away? Or cause your car to speed into a concrete abutment? Or hack into the local pharmacy and switch your medication and induce a heart attack?"

"Because ignorance isn't bliss in a world that is highly vulnerable to destruction by a few keystrokes initiated from across the globe," Wolf said.

"You are a ray of sunshine today, Mr. Wolf," McCrea chuckled. "Unfortunately you are also correct. Being in law enforcement we get to see and hear about things that often don't make it into the news."

"If the Chinese, or Russians or Iranians manage to disrupt our energy infrastructure, tens of millions will have a real life lesson about the wages of appeasing criminals and sociopaths," Wolf said. "Having been sneaking around in some of society's most prominent citizens over a decade, I've heard and seen how our self-identified globalists have deluded themselves about the motives and objectives of the dictators they party and drink vodka with."

"Never thought about that," McCrea replied. "Your exposes don't talk much about that aspect. Might be a good idea to publish something that discusses this topic. 'Western Globalists: Useful Collaborators'. Something like that."

"I'll leave that up to the political pundits," Wolf said. "Besides, haven't you heard? I've retired from muckraking and overturning the rotten apple carts of the high and mighty."

"Meanwhile here you are mucking around looking for a techno-killer," McCrea replied, looking smug. "Once a cop, always a cop."

"A man's gotta do something to keep his mind active," Wolf quipped.

"Well you had better keep your active mind tuned to the possibility that you might be a target too, that killer gets wind Grayson Wolf is hunting for him," McCrea said. "I'm serious about that. Anyone who knows anything about you knows first and foremost that you'll find whatever you're looking for. Please be very careful, Mr. Wolf."

The policewoman was right, of course. Had she known about Wolf hunting down a second killer, she would most likely have thought him crazy to be roaming around the countryside without being accompanied by several bodyguards at all times. But if Wolf had learned one thing in his years of sneaking and hiding, a determined hunter will get to his prey in the end. Besides a heightened awareness and being prepared by planning far ahead, the next best defense is randomness of movement and action. Arbitrarily taking the left exit instead of the right one. Indiscriminately leaving or showing up at a function. Reserving an Uber then waving down a taxi instead. And on it goes, paranoia fueling thought and action.

Wolf thanked McCrea, assuring her that looking over his shoulder and around corners was sacrosanct. Each promised to keep the other informed of any breaks in the case and Wolf drove back to his hotel in Boston. Entering the lobby, he was confronted by several uniformed police who were accompanied by what he assumed were three plain clothed detectives.

The detectives produced identification that Wolf studied carefully, then verbally affirmed that he was Grayson Wolf.

"How may I help you, officers?" he said, a droll expression on his face.

"We are placing you under arrest for harboring, aiding and abetting a fugitive," the detective who identified herself as lieutenant Baxter said.

"That's a new one on me," Wolf retorted.

"Turn around please," she ordered.

"Bondage, I like it," Wolf joked.

Baxter held his eyes and did not smile, though he sensed she wanted to. He turned and the detective places the cuffs on his wrists, though not as tight as she could have. Wolf shot her a grin as a second detective hustled him out of the building into a waiting patrol car and got in the back with him. Detective Baxter did likewise, Wolf now sandwiched between the detectives.

"May I inquire who I'm supposed to have harbored, aided and abetted?" Wolf asked.

"Barry Silverstone," the male detective said.

"Mr. Silverstone's alleged crime took place in New York, not in your jurisdiction," Wolf pointed out. "I see a false arrest lawsuit in the Boston police department's future."

"We are arresting you for extradition to New York, Mr. Wolf," Baxter said. "Quite legal, I assure you."

The detective was right, of course. Wolf couldn't help grinning at the thought that this was the second time in less than a year he was arrested and extradited to New York.

Well, at least the trip south was free.

Chapter 15

Big Apple Deja Vu

"Good morning, Detective Vanderhelm," Wolf said, flashing New York's finest a full-toothed grin. "We meet again. How was your Christmas? Wife and kids happy? New year treating you well?"

Vanderhelm shot him a long-suffering look. "You're a funny man, Mr. Wolf. I'm looking forward to hearing all your cute comments when we lock you up, which we will do this time around."

"Sorry to bust your bubble, detective, but you'll need to wait one more go around," Wolf rejoined. "Third times the charm, not the second."

"You are being charged with harboring, aiding and abetting the fugitive, Barry Silverstone," the other detective sitting across the table from Wolf said.

"Shelling, right?" Wolf replied. "Detective Shelling, I maintain like I did last summer when I was in one of these rooms being charged for rape: not guilty. And now, I'm done talking."

For the next half hour the detectives fired questions at Wolf interspersed with accounts of incontrovertible evidence against him and peppered with descriptions of how life will be for him residing in one of New York's finest prisons. Wolf gazed uninterestedly at each man in turn, his expression devoid of emotion.

"We get it," Vanderhelm said, looking resigned. "The big, bad Wolf got nothing to say. That's too bad for you because your buddy in crime, Colleen Silverstone is doing plenty of talking in the room down the hall. And the moment she mentions your name in conjunction with meeting her father, I'm going to have my own wolf pelt to spread in front of the fireplace."

A grin touched Wolf's lips. They could waterboard her, pull out fingernails, pump a quart of truth serum into her veins all to no avail. Colleen Silverstone would never talk.

"Don't be stupid," Shelling said. "You and Colleen Silverstone were seen together in Boston and then both of you disappeared for days. It's not hard for anyone to image how someone as attractive as Silverstone could encourage you to help her father evade arrest. Believe me, Mr. Wolf, we've all been there when it comes to doing unwise things when it concerns women. I understand how a good looking woman like Silverstone could wrap a man around her little finger. You tell us where she took you and I guarantee the prosecutor will be very grateful to you when it comes to recommending jail time."

Wolf struggled to keep a tight rein on his desire to laugh as the detective unwound his spiel. It was entertaining to observe the shifting tactics used by the detectives to entice him to cooperate.

As for Shelling's comments about Colleen, she certainly had the looks, personality and skills to wrap men around her little pinky, except Wolf knew she never needed to play such silly games. Colleen came at one directly; the force of her personality and powers of persuasion more than sufficient to attain whatever objective she set out to achieve. Seeing Colleen's image in his mind's eye, Wolf had to admit that her stunning looks were a potent asset, one that even he wasn't immune to.

"If you keep wasting our time, then there's not much more to say, Mr. Wolf," Vanderhelm said. "The clock is ticking...tell you what. Detective Shelling and I are going to take a short break to give you some time to think about your future. When we come back, I'm going to ask you for your final answer and I hope for your sake it will be the right one."

The detectives trooped out of the room, leaving Wolf shackled to the table. Doing so was totally unnecessary, but Vanderhelm was holding a grudge from his last encounter with Wolf and obviously decided to make his prisoner's life as miserable as he could while he had him in his possession. Wolf peered up at the surveillance camera located in the top corner of the ceiling, rattled his chain, slowly shook his head and grinning throughout the performance. Were he really annoyed, Detective Vanderhelm and the NYPD would discover firsthand the kind of trouble Wolf could rain upon their heads. However, he had too much respect and admiration for the men and women in one of the best urban police departments to let this little inconvenience diminish his regard.

The short break seemed to drag on and on, Wolf beginning to wonder what was happening outside the walls of his bare cubicle. He was debating banging his retraining chain on the metal table much like prisoners rattle objects against their cell doors in protest, when the door to the room opened and two different plain clothed men entered. The look of their clothing and expressions screamed Federal agents. And maybe something more...

"Mr. Wolf, I'm Johansen, FBI," the tall one said. "My associate, Agent Patterson."

The agents took a seat. Johansen continued.

"This is now a federal matter. Unless you cooperate right now, you will be charged with half dozen crimes including obstruction of justice, aiding a wanted suspect to evade capture and accessory to murder. And I've got a couple conspiracy charges I can tack on just because I can."

"Bullshit," Wolf said. "You can't make any of those absurd charges stick. Go fish."

Johansen leaned toward the table. "Mr. Wolf, we are the FBI. I can assure you that we can dig up enough dirt pursuant to your recent jaunt with Ms. Silverstone to bury you with. You might think you can jerk around the detectives that spoke with you earlier, but we're not inclined to waste time playing footsy with you. You cooperate fully now and we don't haul you down to DC this afternoon and lock you up until a federal judge gets back from his vacation for a bail hearing."

Wolf gazed at the other agent. "I know that the upper echelon of the agency seems to think they're the law these days, but what about you, Agent Patterson? You going along with this level of intimidation of citizens?"

"I strongly suggest you cooperate like Agent Johansen be asking you, Mr. Wolf."

Wolf's expression became thoughtful. This was more serious than he had imagined.

"If I tell you everything, will you let me walk on my own recognizance?" Wolf said. "You know where I live and you also know

I never run from a fight. I will show up in court to take you on. What do you say, agent? Is it a deal? I sing and fly outta here?"

"You will tell us everything?" Johansen asked.

"Everything I know," Wolf said.

"In writing," Johansen demanded.

"Give me pen and paper."

*   *   *   *

"You're lying," Colleen said, examining the two FBI agents sitting across the interrogation table much like she'd look at something mangled laying on the street.

"I warned you, Ms. Silverstone," Johansen said. "I told you that we would be questioning Mr. Wolf next and that now was the time to strike a deal and tell us where your father is hiding. You refused and it turned out that Mr. Wolf much preferred the deal we offered him and he's currently walking out the front door."

"Your furry friend sang like he was howling at a full moon," Patterson crowed. "Got it all in writing. Told us how you conned him to come with you to visit your father in Maine, how you brought supplies to him, how angry he was with you and how you made him the kind of deal he couldn't refuse, saying you convinced him your people could find him anywhere. He told us he overheard you and your father talking about the murder of Justin Bellamy and discussing ways of getting away with it...and he goes on several more pages after that."

"We'll be taking you back to DC today. Ms. Silverstone," Johansen said, standing up. "We'll be back in a little while to pick you up."

Colleen was stunned. It was impossible that Wolf would throw her under the bus and yet he had. How else would Agent Patterson have known such details as Barry hiding in Maine that he itemized for her, some of which were outright lies. That son of a female wolf traded his freedom to walk away from prosecution, but he was going to discover that his little lie about her threatening him with harm was going to come true with her delivering the harm with her own hands!

The door opened and a uniformed NYPD officer entered.

"I'll be escorting you to the cafeteria for lunch," she said.

"Isn't that unusual treatment for a prisoner?" Colleen asked.

"Technically you're not our prisoner," she said. Looking quickly around, she added, "The captain isn't happy about the feds butting their nose into our business. They're in a meeting and it's getting heated so the cap said to treat you to lunch 'cause they might be at it for a while. Just don't try to escape."

Colleen grinned at the officer. If she felt threatened, she would already be out on the street and out of sight ten seconds later.

"Lunch first, escape attempt second," Colleen joked.

By the time her fate had been sealed, it was getting on to midafternoon. The FBI agent collected her from the interrogation room she returned to after lunch and led her in handcuffs to a waiting car, placing her in the back seat.

The streets of Manhattan are jammed with vehicles and the car made slow progress. Colleen was musing about the reason for her arrest being to flush out Barry, thinking that she'd be long out on bail and retired before that would ever happen, when she asked why they were traveling through the West Village instead of heading for JFK airport.

"We're making for the I-73 bridge," Patterson said. "Apparently DC doesn't want to waste more money on the Silverstones than absolutely necessary."

The FBI wants to discomfort Colleen Silverstone, she thought. She sat back and settled in for the long slog to Washington.

"Crap," Patterson said. "Frikken detour."

Looking ahead, Colleen saw as a van in front slowed and began to make a right turn. Barriers blocked the street and a workman was waving vehicles into a narrow alley where traffic soon came to a standstill.

"Seriously?" Patterson blew the horn, a typical and futile response by drivers and especially by drivers in New York. "Come on! Move already!"

"What the hell?" Johansen said.

Colleen saw two armed masked men exit the van in front and rush toward their car, rifles pointing at them. A quick burst of gunfire ripped through the car's front tires. Moving toward Johansen's side the man pointed his rifle directly at the agent.

"Get the fuck out of the car!"

A second later, Patterson's window was smashed in by a third masked assailant who had come up from behind the car.

"Out!"

Patterson got out and stepped away from the vehicle.

"This way—slowly. Hands up! Hands up assholes!" the gunman in front shouted.

The assailant who had smashed in Patterson's window opened Colleen's door. "Out!" He waved his rifle toward the van in front. "Move!"

"Good work," the gunman standing at the van said. "She'll bring a pretty penny."

So this was a kidnapping. Taking the head of the top security firm in the country. A pretty penny, indeed. Embarrassing as hell, too. Too bad she was handcuffed. Could things get any crazier?

"On you stomachs!" one of them gunmen shouted.

Without warning, the assailant who covered Patterson struck him on the head with the butt of his rifle. The agent collapsed in a heap.

"Keep moving, baby," one of the assailants-cum-kidnappers ordered.

Looking back, she saw the one who had struck Patterson rifle through his pockets, then handcuffed the agent with his own restraints. The thief walked over to Johansen, kneeled down and presumably doing likewise to him, dragged him toward the car and handcuffed the man to the tow ring underneath the bumper.

"Get in and sit still, baby," the gunman said, pointing his rifle at her.

Moments later the other assailants hopped into the van and drove off. In the span of few minutes they were driving across the I-73 bridge into New Jersey. A few miles later the driver turned off the Interstate, drove through an industrial area arriving at their destination some minutes later as he drove the van into a small warehouse, its automatic door lowering after the van came to a stop.

One of the men hustled Colleen out of the van and pushed her against the side of the vehicle, his forearm pressing against her upper chest. His veiled face came within inches of hers. She could feel his hot breath wafting through the mask.

"How's it feel to be manhandled, Ms. Silverstone?"

He removed his mask. His grin lit up the dingy space.

"Miss me?"

For perhaps the first time in her life Colleen was speechless as she stared at her kidnapper. The man unlocked her handcuffs.

"If you promise not to escape, I've got some business to attend to," Wolf said, blowing her a kiss.

He walked over to the other two men who had stood some distance away. Unlike Wolf, they kept their masks on. She heard Wolf thank them and hand them a small package. They said something she couldn't make out, turned and left by a side entrance.

"Are you out of your mind!" Colleen said. "You attacked and assaulted FBI agents. In New York, no less. By now there's a massive manhunt underway by air, land and sea, Wolf. What on earth possessed you to do something this reckless?"

"How about we get the hell outta Dodge first and then continue your stream of reprimands," Wolf said.

Colleen shot him a frustrated look and started to get into the van.

"Uh, uh," he said. "Follow me."

Wolf led her to an exit at the back of the warehouse and proceeded to snake through narrow passages between buildings until they came to a car covered by a tarpaulin. Wolf pulled the cover off, opened the truck and stuffed it in and closed the lid..

"Nice ride," Colleen said, admiring the late model BMW. "Beats the that crappy van you used to kidnapped me."

They got in the car and Wolf drove back to the Interstate heading west, turning north on I-287 a few miles later.

"Assuming this ride is longer than fifteen minutes, perhaps now is a good time to tell me what the hell you are doing," Colleen said, looking over at him. "Start with you selling me out and go from there."

Wolf shot her a sardonic look. "I gave you up because they were kidnapping you for real; maybe even kill you. The fact that the FBI would be willing to let me walk was itself a confirmation that something hinky was going down. I had to get you out of their custody and do it immediately."

"Wait," Colleen said. "Go back to the kidnapping or killing me part. I don't dispute that the FBI's reputation has become besmirched of late, but kidnapping and killing isn't in their wheelhouse, at least not yet. What do you base your claim on?"

"The FBI agent named Patterson," Wolf said. "His name is not Patterson and he's not FBI and neither is his associate, Johansen: they're both hired guns. Patterson was an enforcer for a thug, former thug, named Jerry Zaleski. Four years ago when I was slithering through the lives of the rich and thieving, one of the people I'd see attending functions was Jerry Zaleski."

"Rich and thieving like Barry Silverstone," Colleen said, sardonically.

"Yes and many others, as you well know since it produced *Screw You Suckers!*" Wolf confirmed. "Zaleski had several bodyguards, one of them a guy named, Zeke. I always got the impression Zeke was like a backup, a shadow. So when Zaleski went down in a hail of bullets, Zeke must have escaped, or possibly, been the inside man all along. When agent Johansen introduced Patterson, I thought I had seen him before, but when he opened his mouth to speak, I knew who he was. It became clear that someone was after you and I suspected the point of their charade to question me was to see how much I knew. Fortunately I knew much more than they realized and managed to trick them to make a deal allowing me to walk on my own recognizance if I gave you up."

"It was you who knocked down the one called Patterson," Colleen said.

"Yes and it felt good," Wolf said. "I took their fake IDs—figured we'd need that for later—took shots of their mugs and told the one called Johansen that I knew they were fake FBI and that the real FBI was on their way."

"Was that true?" Colleen said.

"Yes indeed," Wolf said, grinning. "Had my associate call the local district office to give them their location and to contact the NYPD precinct for confirmation."

"Where did you manage to recruit a strike team within two hours of being released from custody?" Colleen asked.

"Have you forgotten that I spent a significant amount of my time rummaging through the shadows and back alleys in my previous life as national muckraker?" Wolf said. "One picks up a lot of interesting information from a lot of interesting people doing what I did."

"I was lucky that my fake FBI agents and the precinct captain had a jurisdictional pissing contest which delayed them from taking me two hours earlier," Colleen said. "When the FBI showed up at the precinct claiming jurisdiction, I was sure that it was a politically motivated move by a very unhappy senator in DC."

"No luck involved about that pissing contest whatsoever," Wolf said. "After calling my interesting contact to assemble my army, I contacted Cooper and told him to pressure whomever he thought could convince the captain to put up a fight about jurisdiction. Obviously he found someone."

Colleen was impressed by Wolf's resourcefulness, decisiveness, his, albeit it, dubious associates and the unexpected armed assault on what she assumed was an FBI vehicle.

"May I ask what this campaign cost you?" she said. "Minutemen, equipment and transportation don't come cheap."

"My treat," he replied.

"Just curious," Colleen said. "And don't worry about me wanting to pay you back: I never negotiate with kidnappers."

"One hundred gold eagles," Wolf said.

"I see," she said. "Nice to know you think I'm worth that much."

Wolf shot her a droll look. "I negotiated them down from five hundred eagles."

Colleen laughed. "I like a man who's a tough negotiator ... I have to admit to being surprised at your chutzpa to take such direct and aggressive action."

Wolf passed a slower vehicle then returned to the right lane. She noticed he kept his pace at or near the speed limit.

"Maybe you'll consider hiring me as one of your field agents now that I've proved myself to you," he joked.

"Let's see how things turn out first," Colleen replied. "It's easy to bust something; much harder to put it all back together again...which brings me to the question: where are you going?"

"North to a little house on the prairie," he replied. "We'll hide out with your father. We'll be one big, happy family of fugitives."

Chapter 16

On The Run

"Seems a little too quiet," Colleen said, as she drove along the driveway to the cabin."

"It's almost eleven," Wolf said. "Barry's probably sleeping."

It took almost seven hours to reach the cabin in the northwest corner of Maine. Wolf had driven the majority of the way with Colleen, who knew the way into the remote area, driving the last leg of the trek.

She stopped the car near the entrance and Wolf collected their few belongings from the back seat. Colleen walked to the door and knocked hard. Wolf came up beside her. When no one answered, she called Barry's name several times. Nothing moved inside the cabin.

"This is not good," she said. "I wish I had a—"

"Gun?" Wolf answered. He handed her a pistol with his left hand, holding a second one in his right. "Shall we kick it in?"

"Not unless you want to fracture something," Colleen said. "If Barry's in there, the door is bolted from the inside. Since I assumed he was here and he might not be..." She grasped the door handle and opened the door.

"Why do I have this strong feeling of déjà vu all of a sudden?" Wolf said. "Cold, dark, cabin, you, me and guns in hand."

"Just try not to shoot me when I walk into a room you're occupying," Colleen replied.

"Now that's just plain mean," Wolf retorted, switching his flashlight on. It was one of the sundry pieces of equipment and change of clothing they had purchased along the way.

A quick search revealed the place was empty. Most of Barry's clothing was still there, but it appeared that he had packed and left the cabin on his own since there was no sign of struggle anywhere in the house. Wolf walked back out and shined his light toward the large stacks of firewood, nodded knowingly and came back in.

"Car's gone," he said. "Looks like Barry decided to move on to safer pastures. Does he have other safe houses?"

"Not that I'm aware of," Colleen replied. "I know that if I were Barry, I'd have a dozen safe houses." She walked over to the stove and carefully placed her hand on it. "Cold. He's been gone for a couple days at least."

"Let's get a fire started if we don't want to freeze in our beds," Wolf said. "Isn't there a light? He has solar and storage batteries, if I recall."

Colleen found a switch and an overhead light fixture came to life. Wolf started to place wood into the stove when she stopped him.

"There's a systematic way to load a high-efficiency wood burning stove and it's not by stuffing wood into it."

Wolf shot her a droll look, stood aside and executed a dramatic flourish toward the stove.

"Have at it."

Colleen fired up the stove, its radiant heat warming the small space to a comfortable level within thirty minutes. Adding more wood, she shut the dampers to permit a very slow burning cycle and they went upstairs.

"Good night," Wolf said, and entered the bedroom on his right.

Colleen remained standing in the hall, looking at his closed door, marveling at the thought that she had spent more time with Wolf since meeting him ten months ago than she had with any man for years. The man who had excoriated her stepfather in *Screw You Suckers!* and whom she had her investigators dog in turn. She sighed and entered her bedroom, pulled the thick quilt up to her chin and closed her eyes.

But sleep escaped her. It was the first opportunity to reflect upon the events of the last two days that began with her surprise arrest at her home in Aurora, Colorado, her extradition to New York later that afternoon, interrogation this morning and her most unexpected kidnapping/rescue by Wolf. Someone had gone to a lot of trouble to frame her stepfather for the murder of Justin Bellamy, but Barry managed to run and hide. She supposed the conspirators thought kidnapping his daughter would flush Barry out in the open, their plan rudely interrupted when she was taken by heavily armed ruffians during a brazen attack upon their fake FBI transport.

Most frustrating about this entire affair was that neither the police or SSIS's investigation had uncovered any viable suspects for Bellamy's (and Maggie Talbot's) murder. Whoever was behind the murders, the fake FBI and who knows what else still to come, must be buried deeply in Bellamy's history or organization. Most likely both, Colleen surmised.

She continued lie in the dark, going through a dozen possibilities and arriving at the same frustrating conclusion that there were no clues and no suspects. The only thing for certain was that thinking about cases lying in bed night after night would result in waking up in the morning feeling exhausted from lack of sleep.

"I'm getting too old for this shit," she mumbled, chuckling at the Danny Glover's well-worn meme.

Concentrating on her breathing, she gently ushered further thoughts of murder, mayhem and Barry out of her mind and eventually fell asleep.

She woke with a start, her pistol instantly pointing at the shape of a man bending over her bed.

After recuperating from the surprise, Wolf laughed at the irony of having a gun shoved in his face.

"What was that admonition about me not trying to shoot you when entering a room I was in, Ms. trigger-happy Silverstone?"

"You should know better than to enter a lady's boudoir without knocking. Especially one who's armed and dangerous," Colleen retorted.

"I did knock," Wolf said. "Then entered. I gently called your name and was rewarded for my efforts by you nearly shooting me in the face."

"My finger wasn't on the trigger unlike some novices who shall go unnamed," she replied. "What time is it?"

"You're rather demanding for a woman who almost shot her rescuer and breakfast chef," Wolf grinned. "Nine 'o'clock."

"Nine?" Colleen said, looking alarmed.

"I heard that women your age need more sleep to, ah..."

"Before another word comes out of your mouth, know that I'm pointing my gun at your puny manhood," Colleen growled.

"How feminine of you," Wolf said, grinning. "Now, if you're done threatening to deprive the world of future Wolfies, join me for a late breakfast."

He raised his hands over his head and backed dramatically out of Colleen's bedroom.

"You're a decent cook," she said, after accepting a second helping of scrambled eggs, ham and fried potatoes.

Wolf refilled her cup with coffee. "Glad you didn't shoot me after all?"

"There's always later," she replied, smiling up at him. "I've been thinking about everything that's transpired since that Saturday in Baltimore."

"When you weren't up before I was, I knew you must have gone to bed late," Wolf said. "Have you thought of something?"

"Nothing," Colleen said. "A month of searching and I've got nothing."

"I still find it hard to believe that Barry doesn't know more about all this than he's claiming," Wolf said.

"I'm certain Barry knows a whole lot of plenty, but it makes no sense for him to hide anything that would allow me to track down the people who are framing him for Bellamy's murder," Colleen replied.

"I suppose so," Wolf said. "But he thinks whomever is behind this believes that he *does* know something that might get back to them. Barry and Bellamy were long-time friends; one might assume they shared all kinds of secrets—God knows they shared everything else including their girlfriends."

Colleen shot him an amused look. "You really like to poke the bear even when she's sitting across the table."

"Come off your high horse, Ms. Silverstone," Wolf shot back. "You know everything I wrote about Barry and lot more is true. If we were talking about any other wastrel you wouldn't bat an eyelash."

"Okay," she said, her eyes narrowing. "Your mother had an affair when you were five."

"Excuse me?" Wolf said. "That's a cheap shot."

"It's true," she said. "Shall I give you details or do you get the point?"

"It's true?" Wolf said, studying her face. Colleen was expert at subterfuge, misdirection and able to control her expression to confirm or deny anything.

"Yes."

"You investigated my family?" Wolf said.

"You investigated mine." Colleen pointed out.

"My family isn't involved in shady deals and shady people," Wolf corrected.

"Perhaps, but how do we know that without investigating them?" Colleen retorted. "Sorry...but you can be aggressively insensitive, Wolf."

He sighed and said, "You're right, Colleen. Rubbing shoulders with our not-so-respectable citizens for years will desensitize a person. I have been waving Barry's questionable behavior in front of your face; I guess I deserve your kick in the pants."

"About your mother," Colleen said. "I extrapolated her relationship based on limited information. Your parents must have hit a rough spot in their marriage and your mother was seen in the company of another man a few times. Could have been totally innocent; there is no proof of an intimate relationship. Your comment about Barry caught me at a movement of weakness..."

"Considering my numerous slights pertaining to Barry, I can't say we're even, but I can say, let's forget it and move on," Wolf said. "Which brings me to the question: move on to where? Ask around the neighborhood to see if anyone saw Barry leaving? Get Cooper to requisition satellite images of this cabin to see when Barry drove off and which way he went? Forget about all this and spend the next few week holed up here snuggling in front of a warm stove? ... don't give me that look; you know you want to cuddle up with the Wolf."

"I know you suffer from bouts of delusions," Colleen retorted. "The satellite idea, however, is a viable one. I'll call Cooper and have him move on it."

She made the call, selecting speaker mode allowing Wolf to hear the conversation. Cooper used her phone's GPS to select the appropriate satellite covering that section of New England. It took him less than a minute.

"Got the satellite," Cooper said. "Looking at a live shot...narrowing the field...I see the cabin, your car and..."

"What? Something wrong," Colleen said, when Cooper stopped talking.

"Are you expecting visitors?" Cooper said. "You've got two vehicles stopped at the end of the driveway."

"Not expecting visitors...gotta go," Colleen said. "I'll get back to you." She terminated the call and said to Wolf, "Grab your coat..."

They cautiously opened the door and with guns drawn, made a dash for the car.

"Open the trunk," Wolf said.

"Get in!" Colleen ordered.

"I've got rifles back there," he said.

Colleen opened the trunk and started the car. Moments later Wolf hopped in, placing two rifles and a bag filled with extra magazines on the floor. Colleen slowly drove the car around the cabin then aimed toward Baker Lake.

"What are you doing?" Wolf said, as she edged the car along the footrail.

"Trying to escape their trap," she said, the car lurching over a thick root cutting across the trail. "Did you think we were going to shoot our way out Bonnie and Clyde style?"

"Does this lead to a road?" Wolf asked.

"No."

"Okay," Wolf said, drawing out the k sound. "What's the plan?"

"Crossing the lake."

"Crossing the lake?" Wolf repeated, incredulously. "This car isn't a James Bond special that turns into a submarine. How do you plan to get across?"

"Drive across it," Colleen said. "It's got at least six inches of ice on it."

Looking ahead, Wolf spotted the lake, it's snow and ice covered surface gleaming in the late morning sunlight. Colleen continued moving the car toward it.

"Six inches doesn't make one feel confident," Wolf said. When Colleen shot him a mocking look, he added, "Six inches of ice, smart ass."

"Let's hope it gets the job done," she said, her smile lighting up the interior.

They were approaching the lake. Colleen stopped the car and scanned the coastline.

"There," she said, pointing toward the left. "A gentle, smooth slope. Perfect entry point onto the ice."

She drove carefully toward the spot she had pointed to when several shots rang out, the sound of a bullet striking the car. Colleen started down the slope, picking up speed. More gunfire erupted. The car rolled on the ice as Colleen continued to accelerate gently to prevent the car from skidding out of control.

Wolf lifted one of the rifles, inserted a magazine, lowered the window, and pointing it behind the car laid down a burst of suppressive fire. His shots must have landed close to the gunmen on the shore because they stopped shooting. Looking down momentarily, he saw a different threat to their attempted escape.

"The ice is cracking," he shouted, releasing the spent magazine and inserting a fresh one into the rifle.

"Cracking directly under us?" Colleen said, still accelerating.

Wolf stuck his head out the window and peered down. "Behind the car," he said.

"That's good news," Colleen said. "Hold on, we're approaching land." She gently pressed on the brakes, the stuttering sound of the anti-brake system indicating it was doing its best to slow the car as Colleen expertly steered the car in a reasonably straight line. She suddenly released the brakes and pressed the gas pedal as the car lurched over the shallow edge of the shore, its momentum carrying it upward the slope, Colleen feathering the accelerator to maintain its forward motion.

It was a short, but bumpy ride to the road skirting the lake on its northern side, Colleen gaining speed. The sounds of gunshots reached them, but fortunately their projectiles did not.

"Don't waste your ammo," she said, when Wolf was preparing to return fire.

The road made a turn and the lake disappeared behind a stand of pines. Colleen stopped the car.

"Why have you stopped?" Wolf asked, looking back toward the lake.

Colleen thought for a moment and said, "It'll be just a matter of time before they come around the lake … Hmmm that might work if there's one there." She pressed the accelerator and the car sped down the road.

"What might work?" Wolf asked. "Where are we going?"

"There's only one county road in the area and that's the one we came in on," Colleen said. "I need to know—call Cooper and tell him we need that eye in the sky."

"Okay I see you," Cooper said, a short minute later after Colleen told him what she needed. "Based on the profile, I'm sure it's one of the cars that visited you. It's moving slowly northwest, probably checking every dirt track intersecting the road in expectation of you showing up. The other vehicle is doing the same thing, except going east."

"How far west is the airstrip?" Colleen said.

"Four and a quarter miles," Cooper said. "But you've got to take the next exit south and get on the county road because the track you're on is going to take a sharp north soon after that and that goes into nowhere."

"Will I get ahead of the punk brigade?" Colleen asked.

"By a good half mile," Cooper replied. "They might not even see you entering the road."

Colleen gunned the engine and sped down the narrow dirt road. She was traveling so fast she almost missed the turnoff, the rear wheels sliding into the turn as she barreled through.

Going fifty, they reached the main road in just over a minute, Colleen quickly accelerating up the lane. Cooper had confirmed the presence of a plane giving her real-time reports about their progress, when he suddenly issued a cry.

"I think they might have spotted you because they've started moving faster in your direction."

"How far to plane?" Colleen said, increasing her speed.

"Two miles," Cooper said. "You're pulling ahead, but they're less than half a mile back. The road is clear ahead…"

Colleen pressed down on the accelerator, the BMW flying down the road.

"Three hundred yards, Colleen," Cooper warned.

Colleen made the turn, speeding down the access road. A small structure came into view with a small airplane some distance past it.

"A Piper, great!" Colleen said, speeding past the shed toward the plane. "Grab the guns; get ready to hold them off!"

"They drove past the intersection," Cooper said, excitedly. "That last curve must have blocked their view…still going."

They sprinted toward the plane. Colleen opened the pilot's side door.

"Coming back!" Cooper shouted. "Approaching the road to the airstrip!"

"Other side!" Colleen cried.

Wolf jerked opened the door, tossed the rifles inside and hopped into cabin, shutting the door after him. He heard the motor start and the plane rolled toward the airstrip, which turned out to be little more than a level section of land.

"How'd you get the key?" Wolf said, as the plane picked up speed.

"Older model, no key needed," she replied. "Shit, here they come!"

Wolf watched as their pursuers must have realized that their prey was in the plane and swerved their SUV toward the airstrip to prevent the plane from taking off.

"Come on! Come on you piece of shit!" Colleen said, as the plane picked up speed. The SUV was closing in fast. Wolf shot a glance at Colleen, incredulous at seeing only a calm, cool expression. Looking ahead, the plane was rushing at the SUV, now stopped on the runway, its occupants running to escape the immanent collision. Wolf involuntarily tensed up for the impact.

The plane rose suddenly jerking Wolf in his seat, then dropped down again, the wheels glancing off the ground, gained more speed and lifted into the sky, gaining altitude.

"What happened?" Wolf said, issuing a puff of air from holding his breath. "How did you miss the car?"

"Pulled back hard on the control causing the plane to pop up, momentarily, then immediately ease the control back down," Colleen said. "I wasn't going fast enough to take off, but had enough lift to pop it up and over the car. Good way to crash your plane, but the risk was worth it. The wheels touched down, but we made it."

"I didn't know you could fly," Wolf said, looking at her with undisguised admiration.

Colleen gave him a droll look, a sly grin playing on her lips. "I guess practicing on my flight simulator during dateless Saturday nights year after year finally paid off."

"I'm glad to finally discover what Colleen Silverstone does for fun on her weekends," Wolf sarcastically said.

A persistent beep sounded. Colleen issued a snort.

"We're running on reserve fuel," she said. "How inconsiderate for the owner not to keep the tank topped off."

"How much longer can we fly?" Wolf asked.

"Twenty minutes, tops," Colleen replied. She lifted her phone. "Cooper: you still with us?"

"Always, scary boss lady," he joked. "Twenty minutes at a top speed of seventy five not getting you all that far. I'm looking ... okay, there's a strip, Newton Field, forty miles due south near the town of Jackman, but you're not going to make that."

"For sure," Colleen said. "Twenty minutes of fuel gets me about twenty-five miles, give or take a mile or two. Fuel consumption in one of these old Piper's is more a matter of estimation than certainty. Actual fuel usage is dependent on the age of the motor, its schedule of upkeep and maintenance, wind resistance and sheer and so forth."

"You could fly toward Jackman and hope to spot a field large enough to land on but I wouldn't count on that," Cooper said. "Best bet is to turn southeast and attempt a landing on that county road you came in on."

"And risk the chance of them catching us?" Colleen replied. She thought for moment, shot Wolf a wicked grin and banked the plane hard right.

From the position of the sun, Wolf knew they were flying west. Cooper hadn't mentioned any nearby airfields in that direction. The only thing west was—

"Quebec is the best option," Cooper said, obviously seeing the plane turn toward the Canadian border from the satellite's live-feed. "No airfield within range, but lots of roads. Route 277 has three straight miles of paved road just over the border. It's a shade over twenty miles."

"We should be able to make that," Colleen said. Cooper gave her the directional bearings and she adjusted her direction.

"Let's hope the Canadian's don't shoot us out of the air when we cross into their airspace," Wolf quipped.

"Half way there," Cooper reported. "How's the fuel?"

"According to the gauge, we'll make it with a cup's worth to spare," Colleen replied.

"I can't wait for the local gendarme to haul us in for being suspected gun runners," Wolf joked, looking at the rifles and ammunitions propped alongside his seat. He made a noise, adding, "Or for human trafficking."

"Are you forgetting I'm the one flying this crate?" Colleen said.

"I was talking about me," Wolf retorted. "I'd be in big demand with all those cute French Canadian femmes. Be sure to add ten percent on top of my stud fee to make up for the exchange rate."

Colleen laughed. "Every mission need a comic relief."

A short time later, Cooper informed them that they had crossed the border into Quebec. "Two miles to the road."

A piercing alarm sounded.

"We're running on fumes," Colleen said. "There's the road; a mile or so ... come on baby, you can do it."

Colleen reduced her speed and brought the plane lower as they closed in on the road ahead. The engine began to sputter.

"Almost there ... almost there..."

The engine stopped, its persistent and comforting rumble now replaced by the hissing of air rushing past. The plane slowed and dropped lower. And lower.

The tops of trees rushed upwards, greedily stretching their branches toward the doomed airplane with great expectations of their reward.

Chapter 17

Bienvenue au Canada

Seconds from clearing the stand of trees, the wheels cut into the crown of a particularly tall one, forcing the plane's nose to dip downward as it cleared the foliage. Colleen pulled back hard on the controls, the plane's nose sluggishly rising as the road rushed up to meet it. The airplane struck the pavement hard enough to break off the right landing wheel causing it to tip and skid noisily along the surface. Rotating in a leftward direction, it slid off the road, coming to a bumpy stop a few seconds later in the foliage lining the road.

"You okay?" Colleen said.

"Shaken and stirred, but still intact," Wolf replied.

He grabbed the guns and magazines and got out of the plane. Colleen came around to his side, which was facing the foliage.

"Frisk me," she ordered. When Wolf looked puzzled, she said, "They knew were we were which means they bugged me. Search me: begin with my arms."

She held her arms away from her body. Wolf's hands fingered carefully through her sleeves, working his way toward her neck and down her back.

"I'll handle that part, thank you," Colleen said, when Wolf's hands moved across the tops of her buttocks.

"I think I've got something," Wolf said, examining the back of the waistband. He held up a short, thin object for her to look at.

"That's a tracker," she confirmed. "They must have placed it there when they cuffed me; perfect time to do it since I wouldn't notice with all the jostling. Keep looking; these people were prepared for me to get away from my fake FBI detail, or even planned to let me escape so that they could see where I went."

A thorough search revealed no further tracking devices on her person, Colleen checking her shoes just to be sure. She tossed the tracker on the ground and stomped on it several times. She took one of the rifles and slung it over her shoulder, Wolf doing likewise.

Peering at her, he chuckled and said, "Great, now we look like the avant garde of an imminent American invasion."

"We can't leave them in the plane," she said. "We'll surrender our weapons once we meet with local authorities. Let's move, grunt."

They hadn't gone far when several cars drove toward them, stopping some distance away. Colleen held her arms out to the side and told Wolf to do likewise then walked slowly toward the cars. Several people exited their vehicles as they approached, the locals peering warily at the strangers who fell from the sky.

Colleen said something in French, Wolf catching some bits of it. One of the men answered in French, then switched to English. Colleen explained that they were flying to meet a hunting party in Maine when she noticed the fuel gauge dropping faster than it should. She figured one of the fuel line couplings must be leaking and would be out of fuel long before reaching the Newton Airfield in Jackman, Maine, so she crossed the border to land on a paved road.

"As you can see," Colleen said, pointing back at the broken plane resting in the ditch, "we almost didn't make it."

One of the men offered to drive them to the district police located in Lac-Etchemin, twelve miles west. His name was Andre and he insisted that Colleen sit up front with him. Wolf shot her a sardonic look as he got in the back of the car, resisting the urge to make a comment regarding Andre's act being a classic French cliché.

Wolf's assessment was confirmed over the next ten minute ride to the town as their driver chatted on about guessing Colleen's profession, fashion model being his top pick. When she asked him whether fashion models were known to hunt and fly planes, Andre demurred, saying that she was putting him on, certain that her companion in the back seat was the pilot and that the rifles were props for a camera shoot.

"You are a most observant man," Colleen cooed. "Of course a beauty like myself would never be caught toting a real rifle through the bushes to hunt for game. That is what I have big, strong men like you for. I'd wager that you would never have crashed a plane I was flying in unlike that skittish pilot in the back that my agency hired at the last moment."

"No, no," Andre assured her. "You must fire this agency and sue this pilot for threatening such magnificent beauty."

Wolf rolled his eyes and grinned. It was amazing how easily men made fools of themselves while anywhere near Colleen. Of course he included himself in that blanket assessment, but at least he managed to restrain his tongue from such babbling—most of time.

Thinking about why he was so strongly attracted to Colleen, he was quite certain that it wasn't simply a matter of sexual attraction, but something far more substantial. Over his many years as muckraker, he had met and interacted with many women he found physically beautiful but repelled by their willingness to associate with some of the most deceitful, untrustworthy men in the country. In a handful of cases, it was the women who ran fraudulent operations; either way, the ugly, repellent and dissolute values simmering beneath the veneer of beauty always seeped to the surface, permanently blemishing their attractiveness and lives.

Colleen was everything that such women were not: honest, trustworthy, uncompromising, principled, intelligent, motivated and brave. Such attributes tend to make one successful in whatever venture one sets out to pursue. It also is a bright maker of integrity, that summation where there is no contradiction between one's attractive values inside with one's physical beauty outside.

If love was recognizing one's highest values in another, then what values drew individuals to the liars, the frauds, the wastrels living off the success of their victims?

They arrived at the Lac-Etchemin police station, Andre declining Colleen's offer of payment. She thanked him with a kiss and exited the car, grinning mischievously at Wolf, who shook his head disapprovingly.

The police station was located in a short rowhouse sandwiched between a coffee shop on one side and a hair salon on the other. Seeing two armed individuals march through the door, the two officers inside rose out of their seats, peering nervously at the visitors.

"Good morning," Wolf said, reaching inside the jacket for his identification. He identified himself, mildly surprised to see no visible reaction on the face of either officer upon mentioning his name. He wasn't sure if their ignorance of his name was an advantage or disadvantage. He introduced Colleen who also presented her ID.

"Ms. Silverstone," one of the officer said, his face lighting up with recognition. "It is with great pleasure and honor to meet you! I am Gendarme Landry and my partner Gendarme Demers."

"An honor to meet both of you," Colleen said, smiling affably.

"Silverstone Security and Investigative Services is very respected and much appreciated in our country," Landry continued. "How may our humble station be of service to you?"

Colleen shot a humorous glance at Wolf and explained their situation. Both gendarmes listened raptly as she told of their escape across the frozen lake, their near collision with the SUV at the airstrip and the crash landing on Route 277.

"I apologize for bearing weapons so publicly, but I did not feel it was safe to leave them in the plane. My associate and I carry one pistol each and the rifles you see and would like to surrender them to you."

Colleen removed the rifle from her shoulder and placed it on the nearest desk, followed by her pistol. Wolf did likewise, though he felt vaguely uncomfortable without a weapon. The second gendarme, Demers, logged the weapons into the computer, gave them a receipt and locked them in a safe.

Colleen assured them that she would pay for the removal of the plane and any damage to the road the crash caused as well as any fine associated with their illegal entry into Canada and carrying concealed pistols.

Gendarme Landry assured them that everything would be taken care of and not to concern themselves with anything. He drove them to the best hotel in town and said he'd have a rental car brought by within the hour.

The hotel was surprisingly attractive with numerous amenities including access to the adjacent lake, swimming pool, and several well-appointed suites, one of which they chose. Wolf stood in front of the walkin closet in his bedroom and laughed.

Walking over to Colleen's bedroom, he said, "You should see the size of the closet."

She got the hint, proceeding to get directions from the desk clerk to a nearby store offering a reasonable selection of clothing for both men and women. They each bought two changes of clothing, an extra pair of shoes and a travel bag to carry it in. An hour and a reasonably modest payment later, they were back in their suite hanging up their new duds in their respective bedroom closets.

Colleen had ordered lunch from room service and the pair sat down to hot soup, sundry sandwiches and both hot and cold drinks.

"Let's hope our helpful gendarmes don't decide to access the base der données de la police where they might discover that Colleen Silverstone is a wanted fugitive," she said.

"I'm sure that the FBI knows about our fake agents and you're in the clear," Wolf said.

"Perhaps, but they might not have communicated that with the NYPD," she replied. "More than likely the local cops where first at the scene and assumed that I engineered a getaway."

"Why worry? You've got these big strong Frenchies at your beck and call," Wolf said, giving her a droll look. "Just promise each a kiss and they'll fetch whatever you want."

Colleen lowered her cup and smiled sweetly. "Why Mr. Wolf, I think you might be jealous."

"Not at all," he retorted, perhaps a little too quickly, he noted. "Just pointing out the advantages you have to offer in our efforts to stay out of a jail cell and get back to the US with minimal ado."

Her smile grew larger, Wolf doing his best to project a sense of casual disinterest while struggling to resist giving way under the combined assault of her brilliant white teeth, luscious lips and sparkling eyes.

"I really wish we didn't hand in our pistols," he said, hoping to ease his rising desire by changing the subject. "I feel exposed; our pursuers could cross the border as easily as we did if they believe we did."

"You'll be happy to know that I didn't hand in all my weapons." Colleen stuck her right calf toward him and pulled up her trouser revealing an ankle holster and small pistol. "And if we need serious firepower I know just where we can get that."

"Where? I didn't spot a gun store in town," Wolf said.

"The police station," she said, grinning. "Gendarme Demers is very sloppy about concealing the safe's code when entering it: five-seven-one-three." Seeing the surprised look on Wolf's face she added, "I guess I'm more than just a pretty face."

"Yes, you are," Wolf said, holding her gaze. For a wild moment he imagined his sincere reply pierced her tough emotional armor, but the impression passed. "How long do you expect to us to vacation in this lovely town and what is our next move?"

Colleen flashed him a knowing grin and said, "Cooper's last report confirmed that our pursuers assumed that we had escaped south and were heading back toward New Hampshire. So, for the time being, we're clear for now. But people, including police officers, talk and apparently I'm known and loved in these parts thus others will know sooner than later that I'm hiding out at Lac-Etchemin."

Wolf shot her a droll look. "You're really enjoying this highly unusual reversal of name recognition, aren't you?"

"By name recognition, you mean the notoriety associated with Grayson Wolf as compared to the esteem and respect accorded to Colleen Silverstone?" she teased.

"The only question remaining is why Colleen Silverstone would ever risk her stellar reputation by associating with a reprobate like Grayson Wolf?" he countered.

"Drawing fire away from me comes immediately to mind," Colleen replied, flashing a self-satisfied grin.

"Good to know I have some value to you beyond comical relief sidekick," Wolf said. "May I ask you a personal question?"

"That depends upon the personal nature of the question," she replied.

"Ever plan on getting married? Having children?" Wolf asked.

"Back atcha, comic relief sidekick."

"Deflection; classic," Wolf said. "Okay, me first: I hope so and I hope to. Your turn."

Colleen held his eyes. "No and no."

"Another prospect down," Wolf grinned, his hand crossing out a name on an imaginary list. "At this rate I might have to import a Russian bride."

"You would not want to marry me," Colleen said.

"Because you would besmirch my fine reputation?" he replied.

"Because of the second no," she said.

"You don't want children."

"I am not able to have children."

A very personal revelation indeed and it brought conversation to a swift halt. Wolf thought of what to say, choosing a traditional one.

"I'm sorry ... An accident?"

"Getting shot," Colleen replied. "I was in the service and saw action. Some of that action reached out and touched me."

"I knew you were an intelligence officer, a designation that covers a lot of ground," Wolf said.

"Six years, three in highly contentious parts of the world," Colleen explained. "Two purple hearts, couple others and an honorable discharge."

"By couple others, you mean metals of distinction?" Wolf asked.

"Recognition for doing my duty as a soldier," Colleen replied, her tone indicating that no further explanation would be forthcoming.

A sly grin slid across Wolf's face. "We could adopt."

Collen laughed. "See, this is why I keep you around. You're cheap entertainment."

"I must be pretty good at my job because you do smile a lot more when you're with me than when your not," Wolf stated.

"And you know this how?" she challenged.

"I'm a crack investigator; haven't you heard?" Wolf replied. "You better watch out: I know if you've been bad or good, where you sleep and where you wake up."

"So, you're admitting to being a stalking Santa," Colleen said.

Wolf made an affirmative shrug. "I do very much enjoy our little adventures together. The near-death encounters, the longing looks, sleeping together—in close proximity, exchanging suggestive banter. Good times all around."

"Me too," Colleen admitted, smiling agreeably. "And I very much want the good times to keep on rolling. Which means we need to get back to the States and hunt down whomever is pulling the strings behind Bellamy's murder, my fake FBI kidnapping, the gunmen back at the cabin and who knows what else ... what's most surprising and frustrating, is that we can't get a handle on any of it. I operate a reasonably extensive and highly effective security agency and though I have operatives sniffing around in a dozen corporate and public offices, no one has come up with anything. It's like living through one of those never-ending episodic shows where a shadowing figure keeps coming after the protagonists who's got to keep running or die."

"Whoever that shadow is, he or she must be connected to Bellamy," Wolf said. "And the chances are ten to one that if they are connected to Bellamy they are connected to New World Fund in some fundamental way. I'll go through my notes and files pursuant to my nine-month tour slinking around the under-Bellamy of his fund and friends. Something incidental popping up out of the blue has more than once busted open the social carbuncle allowing its putrid contents to spill out for closer examination."

"Would you be willing to let me go through those records with you? I might spot something meaningful that you might not consider important," Colleen said.

"You'd have to accompany me to my lair in Virginia," Wolf replied. "After all, I've seen yours; it's only fair that I show you mine."

"I just love your kindergarten references," Colleen said.

"I say we sneak across the border," Wolf suggested, ignoring her dig. "If we get stopped, we say we were lost in the woods. We're not illegals crossing the border; we're citizens and have identification. You said it yourself: your enamored gendarme is going to blab about meeting you and waiting around here makes us sitting ducks."

"Had we not attracted attention when we landed, I would have been inclined to head back and cross the border right away," Colleen said. "Running a business predisposes one to follow rules and protocols, not act on the spur of the moment like you are wont to do."

"Aren't you forgetting that you may still be a wanted fugitive?" Wolf said. "We show up at the border crossing they will check their computer to make sure things are on the up and up. What if you're detained? Do you really want another team of fake FBI to collect you again? My contacts in Maine are far and few between; I might not manage to rescue you a second time."

"I'm going to hear about that for a long time, aren't I?" Colleen said, giving him a sardonic look.

"Remind you about being rescued from a pair of stone cold killers during an audacious assault in broad daylight on a Manhattan street?" Wolf grinned. "I'd say pretty much forever ... I suggest we eat an early dinner, buy some protein bars and cross the border before nightfall."

"Crossing the border is the easy part. Hypothermia not so much," Colleen said. "We'd have to cross the border somewhere near Sandy Bay where Route 201 begins. From there it's about ten miles to Jackman where we can lay over until the next day. There we can either rent a car or maybe a plane at Newton Field. If we're lucky we might catch a ride; if not, I hope you're up to a ten to fifteen mile march in the dark while freezing your butt off."

Wolf's reply was cut off by a knock on the door. Colleen slipped the pistol from her ankle holster and moved out of the door's line of sight. Wolf walked to the door and stepped to the left, having learned a long time ago not to open a door the normal way. An irate husband thinking Wolf was having an affair with his wife had forcefully shoved the door when he opened it knocking him on his ass.

"Who is it?" Wolf said.

"It is Gendarme Landry...I have important information I must discuss with Mademoiselle Silverstone."

Wolf shot a look at Colleen who nodded. Using his right hand, Wolf reached over, twisted the handle and opened the door.

"Please come in," Wolf said.

The police officer entered and Colleen appeared around the corner. She greeted him and invited him to sit, which he declined.

"I am sorry to bother you," he said. "I have come to tell you personally that there is a standing arrest warrant issued by the New York police."

"Are you here to take me into custody?" Colleen asked.

"No, Mme. Silverstone," Landy said, smiling. "The warrant does not extend to Canada."

"Gendarme Landry," Wolf said. "I can assure you that this arrest warrant is not current. Events have moved very quickly since yesterday morning, the details of which have obviously not reached the NYPD. Ms. Silverstone has done nothing wrong; it is all a mistake."

"Yet you did say you were being pursued," Landry pointed out.

"We were, but not by police," Colleen confirmed. "I wish I could tell you who it was who attacked our cabin in Maine, but I do not know. I can tell you that it has something to do with the murder of financier Justin Bellamy in his New York residence before Christmas. Why these people are after me, I have no clue, except to say someone thinks that I know something incriminating and wants to stop me."

"Your reputation is well known, mademoiselle," Landry said. "I have not been ordered to detain you and will not lift a finger to interfere with your movements while in my jurisdiction."

"Gendarme Landry," Colleen said, smiling warmly at him. "Would you consider lifting a finger to help me?"

"It would be my honor and pleasure to lift all ten fingers to assist you in any way possible," Landry replied.

"You realize this is insane," Wolf said, after Landry had gone.

"What's the matter, Wolf? Chicken?" Colleen quipped.

"What if the border officers decide to search his vehicle?" Wolf retorted, ignoring her Back to the Future catchphrase. "It's one thing to get caught walking across the border and claim we were lost, it's a whole different matter to be discovered in the act of being smuggled into the country and by a gendarme no less. What'll we tell them: we were freezing, got into his car and woke up during a border inspection?"

"You're worrying unnecessarily," Colleen said. "You heard what Landry said; all the border cops know each other and cross back and forth over the border all the time. No one is ever stopped and searched. It's a wink and a wave. Now get ready; he'll be back in fifteen minutes."

It was a thirty-mile drive to the border crossing at Sandy Bay. Two miles out Wolf and Colleen got down on the backseat floor huddling under sundry coats, blankets and bags randomly scattered across the back.

"Border crossing ahead," Landry said, slowing the car.

He drove through the Canadian side, coming to a halt soon thereafter at the American checkpoint. Wolf and Colleen kept as still as they could under their covers.

"You again Emile," they heard the American border agent say. "She must be a real special girl."

"Qui, qui, James," Landry replied. "So is her sister."

The American agent laughed and said something they couldn't understand, the coats and blankets muffling his words. The officers exchanged a few more words then the car drove on. After a minute or two Landry told them they were clear and to come out from under.

Colleen shot Wolf a smug look and said, "Chicken."

At that moment the flashing of blue and red lights flickered from behind their car.

"Fried or baked?" Wolf quipped.

Chapter 18

Nous Saluons Le Retour

"Get under cover, rapide!" Landry ordered, as he pulled his car to the side of the road.

The police car pulled up behind him, followed by an officer coming up to his door. Landry rolled down the window.

"Oh, it's you, Emile," the officer said. "Sorry about pulling you over; we're on high alert today over chatter that smugglers are trying to bring a bunch of illegals into Maine. We've been randomly pulling cars over all day. You haven't spotted anything suspicious on your trip over here?"

"Nothing," Landry said. "Been quiet all week at Lac-Etchemin, Paul. I see anything while visiting your fine mademoiselles, I will make report pour sûr."

"Have a good time and don't wear our ladies out," the officer replied, chuckling. "Oh, you'd better check your left rear tire pressure; looks a little soft. Later..."

The officer walked back to his patrol car and Landry drove on arriving in Jackman a few miles later. The gendarme took a left on a drive leading to a lodge.

"My aunt and her husband are the proprietors," Landry said. "I will leave you in their good care. You will be able to rent a car at Power Center Transport; half mile south. Good luck and stay safe."

"Thank you Emile; I will not forget your kindness," Colleen said. She handed him a card. "If you ever need to call me."

Wolf collected their few belongings and they entered the lodge. Being in the dead of winter, there was lots of vacancies, Wolf selecting a cabin with two bedrooms. When the owner shot him a curious look, he said that his girlfriend snored like a sawmill at full blast thus requiring his own bedroom.

"Sawmill at full blast?" Colleen said, after they entered the cabin.

"Would you have rather I told her you suffered from Irritable Bowel Syndrome resulting in involuntary blasts of gas throughout the night?" Wolf retorted.

Colleen laughed. "Did you see the way she looked at you when made that comment about snoring? She appeared genuinely relieved when you chose a cabin knowing my night clatter wouldn't disturb the slumber of guests inside the lodge."

They both laughed, though perhaps more from having been successfully smuggled into the country than at Colleen's remark. What few belongings they had were stored in their bedrooms followed by a planning session a few minutes later.

"First thing tomorrow morning we rent a car followed by a shopping trip, phones being the first purchase," Collen said.

"It's a pain not being able to call our people, but it beats being tracked," Wolf said. "Whoever is after you, these people are well connected and that means they have the juice to track us using our phones' GPS. Even using prepaid phones is a risk and you can forget about using a credit card for anything; mine, too. "

"We can use cash for basic things, but renting a car will require a credit card," Colleen said. "We'll rent a car last and get on the road immediately. Once we get back to New York, I'm walking into the FBI district office. If our predators think I've spoken with the FBI they should stop going after me."

"Not if their objective is to use you to flush out Barry, which you thought was their goal," Wolf said.

"Considering they were shooting at us as we skated across the lake and okay with me being incinerated crashing the plane into their car, I'd say preventing me from talking has become their number one priority," Colleen replied.

"If Barry was trying to protect you by not telling what he knows, he failed most spectacularly," Wolf said.

"You're absolutely right, Wolfie," Colleen replied, peering at him knowingly. "And as you should know so well, having dogged Barry and his accomplices for over a year, Barry Silverstone has managed to *not fail* for many years now..."

"Right," Wolf said, enlightenment striking him. "Barry doesn't know anything more about Bellamy's murder than he's told us."

"We might not get along, but Barry wouldn't knowingly put me in danger," Colleen said.

"He and I definitely don't get along," Wolf replied. "But I give him credit for the fact that Barry is very proud of his stepdaughter and her accomplishments."

Colleen shot him a sarcastic look. "Is that so? And you know this, how?"

"I don't think you realize I probably spent more time in Barry's company when I was undercover for a year than you have over the past decade," Wolf explained. "He talked about you quite often; Bellamy would joke about you being his downfall one day. It's how I got to know about you and knew I could trust you."

Colleen held his eyes for a long moment. "I never gave much thought about your life undercover while investigating people; of course you would hear all kinds of things. I was in intelligence, but my activities were of brief duration, often ending in violence." She smiled warmly at him. "Thank you for sharing that bit of intelligence."

"It's nice to know what our parents think about us," Wolf said. "Even if we're not looking for it; that they approve and are proud of what we're doing ... and even if *we* disapprove of *their* activities."

"You ever think of becoming a family therapist?" Colleen teased.

"Barry is everything I said about him in my book: shyster, conman, double-dealing, money-grubbing weasel and more," Wolf replied, ignoring her. "However, based on what I do know about him, he isn't the depraved animal Bellamy was. I know we believe whoever is after you killed Bellamy, but it could just as likely be someone he had defiled in his past. I know that if he'd done to my daughter what he did to Sara Lewis, I'd be plotting to take that bastard out."

"Knowing Bellamy's history, I agree it might be a remote possibility," Colleen said. "But my gut tells me it's someone behind Bellamy's decade-long, stellar success of his New World fund."

"You're probably right; they'd have the most to lose and want to shut up anyone closely related to that suspiciously high and seemingly endless streak of investment success," Wolf said.

"Beginning with Bellamy himself after you tricked him to reveal he was visiting his spawn in Colorado during the time of the rape," Colleen replied. "Knowing him, in exchange for a slap on the wrist, he'd make a deal bringing down a whole passel of notables, so he's gotta be silenced with others close to him, like Barry."

"And Maddie, bringing me documents that they thought might incriminate them," Wolf said. "I'm used to being hated and threatened for my exposes, but have to admit having people after us trying to kill me is somewhat unsettling."

"But hasn't dampened your sense of humor," Colleen said, grinning. "We'll I've got news for them: they have really pissed me off and I plan to go after them, beginning by having a heart-to-heart conversation with the FBI section chief in New York tomorrow. The bigger the noise we make, the more likely these scum will make a fatal mistake."

"Hopefully before they get one of us," Wolf quipped. "And by us, I mean me."

Colleen laughed and said, "I've got bad news for you, Wolfie: the comic relief is always the first one to get whacked."

"How did you manage to rent a car without using a credit card?" Colleen said, getting into the Jeep when Wolf picked her up in front of the Moose Outfitter store the following morning.

"The name Grayson Wolf works its magic even in remote Jackman, Maine," he replied, smugly. "And I didn't have to kiss anyone, unlike some people I could mention."

"My kisses are far cheaper than what you paid to rent—" she glanced around the interior, "this fine example of 1990 engineering."

"It's either this or we hitch a ride on an eighteen-wheeler," Wolf replied.

He didn't elaborate about the rental arrangement, which was in fact a purchase costing seven gold eagles, valued at near ten thousand dollars, twice what the used Jeep would sell on the local market. The goal was to travel without being noticed and gold facilitates that most effectively.

*   *   *   *

Several hours later as Wolf and Colleen were passing Provincetown, Rhode Island on their way to New York, Susan Baker and her legal team arrived at Browning University a few miles east of the Interstate. After Ivygreen College broke ranks and negotiated a separate settlement with Center for Individual Rights in exchange for being removed from the Center's class action suit, additional colleges and universities decided to invite CIR representatives to discuss individual settlement possibilities. One of those colleges was Browning University and Susan Baker was sent to negotiate a separate settlement.

Approaching the college's administration complex, Susan noticed a large cluster of students crowding the stairway, effectively blocking the entrance to the building. She didn't need to read the placards to know that this protest was organized in her honor. Someone must have spotted Susan and her two associates approach because harsh chanting erupted.

Susan slowed her pace, warning the attorneys to not respond to taunts as they encountered the protesters. At least this time the confrontation was in the open, not like what happened previously at Ivygreen College where Juan, Terrance and she had to blockade themselves in the conference room.

"I don't think they're going to let us walk up the steps," Anthony Davenport said.

"Are we going to try to elbow our way through, Susan?" Barbara Chambers said, looking worried.

"Stay together," Susan said. "Get your phones ready to transmit our encounter to Brett."

They walked up to the mob blocking the entrance and halted.

"You are violating college regulations and our right to enter the building," Susan said, loudly.

A chorus of fuck you's and other disparaging comments ensued. Someone initiated chanting "CIR has got to go". After multiple repetitions, "Na-zi bottom feeders" took its place soon morphing into "free speech is hate speech", which went on for some time. Perhaps annoyed at the fact their verbal targets not only failed to retreat as expected but peered at the mob with amused expressions, the chant changed to "fuck the pro-vost", the latter obviously directed at the man responsible for inviting the CIR legal team to Browning.

Concluding enough footage of childish nonsense was transmitted back to Brett at CIR, Susan was going to call the provost informing him that if campus security did not clear the steps she would have no choice but to leave, when a dozen campus police outfitted in riot gear appeared taking a position between the attorneys and protestors. One officer stood in front of the phalanx, microphone in hand. Having witnessed other campus confrontations over the past six months, Susan didn't expect much. The police would huff and puff gaining little more than jeers and ridicule, reinforcing the lesson learned by students from sea to shining sea: rules, decorum and the rights of others do not apply to them. She saw the lead officer raise the microphone to his mouth.

"You are in violation of Browning University code of conduct including disorderly conduct, unauthorized demonstration and obstructing entry and egress. You are to clear the steps immediately."

This announcement was met with a rousing chant of the always popular, "hell no, we won't go".

"This is your second warning. You are to clear the steps," the officer said, his words echoing off the building.

"Hell no, we won't go!"

"In one minute my officers will clear the steps," he said. "Anyone failing to comply will be forcefully removed and detained. Detainees will be placed on school probation for the rest of the semester and parents notified. If you have a scholarship, that money will be frozen until further notice. You have one minute to clear the steps beginning now."

Susan was genuinely stunned, as were the student protestors, because small knots of them started to move off the steps, followed by larger numbers, clearing the steps by the end of a minute.

"Well, that's a first," Susan said, seeing the steps devoid of even one protestor. "Proving once again that money talks and bullshit walks."

"It's easy to be a member of the resistance when mommy and daddy are paying the bill," Anthony said.

The group ascended the steps and entered the building where they were met by the provost himself. He extended his hand.

"Reginald Marshall," he said, introducing himself. "Sorry about the reception. I wanted campus police stationed at the entrance prior to your arrival, but was opposed by other administrators."

"I'm Susan Baker," she said, shaking his hand. "A pleasure to meet you, Provost Marshall; my associates, Barbara Chambers and Antony Davenport."

"How did you manage to convince the powers-that-be to threaten students with probation and loss of scholarship money?" Barbara asked.

"Let's just say that some administrators are more critical to the operation of the college than others," Marshall replied.

Engaging in negotiations requires preparation and an important aspect is knowing the background of the individuals one faces across the conference table. Provost Reginald Marshall was a former Air Force fighter pilot with a no nonsense, but fair-minded reputation as a college administrator. Susan was looking forward at the prospect of dealing with a college administrator who hadn't spent his entire life in academia.

Marshall escorted them to a conference room where half dozen school representatives were seated on the far side of a large, oaken table. As Susan took a seat between Anthony and Barbara facing the sour looking group, she shot a look at Marshall's chiseled face wondering what a man like him was doing here.

Introductions were made, niceties concluded and negotiations began. The Browning Students for Individual Rights had gotten one hundred thirty two signatory for the class action suit. CIR was planning to sue Browning University for one hundred million dollars knowing that in the end, a judge would knock fifty percent or more off that amount. To encourage more colleges to engage in negotiations, the CIR Board had instructed its attorneys to offer a lower settlement amount.

"As you can see from our brief detailing the number, degree and length of time Browning University has failed to uphold its contractual obligations to all its students, our settlement offer of twenty five million is more than generous," Susan said.

"Would you consider twenty million?" Marshall asked.

"Five million," Browning's lead attorney, Lowenstein, interjected, ignoring the provost.

Susan's gaze fell on Lowenstein. So much for being reasonable.

"Thirty million," she said, holding the man's eyes.

"Eight million," he retorted.

"Thirty five million," Susan countered.

"This is ridiculous," Lowenstein said. "Your entire case is nothing but a cheap fishing expedition to extort money from the college. Ten million. Final offer."

A cheap fishing expedition to extort money from the college, Susan thought. Obviously every attorney representing universities and colleges named in CIR's class action suit have been busy chatting amongst themselves. At least Lowenstein could come up with something more original, like money grubbing Nazi lowlife.

Susan shot a glance at Marshall, then peered at Lowenstein.

"Twenty million. Final offer."

"Mr. Marshall," Anthony said. "The administration invited us to negotiate a fair settlement. If the college prefers to be included in our class action trial, it is not unreasonable to think that the final settlement would exceed twenty five million dollars, not to mention the additional millions of legal fees the college will incur."

"The monetary damages won't end there," Barbara said. "Our unique class action trial will bring critical and unwanted public attention on the way the university has nurtured a campus atmosphere of unequal treatment based upon views and opinions contrary to the official school political and cultural orthodoxy; that the administration has routinely ignored bullying and intimidation on school social media and person-to-person when suffered by non protected classes ... for another dozen examples please refer to the brief in front of you."

"I'd wager the college would experience a precipitous drop in applicants resulting in declining enrollment," Susan said. "My colleagues and I will retire to the cafeteria while you consider the offer. If we cannot come to a resolution today, then we have been instructed to withdraw the offer and include Browning University in the class action filing."

"Thank you, Ms. Baker," Marshall said. "We'll discuss the settlement offer and I'm sure you can expect a positive answer within an hour."

Lowenstein and his colleagues shot a disapproving look at the provost as Susan slid documents back into her briefcase. She thanked the man and stood up, leading her team out of the conference room.

They had done what they came to do. Normally, negotiations take much longer than a half hour, but CIR had nixed engaging in extended discussions, preferring to wave each colleges' dirty laundry in front of their faces so that they could not fail to miss the stink that would become public knowledge when paraded in front of a national court for the world to see.

By four that afternoon, Susan texted "mission accomplished" to CIR's Director Diana Cruz. She and her associates drove to the airport where they would spend the night and prepare for an early morning flight to join Juan and Terrance in Los Angles as they prepared for a frontal assault on some of southern California's internationally renowned universities.

Chapter 19

Intimate Contemplations

By two forty five, Wolf rolled up to 26 Federal Plaza near the southern tip of Manhattan and parked across the street from Javits Federal Office Building. They took the elevator to the 23rd floor and entered the lobby to the offices of the FBI.

Colleen brought forth her ID and identified herself; Wolf did likewise. Heads within earshot turned in their direction. Colleen explained her purpose for coming here; the receiving agent asking her to wait while he called the supervisor in charge. Less than a minute later the pair were escorted to the office of Assistant FBI Director Sheldon Derek of New York District.

"The only reason you have not been handed over to the NYPD, Ms. Silverstone," Derek said, "is because of the extraordinary events surrounding the incident two days ago. FBI imposters walk into the police station, interrogate the two of you, take you into their custody and wind up lying in an alley handcuffed to a car bumper. You want to explain what is going on?"

"I was hoping your people might have been able to extract that information from the two imposters I left for you," Colleen said.

"You engineered your own rescue? How?" Derek demanded.

"I've got lots of friends who look after me," she replied. "Did you find out anything from them?"

The associate director shot Wolf an inquisitive look. "How are you involved with Ms. Silverstone, Mr. Wolf?"

"I'm her comic sidekick," he replied. "And part-time lover."

Derek's expression hardened. "I've heard about your flippant attitude toward the FBI and see now that it is not exaggerated."

"On the contrary, Director Derek," Wolf retorted. "I have great respect for the rank and file of the FBI who protect our nation against enemies foreign and domestic. I assure you that my flippant attitude is reserved for your associates in the upper ranks who conspire with enemies foreign and domestic to attempt the overthrow of an elected president ... would you care to comment for my next expose? I'm thinking about calling it, FBI: What's It Good For? Absolutely nothin!"

The two men stared silently at each other for a long moment. Colleen interrupted their visual tug of war.

"Mr. Wolf and I were engaged in a joint investigation when we were detained and brought to New York. When I was freed from the FBI imposters attempting to kidnap me, I called Mr. Wolf who agreed to accompany me and continue our investigation."

"The NYPD still wants to question you—both of you—pursuant to Barry Silverstone and I'm inclined to deliver you to them," Derek said.

"I'm sure the precinct captain is most anxious to talk about how his officers let two fake FBI agents bamboozle them and kidnap a prominent businesswoman," Wolf said. "He'll most likely have the press and national TV present during our interrogation, too. When the media asks how these jokers managed to get authentic federal identification, I'll point them to the Assistant FBI Director of the New York District for answers."

Wolf saw Colleen press her lips together to curtail a smile emerging, or worse, laughter, but he wasn't trying to be funny. Wolf's contact with the FBI over the years was problematic at best as the subjects of his exposes tapped political friends to pull strings at the FBI to harass him at unexpected times and places. Add the current revelations about top FBI personnel colluding with one political party to undermine a national election and Wolf was seriously considering coming out of retirement and raking the muck in FBI basements.

"Assistant Director Derek," Colleen said. "The FBI, including your office, has been assisting in the investigation of Justin Bellamy's New World Fund for years now looking for insider trading, fraud, bribery or other such activity to account for the miraculous success of the New World Fund. To date, no evidence of such activity has surfaced."

"Your point?" Derek said.

"Suddenly the star of the show is murdered along with a lawyer working in the financial area who had called Mr. Wolf to meet with her," Colleen said. She looked expectantly at Wolf.

"December 12th, Madeline Talbot texted me to meet her for lunch at the Baltimore Convention Center the following day saying she had something to give me pursuant to the New World Fund. She provided no further details," Wolf said. "I agreed to meet her and when I got to the restaurant, she was not at her table. I searched for her and found her in the bathroom unresponsive. I tried to revive her but it was too late." Wolf smiled. "But you know all that already."

"The point," Colleen said, continuing, "is that we believe the objective of Bellamy's and Talbot's murders were to ensure that certain information about the extraordinary success of New World would never become public. Barry Silverstone, Bellamy's long-time friend who was visiting Bellamy the night he was murdered, was the perfect fall guy. When Barry got wind of the murder, he was smart enough to know he'd be the number one suspect and disappeared from sight that same Saturday Talbot was murdered."

"Which is why your father is also a suspect for Ms. Talbot's murder," Derek said. "The documents she was planning to hand over to Mr. Wolf could just as easily have been material incriminating Barry Silverstone."

"Except his vanishing act caught the real murderer off guard," Colleen replied. "I think the real culprit believes that Barry knows whatever it is that got both Bellamy and Talbot killed. Furthermore, that same person also believes that Barry has shared that information with me."

"What makes you think that?" Derek asked.

"Because a group of hired guns tried to ambush me in Maine, shooting at me as I was trying to escape and tried to crash a truck into an airplane I was taking off in," Colleen explained. "That is why I came here, to give this killer the impression that I'm sharing whatever information they think I know with you so that they'll take the target off my back."

"But you have no such information to share with me," Derek said. "Or so you claim."

"I do so claim and my record of service along with my company's stellar reputation and consistent cooperation with federal agencies over the past decade should be more than sufficient guarantor," Colleen replied.

"A claim no one representing your agency could make," Wolf said. The Associate Director gave him a wearied look and he continued. "All I ask is that when your buddies raid my humble abode at four a.m. someday, they'll come with least three dozen heavily armed agents accompanied by CNN like during that dramatic raid on the seventy-year old and his disabled wife down in Florida. If you give me a heads up, I'll make sure to have my aging grandparents visiting at the time, too."

Colleen looked knowingly at Wolf. Having worked with him in Colorado last summer, she would understand he was prodding the man to see what would pop up from underneath the agent's veneer of patience. The Associate Director's veneer appeared to remain intact, the man peering at Wolf with a blank stare.

"I think we're done here," Colleen said. "Unless you plan to arrest me or Mr. Wolf, we are leaving. Feel free to let NYPD know I'm in town and inform them I'm coming to see them next."

"The parking garage is that way," Wolf said, pointing toward Worth Street.

"Forget the car," Colleen said. "I'm having some of my people pick us up. I prefer riding with armed bodyguards; at least while we're in New York. Whoever this evil overlord is, he's pulling the strings from this city."

"I'm not averse to bodyguards," Wolf quipped, tossing the car keys in the nearest trashcan. "Are we really walking back into that police station?"

"Feel free to lounge in the car if you wish, but I'm going in and have my lawyer get me out five minutes later," Colleen said. "It's enough having criminals after me without having to look over my shoulder for cops, too. Besides, we both know their accusation of aiding and abetting a fugitive is bogus. The people behind this influenced the NYPD to issue arrest warrants in order to use me as bait to draw out Barry."

"Why include me?" Wolf asked.

"Added bonus. Have you forgotten that you are the scourge of Bellamy and...um, others like him?"

"Including the mystery scumbag aiding and abetting Bellamy to keep the New World Fund money flowin' 'n growin' scheme," Wolf concluded. "There's always a ripple effect; you never know all, or even most, of the people effected by taking down a Bellamy—or his son."

"Or the son's nasty, malicious girlfriend whose father is a US Senator," Colleen said. She pointed toward a vehicle standing at the curb ahead. "There's my team. Let's go..."

"Good afternoon," Colleen said, cheerfully. "Mr. Wolf and I are here to see detectives Vanderhelm & Shelling."

The desk sergeant's eyes widened slightly. She informed them that neither detective was in the station, but that the captain would definitely want to talk with them.

"Not to worry, Captain Keller. Neither I nor Mr. Wolf is interested in suing the department," Colleen said, after the man introduced himself and subsequently apologized for the unfortunate incident two days ago. "We came to turn ourselves in; we are wanted fugitives after all."

Wolf noticed the subtle twitch of her lips following her declaration of surrender. Whereas he favored an overt approach to provoking authorities as he had done earlier with the FBI Associate Director, Colleen preferred to slip in her needling as calm, understatement. Yet another way she and he made a good team.

"Considering the circumstances, I'm vacating your warrants," Keller said. "Our investigation of the incident showed that the anonymous tip was part of the conspiracy to use the NYPD to bring you in so that the FBI impostors could walk out the door with you. It's all connected to the Bellamy murder, but what I don't understand is, why you?"

"Because instead of being arrested for Bellamy's murder like they expected, Barry Silverstone vanished," Colleen explained. "You see, Captain, I'm sure Bellamy was killed to keep him from talking about how he managed to keep his fund pumping up huge gains year after year. The man was going on trial for raping at least one women with his son. The feds would very likely trade the how and the who in exchange for a light sentence or maybe none at all and witness protection to boot."

"In my line of business, the simplest reason is usually the right one," Keller said. "Money, sex and revenge. It's a rare day in this station when we're dealing with mysterious villains manipulating us to haul in suspects and having them kidnapped by fake FBI with authentic IDs. I'm more than happy to forget this whole mess and let the feds run after these shadows. Give me a good 'ol murder any day."

Back in Colleen's downtown Manhattan hotel suite that afternoon, Cooper was on speaker updating both on their separate and collaborative investigations. After communicating his relief that both Colleen and Wolf were still in one piece, he expressed genuine frustration at not being able to discover any viable connection to whom was behind Bellamy's and Maddie's murders, Colleen's attempted kidnapping and subsequent attack in Maine.

"Give me good news, Obi Wan Cooper; you're my only hope," Wolf teased, when he asked about progress pursuant the hacker.

"Although we've got no likely suspects for the hacking attacks yet," Cooper said, "Brett and I have compiled a comprehensive list of every sex change operation conducted by ATTC nationwide as well as any suicide and very unhappy customer related to that outfit. Brett is organizing that list, so check with him, Wolf."

"It's nice to have you on our side, Cooper," Wolf said. "You and Brett are among the best, um, digital disassemblers in the country."

"Yes sir, we are. And we will corner that stealth hacker sooner than later," Cooper crowed.

"Pretty sure of yourself, are we?" Wolf chided.

"Yes and do you know why?" Cooper retorted.

"No, but you're going to tell me," Wolf chuckled.

"Because this hacker or hackee is very good," Cooper explained. "And when you're that good that makes you a member of a small minority, thus increasing the chances of being discovered. And I will get that digital killer. Count on it."

"I am and I know you will," Wolf said. "Thanks for all your help, Cooper."

"What's your next move, boss?" he said, speaking to Colleen.

"Wolf is inviting me to his lair in Tyson's to explore the dark corners of his expose files," she replied.

"Better be on the alert," Cooper warned. "I hear he's a real ladies man. Kat told me all about his smooth style, flashing his big blue's at her and, bam! Next thing he's off on another hunt."

"Cooper, you obviously know nothing about your boss," Wolf replied. "The woman goes around kissing men willy and nilly to get what she wants. You should have seen her wrap the male population of a Canadian town around her pinky. Brazen, brazen woman."

"If you two female-deprived gossips are done, some of us have real work to do," Colleen said, terminating the call. Looking over at Wolf, she added, "Grab your bag, we've got a flight to catch."

"Pushy broad," Wolf snarled, flashing her a canine tooth.

"Best you remember that."

*　　　*　　　*　　　*

It was her first visit to Wolf's Center For Individual Rights and though Colleen initially declined his invitation to stay at his home, his teasing about her succumbing to his charms did the trick. Colleen had never been concerned about capitulating to any man's charms—at least not since middle school. Her initial reluctance staying at Wolf's penthouse five floors above CIR wasn't about what others would think. After all, they had been staying together in hotel suites several times over the past two months traipsing after the killer of Bellamy and Maddie.

Thinking about this as she got dressed the morning after, Colleen concluded that the difference between staying together at hotels and sleeping over in Wolf's home was relational. There was a far greater feeling of intimacy connected to one's home than a hotel or cabin in the Maine woods. If one was to succumb to another's charms, staying over at an eligible bachelor's home would be the more likely scenario.

And she had to admit, looking at herself in full-length mirror, she had grown fond of Grayson Wolf since her frosty reception of him back in Denver last March. Which was probably the reason why she took up his offer to stay at his home. A bedroom was a bedroom whether in a hotel, cabin or Wolf's home. Colleen Silverstone had risen to every challenge throughout her life—especially when the challenge presented was any whiff of self-doubt.

"Well good morning Ms. Silverstone!" RJ said, cheerfully, as she exited her bedroom.

"Good morning to you, Mr. Jano," Colleen replied, gazing coolly at Wolf's friend who shot her a suggestive look. She knew the man loved to tease and toss innuendoes around, but still surprised seeing him, especially exiting a bedroom. This is why she should have declined Wolf's invitation to stay with him instead of at a local hotel.

"Please call me RJ," he replied, still grinning, giving her the once over. "Wolf talks a lot about you...meeting you in person, I can see why."

"Give it a rest, RJ," Wolf said, entering the living room. "Ignore him, Colleen. He's just jealous of the outfit you're wearing because he knows it looks far better on you than it would on him."

RJ laughed. "And Wolf is wishing he helped you get dressed in that gorgeous outfit this morning."

"What makes you think he didn't?" Colleen said, her sanguine tone obviously catching RJ off guard.

Scrunching his face, he peered from one to the other. His expression brightened momentarily and he said,

"Not buying it, hot mama. I know my bro and his expression is not aglow from a night of delight."

This time is was Colleen's turn to laugh. "Just how close are you to your *bro?*"

"As close as two peas in a pod," RJ said, grinning.

"I'm beginning to understand Wolf much better now," Colleen said, smiling at RJ.

"You mean why he's such a good comic sidekick to your badassness?" RJ quipped.

Colleen glanced over at Wolf. "And they say it's only women who tell each other everything."

"He doesn't tell me anything," RJ said. "I've got that special gift that keeps on giving. There's very little I can't conjure from the vibrations coming at me from all sides."

"RJ is special alright," Wolf deadpanned. "A very special pain in the ass, especially when anywhere near me."

"See how he loves me?" RJ joked. "The man is a glutton for pain and I'm highly proficient at delivering it. Which reminds me: be prepared to expect lots 'a pain 'n suffering at the Board meeting this morning. The evil ivory tower empire is striking back."

"What are you talking about?" Wolf asked.

"While you've been busy doing God knows what with your not-girlfriend the past weeks, a backlash to our legal assault on the colleges has ensued," RJ said. "Eat a hardy breakfast, 'cause you'll need it once the meeting begins. I shall leave you now..." RJ walked toward the exit and said as he opened the door, "When you come in the office, the two of you might as well act like you've had a great night together 'cause everyone will be thinking it anyway. Cheers!"

Colleen shot a meaningful look at Wolf. He shrugged helplessly and poured coffee. This was exactly why she should have insisted staying at a hotel. The question reverberating in her head was, why didn't she?

"It's a pleasure to finally meet you in person, Ms. Cruz," Colleen said, shaking the CIR director's hand. "Wolf has nothing but praise when speaking about you."

"Thank you, Ms. Silverstone," Diana replied. "It's an honor meeting you. Please call me Diana."

"While the two of you get acquainted, I'll go see Brett," Wolf said. "Try not to spend all your time talking about me."

Both women shot him a get-thee-gone look and Wolf walked over to the head of CIR's computer and security division. Brett waved at him as he entered the office.

"Your text said you have something interesting for me," Wolf said.

"Yeah," he replied. "Sorry about taking so long to examine the Ivygreen surveillance video. We've been up to our necks assisting Juan and his team with all the legal stuff going on." Brett moved his mouse around and clicked here and there and the video appeared on the monitor. "Okay, now watch carefully as I run it in slow motion..."

Wolf did as instructed, watching as the oncoming truck suddenly sped forward striking the hapless Ivygreen counselor before she could react and get out of the way. The video continued and he saw the two other cars on the lower portion of the field of view careen into parked cars. Though it was the first time Wolf had seen the surveillance video in slow motion, he didn't spot anything different or unusual from what he could remember seeing the first time he was shown the video.

A knowing grin appeared on Brett's face. "You didn't spot it, did you?"

"Maybe not, but I definitely spot that smug expression looking up at me," Wolf retorted.

Brett snorted and played the video again. "Okay, coming up... I'm going to pause it ... right ... now."

"Besides seeing the truck frozen at the point of impact, what do you see that I don't?" Wolf asked, peering at the image on the monitor. Brett pointed at what appeared to be a light shadow near the top-right of the frame. "Okay, what is it?"

"Unusual shape for a shadow," Brett said. "Too small for a cloud, not curved like a streetlight shadow. It's rectangular: darker in the center, lighter and circular sections at the corners ... now what kind of object hovering above the parking lot could cast such a shadow?"

Enlightenment struck, though Brett's sardonic tone also helped to unravel the mystery.

"It's a drone," Wolf said. "Like, duh!"

"Yup, we're still failing to think three—or four—dimensionally," Brett said. "This hacker has been using drones to observe the movements of his victims and transmit the hacks to take control of vehicles. It's a bit more complicated than that, but this is how he's killed the first woman and the college counselor."

"She died?" Wolf said, surprised.

"Two days ago," Brett said. "Your phone, Colleen's too, was offline and then I got busy with the legal stuff and forgot to get back to you; sorry about that."

"Quite alright; we've all been busy," Wolf replied. "Did that get us any closer to tracking this distance killer?"

"I've let Cooper know," Brett said. "SSIS has satellite access and if Colleen gives him authorization, maybe we get lucky and spot the drone from the satellite footage. Long shot, but better than nothing."

"I'll ask Colleen and let you know," Wolf said. "Good eye, Brett; you're worth the fifteen cents above minimum wage."

"I'm glad you think so, because I deserve a five cent raise after three years," he replied.

"Don't hold your breath," Wolf said, over his shoulder as he stepped out of Brett's domain.

He returned to Diana's office where the two executive women appeared to be engaged in a friendly conversation. Promising to attend the Board meeting, Wolf escorted Colleen to records storage. On the way he updated her on what Brett had discovered about the hacking murders and she agreed to direct Cooper to request Satellite footage of the dates surrounding the car-related murders. Once in the secure storage facility, Wolf gave her access to documents and notes pursuant his research of the underbelly of financial and stock-trading institutions and the movers and shakers behind their corporate faces.

By the time Wolf got to the Board meeting, the discussion was well underway with Teena Sanoe talking about the threat of violence on and off college campuses. A key element of CIR's class action suit aimed at colleges centered on administrations remaining silent when confronted with student complaints about feeling increasingly threatened while in classes, on campus and on school social media if they expressed views contrary to what others deemed acceptable. By the time Wolf took a seat, he understood that Teena wasn't referring to bullying or shaming, but actual physical violence.

"While visiting Havens College, someone torched the rental car that Terrance Smith and his team drove," the security chief said. "Juan himself was accosted by a group of thugs screaming obscenities and spitting at him when he left a Georgetown restaurant last week. We've taken calls from over a dozen leaders of Students for Individual Rights reporting that harassment and intimidation is rising at their universities. It's Virginia Patriots College all over again except now it's all over the country."

The security chief nodded at Diana and sat down. She mentioned the recent success by Susan and her team at Browning University then invited Juan to speak.

"Threats aside, I am delighted by Teena's report. The rising animosity on the campuses dramatically underscores virtually every one of our claims of unequal treatment and evading the bullying going on these campuses. Administrators label unpopular views as hate speech while turning a blind eye to real hate speech designed to intimidate students into remaining silent about contrary views. While college presidents prattle on about collegiate atmosphere, social opportunities, freedom to explore ideas and so forth the reality on their campuses belies their lofty claims. It's true about SIR groups calling us to report abuses; however, what's far more important is that group members are recording these abuses on video, oral and written testimonies. If there is increasing violence, we will capture that and use it in court to underscore the administration's inaction and failure to equally protect the rights of every student enrolled in their institutions. A lack of decisive action in the face of mounting threats, intimidation and physical violence, is a de facto admission of consent."

Jewel King raised a hand and was recognized. "According to the Journal of Higher Education, fall applications to many of the colleges we are including in the class action is down an average of eight percent. For some it's over twelve percent."

"Friends, thanks to Juan's stroke of genius during the Virginia Patriot's debacle last May, we may be witnessing the high water mark of the Ivory Tower with its bloated administration," Wolf said. "Little over a generation ago, students could attend a state university and pay for it working during the summer. The unholy collusion between academia and the sugar daddies on Capitol Hill have managed to drive millions of students into a trillion-dollar hole of debt they will struggle for decades to repay. How many more will venture fifty or a hundred thousand into debt for an education peppered with anti-American values and skills that are outdated before they even graduate? The revolution is way overdue and we are going to ensure that at least some students get the refund they deserve."

"You'll need to excuse me, but the revolution is calling me west," Juan said, getting up from his seat. "Susan and her team are currently in the air on the way to LA to meet up with Terrance and his team of legal terrorists—that's what the California Board of Regents called him—and I've got to join them tonight."

Diana thanked everyone and concluded the Board meeting, shooting Wolf a look to hang back. Once the room was cleared, she asked him what was going on.

"Brett tells me that you and Colleen were attacked in a cabin out in the backwoods of Maine, commandeered a plane, crash-landed in Canada, were smuggled back across the border into the US and wound up having a sit-down with the FBI chief in NYC," she said, providing an accurate account of Wolf's adventures over the last forty-eight hours.

Wolf made a droll face. "Hanging out with Colleen can be a breathless experience."

"I'm sure," Diana replied, giving him a humorous look. "Just don't get yourself killed; we still need your talents around here ... What is she hoping to find sifting through your case files?"

"Some clue that might lead us to whom might be behind Bellamy's and Maddie's murders," he replied. "Whoever these people are they tried to kidnap Colleen and failing to accomplish that, sent a hit team after us. It's a confirmation that these people are getting nervous and nervous people do desperate things that wind up becoming mistakes. They've failed and now we're going to dig deeper and harder."

"Just watch your back," Diana said, sounding worried. "Even Colleen Silverstone and Grayson Wolf can make mistakes, too."

"I hear that," Wolf quipped. "Good thing that I have Diana Cruz running this operation in case the Grim catches up with me ... I'll go see if Colleen's found anything useful and after that, I and guest have been invited to lunch at Jeff Kramm's villa. His way of asking for a progress report about what I've discovered to date about the sex change industry."

"You ought to send the man a bill when you're done working for him, because it's the only way you'll ever get paid," Diana said.

"We'll see...he might surprise us yet...later alligator," Wolf said.

Chapter 20

Here A Clue, There A Clue...

"Nothing and less than nothing," Colleen complained, when Wolf asked if she had discovered anything from his case files. "I've studied the photos, but no one stands out as having either sufficient motive, moxie or the connections required to order a series of sophisticated murders, recruit muscle to kidnap and attack targets all while maintaining their anonymity."

"Then it has to be someone remotely connected to Bellamy and his company," Wolf said. "Someone critical to the decades-long stunning success of the New World Fund."

"Well unless it's God providing the insider information, Bellamy had to have bribed insiders from a couple hundred startups and corporations for that damned fund to have made sky-high returns from industries across the board for over a decade," Colleen replied, frustrated. "The FBI and the SEC have been investigating Bellamy and New World since its inception and never found even *one* insider providing information."

"When only the impossible remains, the impossible becomes the possible," Wolf said. Colleen shot him an exasperated look and he continued. "Bellamy's stellar returns comes from hundreds of diverse companies, but no evidence exists of insiders providing critical information to fuel that success. Therefore it is *one source* with access to hundreds of companies supplying the information to enable New World Fund to secure sky-high returns year after year."

Colleen stared at Wolf, obviously digesting his observation.

"A major consulting firm? Major financial bank?" she hypothesized. "More likely a small cadre that, when you add them together, blanket the major business and developmental centers across the country."

"Now all we need to do is identify these evil actors, hunt them down and kick their collective asses," Wolf teased. "Seriously, though, it's worth tasking Cooper and Brett to get one of their people to do such a search."

"Agreed," Colleen said. "Did I hear you say something about being invited to lunch when you came in?"

"Yes; we're invited to break bread with Jeffrey Kramm," Wolf said, letting the name sink in.

Colleen shot him an incredulous look. "Jeff Kramm of *The Washington Progressive* invited you to lunch? Is he sponsoring a masochist event and you're the sadist special?"

Wolf laughed. "Jeff and I are good friends."

"You're punking me, aren't you?" Colleen shot back. "I recall you saying something about his daughter's suicide being part of your gender change investigation, not that you're working for him."

"Calm yourself woman," Wolf intoned. "I'll tell you all about it as you follow me upstairs and we get ready to go."

Wolf had no trouble being admitted through Kramm's gated entrance and past the home's armed security. Observing the respectful and deferential manner the paladins treated his companion, they knew who Colleen was. When she complimented them on their proficient inspection, the guards smiled and thanked Colleen, though Wolf suspected their gratitude had more to do with feeling relief than approval. A domestic escorted them to one of the informal dining rooms in the Kramm mansion where they were met by their host and hostess.

"Nice to see you again, Mr. Wolf. Thank you for coming," Kramm said, adding as he glanced at Colleen, "A pleasure to meet you, Ms. Silverstone."

"Thank you, Mr. Kramm," Colleen replied.

Kramm smiled and introduced his spouse.

"So nice of you to join us," Ms. Kramm said, her comment directed at both of her guests. She glanced toward the table. "Shall we?"

Appetizers were served, followed by the main meal. Small talk dominated the luncheon, the unspoken rule apparently being to avoid potential unpleasant references until sometime after the meal. Leaving the dining room behind, Kramm led the party to the comfortable sitting room. The fireplace was lit, the blaze filling the space with radiant warmth and a golden glow.

Sundry drinks were served, Wolf selecting a full bodied, Spanish sherry. Kramm raised his glass and said,

"To out lovely guests." They all took a sip of their drinks. Kramm looked expectantly at Wolf.

Wolf provided a summary of what his investigation had discovered. When he identified the three victims of the murderer, Kramm's unchanging expression suggested the media mogul had been informed about their deaths. That struck Wolf as rather suspicious, thinking that Kramm would have much bigger things on his mind than three unrelated deaths. The man must have caught something in Wolf's demeanor because a knowing smile touched his lips.

"I know about the victims because I have contacts who keep me abreast of your movements pursuant to your investigation," Kramm said.

"Gee, that's not worrisome at all," Wolf quipped.

"I'm not having you followed or tracked," Kramm assured him. "I know what you are investigating and simply have my people inquire about whom you questioned and so forth. What I've learned is that you've managed to discover that three supposed accidents were in fact murders and that you believe them to be the work of some super smart hacker causing equipment to malfunction. Any clue who that killer might be?"

"No clue at this time," Wolf said, choosing not to reveal the information about drones that Brett discovered. "We believe that the killer might have had someone close to him befall something similar to what happened to your daughter and is going after the people and organization he feels responsible."

"By 'we': are you helping Mr. Wolf in this investigation, Ms. Silverstone?" Kramm asked.

"Only tangentially," Colleen replied. "Actually, Mr. Wolf is assisting me with an investigation that I need his help with."

"The murders of Justin Bellamy and Madeline Talbot," Kramm said.

"I'm not at liberty to disclose the nature of my investigation," Colleen said, smiling amiably.

"Of course; I understand," Kramm said. Glancing at Wolf, he said, "Is there anything else you've uncovered about the Boston Affirmative Transformation Treatment Center that is pertinent to Stephanie's depression and her decision to end her life?"

"Just that Stephanie's situation, meaning her decision to change her sex, is a booming business," Wolf replied. "Based on the data, the number of young people, mostly women, choosing to transform into males has been growing significantly over the past five years and so have complaints, regrets and suicides."

"Could the killer of these people you've mentioned possibly be someone who herself has undergone a sex change and angry about doing so?" Ms. Kramm asked.

"That certainly is a possibility, Ms. Kramm," Wolf said. "Having looked into the sex change industry, there's lots to be angry about. It's one thing to recognize that a tiny percentage of individuals were genuinely born into the wrong sex—gender dysphoria—and to be able to provide appropriate intervention to help correct nature's error. It is an entirely different matter to inflate and promote such a condition for purely personal and monetary gain. A fourteen year old who asserts they are transgender has his or her stated identity immediately recognized and offered 'affirmative care' by the medical community. Could you imagine the medical community embracing other social contagions such as cutting and bulimia with open arms? Campus counselors, like Heather Franken of Ivygreen, happily refer students to clinics, including Planned Parenthood, dispensing testosterone to young women without any psychological evaluation on their first visit. Social media is filled with mentors who cheerfully discuss their own physical transformation and encourage viewers to do likewise. Transgenderism overwhelmingly effects girls and has become so prevalent that a university researcher has identified the fad as Rapid Onset Gender Dysphoria. And I don't need to tell you about all the negative side effects of anxious, confused young people rushing to make permanent physical changes."

Kramm nodded. "We know it all too well, I'm sad to say."

A thought struck Wolf. "Mr. Kramm, do you recall if Stephanie had a boyfriend at Ivygreen? Or perhaps a close friend who might have chosen a physical transformation? Someone who was very close to her who might be quite upset about what happened to her?"

Both Mr. Kramm and Ms. Kramm looked thoughtful for a moment.

"She used to talk about a boy she was fond of during her Freshman year, um, Dan, or Stan Mayor, Myer perhaps," Kramm said. "Stephanie said very little about her life at Ivygreen once she came back home and as I said when you came here the first time, she destroyed everything: yearbook, photos, letters, emails, social media accounts…"

"Dan or Stan Mayor or Myer; that's more than we had before," Wolf said. "I'll have my technicians see what they can glean from the Ivygreen website; we should be able to find this boyfriend easily enough."

They thanked the Kramms for lunch and got back on the road. Wolf contacted Brett instructing him to track down Stephanie Kramm's former boyfriend when he had a spare moment.

"If this boyfriend exists, Brett shouldn't have too much trouble finding him," Wolf said, on his way to the Washington Beltway. "He'll be able to give us a clearer picture of Stephanie while at the college and also give us names of her friends at the time."

"What about talking to her professors and academic counselor?" Colleen said. "They should be able to give you another perspective about the girl."

Wolf shot her a clueless look. "How could I have missed something so obvious? Oh, I know: because I've been spending my time with the bride of doom being chased, shot at, crashing planes and being smuggled across national borders."

Colleen's laughter filled the car. It had an authentic quality of appreciation and he very much enjoyed hearing it.

"Bride of doom. That will go to the top of my list of personal descriptions," she said.

"I bet it's a long list," Wolf teased.

"It is," she confirmed, looking smug. "I consider it a measure of personal success and pride to have such a colorful and diverse collection of reactions and portrayals from those whom I encounter."

"In that case, I claim that I am far more successful and prouder than you are," Wolf said. "Furthermore, I'll bet you that the descriptions in my list are far more colorful that the ones in yours."

"Considering that several on your list came from me, I am inclined to believe you and yield my crown to you," Colleen said.

Wolf was nearing the Beltway when he was cut off by a truck that entered the road from a driveway. He issued a derisive snort.

"My nemesis strikes again! Those damn Shred Pro trucks never fail to impede my way," he complained. "Seems like four out of five morning on my way to the gym a Shred Pro truck gets in front of me and we put along for a mile. They're everywhere and they all get in my way!"

"They're everywhere..." Colleen said.

"Yes, everywhere; I run into them in Boston, in Manhattan, in DC and right here in Potomac," Wolf complained.

"Wolf."

The sound of Colleen's voice made him turn his head toward her. "What's wrong?"

"Wolf...they're everywhere: Boston, New York, DC, Virginia and in Potomac," Colleen said. "I'm sure that I spotted several Shred Pro truck photos in your files."

"That's a very thin thread," he replied. "UPS and FedEx trucks are everywhere, too. I'm not bothered by them much because their drivers are in a hurry to get where're they're going."

"I agree, but what else do we have?" Colleen said. "If you'll allow me, I want to conduct an image search through your computer database and see if more crop up. I'm grasping at straws, but at least I've got a damned straw." She lifted her phone and did a Google search for Shred Pro. "Wolf: during your investigations, did you ever meet or hear about Troy and Rebecca Searles?"

"I can't recall," he said, passing yet another Shred Pro truck on the Beltway. "Did you get their names from my files?"

"Unfortunately not," she replied. "I'm on Shred Pro's website. They own the company ... I'm texting you their photos; if you ever saw them in the past you might recognize them ... I'm going to call Cooper and have him dig into the whole lot."

Wolf's phone dinged indicating an incoming text. Using voice command the photos Colleen sent appeared on the dash monitor. He glanced briefly at the faces.

"Based on a glimpse I don't recall seeing either one at any function where I was present," Wolf said. "If they are connected to Bellamy in some way, I bet Barry would know."

"I've texted it to his phone, answering service and his private line at the law firm," Colleen said. "But considering Barry is on the run and hiding somewhere, the chance of him touching anything electronic is nil."

"I've asked this before, but you have no clue at all where Barry went to ground?" Wolf said.

"Having reviewed your files, I've learned that you know far more about Barry than I do," she replied. "We barely speak to each other and rarely meet. Ironically your book actually brought us closer together and by closer, I mean we talk a couple extra times than normally. Except for the little house on the prairie, I have no knowledge of other Barry hideouts ... hmm."

"What?" Wolf said, hearing the shift of tone in her voice.

"I think Barry might have flown out of the country," she said. "He's got connections everywhere; he could be in Brazil, Spain even Israel."

Wolf was about to ask Colleen how a wanted fugitive could leave the country, but realized how ridiculous he'd sound. Just two days ago he and Collen were smuggled into the US from Canada. If he'd learned anything over the past dozen years immersing himself into the underbelly of the rich and famous is that money can buy anything.

"I know what you're thinking," Colleen continued. "But thanks to our brouhaha at the NYPD, Barry's status has been downgraded from prime suspect of Bellamy's murder to person of interest. He could have come out of hiding and be legally flying to Timbuktu as we speak."

"You're right," Wolf said. "If we're lucky he'll check his messages and get back with an answer about the photos. Right now I'm more interested about Brett's text regarding Stephanie's boyfriend."

"May I ask why you're doing this?" Colleen said. "Kramm's got a media empire at his fingertips and instead of having his people looking into his daughter's suicide he's recruited Grayson Wolf to do his bidding and do it for gratis. I might suspect that your retirement claim is just a smokescreen to put the evildoers at ease so that you can stalk them and pounce when ready to devour them."

Wolf made a deep growling sound. "Once a predator always a predator. Pursuant to our class action against the universities, looking into Stephanie's suicide after two years at Ivygreen was a no brainer. I knew about the transgender popularity on campuses and Kramm's invitation just gave me a push. What I didn't expect to find was a computer-hacking serial killer and the Wolf hunt was on."

When Colleen issued a chuckle, he asked her what was funny about what he had said.

"I was about to wax on about the danger of you hunting down a killer," she replied, shooting him an ironic glance.

Wolf grinned knowingly. "As opposed to the safety of hanging around with the head of the leading security firm."

"No moss growing on you," Colleen quipped.

"Good to know you recognize my natural genius," Wolf retorted. He drove into the underground garage of The Patrick Henry Building. "Let's go see what Brett has to tell us about Stephanie's college boyfriend."

Brett waved them over to his office, a wild exaggeration for the collection of electronic equipment, monitors, tables and seats crowded into the far corner of the room. An enigmatic smile played on his lips.

"His name is Stanley Meyers," he began. "Graduated from Ivygreen three years ago. Did a Masters at MIT. Lives in Albany, New York. Currently working as an independent contractor."

Colleen glanced at Wolf who in turn shot Brett a long suffering look and said,

"And what is the big reveal waiting behind that smug grin itching to spill forth?"

"Only that Mr. Meyers has a computer science undergrad degree, a masters in software engineering, that he runs his own business where he sets his own hours and gets to travel here and there as needed," Brett said, all in one breath. "Not that any of that—and having been Stephanie's boyfriend—would make him any kind of viable suspect as a hacking mass murderer."

"If you worked for me, Brett, I might think you are one sarcastic wiseass," Colleen joked.

Brett shot Wolf a rebellious look. "How come you never give me compliments like that?"

"No problem, Mr. Sarcastic Wiseass," Wolf retorted. "From now on, in-your-face compliments only. I'll give your bonuses to our social fund."

"Just remember I know where you live," Brett rejoined.

"*Everyone* knows where I live," Wolf said. "Shoot Meyer's info over to RJ and ask him to make an appointment at the end of the week or early next week."

"Done," Brett said. "And that's why I always get the bonuses."

"Any news from Juan?" Wolf asked.

"Just that he got to LA," Brett replied. "And that Teena has hired additional muscle to keep our people safe from the rabble."

"Good thing you're not there," Colleen teased. "The rabble would make mincemeat out of Grayson Wolf."

"They wouldn't dare lay a finger on me," he replied. "Wolves are a protected species in California."

"Clearly Teena is concerned about the rabble turning our legal eagles into mincemeat," Brett said. "Considering the potential settlement the state might wind up shelling out for their failure to provide a safe environment on campus for anyone daring to offer un PC views, it's gonna rile up the leadership and its foot soldiers."

"From what I understand, the possible settlement might exceed five billion dollars," Colleen said.

"We have over twenty-five hundred signatories from California's twenty-three state colleges," Wolf confirmed. "The suit will be ten times that amount which is a much needed symbolic two-by-four smack on the faces of the college administration. The final award will be closer to five billion or even less. Whatever the final figure, these colleges are going to be held accountable to ensure equal protection and freedom of speech for every student from now on unless they want to drain the state treasury."

"That's just the state colleges," Brett said. "There's over seven hundred higher ed institutions in the state. We've got another hundred in our sights."

"And that's just California," Wolf said, ominously. "We are going to teach colleges across the nation a civics lesson they will never forget. There's nothing like a financial hanging to get their undivided attention."

Chapter 21

West Coast, East Coast

If Juan Mendez was hoping to exit the LA airport unnoticed, he was quickly disabused of that wish. Juan's legal broadside against a thousand colleges and universities across the nation was the equivalent of Patrick Henry's liberty or death, the shot heard around the world and Bunker Hill all rolled into one. Thanks to Teena Sanoe's foresight, no fewer than four bodyguards were at hand to escort him through the media gauntlet and into a waiting SUV with tinted windows.

Since the previous summer, Juan and his CIR attorneys had been busy identifying public and private colleges whose policies created an unequal and hostile learning environment for students expressing views and opinions that clashed with the political and cultural biases of the administration. This yeoman's task was quickly accomplished by members of Students for Individual Rights located on most college campuses who identified specific abuses and also gathered names and contact information for students who felt victimized by a policy of pervasive and systematic unequal treatment.

Juan had planned a two-prong strategy which he hoped would provide both initial success and a stream of revenue needed to launch the series of class action cases across the nation. The first prong of his plan was proceeding better than expected as a string of private universities beginning with Ivygreen opted to engage in separate negotiation to settle student complaints outside of court. Six colleges had agreed to pay a total of two hundred and fourteen million and make policy changes that ensured equal treatment for all students. As agreed, CIR received thirty percent of the settlement amount, eight hundred seventy plaintiffs receiving an equal share of the balance amounting to $165,000 each. When added to the twenty million dollar legal war chest, CIR's share of over sixty million dollars would enable Juan to go up against a sizable adversary such as the California Higher Education Commission.

Preferring to stay close to the airport, Jewel King, CIR's Events and Scheduling manager, had made all necessary arrangements at the Los Angeles Airport Marriott, a team composed of over a dozen attorneys and paralegals received Juan in a dedicated conference room.

Waving a warm greeting, Juan, as was his habit, got right to the business at hand.

"Shortly before arriving, I received a call from the lead attorney for the defendants offering an out of court settlement amount of seven hundred million and all the changes we demand." He paused, then peered at the group. "That amounts to about one $190,000 each for our two thousand seventy defendants and around two hundred ten million for CIR. As you know, we are obligated to inform our clients about the proposal: will we encourage them to accept or reject it?"

"Reject it. Collectively, the California colleges are among the leading proponents of PC," one of the attorneys said. "Administrators in every one of their twenty three colleges have acted for years with impunity failing to protect the right of every student to express their views without being subjected to mob retribution in dorms, classrooms, on social media, accosted and threatened while walking across campus."

"Turning down the equivalent of a full free ride for four years of college for possibly less in a court settlement solely to shine a light on years of abuse might be a hard sell," Terrance said.

"Then we appeal to their sense of justice and personal integrity," another attorney said. "You gonna let them buy your silence? Let them hide in their ivory tower and get away with their misdeeds? I think we can convince a majority to reject the offer and go to trial."

"Is everyone in agreement with rejecting the offer?" Juan asked. All heads nodded in agreement. "Let's contact our clients, lay out the settlement offer and ask them to reject it based on a list of reasons. Instruct them that we need their reply by Friday, five PM."

Typically communication with, and responses by, clients in class action cases can take weeks. But Juan had structured the client agreement to facilitate a rapid response to contact by the attorneys. With text, email, messenger or other preferred rapid method of contact, giving the student of the class action forty eight hours to respond was plenty of time. All that was needed was for a simple majority of the two thousand seventy clients to respond in time, for a majority of respondents to agree with the attorneys' recommendation and the decision was made.

*   *   *   *

A few minutes after ten thirty the following morning, the plane carrying Wolf arrived in Albany, New York. RJ had arranged an appointment with Stephanie Kramm's college boyfriend, Stanley Meyers and Jewel made the travel arrangements. Colleen had originally planned to accompany him, but business called her back to Colorado. Upon her insistence, she provided a personal bodyguard to take her place, overriding Wolf's objections, saying she'd be distraught if her comic sidekick got whacked. Wolf retorted by saying he loved her, too.

Meyers' office was a fifteen minute ride downtown, Marci the bodyguard taking the wheel. Wolf knew that Colleen had purposefully selected one of her female security personnel as payback for his, love you too, tease. Upon reflection, however, having a woman instead of a man accompanying him to a meeting with a potential serial killer could work to his advantage. On the elevator ride up to Meyers' floor, Wolf explained his charade asking the guard to play along.

"Thank you for meeting me, Mr. Meyers," Wolf said. "This is Marci; we're on our way to Niagara Falls and you being on the way was very convenient."

A sudden change of Meyers' expression informed Wolf that the man must have realized who had an appointment with him and it was not a Mr. Grayson, but the infamous Grayson Wolf. Wolf had worked hard over the years to keep his face out of the public eye, but our electronic age where every man, woman and child possessed a phone, avoiding being photographed by a phone camera was nearly impossible.

"Um, please come in, Mr. Wolf," Meyers said. He pointed at some chairs. "How may I help you?"

"I understand you were friendly with Stephanie Kramm back in college," Wolf said, taking a seat. Marci remaining standing behind him. "You are no doubt aware that she took her own life last fall."

Meyers nodded. "Sure. Was big news." His eyes got bigger and he said, "Was it not suicide? Are you investigating a murder?"

"It was ruled a suicide," Wolf confirmed. "I'm doing research for future Tara Mason mystery books and was given permission by her father to look into her past, speak with people who knew her and so on. I thought you would be able to shed some light into what Stephanie was like before she, um, changed. I'm more than willing to pay for your time."

"Happy to tell you what I know, Mr. Wolf. No payment necessary," Meyers replied.

"Thank you," Wolf said. "When did you first start dating Stephanie?"

"I met her in the fall of my Freshman year, but we didn't start dating until the following spring," he said. "Stephanie was smart, beautiful, funny; she was perfect. I was in love and more every day; she loved me, too. By summer we were talking about getting married..."

"What happened?" Wolf asked.

Meyers' face transformed from its golden glow to one of loathing. "The coven of witches happened. They were a self-appointed transgender avantgarde, going on endlessly about how femininity was a cry for help, that many women were suppressing the fact that they were really men born in the wrong body, on and on. One of them was Stephanie's roommate and she targeted Stephanie, constantly badgering her about being a man, covering up her true self, stuff like that."

"What do you mean, targeted Stephanie?" Wolf asked.

"Stephanie was popular, really smart, and nonjudgmental. Too nonjudgmental and a too willing to give people the benefit of the doubt," Meyers said. "Her roommate was like her evil twin: scheming, nasty, ugly piercings on her face, always complaining about how unfair everything was. Anyway, she just kept on Stephanie, slowly poisoning her mind and getting her to attend their transgender bitch-sessions. I tried to talk to Stephanie, tell her to get away from them, that they were toxic, but she started to defend them and said I was trying to keep her from changing to her real self...anyway, by that November she broke up with me. Later she had a sex change and after the next summer I never saw Stephanie, or Stephen as she called herself, again. Those bitches ruined her life and are responsible for her death—oh, and here's the best part: none of those transgender assholes ever changed their sex. I guess they saw what it did to Stephanie."

"Were you aware of anyone that felt hostility toward them or expressing hostility toward doctors or organizations involved with Stephanie's sexual transformation?" Wolf asked.

"I felt lots of hostility toward the whole bunch; still do" Meyers growled. "I'm sure others felt the same, but people kept their mouths shut if they didn't want to be ostracized. This is Ivygreen College we're talking about; the progressive nirvana of the east. I heard it's gotten a lot worse since I graduated three years ago."

"Do you remember the name of Stephanie's roommate?" Wolf asked.

Meyers scrunched up his face in thought. "Erin ... Shift or Shaft; something like that, though shaft would be the most appropriate name for that nasty bitch."

"Thank you for your time, Mr. Meyers; I very much appreciate all your assistance," Wolf said, rising from his seat.

"I wish I could tell you more," he replied. He looked pointedly at Wolf and said, "I know a little about how you operate, Mr. Wolf. Please tell me you're really investigating the reasons behind Stephanie's suicide."

A grin touched Wolf's lips. "I can't confirm anything...but I can tell you that I'm always in an investigative mode ... thanks again."

"Expose these people, Mr. Wolf. Put their names in bold letters on your organization's website," he replied. "Oh...wait a second..." Meyers walked over to a bookshelf and returned with a leather-bound book. He flipped through the pages until her found what he was looking for. "Here she is... Erin Sheff. That's Stephanie's roommate."

He handed the yearbook to Wolf. Looking at her photo, Meyers description of the "nasty bitch" had been amazingly accurate. Looking at her sullen face with its multiple piercings, adorned with dark eyeshadow and black lipstick, one could easily imagine her to be something out of JRR Tolkien's land of Mordor.

"Lovely," Wolf said. He brought forth his phone and took several snapshots of the page.

"Piece of work, that's for sure," Meyers said. "That photo was taken on one of her best days. You see her, be sure to get a total body scrub down from the nearest Center for Disease Control."

Wolf grinned and said, "I have lots of experience with protecting myself after mucking around disease ridden quarters for many years."

"It's a pleasure meeting you, Mr. Wolf," Meyers said, shaking his hand. "Please let me know what you find, if you would."

"I will. Thank you and have a productive New Year."

Out in the hallway Wolf uploaded the photo to Brett and by the time he got into the car, Brett had already located Erin Sheff.

"These days she goes by the name of Madrigal," Brett said. "Just one name and no mister or mizz; just Madrigal. She runs an art studio called Trans Art outside of Boston and lives there, too. I've already texted her address."

"Thanks Brett," Wolf said. "Do me a favor and dig into her past. She was Stephanie Kramm's roommate and according to Stanley Meyers, responsible for encouraging Stephanie to change her sex."

"Already on it," Brett replied. "You should have some dirt before the end of the day."

"Marci, you up to driving to Boston?" Wolf asked.

"Absolutely, Mr. Wolf," the bodyguard confirmed.

"Great; let's get some lunch first and then hit the road. I'll make reservations at the Royal Sonesta...any problem sleeping with me?"

Marci shot him a humorous glance. "Ms. Silverstone warned me about you're tendency to tease and said to call your bluff." She peered suggestively at him for a moment, then added, "What's it going to be, Mr. Wolf? Are we shacking up or do I have to find other entertainment for tonight?"

Wolf laughed. "I'll make sure your room has all the required amenities to ensure a successful evening of alternative entertainment."

Marci grinned and drove the car out of the parking lot and onto the street heading for a local restaurant. Forty minutes later they were on the Interstate heading for Boston. Somewhere past Springfield, Wolf's phone warbled, indicating a call from Brett.

"Got something? Wolf said, taking the call. "You're on speaker."

"I've been digging through magical Madrigal's history and what I found is interesting, to say the least," Brett replied. "I've uploaded summary details, but thought a live update would help you take your mind off that hot bodyguard your spending all that time with."

Wolf shot a glance over at Marci, who kept her eyes on the road ahead, though he did spot her lips twitch.

"You do realize that you are living in the #Me-Too age and referring to women as hot might deflate their delicate ego and make them feel like they're back in the days of Kinder, Küche und Kirche," Wolf replied.

"Exactly where they should be," Brett retorted.

"Marci looks like she'd love to have a private conversation with you about your enlightened views about a woman's place in the world," Wolf laughed.

Brett's chortle sounded in the car. "I'd be delighted to have a private conversation with Marci. How's this weekend?"

"I'll let the two of you work out the details on your own time," Wolf said, grinning at the woman. "What's the scoop on Sheff?"

"The name Heather Franken ring a bell?" Brett said. "The counseling department at Ivygreen has a junior counselor program where students volunteer to listen to problems and encourage their peers to seek counseling. It's supposed to reduce meltdowns, panic over tests, boyfriend/girlfriend drama, and so forth. Sheff was a junior counselor for her floor at the dorm under the supervision of Franken."

"That's interesting," Wolf said. "It could give Sheff a greater level of influence—for better or worse. Meyers was quite clear Sheff was targeting Stephanie because she was everything that Sheff wasn't. But there's more, isn't there?"

"I guess the sages were right when they said that familiarity breeds people who take others for granted," Brett said. "To maintain a shred of mystery, I'll let you discover that very juicy bit of 'more' by perusing the Sheff dossier I sent you. Chao, baby!"

He heard Marci issuing a snort and asked her what that was for.

"Brett must be very good at what he does to get away with blowing off the man paying his salary," she explained.

"It's more a matter of Brett knowing where all my bodies are buried," Wolf joked. "Besides that, he is among the best. The only person with more skill that I know of is Cooper and Colleen would never let him go ... how did you wind up working for Colleen?"

"Like many of my colleagues, I was recruited directly by Ms. Silverstone shortly before my military term of service was up two years ago," Marci said. "I had been thinking about applying for the FBI, but didn't like what I was hearing about the agency and found SSIS to be a better fit. Considering all the crap about the FBI that's become public recently, I definitely made the right choice."

"I know you did," Wolf said.

They spent the rest of the ride in silence, Marci focusing on driving and keeping an eye out for possible threats and Wolf reading through Erin Sheff's history that Brett had sent. There was a lot about the woman's relationships (a bisexual extravaganza), her activism (including being arrested for destruction of property and making verbal threats) all of which tapered off significantly once she began college, her vocal support of transgender issues taking precedence.

Near the end of the dossier, Wolf finally discovered that promised 'juicy bit' of information Brett had alluded to. He couldn't wait to meet Madrigal and use it as cudgel if required to ensure her cooperation.

It was too late to visit Madrigal's studio and after talking with Diana about CIR business and getting the latest about the status of Juan's progress in LA, Wolf decided to call Colleen next. Expecting a sardonic reception, he was surprised when she said,

"It's nice to hear your voice."

Taken aback by her sincere tone, he became immediately suspicious. Was she toying with him, her way of turning the tables for all the times he made vaguely suggestive remarks? Or more ominously, was she in trouble and this was her way of tipping him off?

"Are you still there?" Colleen said.

"Yes," he hurriedly replied, realizing he hadn't responded. "What's with the happy talk? If I recall, hearing my voice tends to raise your blood pressure." Great, he thought. That doesn't sound suggestive at all.

"Thanks for reminding me," she replied, her tone businesslike. "How is your investigation going? Did you meet with Stephanie's old boyfriend and what have you discovered?"

Wolf immediately regretted his comments. He knew from her change in tone he had missed a rare opportunity to begin a conversation with Colleen the woman and not business CEO. His tendency to issue retorts and engage in repartee was a strategy designed to keep women at arm's length, a crucial requirement for being a successful operative scrounging around the underbelly of upper society largely unnoticed. In the bright light of day as himself, that automatic habit worked just as effectively to deter women from discovering the man behind the operative.

It occurred to Wolf that Colleen, too, must struggle with balancing her professional and personal life and that the role most frequently employed would tend to dominate over the other. He updated Colleen about his meeting with Meyers and the upcoming visit to Stephanie Kramm's old college roommate tomorrow. She gave him a quick sketch of the backlog of projects and meetings that had piled up since that call from her stepfather to meet at Baltimore back in December.

Their professional updates over, Wolf was about to wish her a good evening when he said instead,

"Colleen, would you like to go to dinner with me this Saturday?"

There was a monetary pause. "Yes," she said.

"I'll pick you up at your place at seven...good night, Colleen."

"Good night, Wolf."

Madrigal's art studio was sandwiched between a dry cleaner and Tai takeout on Forest Ave in Bedford, a few miles north of Boston. There was no parking along the street and Marci pulled into the local theater's lot a few building up.

Approaching the studio's entrance, Wolf's hand reached for the door when Marci stopped him, opening the door first.

"Never know what surprises one will find on the other side," she said.

The aroma of paint hung in the air as Wolf entered the interior lit by spotlights aimed at strategic areas where people were busy applying smears of color on large canvases. No one noticed them walk through the studio.

"Seriously?" Marci said, looking askance at the various artistic expressions on canvas.

"Art is in the eye of the beholder," Wolf taunted.

"In that case, better to be blind," Marci retorted. "...Ms. Madrigal up ahead."

Wolf and Marci approached a group of women peering at what appeared to be a large pile of dirty rags, pierced with various sized angular planks, each piece splattered with dull, earth-toned paint capped with iridescent red. Wolf easily recognized the studio's owner who apparently added tattoos crawling up from her neck since her days at college.

"Good morning, Ms. Sheff," he said, purposefully using her given name.

"It's Madrigal," she replied. "What do you want?"

"A few moments of your time," Wolf replied. "I'm inquiring about a friend of yours back in college: Stephanie Kramm."

"Sorry, but I'm busy with students."

"I can come back during lunch," Wolf said, pleased to see that the woman didn't recognize him.

"Sorry, but I'm swamped getting ready for our art show."

"I see," Wolf said, faking regret. "I'll inform Mr. Kramm about your connection with ATTC and let the paint splatter where it may."

Madrigal's face became very still. Wolf could see his comment had the expected impact and he counted the seconds until—

"Let's talk in the back." Entering a cluttered room doubling as an office, she said, "What do you want to know?"

Wolf found it interesting that she didn't bother to ask who he or his associate was. Probably assumed they were private investigators or perhaps journalists.

"Are you aware that Stephanie Kramm committed suicide last October?" Wolf asked.

"Read something about that."

"We've been told that you were instrumental in Stephanie's sexual transformation," he said.

Madrigal's disagreeable expression deepened. "Stephen. Allst I did was to help him discover who he really was."

"For a fee," Wolf said.

"I've got nothing to do with his suicide," she said.

"Stanley Meyers, her college boyfriend, would dispute that," Wolf countered. "He said that you badgered Stephanie from the first day you were roommates, getting her to attend your transgender group, working on her self-image, the lot of you trying to convince her that she was really a man under her beautiful feminine form. That you hooked her up with Heather Franken, the Ivygreen's gender bender counselor, who was paid a handsome stipend for referring potential clients to the Affirmative Transformation Treatment Center in Watertown."

"It was never about the money," she retorted. "There are lots of women and men who are born the wrong sex. I was helping them to see that they could change and live a happy, normal life."

"I'm all for living a happy, normal life," Wolf replied. He was tempted to joke that he changed his sex three times, but said instead, "How come you and none of your fourteen member transgender advocacy group ever changed their sex. Surely advocates of gender change would be on the forefront of making such a transformation to a happier, normal life? But not one of you did. Why?"

Madrigal's eyes looked everywhere but at Wolf. He gazed up at Marci who was standing guard at the door, the woman giving him a disgusted look. Wolf continued.

"Did you know that Heather Franken was murdered a few weeks ago?"

Madrigal's head shot up. "Murdered? Who did it? Why?"

"Did you know that LeeAnn Hicks, a ATTC sex change surgeon was murdered shortly before Franken?"

Madrigal eyes got larger. "What...?"

"Did you know that Joseph Ferrara, the founder of ATTC, was burned to death in his home shortly after Hicks was murdered?"

A look of panic appeared on Madrigal's face and she backed away from Wolf, bumping into the cluttered piled along the wall.

"Who are you? Did you kill them!?"

"Relax; neither of us is the Angel of Death," Wolf said. "I can understand your concern, however. There is a serial killer on the loose getting even with people connected to ATTC. The reason I'm here is to find out who that person, or persons, might be. Is there anyone you can think of that might be angry at ATTC and their associates? Angry enough to have killed three people and most likely will kill more."

A clearly frightened Madrigal appeared to be racking her brain trying to think of possible suspects. Wolf watched as her eyes darted here and there as she sifted through her collection of names from the past.

"Jessica Demming," she said, suddenly. "Jessica was in our group and during her senior year she got a bunch of hate mail. We always got hate mail, notes under our doors, undisclosed emails, calling us names and such. Hers were really vile, saying she should kill herself, she was evil and so forth. That's the only name I can think of that might have anything to tell you."

"Do you have contact info for Jessica?" Wolf asked.

"Nah. After graduation we all went our own way," Madrigal said. "Some of us stayed in contact for a year, maybe. Haven't heard from any of the group for at least four years. I do know that Jessica came from out west; Iowa maybe? You won't tell Kramm about my, um, past connections?"

"No reason to do so," Wolf said. "Do remember that a serial killer is out there getting even with people who the killer feels responsible for harming someone close to them. Make sure you double lock your door, check your car before getting in, and I wouldn't trust everything that is sent to you electronically. This serial killer has killed people hacking their cars and homes, too. Take care."

"You really laid it on thick back there, Mr. Wolf," Marci said, upon leaving the studio. "That woman is going to be paranoid twenty-four-seven."

"No more than she deserves," Wolf said, coldly. "Most likely Stephanie's suicide is not connected to this serial killer because if she was, Madrigal would be dead already considering her role in manipulating that poor girl into changing her sex. My hope is that she feels compelled to look over her shoulder for the next ten years."

"Not a fan of forgiveness I take it," Marci replied, grinning.

"A fan of justice: getting what one deserves," he replied.

"I'll be sure not to get on your bad list," Marci joked. "Where to now? Iowa?"

"Colorado for me," Wolf said. "Thank you for your excellent protection, Marci. Am I permitted to offer you a gratuity?"

"No sir," Marci replied. "Thank you; it's been interesting working with you, Mr. Wolf."

"Ditto," he said.

Marci drove out of the theater's parking lot and headed back to Boston.

Chapter 22

Victim Zero

The woman sure could take a man's breath away. Wolf gazed silently at his lovely date standing in the open doorway.

"Come in," Colleen said, the glint in her eyes communicating her triumph over a welcomed adversary.

It was the first time Wolf had entered her home and he scanned the area gathering whatever insight about Colleen he could glean from what most likely would be his one and only opportunity. He was familiar with Colleen's reclusive private life to safely assume that few people, especially men, were invited into her residence.

To be honest, the part about men not being invited was pure speculation—or was it hope—since compared to Wolf, very little was known about Colleen Silverstone's private life and even less about her romantic assignations. The woman, after all, had been a successful intelligence officer and would know better than almost anyone how to cover her tracks.

"Beautiful," Wolf said, gazing at the tasteful simplicity of the living room, though his assessment was mostly directed at Colleen.

"I'm glad you like it. Want to see the bedroom?"

She laughed gaily at his surprised expression.

Quickly recovering from being blindsided, he said, "Seen one bedroom, you've seen them all."

"May I inquire where you are taking me for dinner?" she asked.

"I was aiming for the diner down the street, but they were booked for the evening," Wolf teased. "Hungry?"

"Starved."

"Let's roll."

Exiting the building, Wolf escorted Colleen up to a waiting black Lincoln Navigator. A driver in evening attire stood by the opened rear passenger door.

Colleen stopped and faced Wolf. "You hired one of my security detail to escort us to dinner?"

Wolf grinned and said, "Carrying precious cargo, so I hired the best. Bullet proof panels, windows and a backup guard you see standing on the far side."

"Precious cargo," she deadpanned.

"You do know who I am, right?" Wolf said.

"The comic relief has returned," she said, and got into the vehicle.

Twelve minutes of inconsequential conversation later the vehicle came to a halt. Colleen looked out the window then over at Wolf who presented her with a pregnant smile.

"Nondescript, single story brick building," she stated. "Dinner in Denver's historic Five Points neighborhood. I'm intrigued."

Wolf took Colleen's hand and helped her out of the vehicle, the bodyguard shutting the door and following them to the building's entrance, which opened upon their approach.

"Good evening," a young woman said, smiling warmly. "I'm Emily, welcome to the Night Owl supper club."

Supper clubs were all the rage these days. Disconnected from a fixed location, top notch chefs were free to create one of a kind menus, experimenting with style and mood of the moment. This evening's event was also unique in that there were only two guests.

Gazing at each other across at a candle-lit table nestled in a low-lit corner of the room, Colleen took a sip of wine and said,

"Not many people surprise me these days; well done, sidekick."

"Thank you," Wolf said. "Considering how rusty I am at, ah, socializing, I admit to being surprised about surprising you. I must warn you, however, that I have no clue about the menu. When I arranged for this dinner, I said surprise us with something tasty; let's hope it'll be edible."

Dinner was a great success with every course, including the selection of scrumptious desserts, most edible indeed. Dinner conversation, however, was a bit more restrained on account that

Wolf—and perhaps Colleen, too—felt a certain awkwardness being together for the first time in a non-professional manner. They were not pursuing a killer through a forest, being accosted by a bear and jumping off a overhang into a swiftly moving stream. They were not interviewing suspects or being shot at while escaping across a frozen lake.

Looking at Colleen across the span of a dinner table, Wolf was not gazing into the dispassionate eyes of a dangerous operative, but the glowing eyes of a very beautiful woman. The contrast created an uncomfortable sense of disorientation and uncertainty.

"You grew up in New York," Wolf said.

"Yes; Upper east side, couple blocks from the UN," Colleen said. "I was three when my father died and five when mom married Barry and we came to live in New York."

"What made you pick Denver to establish SSIS?" Wolf asked.

"It's not New York and it's elven hundred miles from Barry," Colleen said, a smile playing on her lips. "Denver is an important military hub from which to recruit personnel. And it's physically beautiful—mountains, plains and clear skies."

"Did you like growing up in Manhattan?" Wolf asked.

"Not really; too restrictive," she replied. "It's easy to get around, though these days the subways are getting worse and the traffic, as you know, is insane. As is the cabal running the joint."

"New York has been a most fruitful boon to my career as national muckraker," Wolf said. "Half of my best selling exposes focus on the horde of scumbags infesting the city."

Colleen shot him a humorous look. "Yes, I know."

Wolf issued a knowing snort. Ten months ago, upon his first meeting with Colleen at her office, he had serious doubts whether he'd leave intact. Now she was actually smiling at the man who had singlehandedly publicly excoriated her stepfather in a bestselling novel-expose read by millions. What else might happen as the evening progressed?

Wolf stood up. "Let's powder our noses then proceed to our next mission."

Wolf's comment was a cryptic referral to Denver's foremost dance spot, The Mission Ballroom. Originally scheduled to be opened in the summer of 2019, the center was completed six months earlier with a grand opening on the last weekend of January. The Ballroom featured various stages, some that moved and shifted with a capacity for four thousand guests. The grand opening had been sold out for months but for the magic of on-line bidding, Wolf, who loved to dance, had secured a pair of tickets.

"This is an amazing place," Colleen said, gazing at the glittering expanse of interior space. "How did you know I enjoyed dancing?"

"I didn't," Wolf said. "I assumed anyone rubbing shoulders with the elite would most certainly be a proficient ballroom dancer."

"I am proficient," Colleen said. "It remains to be seen whether you are."

"Better tighten your nickers, baby," Wolf retorted.

"Baby?"

"That's right, honey," Wolf said, taking her by the arm and leading her to the dance floor.

After several Salsas, two Tangos, one Waltz and one Foxtrot, Colleen surrendered and the pair drifted over to the restaurant, managing to secure a small table as a couple were leaving. Wolf went for drinks, returning a few minutes later with a tray filled with a bottle of sparkling water, red wine and a large glass of beer.

Colleen reached over and took a large draught of Wolf's beer. Next, she filled a glass with bubbly water and drank it, then refilled it. Lastly she poured herself a glass of wine.

"Impressive," Wolf said, laughing.

"Thirsty," Colleen replied.

"I'd like the record to show that Colleen Silverstone threw in the towel first," Wolf said.

"I'd like the record to show that Grayson Wolf was keeping score while on a date," Colleen countered.

Until that moment, Wolf had been successfully evading thinking of being on a date. He was simply going to dinner with a friend and colleague with some dancing thrown in for good measure. It was an opportunity to get to know a little more about Colleen and definitely not a date.

Colleen's comment broke the illusion. He was on a date and enjoying her company immensely.

"Care for more gliding across the dance floor?"

"So you can show off again? I'll pass," Colleen said, giving him the stink eye. "I'm ready to go home...unless you had other plans?"

"Other plans?" Wolf said, his pulse quickening a notch.

"The entire evening's been one nice surprise after another. Just letting you know I'm open to any further surprises you had in mind," Colleen explained.

"Oh," Wolf said, feeling foolish. "Two surprises is all I could arrange."

"Home it is then," she said.

The security detail dropped their charges off in the lobby of Colleen's secure building and bid them good evening. Wolf accompanied Colleen up the elevator and to her door.

"Would you care to come in for a nightcap?" Colleen said.

"Thank you, but no," Wolf replied, matter-of-factly. "I've got an early flight out to Des Moines, Iowa then a drive north to Ames. Brett was able to track down one of the names Stephanie's former roommate remembered and I'm hoping her parents will be able to tell me where she's living now."

"I see," Colleen said. She held his gaze for a long moment, then said, "Thank you for dinner, dancing and all your surprises, Wolf. Please watch your back."

There followed the traditional pregnant pause as the boy said goodnight to the girl at her door after a date. Wolf smiled and said,

"Don't worry; what could possibly happen in Ames, Iowa? Thank you for a wonderful evening. Good night, Colleen."

He turned and walked back to the elevators, relieved that he didn't say, or do, something foolish. But his inner voice rose up and called him a chickenshit.

"Shut up," he said, to himself as he waited for the elevator to arrive. Over the years, a juxtaposition of Grayson Wolf and dating was a rare occurrence. His clandestine activities made avoiding romantic entanglements the most prudent choice, Wolf acting upon the maxim, when in doubt, get the hell out. It was hard to break old habits, especially in light of what happened to him last summer when he did enter the home of a woman.

Wolf had picked a Sunday in the expectation that he could catch Jessica's Demming's parents at home. He purposely waited until shortly after noon, guessing that if they attended church, they'd be home by now.

They weren't.

Probably at a restaurant, Wolf thought, and got back in the rental. He lowered the seatback to a more comfortable position for the duration. His thoughts returning to last evening, he lifted the phone and called Colleen. Disappointingly, her phone went to voice mail and he left her a brief message thanking her for a lovely evening and that he'd call again. He'd just ended the call when his phone warbled. Wolf issued a snort and said,

"Yes, RJ, I had a good time and no, RJ, I didn't sleep over."

"Well that's disappointing," RJ said. "But there was at least a satisfying kiss at the door, yes?"

"Don't you ever get tired of playing matchmaker?" Wolf countered.

"So, no kiss," RJ deadpanned. "I'll stop matchmaking when my oldest and bestest friend in the world finds true love and gets to enjoy romantic bliss."

Wolf was about to wax on about not wanting any romantic entanglements during the middle of murder investigations, but said instead,

"Perhaps you have forgotten that I'm the man who publicly keelhauled Colleen's father in my book? The fact she was even willing to accept an invitation to dinner was an important step. I like Colleen and don't plan to ruin our budding friendship by leaning in, if you get the picture."

"Faint heart never won fair maiden," RJ retorted. "But perhaps in your case, slow and steady wins the race."

"You are just full of aphorisms today, bro." Wolf said. Seeing a car pull into the Demming's driveway, he said goodbye and walked over to them.

Typically Wolf would introduce himself using a fictitious name to prevent his cover from being blown. But he was retired from that life and offered his full name.

It was a rare individual who, upon being introduced to Grayson Wolf, didn't know who he was. The Demmings were not among that small minority.

"A pleasure to meet you, Mr. Wolf," Mr. Demming said, surprised. He introduced his wife, Wolf offering words of greeting to both.

"Please come in, Mr. Wolf," Ms. Demming said. Once in the house, she offered him something to drink, which Wolf accepted.

"I apologize for troubling you on a Sunday afternoon," Wolf said. "I've come to ask about your daughter, Jessica. I'm doing some research for a friend and I was told that your daughter might be able to help me. I assume she's not living with you and I was hoping you could provide her contact information."

When both Demmings gave him the same unhappy look, Wolf braced himself for the worst.

"I'm afraid Jessica died last September," Mr. Demming said.

"I didn't know; please accept my deepest condolences," Wolf replied. "May I ask about the circumstances of her death?"

"Car accident," Mr. Demming said. "The police said she must have fallen asleep and her car veered off the road into a ravine."

"A ravine?" Wolf said, wondering were in Iowa there was anything higher than a mole hill and deeper than a roadside ditch.

Mr. Demming obviously understood his question and said,

"Jessica was living in Helena, Montana at the time."

"I see," Wolf said, remembering his own near-death experience being run off a Colorado road last spring. "I apologize again for bothering you and especially for being the cause of further pain pursuant to your daughter's untimely death."

The Demmings assured Wolf that they had come to accept Jessica's death.

"Truth be told, she was a difficult teenager, easily influenced by her peers and once she started college, she became even more distant," Ms. Demming said. "We miss our daughter, Mr. Wolf, but I'm afraid that Jessica was lost to us long before her death."

"She got into all that sex transfer stuff back in high school; said all the girls were into it," Mr. Deming added. "Please understand that we'd love our daughter no matter her sexual orientation, but those girls she was hanging with were toxic. By the time she graduated from high school, all she talked about was how she was really a boy, which was absurd if you knew Jessica. In college she got deeper and deeper into that group and the few times she came home she wasn't our daughter anymore. Or our son. She was a sullen, obnoxious brat. Sorry, but that's the truth."

Though Wolf knew none of the coven headed by Madrigal at Ivygreen physically changed their sex, it was clear that some, or perhaps all, experimented with male hormones. After all, the college had counselors dedicated to promoting gender change and one could walk into a local clinic to receive testosterone without a doctor's prescription or supervision. Obnoxious and sullen behavior were examples of a long list of potential side effects of testosterone hormone therapy.

Wolf assured the Demmings that he was familiar with the issues surrounding the sex change industry and that he understood their feelings. He thanked them again for their time, offered condolences once more and returned to his rental.

His first act was to book a flight to Helena for five that afternoon as well as reserving a room at the airport Marriott. Next he left a message on Brett's voicemail giving him a heads up about Jessica Demming's death and that he'd talk with him Monday morning. Then he got on the road back to Des Moines.

He hadn't got far when the phone rang. Touching the Bluetooth unit on his ear, Brett's voice came in crystal clear.

"Got you message, boss. What do you want me to do?"

"Brett, I think I've stumbled over victim zero—assuming Jessica didn't fall asleep at the wheel and drive off a cliff," Wolf said. "I'll be flying to Helena tonight and meet with local police tomorrow. I should learn more about her accident. That list of names of women in that Ivygreen gender advocacy group I sent: see if you can track them down. I want to know if any others have experienced accidental deaths."

"On it," Bret said. "Do I get my usual overtime rate?"

"Extra cup of coffee and two bagels? You got it," Wolf joked. "Might even spring for gourmet cream cheese if I get some hot news about any of those women."

"Damn! I'll work twice as hard," Brett replied.

By the time the call ended Wolf was nearing the airport. He checked in the rental and found a comfortable spot in an airport lounge to pass the next couple hours before his flight. He opened his laptop, launched his latest Tara Mason novel and picked up where he had left off writing the week before. Running around the country after serial killers puts a crimp in the time one can devote to fabricating stories of fictional characters running around the country hunting down evildoers.

By the time Wolf got into his bed at the Helena Marriott it was after eleven PM. The irony that the flight included a stopover at Denver wasn't lost on him, Wolf imagining the city taunting him.

After breakfast Monday morning, Wolf dropped by Helena's police department located on Breckenridge Street where he was whisked to the police chief's office within a minute of his arrival. Wolf had never encountered any representative of the law who, when he properly identified himself, didn't know who he was and concerned why the nation's foremost muckraker had deemed to visit them.

"I must say, Mr. Wolf, you are the last person I would have expected a visit from," the chief said. "Are you just visiting or here doing research on some of our local luminaries?"

"Actually I'm tracking a very elusive serial killer," Wolf said. "I'm here to ask for your help."

The chief's eyes widened. "Serial killer, you say? Have you gone into the private detective business now?"

"I wasn't planning to, but it turns out I've been pulled into the job," Wolf said. "I've been looking into a suicide for ah, friend and discovered a serial killer. My investigation has led me here."

"How can I help?" the chief said.

Wolf explained about Jessica Demming, asking to look at the full police report and also speak with officers who investigated the accident. The chief agreed to allow him access to the accident report and said he'd get the officer in charge to meet him when she came in for her shift in the afternoon.

"Any idea who this serial killer is?" the chief asked.

"None," Wolf admitted.

"What makes you think there is a serial killer on the loose?" the chief asked.

Wolf gave the officer an overview of his investigation. The chief was especially intrigued about the killer striking at his victims virtually.

"I thought cars were supposed to be hack proof," the chief said.

"Mostly, especially the high end vehicles like Mercedes, Lexus and the like," Wolf replied. "But according to my people and a few others who are very knowledgeable, apparently a highly skilled hacker can access certain critical features such as acceleration and engine ignition by hacking through the onboard system's Wi-Fi; even its radio. They can also install an electronic override module, though that requires direct access to the vehicle, thus increasing the chance of being seen."

"Damn. Just when I think I can relax in my fancy new truck, I've got to worry about some sonofabitch trying to kill me using my truck to do it," the chief complained.

Wolf could relate. Politicians, police, prosecutors or a hated neighbor all should be aware of the danger getting into a car or even walking among them, as Heather Franken discovered crossing the Ivygreen College parking lot.

"Be prepared to shift into neutral if your truck suddenly lurches forward," Wolf advised. Then he remembered. "Nope, that won't work either. Gear shifts are not physical links anymore. It's all electronic."

"Well, ain't you just a ray of sunshine, Mr. Wolf," the chief said, laughing. "Come on, I'll take you to communications where you can use a computer to access the accident report."

Wolf studied the photos first. As expected, Jessica's car was badly damaged from the plunge into the ravine. He was looking for evidence that she might have been pushed off the road like he had been last spring in Colorado, but didn't see any obvious paint scuffs from impact with another vehicle. Then he read the report. Jessica was driving late at night, assumingly she dozed off—there were no skid marks—the car crashed through the low safety railing around a tight bend in the road and plunged over the precipice.

End of report and end of Jessica. But Wolf was buoyed by what was not mentioned in the report and looked forward to speaking with officer McClure after lunch. Wolf returned to the hotel and spent the remainder of the morning working on his novel.

Taking an extra-long lunch, Wolf returned to the police station well after one p.m., the receptionist escorting him to officer McClure who looked apprehensive upon meeting him. Spotting the suppressed grins of her colleagues, Wolf guessed they were playing a prank on the woman.

"Whatever they told you about my seeing you, they are pulling your leg, officer McClure," Wolf said, smiling warmly. "I'm here to ask you about Jessica Demming's accident."

McClure glanced around the room shooting an evil look at everyone, who laughed good-naturedly in return. She bid Wolf to take a seat.

"The chief allowed me to review your report," Wolf said. "I have a few questions that I hope you can answer."

"Happy to help, Mr. Wolf." She made a gesture with her hand past him, adding, "They told me you were investigating police corruption and wanted to speak to me specifically."

"Folks enjoy threatening their coworkers with the big bad wolf," he said.

McClure grinned and said, "Having blown down quite a number of straw mansions, the wolf is big and bad enough to put the fear of the lord in just about anyone."

"Unfortunately such a reputation also scares away good people, too. But like the sage says, you makes your bed and you lies in it," Wolf explained.

Getting down to business, he asked McClure about whether her investigation showed signs of Jessica being run off the road, saying that he didn't see anything like that in the photos.

"We didn't spot any foreign paint smudges nor suspicious dents, though the car was smashed up pretty good from tumbling into a ravine," she said. "Autopsy didn't show anything that might have affected her ability to drive: alcohol or drugs. She was driving home from visiting friends late at night on a road with many tight switchbacks. Dozing off for a couple seconds is long enough to miss a turn and she crashed through the railing."

"She must have been going fast to crash through the railing, yes?" Wolf suggested.

"The car's computer record clocked her going over sixty," McClure confirmed. "Safe speed on that road is thirty. Going that fast you're gonna crash through the safety rail."

Wolf nodded thoughtfully. "Officer McClure, even if you were really tired, how likely is it you'd doze off while driving along a narrow road with numerous turns and twists? Driving on a long, straight road, it does happen. On a mountain road at night, I'd be feeling a bit uneasy, adrenalin helping to keep my eyes open and peeled on the road ahead. Did autopsy check for an elevated level of adrenalin?"

Having read the report, Wolf knew the answer. McClure's expression showed agreement with his assessment.

"I'll ask the lab to check her blood," she said. "But even if higher amount of adrenalin shows up, something could have caused her to panic, maybe an animal in the road. She tries to brake, her foot slips off, presses on the accelerator and she crashes through the barrier. Are you suggesting something else happened to cause the accident?"

"Yes," Wolf said. "I'm certain the lab will find an elevated level of adrenalin in her blood; high enough to indicate a spike of panic. I'm going to ask the chief to allow me to take her car's computer back with me to have my people go through it."

"What are you expecting to find, Mr. Wolf?"

"The signature of a serial killer, officer McClure."

Chapter 23

Accident by Design

"According to Cooper's research, Shred Pro operates in thirty-nine cities around the nation," Colleen said. "The company provides shredding and recycling services for over five hundred clients."

"Well, that's narrows it down significantly," Wolf quipped. He had flown back from Helena the following day after interviewing officer McClure, bringing back Jessica Demming's car computer for Colleen's tech team to comb through.

"It's so nice to have your smart mouth back in the saddle again," Colleen retorted. "Cooper has also discovered something that even a comic sidekick might think suspicious: Shred Pro has serviced every company that New World has invested in over the past ten years."

"Correlation does not causation make," Wolf said. He gave Colleen a doleful look, adding, "Can we go to dinner soon?"

"I shudder to think what my drill sergeant would have done hearing that whining tone."

"We can't all be tough Amazons," Wolf grinned. "Some of us are just too delicate for burrowing through granite and leaping over tall buildings."

Colleen leaned toward him, holding his gaze. "Are you aware that you've talked more in the last ten minutes than during our date the other evening?"

Looking droll, Wolf replied, "Had I known you expected your dates to talk by rule, I would have regaled you with a litany of my exploits over the years."

"If I invite you to dinner at my lowly company café, I hope it won't diminish my chances for a future date," Colleen said, getting up.

"That all depends on whether you ask me to dance or not," Wolf replied.

Colleen shook her head and headed for the door, Wolf trotting along behind her. Not that he minded.

Colleen's Silverstone Security and Investigative Services cafeteria was far from a lowly affair. Colleen worked to create the best private security service in the nation, her diligence and mindfulness encompassing every aspect of the business including offering employees an attractive cafeteria and top notch food. The upscale facility offered linen tablecloths, servers and accomplished chefs offering a diverse and tasty menu.

Wolf ordered grilled salmon with roasted vegetables and mashed golden potatoes. Colleen went for grilled chicken salad with a side order of grilled vegetables. For an appetizer she selected five-cheese ravioli with red sauce for two.

"About your Shred Pro suspect: I admit that it might be more than a coincidence that they service every company that New World has invested in," Wolf said. "We need to take a closer look at their operations."

"I've got Cooper and his team digging into the company and they will let me know the second they find a lead," Colleen replied.

Wolf thanked the server for bringing them their drinks. He took a draught of his beer and said,

"Let me clarify what I mean by, a closer look. I go and see firsthand how they operate, beginning with the trucks picking up corporate waste documents. I want to observe every stage of the process."

"I'm coming, too," Colleen said.

"Two heads are better than one?" Wolf replied.

"Let's just say we have complimentary skills," she said.

"I get it: you distract them by shaking your booty while I rummage through the waste bins," Wolf grinned.

"*Or*, I shake them by their necks while you pick up what falls from their pockets," she replied.

"Either way works for me," he said, cheerfully.

"Now that's settled," Colleen said, "you mentioned earlier this woman who was killed in Helena might be victim zero?"

"Maybe," Wolf replied. "I've got Brett working on tracking down the women who were in Ivygreen's transgender advocacy group. There were about eight or nine. If any other turn up dead then I'll investigate their demise. The more important aspect of Jessica's death is that she was killed several weeks before Stephanie Kramm committed suicide. If the killer was out to avenge her death, then killing someone before she died makes no sense."

"Unless the killer is avenging Stephanie's deteriorating condition," Colleen said.

"Stephanie was a recluse living with her parents for over three years," Wolf pointed out. "If someone wanted to get even with the people who messed up her life, why wait three years? Most likely it would be someone close to her, someone in love with her. I've spoken with Stephanie's college boyfriend and though he's pissed at these women, I don't like him as the killer."

"That would mean the killer is avenging a different victim of the sex change industry," Colleen concluded. "We need to identify other deaths and individuals suffering physical or psychological injury by a procedure performed at ATTC in the northeast." Seeing the smile playing on Wolf lips, she added, "Your people are already working on this, of course."

"I keep getting pulled into criminal investigations, I'm thinking of launching my own investigative firm and give SSIS some real competition for once."

"I love a man who thinks big."

"Perhaps we should merge our interests and form *one* company?" Wolf said, looking expectantly at her.

The server came by asking if they'd care for dessert. Both declined, thanking him.

"I think dinner is over," Colleen said, and stood up. "I'll be available to accompany you to visit Shred Pro by tomorrow afternoon. Come earlier and meet with Cooper; I'll give him a heads up to provide us with details about truck routes, pick up stops and so forth. That work for you?"

"I'm at your disposal," Wolf joked.

She shot him an uncompromising look and said,

"And don't you forget that."

Wolf arrived at SSIS around ten the next morning. Having become a regular visitor at the high security facility, he faced minimal screening and was allowed by Colleen to retain his concealed pistol inside the building. Meeting with Cooper, he received an itinerary of half dozen Shred Pro trucks making stops that day.

Wolf was about to ask about the progress being made on Jessica's computer, when Cooper shot him an inexplicable glance.

"Something wrong?" Wolf asked.

"Everyone is curious about how your date with Colleen went last week and I was elected to ask," Cooper said.

"It was hot. It was heavy. And it ended spectacularly," Wolf replied, a big grin on his face.

"So, you struck out," Cooper said.

"Firstly, a gentleman never tells," Wolf began. "Secondly, women swoon at the sight of Grayson Wolf. Nuff said."

Cooper laughed and said, "Thank you for confirming my assumption. Just so you know, the odds were ten-to-one—against you."

"I find your lack of faith in my prowess deeply disturbing," Wolf retorted. "If we can move past prurient topics, how are your people coming along with Jessica's computer?"

Cooper held up a finger. "Done. Let me check." He checked his computer, then continued. "The bad news is that there is no evidence of any tampering from a remote hack. Her car was six years old and it's computer could not be accessed virtually."

Wolf sighed. "So just a freak accident after all."

"Hardly," Cooper said. "My topnotch computer forensics team has determined that the computer was accessed via direct link. That means someone physically connected an electronic unit to the vehicle's computer."

"The police weren't looking for a killer so it's very likely that unit is still in the wrecked car," Wolf said.

"I'd think so," Cooper agreed. "If the transmitter is still intact, we might be able to get a serial number and identify the manufacturer and perhaps even where the unit was purchased."

"I'll call officer McClure and ask her to get her forensics team looking for this unit," Wolf said. "To speed things up, would you tell them key spots where to look?"

"Sure," Cooper said. "There's only a few places to put it."

"One more thing," Wolf said. "Could your team comb through whatever surveillance recordings are available for last September from Jessica's residence, her place of work, maybe her favorite haunts and do facial recognition on everyone coming and going? I'd get my people to do it, but we don't have the sophisticated technology or capacity to do that. And I want to pay for it."

"We can do it, but I'll have to clear it with Colleen," Cooper said. "We're up to our eyeballs with projects and all our client commitments; I can't promise you anything, Wolf."

"Understood. Thanks, Cooper."

They shook hands and Wolf left, aiming at the café for lunch.

"Ready?" Colleen said, coming up to where Wolf was sitting.

"Let's roll," he quipped, storing his laptop in its protective cover. "Where to first?"

"To Western Consulting, located in the west Twin Tower," she said. "Instead of following around trucks and trying to get a peek at how Shred Pro processes documents, I asked WC's President and friend to ask for a demonstration as though he were interested in becoming a client. This way we can get a closeup without arising any suspicion."

Western Consulting was a mile from SSIS, Colleen passing the parked Shred Pro truck, driving to a spot behind the building out of sight of the truck. They got out of the car, Colleen leading Wolf though the rear entrance of the building and exiting through its front entrance and walking up to a small group standing adjacent the truck.

"Mr. Sikes, sorry to keep you waiting," Colleen said, to a well-dressed middle aged man.

"Quite alright," Sikes said. "Mr. Benton was just explaining Shred Pro's secure shredding process ... please continue..."

"Thank you, Mr. Sikes," Benton said. "We would provide your business with one or more document waste receptacles like the one next to me." He pointed to a metal unit the size of desk. "Your employees would place a pile of papers into the opening of this rotating drum. Once turned over, the papers are deposited in the container and cannot be accessed again. Notice the four circular openings along the sides...I'll explain their function once the demonstration begins.

"Our people pick up the storage bins on a predetermined schedule and bring them to a truck like this one, dumping their contents into our on-site shredding mechanism in the truck, thus assuring destruction of all sensitive material." He waved at a worker in the truck who initiated the process. Benton continued to explain the process as a pair of arms extended from the top of the truck, lifting the storage unit to the top.

"Now it's flipping the container upside-down and partially inserts it into the top of the shredding machinery. Those round openings on each side of the bins I mentioned earlier: as the mechanism lowers the bin, metal pistons, we call them keys, slip into the openings, which unlocks the sealed mechanism and empties the papers into the shredder ... As you can see for yourselves through the viewing port, the documents are being shredded as I speak. It's just one more aspect of our process of transparency to ensure our customers that their sensitive material is fully destroyed."

Mr. Sikes thanked the Shred Pro representative saying he'd get back to him in the near future. Colleen thanked Sikes for arranging the demonstration and the group reentered the building. Wolf and Colleen continued through the lobby, exiting at the rear and got into the car.

She started the car, but didn't move. Her hands rested on the steering wheel for a long moment. She sighed and said,

"Another dead-end. Shred Pro might have serviced every company that the New World Fund invested in, but unless they had someone in every company passing the truck drivers insider information, there is no way anyone could reassemble a billion bits of paper into a coherent document, not to mention thousands of documents. And if there had been insiders, the FBI investigation would have turned up at least a few over the past ten years. Though I am loathe to admit this, Justin Bellamy just might have been an investment genius after all and his murder may have nothing at all to do with the fund."

"No one is that good for that long," Wolf countered. "I've spent the better part of a dozen years of my life rummaging around in the basements and attics of all kinds of notables from politicians to actors. I've learned not to believe most things I hear and suspicious of anything I see, especially if it's totally transparent, absolutely secure and destroyed in front of my eyes."

"Are you suggesting that we didn't see a tub full of paper shredded?" Colleen said, looking skeptical.

"I'm saying there's nothing as suspicious as showing people what they want to see," Wolf said.

"You keep talking like that and I might suspect you're a secret follower of Immanuel Kant," Colleen teased. "Because we have ears, we cannot hear. Because we have eyes, we cannot see."

"Trust me, my comments are fully grounded in reality, not subjective suppositions," Wolf said. "I've witnessed numerus slights of hand and listened to huge quantities of double talk over the years."

"Operating a security business, I don't disagree with you," Colleen said. "What do you propose?"

"Take a much closer and much longer look at these trucks," Wolf replied.

"What would you be looking for?" she asked.

"Don't know until I see it," Wolf said. "I'm going to need a few things..."

*   *   *   *

"They're playing our song," Juan quipped, as the SUV pulled up to the District Court in Los Angles about the same time Wolf was explaining to Colleen his plan regarding looking more closely into the workings of the Shred Pro trucks.

A huge crowd cluttered the sidewalk, protest signs peppered throughout. A narrow aisle leading to the courthouse steps remained open by virtue of a linked array of uniformed police holding back the press of bodies.

"Ready or not, here we go," Juan said, exiting the vehicle, followed by Terrance and Susan.

A frenzy of voices shouting disparaging comments erupted. The mob pressed against the police working hard to keep the aisle to the courthouse open as the three CIR attorneys hurried along. Sundry missiles fell around them, some striking, most, gratefully, missing their targets.

Every seat in the courtroom was taken, a large percentage of the faces sporting hostile expressions. The only question in Juan's mind wasn't whether the judge would certify the class action suit, but whether the judge would allow the proceedings to be disrupted or not. His question was answered shortly after the judge entered the room, where he peered at the packed house, warning the audience he would have the court cleared at the first sign of any disturbance. His announcement had the effect of cold water tossed upon the spectators, expectations transforming into consternation.

The court bailiff announced the case, identifying the names of the plaintiffs and the defendant. The judge reminded everyone that today's hearing was solely to determine whether there was sufficient cause for the plaintiff's class action suit to proceed.

"I have reviewed the application for class action by the Center for Individual Rights and have determined that the case meets the four prerequisites to warrant class action status. The plaintiffs are sufficiently numerus, important legal and factual issues are common to all plaintiffs, the named individuals have a case that is a typical claim of the class and the named individuals represent the interests of everyone in the class. I therefore certify the case as a class action lawsuit. In agreement with the plaintiffs, I appoint CIR attorney Juan Mendez as class counsel."

Juan rose from his seat. "Thank you, your honor. Because of the unusual nature of our case, CIR had publicly notified all students in the California college system of the nature of our intent last fall and have collected over twenty-five hundred *certified* complainants to date. We will of course request student and alumni contact information and contact these individuals. In order to include only individuals who can show sufficient cause of having their right to an equal educational opportunity abridged or denied pursuant to our suit, I ask the court to approve the submitted survey requiring completion and sworn certification by any claimant in order to be included in the class action."

The judge appeared to look thoughtfully at documents in front of him. He nodded and said, "Approved."

"Thank you, your honor," Juan said. "In consideration of CIR's six month national public awareness campaign where we have invited any harmed student or alumni to come forth, I ask the court for a cut off date June first of this year and set a trial date soon thereafter."

"Approved, on the condition that potential plaintiffs receive three subsequent notifications of joinder deadline at the beginning of the final three months." The judge said.

"Yes your honor," Juan said, "Thank you."

The judge rose and disappeared into his chambers behind the bench, followed by an outburst of voices, most certainly surprised by the swift and positive decision of the judge.

Juan was as surprised as anyone. He had expected to offer further arguments for allowing the class action suit to proceed and felt somewhat deflated, though, upon reflection, once the trial began, the fireworks would begin in earnest.

"I suppose they saw the handwriting on the wall and decided to just get on with it instead of creating further controversy and thus more media attention," Susan suggested.

"That was unexpected," Juan said. "I was sure that they'd make us jump through more hoops just to spite us ... it does seem too easy: especially considering we're in California. With the possibility of our case proceeding this summer prior to school beginning, I'm thinking they might come back with a settlement offer that our clients simply can't refuse, say, upwards of two billion dollars. If so, we're talking $200,000 or more per client."

"And you think a majority will go for it," Susan said.

"What do you think, Terrance?" Juan asked. "Will a majority continue with the trial with a possible quarter million payout?"

"Weighed against the possibility of winning but the court cutting our amount down to less than a hundred thousand per client?" Terrance said, sarcastically.

"So the news of the day becomes the money and then it's back to business as usual for the colleges tomorrow," Susan said.

"The politicians running the state have allowed their schools to become centers of intolerance and intimidation," Juan said. "They'll pay to prevent most of the muck from being dragged out on the public stage of an extended trial. I'll bet they will bury our suit under a ton of money."

"If they do throw, say, two billion at us," Terrance said, "we'll build our war chest with six hundred million dollars, enough to push forward with a hundred class action suits across the country."

"And we can launch a major media campaign educating the public about the PC intolerance on campuses," Susan added. "Either way, we will get our message out loud and clear."

"Assuming their plan is to buy us off and not some other move to get the case thrown out before we even begin," Juan warned.

"The class action suit has been certified," Terrance said. "What could they possibly come up with to derail the trial besides offering a big payout?"

"This is California; the Pro-regressives have a death-grip in the legislature and the courts, too, as we have seen time and time again in the Ninth Circuit," Juan explained. "Who knows what they might throw at us, including having the governor escorting us to the border. If I were to guess, most likely we go to trial, they ask for delay after delay, drag it out for months or years. Sure, we'll eventually win, the court cuts it down to pennies, we sue again and win, the state says it can't pay: after all, they've done a great job mismanaging everything and the debts are piling up and our legal coffers become bare."

"Maybe we should have taken their initial offer," Susan said, looking concerned.

"Too late for that," Juan replied. "We'd look weak."

"Based on your dim prognosis, Juan, we might want to accept the next settlement offer, even if it's only a bit more than the original seven hundred million," Terrance suggested.

"Only thing to do is to move forward and build the case and collect the plaintiffs," Juan said. "We'll know something definitive before June1st."

Chapter 24

Shredder Insider

"Don't worry, they hire temps all the time," the driver said. "Just follow my lead. We roll the units to the elevator, line 'em up and the truck does the rest. Easy-peasy. I'm Carlos, by the way."

"Sonny," the temp said. "Been a while since I've had a job."

"Well, you just keep close to me," Carlos said. "I'll make sure you do everything perfect so the boss will want to hire you."

"Appreciate that," Sonny replied. Peering at the truck, he added, "I'm looking forward to learnin' how this beast works."

"Sonny, my Shred Pro unit turns a ton of paper into a billion teeny pieces; nobody could ever put it back together to read any of it again. It's why we're so busy. An talkin' about busy, we better hit da road 'fore the super comes an hollers at us."

Carlos took hold of the handgrip on the truck's cabin and climbed into the driver's side. Sonny hopped into the passenger seat. The truck started up and a minute later they were on the road to their first stop, a major Denver consulting firm.

"Okay," Carlos said, issuing a puff of air. "This baby is stuffed, so we're gonna be pushin' couple hundred pounds. But don't worry: the wheels are da best and it'll roll right along."

"Not bad at all," Sonny agreed, the bin rolling smoothly along the aisle to the elevator.

Down at the loading dock, the workers positioned the bin adjacent the truck. Carlos warned Sonny to back away, pressed a lever and arms came down from the top of the truck, lifted the bin, flipped it over and inserted it in "the cradle", the name given to the opening where the bin was placed.

"That clunk sound means the keys have unlocked the bin's lid and the papers are being dumped into the shredder … and there it goes!"

The mechanism began to whine and churn and they could see masses of tiny bits of shredded paper rush past the observation glass. Seconds later mechanical arms lifted the bin out of the cradle, the process of flipping it shutting the top of the unit and locking it. The arms lowered it to the pavement, then folded into a notch at the side of the truck. The entire process took less than three minutes.

"Alright, let's roll this baby back to the elevator and we'll be outta here in two shakes and on our way," Carlos said, his upbeat tone aligned with the speed and efficiency of the Shred Pro procedure.

By the end of the afternoon, Carlos and Sonny had completed thirty-four stops and were on their way to the Denver Metropolitan Recycling Center. Carlos drove the truck through a narrow lane, passing over a metal plate in the center and coming to a halt.

"Time to take a huge dump!" Carlos laughed. "Come on, you'll understand."

They got out of the truck and walked to the rear. The metal plate was sliding open under the roadway exposing a steep angular concrete slide. Carlos pressed some levers and pushed a button. The rear door of the truck raised and the shredder machine kicked in. A large rectangular panel opened near the bottom of the mechanism from which tightly compacted rectangular shaped blocks of shredded material began to exit and drop into the opening rapidly sliding down the incline into its depths.

"What goes in must come out. Glad it's the truck and not me," Sonny laughed.

Carlos's belly laugh drowned out the motor shoving out bales of compressed paper. The last bundle dropped through the opening and the machinery ground to a halt. Carlos shut the rear door and the two workers got back into the cab and drove the truck out of the center and back to the garage.

"You did well, Sonny," Carlos said, locking the doors to the truck. "I'll let the super know you a good hand."

"I appreciate that. Thanks, man."

"Hope to see ya mañana; g'nite," Carlos replied. He placed the truck key in a small metal wall cabinet and snapped the door shut, locking the unit.

Carlos and Sonny exited, the driver walking across the street, Sonny turning left and moseying down the sidewalk, ostensibly aiming for a diner two blocks away. Sonny found a seat and ordered a light meal, casually reading the day's newspaper that someone had thoughtfully left for subsequent diners to enjoy if they wished. For dessert, Sonny ordered a slice of cherry pie washed down with a second mug of coffee, then spent another thirty minutes talking to people on his cell.

By the time he got up to leave, it was pushing seven. He placed a Franklin on the table to compensate the waitress for the fact he had loitered in her section for near ninety minutes and made his way back to the truck garage from the rear of the block. The streets in the industrial sector were largely abandoned and he saw no one as he approached a side door at the Shred Pro storage facility.

Sonny had no trouble jimmying the locks, his task completed in twenty seconds. He quietly closed the door then stood, listening for any sign of life. The facility did have a night watchman that dropped by at random times, but the man didn't begin his rounds until eleven in the evening.

Sonny aimed for the key storage box resting on the wall next to the office, it's door yielding to his deft manipulations within seconds. He took one of the keys and walked over to the appropriate truck, started it, opened various panels and doors and shut the engine off.

His first action was to closely study various parts of the shredding mechanism looking for anything unusual or suspicious. Next, Sonny opened an access panel located at lower front bedside a few feet behind the cabin. Using a small, but very bright flashlight, Sonny looked at the rear portion of the shredder, where the paper compressing unit was located that transformed the bits and pieces of paper into tight bales to be ejected at the recycling plant. He knocked the back of the light against the metal enclosure, hearing a dull echo indicating internal space. That would make sense considering the truck had dumped its paper load earlier that afternoon.

Peering along the back, Sony noted the cover consisted of four separate panels each about four feet high and three feet wide held in place by an array of four bolts along each edge fastening the metal cover to the frame of the shredding unit. Sonny took out his cell phone and took pictures. He got out of the access space and shut the access door, then climbed to the top of the truck.

The top panel was open exposing the cradle, that rectangular depression where the mechanical arms placed the paper storage bins to empty them into the shredder. Sonny looked at the two keys on each side, the round steel pins that slipped into the top of the bins to unlock them. He was moving his light along the edge of the cradle, not sure what he expected to find, when he did spot something curious.

All of the keys were scuffed from the action of insertion and removal of the storage bins, but one key, the far right one, appeared to have vertical striations at several points around its perimeter. The scratches were barely noticeable, but there were there. None of the other three keys had similar striations on them. Shining the light at the base of the suspicious key, Sonny was sure that this pin was not fixed, but could be pushed down, into the mechanism. He tried pressing on the top of the pin, but it would not budge; it required far more weight, such as several hundred pounds of a filled storage bin to move it. Sonny took photos of the entire area and numerous close-ups of the striated key.

His work done, Sonny started up the truck allowing him to shut all power doors and panels, turned the engine off, locked the truck's cab doors and placed the key in the metal unit on the wall. He left by the side door that he had entered, jimmying the locks shut and disappeared into the night.

*   *   *   *

"What's the verdict, sonny boy,?" Colleen said.

"Maybe, perhaps and possibly," Wolf replied, looking cagey.

"We'll that clears that up," Cooper said, sarcastically. "I've studied the photos you took of the striated steel pinon and its base. There's no question in my mind that particular post retracts. What it activates by doing so, is the multi-billion dollar question."

"I've got to hand it to you, Wolf, you have great intuition. Good work," Colleen said. "You get tired sitting in your penthouse writing novels about a fictional woman, you're welcome to come here and work for a real woman."

"You've met Diana, right?" Wolf retorted, flashing her a toothy grin.

"Before the two of you launch into a pseudo-sexual bantering session, I'd like to hear Wolf's theory about the Shred Pro truck mystery," Cooper interjected.

Wolf barked a laugh upon seeing Colleen shoot the man a most evil glance.

"You'd better watch what you say or she might turn you into a pillar of salt," he teased. Aware that Colleen's gaze was turning toward him, he quickly added, "Here's what we got so far: One, Shred Pro serviced every company over the last ten years that New World Fund invested in. Two, New World has managed sky high returns every year. Three, the Shred Pro truck I examined has a suspicious metal pin that is able to be depressed when a storage bin is lowered upon it. Four, the rear of the shredder, where the paper compactor mechanism is located, is covered by four small panels that can easily be removed. Five, a sound test proved a hollow space behind those four panels, which *might* be employed as a secret storage compartment. Therefore and thusly, adding number three and four together, we arrive at a process where the movable pinon engages a trap door that dumps the contents of a document storage unit into that rear hollow space where sensitive papers can be sorted through, intelligence gathered and very profitable investments made year after year."

Colleen and Cooper looked thoughtfully at Wolf for a long moment. Colleen spoke first.

"Excellent summary, but conjecture nonetheless. We need proof."

"And by proof," Cooper said, a wicked grin forming, "you mean we need to borrow a truck and test Wolf's hypothesis."

"And by 'borrow'," Wolf said, "you mean steal one."

"All I'm saying is that without a truck to test, allst we got is a Wolf howling in the wilderness," Cooper replied.

"No," Colleen ordered. "There would be only one reason to steal a Shred Pro truck and it would tip off whomever is behind this financial scam."

"What do you suggest?" Cooper asked.

A sly grin slid across Colleen's mouth. "You and I are going to join Sonny on his paper route tomorrow.

"Another day, another hundred ninety three dollars," Carlos said. "Hop on in and let's roll, Sonny."

"That's pretty good pay for haulin' waste paper around," Sonny said. "What's that a year: 'bout forty grand?"

"Almost fifty large," Carlos said. "Don't you be getting' any ideas, compardre. I've been working over eight years. Didn't start with no hundred ninety a day; you gonna need to prove yourself and stick around to make my kind 'a money."

"You can live pretty comfortable on that and feed a family, too," Sonny said.

"Feed a family of seven in my case," Carlos replied. "Yeah, it's a good salary, safe work and three weeks paid vacay. Do my job, stay on schedule and keep my mouth shut, get paid and enjoy life. More people ought to do that."

"I'm down with that," Sonny agreed.

Carlos drove to the first service stop, a legal firm in downtown Denver, backing the truck to a service entrance at the rear of the building. He got out and made for the service door, Sonny making an excuse about having to tie his boot laces, saying he'd be right behind him.

The moment Carlos disappeared inside the building, Sonny signaled Cooper and Colleen who hurried forward. He opened the side door just behind the cab, giving both a hand up and into the narrow compartment behind the massive shredder unit. He made sure the latch was open and hustled after Carlos.

Inside the dark space, Cooper was rapidly unscrewing the bolts holding the lower left cover in place, Colleen holding a flashlight. His task completed, he carefully lifted the panel and leaned it against the back wall, using his flashlight to look inside. Colleen got down on her knees, doing likewise.

"Plenty of room to hold the contents of several bins of misdirected paper," she said, shining the light all around the interior. "But where's the trapdoor?"

"Got to be near the top," Cooper suggested, shining his light toward the upper portions. "Yup ... see, the compactor mechanism takes up most of the space, but there's a two foot height of space the width of the interior above the machinery; plenty of room for a ton of paper to blow into this space—oh, oh. I hear voices..."

"That means—" Colleen's words were cut off by the whine, whirring and clunking of the shredder machinery coming to life, the noise reverberating inside the narrow access space where she and Cooper were standing.

The sound abated and stopped a short time later, as the machinery completed its task. Cooper took a series of photos of the space inside of the back of the shredder, then replaced the metal panel. He carefully opened the side door, peering around for anyone nearby, helped Colleen out and shut the latch before lowering himself on the pavement. The pair slunk away and disappeared around the corner of the building.

Later that evening after Sonny's route was done, the trio met in Colleen's office at SSIS to discuss their findings.

"We still haven't actually tested whether there is a mechanism that diverts a load of paper to the space behind the shredding unit," Cooper said.

"True as that may be," Colleen replied, "we've saw a whole lot of opening above the machinery where a ton of paper could easily be directed and dumped into that space. It's a matter of minutes to unscrew those access panels, remove the paper, sort through them for information about inventions, processes, breakthrough developments and so on which Bellamy and his cohorts used to make their investments and reap spectacular returns."

"What she's getting at, Cooper," Wolf said, "we know enough details to use them as leverage to uncover the vermin hiding in their nests. However, about Bellamy and company knowing about new inventions or innovations from little known companies or startups: how would they know about them if Shred Pro didn't already service them? What I mean is, why would these small operations even pay for professional document removal?"

"I can answer that," Cooper said. "Shred Pro approached them with their special free offer of a six or twelve month trial. Lots of companies dealing with an initial money crunch happily take that offer, especially if they believe it's the best way to ensure complete destruction of sensitive documents, random notes, hard copies of emails and so forth. A six month free shredding gives Bellamy and friends plenty of time to sort through a ton of paper for clues to future profits."

"And the beauty is that they can make profits whether a company or its product is a success or a dud because they can go long or short," Wolf said. "Succeed or fail, Bellamy wins either way."

"Not just the free trial companies," Colleen said. "I'd guess they'd be doing the same thing to companies who contacted Shred Pro to process their paper, too. It wouldn't take Bellamy long to determine which companies were worth the bother of sorting through their paper. There'd be a priorities list."

"Which we have, sort of," Cooper said. "I'm talking about the list of companies New World invested in or shorted over the last decade."

"The bins are they key," Wolf said. "Clearly not all bins are equal, or rather, the depth of the lock release cylinders along the edge are not equal. The depth of the top left cylinder of certain bins is much less so that when the bin is lowered into the shredder's cradle, that one pin is pressed down activating the trap door and the papers flow down into the rear compartment."

"What about the fact that customers can observe the paper being shredded through a glass portal?" Colleen asked.

"I suppose the mechanism is designed to blow previously shredded paper toward the window to make it look like documents are being shredded," Cooper said. "Perception is reception."

"Of course. I think we have a pretty good idea of how Bellamy and his pals managed to cash in for a decade," Colleen said. "Cooper, expand your search about anyone, person or business, ever connected or associated with Shred Pro. I want to know about everyone connected with Shred Pro, including the gardener and maid working for them."

"As you wish, boss," Cooper quipped. Turning to Wolf, he said, "I guess Sonny's not going to show up for work tomorrow?"

"You'd guess wrong," Wolf said. "Sonny will show up and notify the supervisor that he's found permanent employment."

"No loose ends," Colleen said. "This keeps Wolf's cover intact because no one will wonder why Sonny didn't show up and begin to think about reasons why he came and why he suddenly didn't."

"Makes sense," Cooper said. "Wolf, are you planning to hang around or fly back to DC? The Helena police have FedExed the suspected unit used by your serial killing hacker to whack Jessica Demming which should arrive tomorrow morning. We expect to know all about it ten minutes after arrival. Might want to be present for the unveiling." He made a droll face, adding, "And it is a Saturday, the evening of that day of the week being a traditional date night."

"I think you missed your calling as a matchmaker," Wolf retorted.

"Been reading about that," he replied, bemused. "Apparently the virtual dating scene isn't all that's it's cracked up to be and the professional matchmaker is making a big comeback. Some of these people make upward of ten thousand per client. Get one client a week, and I'd be pulling in over half a mill annually!"

"If that's your way of hinting for a raise, you need to turn in your soothsayer credentials," Colleen jested. "And as for our housebroken Wolf, I'll pay for dinner."

"At our usual haunt, is it?" Wolf said.

"Of course," Colleen grinned. "See you the Café in fifteen."

"You are one cheap date, Wolfie," Cooper said, once outside of Colleen's office. "I'm amazed the women aren't lining up around the block to take you out for a night around the town. And by around the town I literally mean—"

"I get it," Wolf said, cutting him off. "I suppose you'll now regale me with tales of all the women you'll be seeing this weekend, yes?"

"Better go freshen up," Cooper retorted, making a face. "Colleen likes her dinner dates looking tidy and perky."

Chapter 25

Hacker Hunting

"How did your dinner date go? Was there dessert?" Cooper taunted.

"If I told you about the delicious dessert offered, would you believe me?" Wolf countered.

"Nope," Cooper said, chuckling.

"Because it's Colleen?" Wolf said.

"Because it's you," Cooper laughed. "You're too busy running here and there and never stopping long enough to enjoy dessert."

"Touché," Wolf said. "In my defense, I did announce my retirement from running here and there on Carolyn Mayor's radio show last December and look whats happened since."

"You got run over by here and there?" Cooper joked.

"Correctamundo," Wolf said. "It's hard getting to enjoy dessert when one rarely even makes it to dinner ... now, if we're done discussing my culinary lifestyle, can we get on to our little electronic fiend the Helena police sent?"

"Party pooper," Cooper quipped. "As promised, my peeps have tracked the transmitter's manufacturer by its serial number. It's a specialized piece of equipment sold to a limited clientele, not something the average schmoe would pick up at a Walmart."

Cooper's pregnant pause that followed was a tipoff for Wolf to expect a basketful of significant and perhaps unexpected details. Taking the bait, he asked Cooper what else they had found.

"Not much," he replied, looking nonchalant. "Just that the transmitter was purchased in one of five specialty shops in Maryland and that a person of similar description was captured by surveillance footage several times near Jessica Demming's apartment and workplace in Helena prior to her death in September."

"Fantastic!" Wolf exclaimed. This was far more than he had expected. "Got a name? Where do they live?"

"Down boy," Cooper said. "Similar description does not a who and a where make. Our prime suspect knows what they're doing. They were aware of cameras; never got a facial shot from any location. They also made an effort to cover themselves from hand to foot, but they can't hide from Cooper's troopers. Snippets of exposed skin reveals the suspect to be African American ... and a woman."

"How could you tell it's a woman? Was she dramatically swishing her hips as she walked past the cameras?" Wolf said.

"Anyone ever tell you you've a smart mouth?"

"All the time," Wolf grinned, adding, "Being a member of the male canine species, I pay particular attention to the female of my species. I suppose it was something about the way she walked, her demeanor and so forth?"

"Glad to hear your observational skills can differentiate between the sexes," Cooper joked. "That's pretty much it: her stride, body movements, size and height. It's not an absolute certainty, however. It could still be a slight male doing a good female impression, but if Demming was victim zero as you believe, then going to such lengths to confound investigators is unlikely."

"Unless Jessica isn't the first victim," Wolf said.

"Unless that," Cooper agreed. "Then all bets about our suspect's sex are off."

Thank you, Cooper and peeps, for doing such a thorough job," Wolf said. "I knew Colleen only hired the best, but you and your team are better than the best."

"I've already sent everything to Brett," Cooper replied.

"Of course you have," Wolf smiled. "Reading one's mind being a prerequisite for being a member of Cooper's Troopers."

"Absolutely," Cooper agreed. "That's how we stay way ahead of our competitors."

The men shook hands and Wolf tracked down Colleen to update her about Cooper's discoveries. Intercepting her on the way out of the building, she grinned and said,

"Up to speed. Cooper still works for me, in case you have forgotten."

"I haven't and thank you for lending me the services of your prodigiously skilled technicians," Wolf said. "I'll be taking a flight back to Virginia later this afternoon. Hopefully I'll see you sooner than later?"

"A lot sooner," she replied. "Tomorrow, in fact. I assume you'll put me up for the night? You know: in exchange for lending you Cooper's Troopers."

"You are welcome to stay at my humble abode anytime," Wolf replied. "No reservations or quid pro quo required."

A generous smile spread across her lips, exposing pearly white teeth. "So noted ... Gotta run. See you tomorrow night."

"I'll leave the light on for you," Wolf quipped. A sly grin touched his lips and he added, "Would you like your own key?"

Colleen took a sudden step toward him and said, "Honey, I don't need a key to get into your place."

She turned and hurried out of the lobby, stepping into a waiting vehicle. Wolf grinned from ear to ear.

"She called me, honey," he said, to no one in particular.

*   *   *   *

"Good morning," Wolf said. "Coffee, splash of cream, kippered salmon and a schmear."

"Good Jewish breakfast," Colleen said.

"Good anyone's breakfast," Wolf replied, placing a mug of coffee on the counter.

"Thank you," Colleen said, taking a sip of her coffee. "Very good ... I should stay at your establishment more often when I'm in town."

"Any time," Wolf said, grinning. "Happy to give you a key—come any time, day or night."

"Aren't you worried I might arrive at an inconvenient time?"

Wolf shot her a droll look. "There has never been an inconvenient time in this establishment."

"Too busy," Colleen said.

"Too picky," Wolf corrected.

Colleen nodded and smiled knowingly. She thought of herself as highly selective instead of picky; either way, however, the end result was the same: solitude. Though she gave Wolf a hard time and would never admit it, she was glad he was in her life, thinking of him as someone even more rare and important than her short list of past lovers: she considered him as a true and unwavering friend.

"May I ask you a personal question?" she said.

"Knock yourself out," Wolf quipped.

"Were you in love with Madeline Talbot? At least prior to your trial last August?"

Wolf held her gaze. "Love...hmm. Maddie was an informant and I have an iron rule never to get intimately involved with an informant or anyone connected to my undercover activities, even afterwards. I was attracted to her and wound up sleeping with her and paid the price. But I don't regret it. Let's just say that had things turned out different back then, there is a good chance I'd be talking to her right now instead of you."

"Damn; I thought I was a hard ass," Colleen said.

"I didn't mean the way that sounded," he quickly replied. "What I meant was that Maddie and I would probably still be together, not that I don't want you here, I do, very much in fact—" He got up, giving Colleen a knowing look. "I can tell by that twitching on your lips you are pulling my leg, which, by the way, you are extraordinarily good at doing. Now, I'm going to place the plates into the dishwasher and get ready to hunt down our hacker."

"Would you mind if I said hello to Diana?" Colleen said, as they stepped into the elevator.

"Of course not," Wolf said, pressing the sixth floor button.

The entire floor of The Patrick Henry Building was taken up the Center for Individual Rights, making Wolf's four-floor commute to work one of the shortest in the region. Colleen headed for the Director's office, Wolf to Brett's domain.

"Colleen," Diana said, "are you and Wolf...?"

Colleen flashed her a warm smile. She liked people who didn't beat around the bush and she really liked Diana.

"No," she said. "We're friends."

"You might say it's none of my business, but Grayson Wolf is my business," Diana asserted. "He's been going through some personal issues and I don't—I want him to be happy."

"The protective big sister," Colleen said.

"Everyone on this floor is protective of Wolf," Diana said. "He never talks about you, you know."

That was rather a strange thing to say, Colleen thought. "Is that a good thing or bad thing?"

"That depends," Diana replied. "Do you talk about Wolf?"

"No," she replied.

"Then you understand why we're having this conversation," Diana said. A droll expression appeared on her face and she added, "You and Wolf might want to have a conversation about what the two of you are not saying about each other sooner than later."

Colleen was about to respond when Wolf stuck his head in the door and asked if she was ready to go. She gave Diana a brief hug and left with Wolf.

"Have a nice chat with Diana?" Wolf asked, driving the car out of the underground garage.

"Yes, we did; I like her a lot."

"Just don't like her *too* much," Wolf replied.

"Afraid I might poach her, are we?" Colleen teased.

"If she were in the market, would you hire Diana?" he asked.

"In a heartbeat," she replied. "I have to admit I envy you."

"Don't worry; I haven't been in love with Diana since she ran off and married that bum," Wolf joked.

"Cute," Colleen said. "You are fortunate to have someone as competent and committed like Diana running the show."

"I see," Wolf said, sounding disappointed. "I was hoping you were jealous ... seriously though, are you thinking about stepping back from being the leader of your band?"

"Yes and it's your fault," she said.

"My fault?"

"I've spent the last eight years working day and night to build my business," Colleen explained. She paused, finding herself a stranger in an unfamiliar land, debating whether she should proceed. Diana's face appeared in her mind's eye and she continued. "Then last March you walked into my office and everything changed."

Wolf glanced over at her. He cleared his throat.

"Are you trying to tell me you enjoy my company?" he teased.

"I'm saying that I've missed being out in the field," she said. "And that I enjoy being in the field with you."

"Before this conversation goes any further, I must inform you that I am involved with another woman," he said.

"I'm sure Tara Mason won't mind sharing you with me," Colleen replied. "After all, both of us women are cut from the same cloth, aren't we, Mr. Wolf?"

"If you mean that I only engage in field work with women who are smart, beautiful, can handle a gun and kick ass, then yes, you fit the bill, Ms. Silverstone."

"I'm relieved to know that I pass your rigorous qualifications," she said. "Just so we are clear, you need to know that I'm absolutely confident about your role as comedic sidekick, but uncertain about other critical attributes as a field operative."

"If you're referring to the attribute about me not being as beautiful as yourself, that shouldn't be a problem," Wolf replied. "A team needs only one siren to distract clueless males."

Colleen laughed. Being in the field wasn't the only thing she had been missing in her busy life.

"I'm sure there are lots of clueless males happy to be distracted by a good looking, furry Wolf," she retorted.

"Okay, we're closing in on the first of our five specialty shops," Wolf said, apparently choosing to ignore her remark. Exiting at Rt. 450, the Annapolis Town Center was facing them and he quickly found a public parking garage. "Let's see if we get lucky."

The electronics shop was a small affair squeezed between the Brooks Brothers and Restoration Hardware stores. Shoppers who blinked twice or walked faster than a leisurely stroll could easily miss the store's entrance.

"May I help you," a middle aged man behind the counter said.

"I hope so," Wolf said.

He explained the reason for the visit, showing the man several enhanced photos of the subject from Helena surveillance cameras. The good news was that the man was the store's owner and sole worker. The bad news was that he was sure no slender Black woman, approximately five foot six had purchased the particular two-way transmitting device Wolf was asking about.

"One down, four to go," Wolf said, walking back to the car. "Next stop, Baltimore—Catonsville, to be more precise."

The visual memory of the clerk manning the counter of Specialized Electronics was tuned to identifying equipment and parts, not humans. He was sort of sure that there had been a couple women that maybe, perhaps matched the person in the photos Wolf showed him, but had no clue when they came to the shop—if any had.

Wolf shot a droll glance at Colleen, thanked the clerk and made for the door, when the employee said,

"You could check the tapes. They're digital and go back like, ten years."

Searching through the previous August and September record produced several Black female customers, one of which was a definite possibility. Wolf downloaded the file and sent it to Brett. He thanked the clerk once more and they returned to the car.

Colleen studied the photo of the woman. "Close but no cigar. She the right height, but a bit too zaftig."

"Better than what we got from Annapolis," Wolf said. "Next stop, Hunt Valley, couple miles north."

The electronics specialty store in Hunt Valley turned out to be a Cold Stone Creamery, the owner having gone out of business before the New Year. Grumbling about the closed store probably being the one the killer bought the transmitter, Wolf shrugged and bought Colleen and himself sundaes. Cold comfort, to be sure, but tasty.

They were rolling west on I-70 on their way to Rockville, when the sound system announced a call from RJ.

"Yo, bro," he said, "there's been an attack on one of our lawyers out in California."

"Not seriously hurt, I hope," Colleen said.

"Oh, there's hurt alright," RJ said. "I'm sending you video that one of the students captured. You're gonna want to pull over and watch."

RJ signed off and Wolf slowed the car and pulled onto the shoulder. The video came available and he transferred it to the much larger dashboard monitor and pressed play. A young woman was walking toward the camera followed by a crowd making sundry disparaging and vulgar comments.

"That's Susan Baker, one of our rising legal stars," Wolf said.

She was walking along, ignoring the nonsense around her when she was rushed from behind, struck in the back of the head and shoved so violently she fell forward. Incensed at the unprovoked attack, Wolf uttered a profanity as the victim fell forward, tucked in her head and shoulder, performing a perfect forward summersault landing on her feet. Mesmerized, they watched as Susan pivoted on her heels to face her attackers, who rushed at her. In the blink of an eye, her right fist struck one assailant in the face, her left fist doing likewise to the second, both tumbling back and falling down. The video continued for a few more seconds, Susan facing the mob, her glare daring anyone else to attack her.

"You go girl!" Colleen said. "Are all your lawyers trained in martial arts?"

"Let's just say that anyone working for CIR is aware that they are a potential target," Wolf said. "It's also one of the reasons why a majority of our employees carry concealed and also why CIR is located in a state aligned with the Second Amendment."

"Well I'm impressed," Colleen replied.

Wolf terminated the link, then called out Susan's name. The ringing of the phone sounded in the car. A woman answered.

"Hello Susan, Colleen Silverstone is with me," Wolf said. "We just saw the video. Are you unhurt?"

"Good as new, Mr. Wolf," she confirmed.

"Ms. Baker," Colleen said, "I'm glad you're not hurt. Congratulations on your impressive recovery and counterstrike."

"Thank you, ma'am," Susan said.

"May I ask you a question?" Colleen said. Getting an affirmative response, she continued. "Upon reflection, is there anything different you should have done?"

There was a pause and she said, "Should not have allowed a group of jeering students to dog me and assume they weren't dangerous; just acting like assholes. Won't happen again."

"I'm sure it won't; take care, Ms. Baker," Colleen said.

"Susan," Wolf said, "keep me informed. I know Juan will take good care of you and if you need anything, you let me know. Stay safe."

He ended the call and got back on the highway.

"Your class action suit has riled up all the hornet nests, Wolf," Colleen said. "You are literally striking at the foundation of the source of power from which the ruling class derive their privileged power over the mass of unwashed hoi polloi and they are not going to go quietly into that good night. There will be blood and we've seen a few drops on that video."

"Considering their mangled rerun of a Seven Days in May coup of a duly elected president last election cycle, all I can say is that if it's blood they want, they had better be storing a ton of it for transfusions," Wolf growled.

Colleen peered at him. "Are you threatening violence, Wolf?"

"I'm saying these fools are playing with fire," he replied. "I, more than most, know that a free society enables crooks and shysters to operate, sometimes for years. But in the end, they get what they deserve and the rest of us live in peace and prosper. But these new politicians running on historically discredited ideas want the power to control and lord over us and the universities are a key source of that ideological poison. There's a bad moon rising, Colleen, and it bodes an ill future unless we fight it."

"The price of liberty being eternal vigilance?" Colleen quipped.

"And the road to serfdom being but a handful of votes away," he retorted. "We're raising a generation of kids who've been micromanaged by their parents, their teachers and whipped into passive compliance by their digital toys. A generation who needs to have a class in 'social courage' just to ask a girl out on a date. Who do you think they will vote for in future elections: mommy promising them free games and snacks or daddy telling them to get a job?"

"I think you are being overly pessimistic, Wolf," Colleen said. "Every generation has its growing pains and eventually the kids become productive members of their society. How often did you hear your parents complain about the deficiencies of our generation? And yet, here we are, muddling along just as well as they did."

"And hunting down killers who most certainly are members of our generation and that of our parents'," Wolf said, agreeably. "Spending half of my life exposing looters and charlatans comes with a price: cynicism, detachment, distrust, just to name a few. And recently I've grown tired paying that bill and announced my retirement."

"And you're having a lot more fun," Colleen teased.

"Actually, I am," Wolf said. "I enjoy hunting down these killers with you."

"Wolves are natural predators," Colleen pointed out.

"Yes, they are and I'm appropriately named because I enjoy hunting down criminal prey," Wolf said. "And talking about tracking prey, we've arrived at the store."

He parked the car in a spot near the store. This was the second to the last electronic specialty shops and Colleen was keeping her fingers crossed for a successful outcome.

"We rarely get requests for anything beyond the latest game console or phones these days and haven't carried a switch transmitter for maybe two years now," the owner said. "CBs are still popular; we only sell the high end ones that can transmit over ten miles or more. We also sell top-rated two-way radios; their range is over thirty miles."

Wolf showed her the photos and particulars of the person they were looking for, but neither the owner nor her employee could confirm a Black woman matching the description had been a customer asking to order the specialty item Wolf had discussed.

"People don't tinker with equipment anymore," the owner said. "Something breaks, they toss it and buy a new one. Sorry I couldn't be more helpful."

They thanked the proprietor and returned to the car.

"Four down, one to go," Wolf said, issuing a sigh. "It's Laurel or bust."

"Never fear, Wolfie," Colleen quipped. "Cooper said five stores in Maryland carried this switch and Cooper is never wrong."

And he wasn't.

At Main Street Electrix they hit pay dirt. And a dirty clerk happy to accommodate their request for an exorbitant payment.

"You want info, I want a sale," the sallow-faced clerk insisted. "That Samsung Q8FN Smart 4 K is just the ticket for what you be asking."

"How about two hundred bucks?" Wolf offered.

"How about two thousand bucks?" the clerk suggested. Looking at Colleen, he grinned and said, "Or a piece of you."

A suggestive grin slid across her mouth. "I can do that." Colleen stepped around the counter, embraced the clerk, his face suddenly registering extreme discomfort. "Now, honeybuns, you are going to give us the information we asked for. And if you're quick about it, I might not deprive the future of any protégés coming from your loins. Capiche?"

When she said capiche, he let out a loud grunt and shook his head repeatedly. Colleen eased her grip on the man's crotch.

"Tania," the clerk wheezed. "Tania Johnson. Lives in Columbia...a townhouse in Owen Brown, close to Broken Land street, road; something like that."

"Got an address?" Colleen said, her tone threatening.

"No...we do cash, no address," he replied.

"How do you know where she lives if she never gave you her address?" Colleen asked.

"Phone," he said. "I overheard her talkin' every so often. I suppose that's were she live ... that's all I know..."

Colleen released her grip and walked back to the front of the counter where Wolf received her with a droll grin. With a slight jerk of her head toward the exit, she started to walk out of the store.

Wolf placed a hundred dollar note on the counter.

"For your trouble," he said, and followed Colleen out.

Chapter 26

Hacker Whacker

"Tania Johnson." Brett's voice filled the car's interior. "She works for Micro One, 4554 National Business Parkway, just west of Ft. Meade. Looking into her life, I don't see any connection to the gender transformation center in Boston, or any other one this side of the Mississippi. As far as I can tell, none of the recent suicides or people suing the Boston transformation center—or any of them—are related to Johnson. I can tell you this: she's a top notch software engineer. Proceed gingerly; she's got killer skills."

"Are you seriously warning the big bad Wolf to be wary of a five-six, hundred fifteen pound computer programmer?" Wolf retorted.

"Computers isn't Johnson's only skill," Brett replied. "The woman is a sharpshooter; she competes in amateur pistol shooting events across the country and has won more first places than not. Last I heard, wolves are still vulnerable to bullets."

"Understood; Wolfie will be wary. Thanks for the info and heads up about our most wanted." Wolf ended the call and said to Colleen, "Neutralizing hostiles is your specialty. What's the plan?"

"Wait, watch, pounce," she replied.

Wolf laughed. "Sophisticated, nuanced, direct."

"You do know you're in range of my specialty?" Colleen said.

"Promises, promises," Wolf grinned. "Do we show up at her workplace or surprise her at home?"

"I assume the company she works for is close by?" Colleen asked. Wolf confirmed it was and she said, "Let's catch her at work; at least she won't be armed. But we'll go in prepared nonetheless."

Micro One was a ten-minute ride from Main Street. The receptionist in the lobby gave them the usual spiel about not being allowed to give out any information about personnel. When Wolf identified himself, the clerk's eyes got larger and said he'd call for the personnel supervisor.

The exchange between the supervisor and Wolf was short and to the point, Wolf saying he only wished to talk with Ms. Johnson about an important personal matter. The supervisor replied that he wouldn't object, however the employee had signed out a short time before, saying she was ill.

"Looks like our little Laurel vermin has ratted us out," Wolf said, walking back to the car. "Let's see if we can catch her at home."

"She has at least a twenty minute head start," Colleen said, getting into the car.

"She can run, but she can't hide," Wolf quipped, driving out of the parking lot. "Her house is a ten minute ride up Rt. 32 where we take Broken Land north to a street called Cradlerock and make a right into her townhouse development a few streets down."

"They've got some offbeat street names in Columbia," Colleen said.

"Unlike common street names like Xanthia and Xenia that your condo is located between," Wolf teased.

"Next time you startle a bear in the woods I am going to enjoy the show," Colleen retorted.

"You know as well as I do that you'd never let anything untoward happen to your favorite sidekick," Wolf replied.

"Only because of the all the paperwork I'd have to fill out," she said, though she knew with absolute certainty she'd do whatever it took to keep Wolf safe.

That realization brought her back to the reality that they were about to encounter a woman who had managed to kill a least four people from the comfort of her home or a nearby car. They could not afford to let their guard down.

"According to Brett, Johnson is driving a 2018 silver Acura RLX; shouldn't be too hard to spot that," Wolf said, exiting on Broken Land.

Colleen's internal guardian was on full alert. Johnson knew they were coming and would be prepared. Colleen cursed the fact neither were wearing body armor, something that she would need to correct at her earliest opportunity once they resumed their hunt for Bellamy and Madeline's killers. At least Wolf and she were armed. Johnson might be a crack shot at immobile targets, but Colleen was an experienced field agent who could place dead-center shots while running and dodging around obstacles.

Wolf turned into the townhouse development, driving to a cul-de-sac and backed into a parking space between two vehicles.

"That's her place, the one on the end across the way," Wolf said. "No car in front."

"And we might never see one, either," Colleen said. "She had at least a twenty minute head start. Assuming she's our killer, she would have a go bag ready and be here and gone in minutes."

"Or be grocery shopping and show up soon," Wolf said. "After all, she's gotta know from the clerk back at the store that we're not cops."

"Based on the fact that police don't threaten to crush sensitive body parts anymore?" Colleen said, a smile touching her lips.

"Something like that," Wolf grinned. "And having seen you in close-up action, I'm planning to wear an athletic cup whenever I'm around you from now on."

Colleen laughed. "Smart move ... um, Wolf, isn't that a new, silver Acura rolling up to her townhouse?"

"It certainly is," Wolf said. "Coming back from grocery shopping as predicted."

They watched Tania Johnson exit her car, walk up to her front door and enter. Five minutes later they knocked on her door, both Wolf and Colleen standing on each side of the entrance in case the occupant were to open the door and start shooting. Each had a hand resting on the grip of their concealed pistols, just in case. The door opened.

"May I help you?" Johnson said, looking cordially at the visitors on her stoop.

"Ms. Johnson, I'm Grayson Wolf and my associate Colleen Silverstone," Wolf said. "May we come in?"

"I recognize you," Johnson said, looking at Wolf. "I'm puzzled, however, about your visit."

"We'd like to speak to you about the Affirmative Transformation Treatment Center in Boston," Wolf replied. "Specifically the deaths associated with that organization."

Johnson held his eyes. "Are you writing an new expose, Mr. Wolf?"

"Not currently."

A grim smile appeared. "Too bad; there's enough dirt there to fill several volumes ... come in."

She stepped back and they entered, Colleen's gaze watching the woman's eyes for any sign of imminent violence. Johnson led them to a nicely appointed living room, signaling them to have a seat. She offered her guests refreshments which they turned down.

"Imagine the person you love more than life itself being slowly mangled and killed in front of your eyes and there wasn't a damn thing you could do to stop it," Johnson said, taking a seat across from them. "The person you were going to marry, that you expected to spend the rest of your life loving. Then one day, she announces that she feels like she's been a man all along because she got hooked on websites that spoke so glowingly of all the wonderful benefits of finally becoming the gender she was supposed to be all along. She begins to hang out with groups promoting gender transformation and finally goes to discuss options with counselors and doctors and without any hesitation—and lots of encouragement—begins the process of hormone replacement then radical mastectomy. Imagine your loved one transforming from a kind, sweet, reasonable human being into some kind of alien monster, increasingly angry at everything and everyone, bouts of physical violence, ranting and raving. Soon enough you wake up one morning realizing that you are living with a total stranger and whatever dreams and plans you had were over."

She stopped talking and sat, stone faced looking at Wolf and Colleen. After an extended period of silence, Colleen spoke.

"I understand someone would feel betrayed and angry, but deciding to kill the people involved in making the changes of a loved one? By what right? Perhaps the loved one committed suicide?"

"There are many ways to commit suicide, Ms. Silverstone," Johnson said. "Some are quick and clean, others are torturously slow and very messy and take years to accomplish. Maybe hearing about the increasing unhappiness and suicides might finally move one to take direct action to punish those who benefit and profit from destroying more and more lives. We're not talking about changing a hair style, choosing to get tattooed or plastic surgery to improve one's looks. The damage is physical, emotional and permanent; it spreads like dry rot to everyone it touches. Something had to be done."

"And hacking into car computers and house gas heaters is what had to be done," Wolf said.

"I have no clue what you are referring to," Johnson replied.

"Ms. Johnson..." Wolf leaned forward on his seat, "I was asked by Mr. and Mrs. Kramm, the owners of *The Washington Progressive,* to look into the matter behind their daughter's suicide. That investigation has brought me to you. I have accumulated solid evidence that you are the computer hacker responsible for the deaths of Jessica Demming, LeeAnn Hicks, Joseph Ferrara and Heather Franken and possibly others."

"You are very good at what you do, Mr. Wolf," Johnson said. "But as much as I enjoy discussing fiction, I will ask you and your friend to leave now." She stood up and looked at her guests expectantly.

Wolf and Colleen got up and started to walk toward the door. Wolf placed his hand on the doorknob and said,

"I'm afraid your mini-crime wave is over, Ms. Johnson. I'd get your affairs in order, if I were you."

"Jessica Demming was paid to pressure anxious and confused women to have their lives permanently mangled as was Franken, a college counselor whom students trusted, paid to refer deluded young women to surgeons like Hicks who never questioned the morality of her actions," Johnson said, her tone icy. Moving toward the door, she continued, "And Joseph Ferrara who built a fortune exploiting young women like my sweet, lovable, beautiful Ellie condemned to a lifetime of misery and regret. Whoever killed those incipient Nazis butchers did the world a favor ... good evening, Mr. Wolf, Ms. Silverstone."

"You have any doubts about her being the killer?" Wolf said, back in the car.

"No," Colleen confirmed. "Doing the world a favor, she said. Doesn't see the irony justifying killing people by labeling her victims Nazis butchers while acting in a similar manner."

"Psychology is a powerful deluder," Wolf replied. "We can talk ourselves into anything, as history so clearly illustrates."

"And increasingly manifested in our own culture," Colleen said. "Got complaint? Shoot up a school. Want your neighbor's daughter, kill the parents and kidnap the girl. Bored? Torch an apartment building."

"It will get much worse, I fear," Wolf said. "Education, the process of gaining knowledge and understanding allowing one to become a competent, independent person has been transformed into a permanent nursery where emotions rule. Feelings become the standard and hurting one's feelings is the ultimate crime."

"And if I'm really upset, I am justified in doling out whatever form of justice my emotions decide is appropriate," Colleen added.

"Whim-based morality," Wolf replied. "What could go wrong with that? ... okay, let's assemble all our evidence and hand it to the various police districts where the crimes took place."

Wolf started the car and drove out of the development back onto Broken Land toward Rt. 32. He was just about to take the exit when his car lurched forward causing him to miss the exit and accelerate toward the end of Broken Land a few hundred yards ahead, the car's speed increasing rapidly.

"Wolf!" Colleen shouted.

Wolf veered around a slower vehicle in front, immediately facing an oncoming car.

"Shit!" Wolf cried, swerving back into his lane, narrowly avoiding a head on collision as the car rapidly approached a line of cars ahead waiting for the light to change.

"Oh no you don't!" Wolf cried, his fingers reaching behind the steering wheel.

The engine roar died as quickly as it had started seconds before and he successfully braked the vehicle, coming to a stop a few yards behind the last car in the queue of vehicles stopped at the traffic light ahead.

"You okay," he said.

"What the hell, Wolf," Colleen said. "If you're trying to impress me with your driving skills, you succeeded spectacularly."

"I'm as impressed as you are," Wolf joked. "You can thank Tania Johnson for the demonstration. Fortunately we were in my car and not yours."

"Are you suggesting I can't drive as well as you?" Colleen retorted.

"I'm saying that I had Brett install a Wi-Fi kill switch in my car, which is why we didn't crash into the cars ahead going ninety," Wolf explained. "Fortunately I remembered it sooner than later."

"That bitch tried to kill us," Colleen said.

"Yup," Wolf said.

"Turn this crate around," she growled. "I have some choice words for her."

Wolf executed a U-turn and headed back to Johnson's house, parking the car behind her silver Acura to prevent it from being used for escape. They exited the car, each brandishing a pistol, conscious of being exposed to potential gunfire from the townhouse.

"Cover the door," Colleen said. "I'll take the rear."

"Please be careful," Wolf said.

"How sweet; you're worried about me," Colleen grinned.

"Sarcasm, the last refuge of the evader," Wolf retorted.

A toothy grin lit up her face and she proceeded to slink carefully around the corner of the building making her way to the rear. Gun raised and ready, Colleen stepped around the back corner, her eyes darting here and there looking for an ambush. Johnson was a crack shot and Colleen would have only a split second to avoid being hit and return fire.

Studying the slider and windows from top to bottom, all appeared to be closed. Colleen hugged the back wall making her way toward the sliding door, finding it locked. The back yard continued uninterrupted across a short open space ending at a row of townhouses beyond. Nothing moved.

All was quiet in the front, too, as Wolf stood pressed against the wall adjacent Johnson's main entrance, his pistol near his head pointing skyward. Then he heard sirens in the distance, their wail rising as they came closer.

Wolf started laughing as he waited for the police cars to come racing into the parking area, which they did a few moments later, officers exiting their cars, taking cover behind open doors. Wolf didn't wait for an order; he got down on his knees, placed the pistol on the ground and locked his hands behind his neck. He did continue laugh under his breath, however.

The Howard County police officers, however, were not amused. Neither was the Police Chief, who, albeit reluctantly, agreed that both Wolf and Colleen had federally issued concealed carry permits allowing both to carry a weapon in every state and US possession.

"Those permits do not allow you to wave your guns around causing panic among the homeowners," the Chief said, peering at the pair. "Explain and it better be legitimate."

Wolf spent the next fifteen minutes giving the Chief a detailed overview of his investigation ending with the near death event on Broken Land Parkway earlier.

"The only reason we're here talking to you is that I had the foresight to ask the head of my technology department to install a kill switch cutting off all external reception of data," Wolf explained. "Even then, it took me a few seconds—and some emergency maneuvering—to throw the switch and regain control of my car coming to a stop a few feet behind a line of cars waiting for the light to turn green. If you check your records, I bet you'll find that the frantic caller was Tania Johnson, who will have had plenty of time to hotfoot it outta Dodge to parts unknown."

The Chief looked at the computer monitor on her desk and said, "Johnson is a software programmer and it was her who called about gunmen outside her home. I've heard about cars being hacked, but how could she have taken over your car in the short time you were at her home?"

"I've been thinking about that," Wolf replied. "My guess is that she was waiting in her car when we arrived at her company. The clerk at Main Street Electrix did warn her we were coming. She would have had enough time to establish a connection with my car's Wi-Fi allowing her to take control."

"Why wait for you to visit her at home?" the Chief wondered. "She must have been following you; why not try to crash your vehicle on the way to her house?"

Colleen answered her. "To find out what we knew and the opportunity to share her pain; to explain why she felt justified killing people connected in some way to the Affirmative Transformation Treatment Center in Boston and the woman Johnson loved whom she lost due to her gender change."

"Love, greed and revenge are among the top causes for murder," the Chief said. "And after the deed, killing to cover up the deed is a strong motivator. I've already put out an APB on her; she can't get too far. If you give me everything you've got on Johnson, I will share it with the Massachusetts police and the NYPD."

"We'll be happy to do that," Wolf agreed. "Oh, you'd better warn your officers that Tania Johnson is not only dangerous with a computer: she's a pistol sharpshooter. It's the reason why Colleen and I approached her house with guns drawn. We weren't taking any chances."

"I'll let my people know," the Chief said. "Thanks for the heads up. We've got a convenience room where you can write your report. There's drinks and snacks; take whatever you want."

They thanked the Chief and followed an officer to the room where they keyed in the details of their investigation into a computer file. One finished they were officially released from police custody and their weapons returned.

"That was fun," Wolf said, slipping into the driver's seat and shutting the car door. "I guess the last order of business for me is to visit the Kramms and make my report and that's that. What's our next move regarding Shred Pro?"

"Cooper is still digging into that landfill so our move is wait and see," Colleen replied. "I'm going to fly to New York tonight to visit my mother while waiting for information allowing us to proceed. As soon as I get word from Cooper, I will call you. I assume you'll be cavorting with your fictional girlfriend in the meanwhile?"

Wolf shot her a toothy grin. "Until I get a nonfictional one. You up for the challenge, Ms. Silverstone?"

"Stop talking nonsense and drive, sidekick."

"Yes, dear," Wolf quipped, laughing.

Chapter 27

Toxic Swamp Gas

"I suppose you gave the scoop about the killings to my competitors?" Kramm said, after Wolf gave him a full report of his investigation.

"Nope," Wolf replied. "The story is going up on CIR's National Update page. Your family is not mentioned. I hope that I've been able to bring some measure of closure, or at least, a deeper understanding of the issues associated with our latest national fad among mostly young women. I'm afraid that many more women and some men will fall prey to peer pressure that feeds their insecurities, anxieties and confusion about their sexuality and take actions that for the most part will be irreversible. Hopefully my investigation will throw much needed light on this gender transformation industry and change the minds of some who may be thinking about going down this dangerous path."

"It's bad enough that despondent young adults commit suicide, but people being killed over it is appalling, though understandable," Kramm said. "Not to mention the truly frightening notion that our cars and homes are vulnerable to being used to harm us, though none of this is surprising given the lackadaisical attitude business and government have shown toward computer security. I am sorry I've put you in harm's way, Mr. Wolf."

"Thank you, but I'm very good at putting myself in harm's way all the time," Wolf said, grinning.

"I know you declined remuneration for your efforts on my behalf," Kramm said. "But like you, I do not like being in anyone's debt. I owe you a personal favor, Mr. Wolf and expect you to collect it."

"I will, thank you," Wolf assured him, getting up. "Please accept my sincerest condolences for the loss of your daughter and wishing you and yours a healthy and productive year."

"And the same to you," Kramm said, shaking Wolf's hand.

*   *   *   *

Colleen scrolled through her phone messages stopping here and there to re-read Wolf's texts he had sent since she had informed him that she had arrived in New York two days back. She didn't bother to deny that she enjoyed his company and liked reading his texts.

"How often are you going to read his messages and not answer him back?" her mother said, appearing behind Colleen on the sofa. "You're not getting any younger and your Mr. Wolf will only take so much rejection before he trots off."

"He's not my Mr. Wolf, mom," Colleen replied, suddenly feeling like she was in a Jane Austen scene. "We're just friends."

"Oh please!" her mother retorted. "He can't take his eyes off you and you smile a lot when you talk about him."

"I've hardly mentioned Wolf since I've been here," Colleen protested.

"You have referred to Mr. Wolf no less than five times in two days," her mother replied. "That's four times more than any other man you have mentioned over the past five years. Honey, you are brilliant, brave, successful and beautiful and I love you—"

"*But?*" Colleen interjected.

"But when it comes to love and romance, you can be as obtuse as a boulder."

"Maybe I'm just not ready for a long-term relationship?" Colleen countered.

"That's a load of crap and you know it, honey," her mother said. "There is no readiness button that switches on during some fictional future. You've been on a personal fast track all your life, Colleen and now you're thirty seven. In a few moments you'll wake up

273

and be fifty seven and that readiness you're waiting for won't be lying next to you ... now seize the moment and text your Mr. Wolf a message that will make his day. Like Nike says, just do it."

Wolf was in the middle of a strategy session with CIR's department heads when his phone made a low sound and he did what he'd never do when engaged with others: he lifted his phone and read Colleen's text.

"I miss you."

"What's wrong, bro?" RJ asked, seeing Wolf's surprised expression.

"I'm not sure," Wolf replied. He held the phone toward RJ.

"What part are you unsure about—the, I, miss or you?" RJ said in his most sarcastic tone.

"All three," Wolf said. "Colleen doesn't say or write such endearing messages. It's either a joke or an SOS."

"Man, the two of you are going to be the death of me yet," RJ complained. "Just get on with it and take her to bed already!"

"Excuse me," Diana interjected. "I can't believe my eyes: Grayson Wolf with a phone in his hand during a phones non licet meeting, a rule that he himself had insisted upon years ago."

"It's his girlfriend saying how much she misses him," RJ said, grinning from ear to ear. "Love takes priority over some boring meeting any day."

RJ's announcement brought the meeting to a halt as the agenda switched from discussing the attack upon Susan Baker and the class action suit in California, to Wolf's love life. Wolf sat passively as the attendees fired a series of questions at him ranging from his current relationship with Colleen to when's the wedding.

Wolf shot RJ an evil glance, proceeding to deny any ongoing intimate relationship with Colleen, effectively deflating any expectations about incipient nuptials. Waving a hand at the assembly, he urged them to return to the business at hand.

Diana brought the meeting to order bringing up a name that Wolf hadn't heard since last December: Retief Mbuso, who worked for Universal Accounting, which did independent audits for colleges.

"You may recall that Mr. Mbuso tipped us off last year about shady accounting practices in the colleges he audits," Diana said. "Turns out the shade is spread far and wide darkening not only dozens of public and private universities and colleges, but so is Universal Accounting traveling on the shady side of the financial street. I'll let Annika give us the down and dirty..."

"Where to begin?" Annika said. "Let's start with the fluff: the college admissions scandal we've been reading about. Anyone in the room not shocked to about wealthy parents paying tens of thousands of dollars for fake test takers, bribing coaches, changing SAT scores and so forth just to get their kids in one of the name colleges?"

"I suppose the good news is that at least these parents recognize that many colleges still admit on the basis of merit," Jewel King said. "Though as we see from Harvard's discrimination against Asians, merit has long ago taken a back seat behind the anti-concept called diversity."

"And look at the harm this policy is doing to worthwhile minority kids who find themselves unprepared for the academic rigor of these colleges," Teena said. "I've got friends and family who sent kids to Stanford, Yale and MIT only to discover that they were floundering. A few quit, but the ones who transferred to local colleges are doing quite well, thank goodness. Diversity is just another form of discrimination; worse, 'cause it sucks people into it thinking they're getting an equal shot."

Annika nodded in agreement and continued. "Now for the real news: the college endowment scandal. A significant percentage of endowment, as high as eighty percent, is designated by the donor for funding a specific cause: a medical center, technology scholarships, a professorial chair, like Objectivist studies and the like. However, money is fungible; once in the bank, it can be moved to wherever the administration designates. Brett, you want to give an example of what we've found?"

"Thanks to Retief Mbuso who's been providing specific evidence of the misuse of endowment funds, we're getting detailed information of who and were they're shifting these designated funds," Brett said. "College administrators are spending huge sums on promoting a pro-regressive agenda and personnel. A random sample: Michigan has a Vice Provost of Equity and Inclusion with a salary of four hundred thousand and his department spends eleven million on diversity, inclusion and so forth. His job? To sniff out racism, sexism, homophobia, transphobia etc., each and every day. California at Santa Cruz has an activist in residence whose job—and I'm not making this up—is to mint student activists, all leftists, of course and train them to be good useful idiots. Tens of billions of donations aimed at improving life and liberty, is being used to undermine the values of liberty and our Western heritage. I can't wait for Juan and our legal tigers to take a huge bite outta them."

"And when our legal team does tackle this issue, the endowment scandal will be a thousand times bigger than this media blip about parents paying to get kids into colleges they aren't qualified for," Annika said.

"What's the plan?" Wolf asked.

"Keep on gathering evidence," Annika replied. "Our current class action assault on colleges is just starting, so it will be many months, years perhaps, before we can take action on college endowments."

"That's not acceptable," Wolf objected. "We should consider gathering sufficient evidence to launch a media campaign naming names, dates, amounts and deeds. If administrators suddenly find themselves having to defend their universities against a rising torrent of accusation and the legal challenges that follow, it might make them more willing to settle our class action suits instead of trying to stonewall with countersuits, legal delays and all the rest to put off the day of reckoning. I move the Board vote on my motion."

The Board did vote and so move and the measure to launch a media campaign passed unanimously. The next order of business was political and Diana called on RJ to present.

"As you all know, we get pressure from politicians all the time," he began. "In most cases, it's Democrats, who by the way, ought to change their name to autocrats because in almost every case, they are upset with our work to protect individuals rights, though none would dare utter such words since I'd push their admission out across the globe. Lately, however, my team's been fielding as many complaints from Republican politicians as Democrats."

"Ah, yes," Wolf jibed. "The me-too chickens coming home to root and spreading their poop amongst us. Let me guess: the Repubs are clucking about the class action."

"Give the Wolf a bone," RJ quipped. "We're undermining our great university system. We're going to bankrupt private colleges. And my personal favorite, we're a bunch of greedy wastrels. That one was from Independent Senator Blahsi, a member of the Senate Education Committee. The same man who's never run a lemonade stand but somehow winds up being worth a couple million. And it's not just complaints and concerns; it's threats. The head of the House Finance Committee promises to sic the Justice Department on us. I'm waiting for the DOJ to charge us with colluding with the Russians to eliminate free lunches for poor kids or to make bus riders walk more than the length of their driveway to the school bus."

"I'd say they'd have a good case to charge you with being a sarcastic wiseass," Wolf joked.

"How are you and your people responding to these threats?" Teena said. "I'd like to know because knowing you, RJ, I'm thinking we need to double our armed security."

"I've instructed my peeps to tell anyone that speaks to them in a threatening manner that we're putting their alma mater on top of our hit list." It took everyone a moment to realize RJ was not kidding. He continued. "Hey, I was inclined to tell these so called lawmakers to screw themselves, but I didn't want any to get hurt."

After the laughter died down, Diana spoke.

"You're seriously telling Senators and Representatives—"

"And governors, mayors and the local dog catcher," RJ interjected.

"One and all," Diana continued, "we're putting them on top of our list?"

"Yes," RJ replied. "And any that really piss me off, I tell them their alma mater is now number one after we dump the California colleges into the Pacific."

Diana peered at the Media chief for a long moment. Seeing the guarded look on her face, Wolf could imagine one of two responses forthcoming from the Director of CIR: lasers shooting out of her eyes reducing poor RJ to ashes in an instant or planting a big, fat kiss on his lips.

A wicked grin slid across Diana's mouth. "Make sure you follow up your threat by putting their alma mater on top of our legal hit list and spread it across every media platform. Let every politician from sea to shining sea discover the wages of sinning against the foremost defender of individual rights. They've been going after us collectively and individually for over ten years and unlike them, we're not beholden to, or swayed by, special interests, paybacks, influence peddling, pay for play and all the rest of the corrupt practices in the political swamps across the country ... RJ, be sure to name names, too. And let's get ready to burn any pol that attempt to use their federal or state goons to harass or threaten us, any employee or supporter."

"Yes, sir!" RJ said, performing a snappy salute.

New and old business addressed, Diana officially closed the meeting and the focus returned to Wolf, everyone wanting the low down about his and Colleen's encounter with Tania Johnson, which Wolf was happy to accommodate. When the topic switched to the killer of Madeline Talbot and Justin Bellamy, the flow of information was reduced to a trickle.

"We've made some progress on a way Bellamy managed to rake in huge investment returns year after year, but as for who killed them and why, we're no further than we were back in December. Colleen's got her best people working on digging into New World Fund, but to date we've got bupkis ... On the other hand, I'm closing in on the last few chapters of my Tara Mason novel, but I'm not going to say more than that. And as for further inquiries about my love life, I'm closed to further discussion, except to say that I do appreciate that everyone is thinking about me and wishing me happy trails."

The group began to disperse when Brett stopped everyone with an announcement.

"Just came in," he said, looking at his phone. "Looks like your friend Tania has been busy...she walked into the DC gender trans center fifteen minutes ago and started shooting...no word on how many people have been shot, but preliminary reports say she went for administrators and medical staff. Police have the place locked down, but they can't locate the shooter."

"I guess she feels she's got nothing to lose at this point and is going out with a bang, no pun intended," Wolf said.

"Frankly I've had it up to the proverbial 'here' with people deciding that they're judge, jury and executioner," RJ said. "I certainly am prepared to defend myself if some ass wipe objected to me being gay by trying to bash my skull in. But going around hacking into cars and home heaters to kill people because her lover changed her sex and it messed her up love life is no reason to hurt the ones who engineered the transformation. The same goes for all the religious wackos over in the Middle East or any other self-serving, righteous idiot shooting unarmed people, like that jerk in New Zealand. Talk about a violation of individual rights!"

"Wolf, you spent over two months looking into this sex change industry," Annika said. "I know there are people who are born into the wrong body, but thousands and growing exponentially? Does Tania Johnson have a genuine complaint about the damage being caused to many who engage in gender changes—not that I'm suggesting what she's doing is justified in any way."

"Based on my initial findings, there is cause to be concerned, if for no other reason than cui bono: who benefits," Wolf said. "An entire sex change industry has sprung up in the last decade raking in millions from insurance payments, grants from local government and doling out that money to pay people like college counselors and student sex change cheerleaders to funnel an increasing clientele of mostly women believing that they're really men in women's bodies. Make no mistake, this upsurge of gender change is driven by social media feeding off the insecurities of young people, many whom subsequently experience a sense of despair. After having made such a momentous and fundamental decision, some feel angry and direct their anger at themselves as we see in the rising suicide rate among trans. And finally, a violent response by those who feel a sense of deep loss over having been robbed of the person they loved who is now physically or emotionally gone. Expect to see more violence as this trans fad continuous to grow."

"Is everyone else always responsible for the fact that they were the ones who hopped on the bandwagon and screwed up their life? I am victim, hear me whine?" Diana said, her tone uncompromising. "Freedom demands personal responsibility, or we are left with chaos ending in some form of unpleasant consequence. All of us at CIR fight for the right of individuals to their life, their property, their liberty and their pursuit of happiness and getting endless grief for doing so. I'm sorry to see people suffering the consequences of their poor judgement, but I will not allow any to get away with evading the reality that it was they who failed to think before acting—repeatedly—and subsequently attempting to make others feel guilty for their own foolish decisions and actions."

"Unfeeling, selfish Director!" Wolf said.

"Thank you, Lady Catherine de Bourgh," Diana retorted, a droll look on her face. "But I stand resolute in my view and shall not be moved."

"You might be *re-moved* however," RJ teased.

"It's over," Brett said, bringing the subject back to the events unfolding in DC. "According to my sources, Johnson came out shooting and the police fired back."

No one asked what the outcome was.

"What a waste," Wolf said, shaking his head.

"Tears for the woman that nearly killed you and your main squeeze, bro?" RJ taunted.

"Tears for Tania Johnson who by all accounts was a brilliant computer scientist; yes," Wolf replied. "Having said that, I agree with Diana: best check your premises before acting because one or more may be wrong."

"That's for sure," RJ agreed. He puckered his lips and peered at him. "So, what are you gonna do about Colleen, Wolfie?"

"Ask her to marry me," Wolf joked. "Happy now?"

"From your lips to God's ears," RJ quipped, a toothy grin lighting up his face.

"Incorrigible." Wolf shook his head and left the room.

Chapter 28

Who Knows What Evil...

Colleen's brilliant smile upon opening the door caught Wolf off guard. He shot her a suspicious look and entered the hotel suite.

"I hear you are going to ask me to marry you," she merrily said.

"What I am going to do is throttle RJ the next time I see him," Wolf replied, looking annoyed.

"So you're *not* going to ask me to marry you?" Colleen said, her tone threatening.

"Cute," Wolf retorted, walking over to the bedroom he stayed in last time he was here with Colleen. He stopped, shot her a droll look and said, "Shall I take my things to your room?" She grinned and pointed toward his door. "I thought so."

He put his things away and came back to the living area. Colleen placed a bottle of water on the elevated kitchenette counter.

"Thanks." Wolf took a seat on the stool across from her. "You mentioned that Cooper and company had found something."

"Several somethings," she replied. "Shred Pro trucks all have GPS and every trip is recorded and stored. Cooper has found a backdoor into their master systems in half dozen key cities where most of the technological and business deals originate and has been running a program to connect truck routes to specific businesses that were startups or that announced major developments. His objective is to compare the routes over time and spot any deviation from any particular truck's route."

"The idea being that a deviation might mean a location where non-shredded papers are delivered," Wolf said. "The fact I'm here, I'm assuming Cooper has found a location or two."

"Yes," Colleen confirmed.

Wolf grinned. "And?"

"And you've arrived just in time because a truck has visited one of these off-route locations in Queens, a dozen miles across the East River," she said. "And I've got a surprise ready and waiting, so chop, chop."

"What's the other bit of news Cooper has discovered?" Wolf asked.

"Tell you in the car," she replied.

Colleen drove out of the hotel's underground garage and headed for the Queensborough Bridge.

"The other news Cooper dug up is about Troy and Rebecca Searles, who are the owners of Shred Pro," she said, the traffic moving slightly above a snail's pace on East 59th. "Apparently Shred Pro's been losing money for years, yet the Searles' continue to live a life of luxury in their fifty million dollar condo overlooking Central Park, winter villa in Spain, beach front home in San Francisco and lots more like it."

"Has Cooper found out how they manage to live so modestly year after year?" Wolf said. "Billion-dollar lottery winners, perhaps?"

"No, and that's what's so interesting," Colleen said. "Where is the money coming from to maintain their extravagant lifestyle?"

"This is where it's good to have the Grayson Wolf on the case, with his many years of experience hobnobbing with the sleazy and greasy," Wolf beamed. "When someone lives high on the hog with no visible means of support, that's a clear signal that they have significant invisible means of support. For the average thug, that means dealing in cash transfers. For the sophisticated thug, that's shell companies, off shore accounts, draining the life out of companies they own and another hundred financial tricks."

"If we get lucky with our surprise visit this afternoon, we'll have a direct go at the Searles with whatever leverage we come up with," Colleen said. Loudly expelling a puff of air, she added, "Finally...traffic's getting worse every day; at least it's moving across the bridge at a good clip."

The traffic along Queen's Blvd. rolled a shade under the speed limit and they were soon traveling east on Interstate 495 then south on

I-627 eventually winding up at a nondescript warehouse off Lawson Blvd. near the southern shore of Long Island. Colleen slowed the car as she rolled past, finding a convenient spot to park out of direct line of sight from the building. They got out and walked into an alley adjacent the warehouse where they were met by a group of heavily armed federal agents.

"You alerted the FBI?" Wolf said, surprised.

A smile touched Colleen's lips. "Look more closely."

"Ah, what's with the crossed ᵮ? What agency are they from, the Templar Knights?" Wolf joked.

"F, crossed T...confusing, isn't it?" Colleen's smile expanded. Turning to the armed cadre, she said, "Let's roll, boys."

Half dozen men stormed the warehouse yelling, BI! BI! which sure sounded like it could be the *F* BI raiding the place. The fake federal agents bound the hands of the three men working at the truck with zip cords and sat them on the ground, their backs to the wall. Brandishing pistols, Wolf followed Colleen into a room directly behind the Shred Pro truck finding several people sorting papers from carts that had been wheeled in from the truck. Surprised, they dropped the papers they were holding and quickly raised their hands pursuant to Colleen's order.

Wolf traded his pistol for a camera and took pictures, while Colleen questioned the workers, who initially refused to answer. When she promised them that she would guarantee their immediate release from (mumble) BI custody, they appeared willing, but suspicious. When Colleen wrote a statement attesting to their release, applied a signature and handed it to one of the detainees, they capitulated.

"We're not doing nothin' wrong," the man said. "We're just doin' our job ... a truck comes in, we unload the paper, then we place it in those hoppers over there." He pointed to several large electronic units on a counter by the wall, then continued. "The papers run through the scanner and the data goes out on the wires. When the scanning is over we return it to the truck and run the shredder. The driver takes the truck and leaves. We're not doing nothin' wrong; that's what we're hired to do."

It was clear to Colleen and Wolf that these men were just doing the job they were hired to do and further questions about where the data was being sent was fruitless. Colleen told the men to leave the room and go home for the day, which they happily did.

"Now what?" Wolf said.

"Cooper," Colleen said.

She retrieved her phone and called the man, telling him what she had discovered. He directed her to key his computer code into the scanner and scan some docs to him, explaining that he'll use the information gained to begin tracking down the location where information was being sent.

"I can't guarantee finding the end user," Cooper said. "If these people have been getting away with this for over a decade, most likely they're good at covering their tracks. But success makes people become complacent, so we might get a break. I'll let you know the second I find anything."

Colleen thanked him and terminated the call. She scanned a few document sending their data to Cooper while Wolf grabbed reams of documents stuffing them into a duffle bag to look at later. Done with scanning, Colleen signaled him and they left the room, Wolf noticing the truck had disappeared.

"Where did the truck disappear to?" he asked, as Colleen drove back up Lawson Blvd. the way she had come in.

"The cross T BI took possession: evidence," she replied. "Looks like your hunch about these trucks back in Denver panned out spectacularly. Not bad for a mediocre fiction writer."

"*Excuse me?*" Wolf countered. "There is nothing mediocre about any part or parcel of me."

A grin slid across her mouth. "That remains to be seen."

"You should only be so lucky," Wolf retorted. "Besides insults, what's next?"

"A visit to a fifty million dollar sky high condo with a clear view of Central Park as soon as we assemble all the evidence," Colleen said.

"I have to admit, it's nice to be able to order up your own private army at a moment's notice," Wolf said. "I could have used that type of muscle a few times over the years. I especially loved the FBI allusion."

"Figured having our friends *assume* an FBI raid was preferable to a possible shootout at the Shred Pro corral," Colleen explained.

"I suppose they'll figure out they've been snookered soon enough," Wolf said. "And I bet on hindsight, they consider themselves lucky to been fooled by your fake FBI ... While we're on the subject, have you had anymore FBI hassles since that raid on SSIS back in December?"

"No further raids at the center; at least not yet," Colleen replied. "We still get the occasional request for additional information pursuant to the little darlings of Senator Grisham and Justin Bellamy and that of Bellamy's associates that my company is or has done work for. We refuse, of course, unless they present a court order and even then we have at times refused to comply pursuant to privacy guarantees."

"Karla Grisham," Wolf said, issuing a snort. "She and her Senator daddy are lucky her vicious behavior didn't become public now with all that brouhaha over the college admissions scandal that's getting juicer with every passing day. Especially if the public discovered that after being involved in setting up girls for date rape, she gets off with a slap on the wrist and a couple hundred hours of public service ladling soup for the homeless."

"That'll teach her never to be a bad girl again," Colleen said. "You can bet you'll hear her name connected to something much worse before she's twenty-five, if no one kills her first."

"In a way I feel sorry for kids like Karla because her parents failed her all her life," Wolf said. "Saw that time after time when I was slinking around with the high and mighty. You see it every day with kids from the rich and famous bragging about college being one big party, getting high, getting drunk, indiscriminate sex, petty and not so petty criminal acts and down the drain they go. It's sad, it's stupid and worst of all, so unnecessary."

"You're more understanding than I am, Wolf," Colleen replied. "These kids may not have the most attentive or caring parents, but they're not mindless animals. They're not living in a vacuum; they make choices and take actions and these actions have consequences, including the possibility of getting your head bashed in. I can assure you that Karla Grisham's kind of maliciousness will drive someone to beat her to a pulp sooner or later; I've seen it time and time again. I'd like to believe she'd see the error of her ways and reform, but there is no incentive to do so since her environment supports her behavior."

"Sooner or later also applies to some of their parents, too, like Justin Bellamy," Wolf said. "Successfully cheating and lying and lording it over the suckers for nearly twenty years and now dead as a doornail because another lying, cheating SOB wanted to make sure he kept his mouth shut."

"It is a form of justice, getting what you so royally deserve," Colleen replied.

"But not to be doled out by those anxious to avoid getting what they themselves royally deserve from a judge and a jury of their peers," Wolf said.

"And when that system of justice breaks down?" Colleen challenged.

"Then we all discover what it's like to live in most of the rest of the world," Wolf replied, darkly.

*　　*　　*　　*

"You tell them that they can either talk with us or to federal authorities," Wolf said, peering at the steward guarding the lobby at One Central Park West.

The man made the call and minutes later Wolf and Colleen were admitted into the humble, forty-fifth floor abode of Troy and Rebecca Searles. A pleasant receptionist escorted them to a lovely sitting room, its huge windows overlooking Central Park illuminating the well-appointed space in the bright, February morning. Several paintings hung on the wall, Wolf recognizing them as Dutch masters, the cost of just one quite possibly greater than the value of the condo itself.

Mr. and Mrs. Searles were seated on a sofa, each sporting a most displeased expression. The receptionist waited expectably; Mr. Searles made a dismissive motion with his hand sending her away: no offer of refreshment for their uninvited guests was to be forthcoming.

"What do you want?" Mr. Searles demanded.

"Good morning," Wolf said, cheerfully, ignoring the man. "I'm Grayson Wolf and this is my associate Colleen Silverstone. How are you and Mrs. Searles on this lovely morning?"

"Besides annoyed at having our morning coffee interrupted, we're splendid," he replied, voice dripping with sarcasm. "Before you begin, let me assure you that unlike others who may tremble at the mention of your name, Mr. Wolf, I do not. I am fully aware of your little tricks and games and the only reason I permitted you and your sidekick access is because I like to be entertained."

Wolf shot a droll glance at Colleen at Searles's comment referring to her as his sidekick, then addressed the man.

"I do love to entertain people, especially those who will soon grace the headlines of CIR's website. We're here to give you a heads up about untoward behavior at Shred Pro."

"Don't know anything about what you're talking about," Searles said. "I don't manage the company. What is it you think is going on?"

"Let's begin with the unique construction of the shredding mechanism of your Shred Pro trucks that can divert documents to an empty space in the rear," Wolf said. "That material is delivered to unscheduled locations, such as the one on Lawson in Queens, where employees empty the secret compartment and proceed to scan documents giving certain people access to proprietary information used to make your ill-gotten investments for a hefty return."

Searles looked genuinely troubled, Wolf thinking the man might have missed his calling as an actor. He shook his head slowly and said,

"Like I said, I don't manage Shred Pro or any other of the companies I own. What you're telling me is very concerning, of course, and I will look into it. Is that all, Mr. Wolf?"

"I'm afraid there's more," Wolf said, scrunching up his face in mock concern. "It's pretty clear to me that you, and perhaps the missus, too, are co-conspirators to financial fraud and the murder of Justin Bellamy and Madeline Talbot."

Searles issued a chuckle, got off the sofa and clapped his hands. "Bravo, bravo. I do so much enjoy hearing about your fictional work. Now, unless you have any further blockbuster announcements, I'm anxious for my mid-morning cup of Kopi. Good day, Mr. Wolf and your lovely, um, *associate*." The emphasis he placed on the word associate left no doubt in anyone's mind exactly what he had intended it to mean.

The lovey associate took several steps toward him, lovely white teeth gleaming between parted lips.

"Enjoy your defecated coffee, Mr. Searles," Colleen said, her face barely a foot from his. "In fact, I suggest using it up in the next few days because in twenty four hours we're going to find the killer of

Madeline Talbot and Justin Bellamy. If my years of experience is any guide, expect your lovely associates to sing like songbirds; and if you're very lucky, the police will get to you before Mr. Wolf does. You see, he's planning to rip to shreds the people responsible for murdering his pregnant fiancé, the love of his life, the woman he was going to spend the rest of his life with, the son he's never going to have now ... enjoy the reset of the day, Mr. Searles—it's going to one of your last."

"Damn girl," Wolf said, walking back to the elevator. "Listening to you back there, I was thinking how glad I was you're on my side. But upon reflection, I'm sure your performance has Searles on the phone this very second calling every hitman in New York to take me out."

"Not every hitman; just the one we want," Colleen clarified.

"And you know this, how?" Wolf said, skeptically.

She placed a finger on her lips and smiled cryptically. The elevator doors opened and they rode silently down to the lobby. Back in the car, Colleen brought forth her phone, swiping and tapping at the screen. A voice was heard: Searles's voice.

"You bugged his home?" Wolf said, alarmed and pleased at the same time.

"I bugged him, the arrogant son of a bitch," she replied. "Dropped in into his pocket when he was busy admiring my lovely visage; it'll record everything he says. I'm hoping he'll call his wet worker, but any call he makes before he discovers my little friend will help us move forward. And just so we're clear, you're the sidekick no matter what that sleazebag says."

"Yes, dear."

"Glad you understand the pecking order, sidekick."

"Sorry, Colleen," Cooper said, later that day. "Recording's all we got. Searles must have used a disposable phone and he's smart enough to talk in code—all the successful thieves do. I've got no clue who, or what, this Syblov is or refers to."

"I assume you're going through everything we've got?" Colleen asked.

"We've searched through our current list of names of anyone associated with New World and Searles," Cooper assured her. "We've applied a hundred variation of Syblov hoping to find some break in the code, but we've got nothing so far. Sorry, Colleen. If I find anything, I will call you immediately."

She thanked Cooper and terminated the call.

"Whoever this Syblov Searles talked to is, this guy is the killer, I'm sure of it," she said, looking determined. "Based on the conversation, I don't get the sense Searles was ordering a hit; more like he was warning him."

"How could you tell that?" Wolf said, not at all convinced since most likely he'd be the killer's number one target.

"Twenty years of intuition," she replied. "Searles was using a throwaway and not worried about being bugged by the FBI. His tone and language *felt* like he was warning the guy we're were looking for him. If he wanted to schedule a pick up, or make a takeout order, or closing the account or similar type of wording with appropriate inflection—or lack thereof—then I'd be looking over my shoulder from now on. Of course, if and when we do catch wind of the killer's trail, then we had better be prepared."

"I respect your intuition, but plan to look over my shoulder, eye the drink served to me and check my rearview mirror consistently until we get this killer," Wolf said.

Colleen's phone jingled. She shot a surprised look at Wolf and took the call.

"Barry," she said. "I'm with Wolf; your call is on speaker. Where have you been and where are you now?"

"Out of reach of friend and foe," he said.

"Mr. Silverstone," Wolf said. "There have been some developments about Bellamy's murder over the last six weeks. The police are convinced that you had nothing to do with his death; you should come out of the cold."

"Not happening," he replied. "Until the killer is caught, I remain a target and turning myself in would make me a sitting duck. This may come as a shock to you, but not all police can be trusted."

Wolf shot Colleen a, like duh, face causing her to issue a snort.

"Barry, have you ever heard of Syblov?" she asked.

"Oh, my God," Barry replied. "I don't know who he is, but I know the name strikes fear in conversations of people connected to

Bellamy's circle of influence the handful of times it was mentioned. Where did you hear it?"

"Troy Searles mentioned it," she replied.

"Troy Searles?" Barry said, his tone puzzled. "I've heard of him; saw him a few times at some events over ten years or so. Never saw him around Bellamy or New World functions. Why were you talking with him?"

"Did you know he owns Shred Pro?" Wolf said.

"I think I heard his name associated with it," Barry replied. "What's a recycling company have to do with anything?"

"Only that's how Bellamy managed to turn New World Fund into a multi-billion dollar investment company and keep it the top earner for over a dozen years," Wolf said, proceeding to give Barry a thumbnail sketch of the scam.

"Son of a bitch!" Barry exclaimed. "I—all of us—knew that Bellamy had some secret pipeline to inside information from dozens of firms and financial companies, but no one ever discovered a clue how he did it. The SEC, the FBI, they kept investigating for years; made me rich just being his attorney...and investing in his company of course... Colleen, you think New World is still getting the inside scoop? If they are, shame on me for liquidating my account days after he got killed, though I didn't lose all that much."

Wolf looked at Colleen who shook her head knowingly.

"Glad to know your priorities are still on what counts the most, Barry," she quipped. "Any clue at all who this Syblov is?"

"None whatsoever," he replied. "Colleen, please be extra careful and look out for your mother, too. Gotta go..."

The call ended and Colleen lowered her phone.

"Well, we're no further than we were ten minutes ago," she said. "At least we know Barry is still breathing. Looks like it's down to Cooper to find a link."

"Link..." Wolf said, his voice sounding distant. "I just thought of someone who has a business based on links..."

He fished his phone out of his pocket and pressed a name on his call list.

"Hello Mr. Kramm," Wolf here. "I'm calling in that favor you owe me."

Chapter 29

Scent of Syblov

Wolf entered the bar, his eyes adjusting to its dim interior, the aroma of stale beer assaulting his nostrils. The place was a classic dive making it the perfect location for a surreptitious meeting with Chuckie, a character of questionable reputation, Kramm's sources had arranged. Gazing at the clientele strewn throughout the place, Wolf was struck by an overwhelming impression of disappointment, resignation and regret so palatable that it crowded out any other emotion, much like a smoldering fire would use up all the oxygen, smothering what life remained.

He nervously took the first steps toward the rear booth where his contact was supposedly waiting for him. For all Wolf knew, the person he was meeting might turn out to be the elusive and mysterious Syblov, an assassin capable of killing a person in the middle of a police convention without anyone being the wiser.

Closing in on his objective, Wolf saw a shadowy figure waiting for him on the far side of the booth. He slipped into the bench seat facing the man, uttering the expected phrase, the man confirming the code with the expected response.

"First order of business: the money," Chuckie said.

Wolf peered at the sallow, shrunken face for a moment, then retrieved a thick envelope from inside his jacket filled with a fifty circulated Benjamin's, sliding it across the table. Chuckie eagerly fingered through the cash, his expression darkening.

"You cheatin' me, man?" he snarled.

"Just protecting my interests," Wolf replied. "That's five thousand. If the information you give me is genuine, you get the other five grand...plus five more."

"Sure you will," Chuckie said, his voice dripping with sarcasm.

Wolf produced his driver's license and held it up to Chuckie's face. "If you recognize my name, then you know my reputation. So, you want a shot at a five thousand dollar bonus or do I find someone else who will?"

Chuckie looked hard at Wolf, blinked a couple times and stuck the envelope into his jacket. His eyes darted here and there across the room.

"No one knows who Syblov is," he said. "At least nobody I know knows and I knows most of the lowlife in fifty miles. Last December when that finance dude got wacked, I was pursuin' my business over that part 'a town. Didn't think nothin' of it until the next week when I hear he was killed on a Thursday night. Turns out I was working the corner where he live, me thinking how weird me being there that evening."

"So you think you saw this Syblov?" Wolf asked, hoping Chuckie's account was going to produce some tangible result.

"Well that's the thing," he said. "I didn't give it another thought until I get the message about you looking for Syblov. I tell the dude I'll get back to him and now I'm going through my pictures trying to find something."

"You have photographs?" Wolf said, excitedly.

Chuckie grinned, showing a mouthful of neglected teeth. "Nothin' like that. I got this ability to see picture in my head as clear as I see you; had it since I was born, I guess. Anyhoo, I'm flipping through like couple hunnerd pictures and I get one of a guy, I think a guy—dressed in overalls, cap, like some repairman—walking past me into this Bellamy guy's building and come out again maybe twenty minutes later and get into a car."

Wolf looked skeptical. "A worker getting into car isn't exactly unusual."

"Maybe not," Chuckie said, his crooked grin growing larger. "Except this repairman came out of the place wearin' a suit and hopped into a silver Mercedes at the corner where I was standing. I'm thinking that might be a clue worth a few bucks."

Wolf was in full agreement with that assertion. "You say you've got a photographic memory; can you describe his face to someone who can create an image?"

"There's the rub," Chuckie replied. "It's December and it's freezing, so he had a scarf covering most of his face comin' 'n goin'."

Wolf's eyes tightened. "Then what makes you think the man getting into the car was the repair man that you saw earlier?"

"Couple ways," he replied. "Same height, same eyes and eyebrows and walked the same way."

Wolf turned around in his seat, challenging Chuckie to describe his eyes, eyebrows, the way he walked and any other distinguishing feature about himself. After providing a highly accurate rendition of his face, mannerisms, gait and posture, a convinced Wolf turned back to face this human visual recorder.

"So what can you tell that might allow me to track this man down besides the shape of his eyes and eyebrows?" Wolf challenged.

"He's white, five foot seven, slight build, about a hundred twenty, thirty pounds or so," Chuckie said. "One more thing, I overheard him saying 'wazzo" or something like that before the car door shut."

"Wazzo? Could be he said Wazzzup in greeting," Wolf supposed. "You saw him getting into a silver Mercedes. What kind: SUV? Sedan? Old, new? Did you catch a plate? Sticker? Anything?"

"Silver sedan; seemed new. Didn't spot a plate on account a bunch of potential customers were coming my way," Chuckie said.

Wolf thanked the man, promising that the rest of the money would follow discovery and apprehension of Bellamy's—and presumably—Maddie's killer. He got up to leave when Chuckie said,

"Wait..." His eyes appeared to lose focus, Wolf recognizing the look as his way of sorting through the images in his mind. "I see a sticker on the lower corner of the windshield. It's black with gold printing, but can't tell what it says."

"Silver Mercedes sedan with a black and gold sticker on the windshield," Wolf said, looking pleased. "That's good, Chuckie. Thanks...hopefully you'll have the ten grand before the end of a week."

He turned and started for the door. Wolf passed the bar when a figure slid off the barstool and followed him out.

The bar was situated near the corner of the block, Wolf making a turn at the intersection. He stood waiting, his back to the wall. He didn't have long to wait as his shadow rounded the corner, halting the second Wolf was spotted.

"Excellent disguise," Wolf said. "I looked for you, but didn't see you anywhere."

"Were you worried about me...or you?" Colleen said, coming up to him.

"Me, of course," Wolf replied, a droll expression glowing on his face.

"Good to know I can count on my comic relief to come to my rescue," she replied. "So, we've got a partial description, a silver Mercedes, a snippet that sounded like Wazzzup and a black sticker with gold print. Frankly, it's more than I thought we'd get. I've already uploaded the information to Cooper, he'll search everything connect within a hundred mile radius. He'll get hundreds of hits, I'm sure."

"I'll take hundreds over the nothing we've gotten so far any day," Wolf said, walking back to the car which they'd parked several blocks away. "That Chuckie character is quite remarkable; too bad he didn't do more with that photographic memory than panhandling."

"You yourself have written about the piles of cash some panhandlers accumulate," Colleen said, getting in the car. "Maybe the Chuckster discovered he can rake in enough money during his working hours to make it worth not having to hassle with the daily rush-hour, paying taxes, pushy bosses and annoying sidekicks."

"And being bored to death doing the same schtick day after day," Wolf said. "Frankly, I couldn't do the nine-to-five routine either. I had enough of that in school; why I quit college and pursued professional gambling until I lost it all and had to find another way to make an interesting living."

"And the rest, as they say, is history," Colleen quipped. "I, on the other hand, did very well in school—after my mother got me out of the public one into a private one. Its strict routine and high expectations was perfect for me and got me into officer's training after graduation and here I am today, a successful, hard-ass business woman."

Wolf was about to utter a complimentary remark about her ass, but wisely decided to check his urge. Sitting in the passenger seat, he was easily within Colleen's striking distance.

"You chose wisely," she teased, correctly interpreting his subsequent silence to her comment. A ding sounded and she used voice command to accept the call.

"Hello boss-lady," Cooper said, his deep voice reverberating in the car's interior. "I've started my search for black stickers with gold print within a hundred miles of Manhattan and being the best of the best, have a result. Actually, I have thirty-one results. I'll feed the variables you gave me into a program that will analyzing every hit sorting it into viable possibilities such as an event, business, parking permit and so forth."

"Good work, Cooper," Colleen said.

"Hi, Cooper," Wolf said. "How long do you estimate before your program spits out a list?"

"Let's give it twenty-four hours," he replied.

"Ten-four, good buddy," Wolf quipped.

"Over and out—unless you've got other things to talk to me about, Colleen."

"I'm good; thanks and have a good evening."

"Thirty-one possibilities; very encouraging," Wolf said. "When Cooper's algorithm whittles it down, we might be looking at a dozen or less prospects. That's assuming what Chuckie heard and seen has anything to do with anything."

"We'll know a lot more when we get Cooper's report," Colleen said. "Once we know what we're dealing with, then we'll go from there. I'll make arrangements for teams of my people to assist us if we need help running down leads; that will speed up our search."

They spent the rest of the afternoon pursuing personal activities, Wolf working on the final chapters of his Tara Mason novel, Colleen conducting business via phone, email and videoconferencing. With the approach of dinner, they came out of their respective rooms spending some time together in the sitting area. Wolf updated Colleen about progress made toward the end of the novel, Colleen giving him a brief summary of the dozen management tasks she completed or working on. Seeing him grin, she asked what he was smiling at.

"The workday over, we relax over a drink, each sharing our trials and tribulations of the day," he said. "Just like an old married couple."

Seeing a change in Colleen's expression, he asked her what was wrong.

"Do you ever feel you waited too long? Put an important part of your life on hold while pursuing other interests?" Colleen asked.

"You mean like marriage; a family?" Wolf said. Colleen nodded and he continued. "Absolutely and one reason why I retired from slithering around the muck exposing the hypocrisy and criminal behavior of the high, the mighty, the famous and their lackeys. It was exciting work and rewarding, too, but been there, did that. Time for other adventures."

"Like hunting down killers?" Colleen said.

"That's just a momentary diversion. Though..." Wolf paused, holding her gaze. "I will admit that working closely with you adds an entirely new dimension to my life, one that I very much enjoy."

"I'm thirty-seven," she replied.

"And you look fantastic for an older woman," he teased.

"And can't have children," she replied, giving him a knowing look.

"Kids are a dime a dozen; we can pick up a few at the local nursery," Wolf joked. "Seriously, Colleen. If you're feeling like you're missing out on something you now feel is important, then you need to act sooner than later. Regrets, like sores, fester and become worse over time."

"And you?" she challenged. "If you don't have children, will your regret fester and grow over time?"

"There's always adoption," Wolf replied. "If I do ever get married, I'll only marry a woman who is exciting, beautiful, smart, brave, industrious, thoughtful and loyal. Someone exactly like Colleen Silverstone."

A warm smile grew on her lips. "I'll let her know you're interested, but I imagine she'd like to finish her current mission before contemplating shacking up with man or wolf."

"So noted," Wolf said, his toothy grin acknowledging the reality of the situation.

Love, as he had discovered, even in the best of circumstances, can be littered with hidden boobytraps. During periods of intense emotion, such as hunting down a vicious killer, love is best placed in a locked compartment to prevent fatal distractions or foolish actions.

Wolf rose from his seat. "Dinner?"

"Thought you'd never ask."

*   *   *   *

Cooper's list of possible Syblov locations arrived shortly after lunch the next day, the task requiring less time than he had predicted. But then, it's always better to under promise and over deliver.

"Okay," Cooper said. "We've got five red-hot possibilities matching all or virtually every variable you provided beginning with a veterinarian center named Watts Canine Clinic in Manhattan."

"Vets and their employees are familiar with drugs," Wolf suggested.

"Drugs, yes," Colleen said. "Nerve agents and Dimethyl Sulfate not so much. I assume you're already checking out the owners and employees?"

"All the way back to their cribs," Cooper replied. "If any have ever used DSMO to rub on a dog or their sore shoulder I'll flag 'em. Perhaps more pertinent is that fact that the clinic's owner and the head vet drive silver Mercedes."

"You do realize that you're not paid by the hour?" Colleen fired back. "You could have mentioned the Mercedes at the start."

"See, this is why you're the head of the leading security firm, boss," Cooper chuckled. "You don't miss a trick and you keep our feet to the fire. Take a look at the list; I'm gonna read off the candidates real slow like for the benefit of your furry companion..."

"I'll remember this indignity," Wolf retorted. "Best you keep indoors the next full moon arising, dude."

Cooper snorted and began to read. "Okay, we've got Watts Clinic with two white males and two silver Mercedes ... Wows Technologies, a passel of white males, several silver Mercedes and a black parking sticker with yellow letters and numbers ... Wowzah Publishing, black stickers and the VP drives a silver Mercedes ... Gold Park 101, lots of Mercedes including silver ones and a black-gold condo owner sticker ... and last, but not least by any stretch of the imagination, the Hampton Bays Yacht Club. Lots of pale dudes with lots of silver Mercedes, every one of them sporting beautiful black and gold stickers..."

Cooper paused, clearly for effect. Colleen shot a look at Wolf and grinned.

"And...?" she said, drawing out the word.

"*And*," Cooper said, enunciating the word slowly, "every black and gold sticker is placed at the lower corner of the passenger side windshield. I were a hot shot investigator, I'd put the yacht club at the head of my list and work my way down."

"Good thing Colleen has a hot shot investigator sitting next to her," Wolf said.

"Cooper, is it possible for you to review their membership list and find out what type of car they're driving?" Colleen said. "And having discovered such public knowledge, perhaps discover who they are, what they do and where they live?"

"I should be able to peruse the public domain to discover such bits and pieces," he replied. "Gosh, golly! Turns out I've already populated a database with such pertinent bits and pieces on everyone from our hot five already...must have slipped my mind. I'll send you the file momentarily..."

Momentarily turned out to be immediately as textual information was displayed on the car's dashboard monitor. Colleen and Wolf looked at the data then over at each other with puzzled expressions.

"Cooper, I thought you said you were sending information on everyone," Colleen said. "I only see one name."

"More coming," he replied.

The screen on the dashboard filled up with more information. Looking closely, it was more about the same man.

"Read the part about the company Mr. Blair Cottier represents," Cooper said.

Colleen scrolled down. Her eyes got wider.

"Wossow, Inc." she said. "You are damn good, Cooper."

"Why you pay me the big bucks," he quipped. "Cottier is a perfect match: white male, five nine, hundred thirty eight pounds, silver Mercedes, black and gold sticker in lower corner."

"Colleen," Wolf said, thinking about something. "Chuckie said he got into the passenger side. A second person was in the car: the driver."

"Got you covered, my Wolfman," Cooper said, having heard the comment. "Check the list: there is a Mrs. Cottier."

"So there is," Wolf said, peering at the screen. "Now we're approaching a 100% match. All we need is to drop by, ask them to confess and come with us peacefully. Piece of cake."

"One more thing," Cooper said. "Though it's February, the Cottiers happen to be currently lounging around their lovely Hampton home. If you roll out now, you can catch them sipping their three o'clock martinis on their heated veranda."

Colleen gazed at Wolf who nodded.

"Will do," she said.

"One more thing," Cooper said, causing his listeners to laugh. "I'm a hoot, I know. Mr. or Ms. Cottier or both know how to fly and they've got a helicopter sitting out on the back forty. Thought you ought to know such mundane details."

"Anything else we should know before we make for Hampton Bays?" Colleen said, sarcastically.

"Hmmm," Cooper said. "Like the fact both are members of the gun club?"

"Better and better," Wolf said. "We'll be sure to load for bear, Cooper."

"One more thing," Cooper said, causing Wolf and Colleen to issue loud groaning noises. "The Mrs. was a chemistry major in college, so don't accept a drink, or a cookie and coat your hands with impermeable exoskin to keep out toxins when shaking hands."

"Thank you, Cooper." Colleen said. Grinning at Wolf, she added, "And please do let us know any other possible dangers lurking around the Cottiers before we engage them."

"Roger that. Be careful. Over and out."

Hampton Bays lies over eighty miles east along the southern shore of Long Island, normally a two and half hour road trip. Colleen pushed the envelope arriving in a shade under two hours, rolling up to the Cottier humble Hampton abode on Red Creek Rd. shortly after one that afternoon. The home was surrounded by what Wolf guessed was at least four acres of tame woodland and open areas tastefully clipped, shaped and manicured. Even the winter months with its oppressive cold and damp climate and bare trees could not diminish the splendor of the view. A long, curving driveway led up to the home some hundred yards ahead.

"The Wossow company must be doing pretty well to provide such a cozy nest for the Cottiers to roost in," Wolf said, as Colleen came to a halt at the closed gate blocking access to the driveway.

"Wossow Inc. is a financial holding company," she replied. "Since it is most likely connected to New World Fund and Shred Pro, I'm quite certain that the company is drowning in cash."

Colleen pressed the intercom and waited. A voice asked who was calling and the purpose of their visit.

"Special Agent Cathy Silver, Home and Land Security Agency and Junior Associate Agent William Gray," she said, not missing a beat. "We are investigating acts of domestic terrorism and your names came up as possible targets. We would like the opportunity to speak with you about this important matter."

There was a long pause. Wolf hummed a ditty typically heard when waiting on hold. Colleen shushed him and struck him gently on his thigh.

"Come on up, officers," the voice issuing from the speaker said, the gate opening shortly thereafter.

"Think we fooled them?" Wolf said, as Colleen drove up the drive.

"Not even one bit," Colleen replied, rounding the circular driveway and coming to a halt next to the walkway to the house's entrance.

Wolf pointed to a car parked in front of the garage.

"Late model, silver Mercedes with a black sticker on the windshield."

Chapter 30

Unwrapped and Undone

"Wolf..." Colleen began, walking up to the door.

"No drinks, no cookies, no touching. Got it." Wolf replied.

They were potentially walking into the lair of a most ruthless killer and Wolf took Colleen's cue seriously. His choice of occupation had required him to remain ever alert and vigilant as he insinuated himself into the lives of the high and mighty and though Grayson Wolf was despised and hated by the targets of his exposes, none were stone cold killers seeking to snuff him out. This was Colleen's arena and forte and he wisely deferred to her leadership.

"Please come in," a smiling woman said, opening the door upon their approach. "I'm Serena; welcome. Please follow me to our sunroom."

Had Wolf been adorned with a coat of hair, his hackles would be firmly erect. Having spent years in the company of posers, thieves, liars and cheats, Wolf's sixth sense was a finely honed instrument of detection and its alarm bell was clanging loudly. To an unsuspecting visitor, Serena Cottier would appear to be exactly as she appeared: a petite, attractive woman possessing a comely face, sparkling blue eyes and a warm, inviting personality. To Wolf, Serena was a venomous spider welcoming them to her web of deceit, deception and death. Upon reflection, he thought it rather an excessive appraisal, Wolf deleting the death part of his imagery, which he felt would not occur at their place of residence.

"Hello," Blair Cottier said, standing in front of a large, floor to ceiling window, the afternoon sunlight brightly illuminating the room.

"May I offer you some refreshment, officers?" Serena asked, her voice silky smooth.

"No thank you," Colleen said.

"You said something about domestic terrorism," Blair said, looking concerned. "Are we in danger?"

"We believe there is a strong possibility you might be a target," Colleen replied. "We are investigating the death of Justin Bellamy and Madeline Talbot, which we believe is tied to an international conspiracy."

"International conspiracy?" Serena said, her eyes growing large. "A political one?"

"An economic one," Colleen said. "Apparently terrorists have been using America companies to defraud the public and rake in billions of dollars which is transferred to off-shore shell companies. We believe that Mr. Bellamy of New World Fund had discovered this sham and was killed to keep him quiet. We think that Ms. Talbot might have accidentally discovered a link to the conspiracy and was killed for it."

"That's just awful," Blair said. Serena, looking frightened, moved next to him and grasped his hand. "I don't understand what we might have to do with any of this. We're not involved with that financial company."

"You represent Wossow Inc.," Colleen said. "Wossow is a financial holding company and that makes it a target for these terrorists."

"I'm the resident agent for the firm," Blair said. "Wossow is registered in Bahrain; It's my understanding that the firm processes monetary transfers for all kinds of institution: non-profits, national banks in third world nations and so forth." His expression became alarmed, adding, "My God! Please don't tell me I'm working for some terrorist front funding murder and mayhem across the globe."

They were good, Wolf surmised. Watching Blair's and Serena's expressions and body language the casual observer would be hard not to believe they were genuinely clueless and innocent. But Wolf knew they were acting and thus their great performance was in fact a dead giveaway.

"I'm not at liberty to go into any details, Mr. Cottier," Colleen replied, "But I am allowed to inform you that the company you represent is involved in fraudulent activity and that places you and your wife in grave danger. You see, we are certain that the firm has one or more contract killers residing in the New York area. But let me assure you, we are closing in on them as I speak. In fact, my people have a good idea where they are hiding out, so it's just a matter of time before we place them in custody."

"Well, that's a relief, isn't it, honey?" Serena said, peering at Blair with obvious concern mixed with the proper amount of hope.

"I assure you I have nothing to do with promoting Wossow's evil goals," Blair said. "Will your agency provide us with guards or should we hire private security?"

Colleen slowly shook her head, her expression registering regret. "Because you are clueless about the people you represent, the agency does not consider you and your wife to be prime targets. However, I would advise you to hire armed security because one never knows what cornered rats will do. We best be leaving; thank you for your time and be mindful about the possible threat."

The Cottiers thanked the Home and Land Agents for coming and escorted them to the door. Wolf followed Colleen to the car, feeling a strong sense of relief when he shut the car door.

"Jeezus Colleen; talk about poking the bear," he said, looking at her with astonishment. "For second I thought you were going to say that you knew who the killer is and it's you!"

Colleen started the car. "I was thinkin about it, but better to let them stew for a while. They'll make their move sooner than later and we'll be there to collect the pieces." She drove slowly around the circular driveway, proceeding toward the gate. "I'm sure we won't need to wait too—"

There was a sharp crack as something smashed through the driver side window, bouncing off the windshield unto the floor at Wolf's feet.

"What the hell!" Wolf cried, as the car careened off the drive into the adjacent trees coming to a halt behind a thick stand.

"Keep your head down," Colleen ordered. "That was a round from a rifle. Open your door and get out—stay low."

"How do you know it was a rifle shot?" Wolf asked, sitting on the ground, his back on the rear door.

"Because a pistol round doesn't have enough speed and energy to penetrate my bullet proof windows—semi-bullet proof windows," she replied.

"I guess they didn't need to stew to make a decision," Wolf quipped. "Now what?"

"Now I'm going back there and slap their bottoms," Colleen snarled.

"I'm coming with you," Wolf said.

Colleen peered at him. "No. These people are real professionals, not like the amateurs we ran into in Colorado, Wolf."

"You're bleeding," he replied, reaching a hand above her left eye. "Christ! That's a graze! They almost killed you."

"They would have," she confirmed. "Didn't count on armored glass. Slowed and deflected the bullet. I'm fine; feels like a scratch."

"I'm coming with you," Wolf insisted.

"Wolf—"

Further conversation was cut off when Wolf pressed his lips on hers. Some moments later, he released her from his amorous onslaught and said,

"I'm coming with you. End of story."

"Fine. Now scoot over so I can get in the back."

Wolf edged toward the rear and Colleen opened the door. She reached in and retrieved several weapons and belts studded with ammunition magazines. She handed him one of the belts which also held a holstered pistol and a short semi-automatic rifle, taking another set for herself.

Colleen edged carefully up the side of the car. She produced a monocular which she placed near one eye peering cautiously toward the building. She dropped down just as the sound of a bullet was heard ricocheting off the roof of the car. There being no sound of gunfire, it was clear the shooter was using a silencer.

"Listen very carefully," Colleen said. "They've got a bead on us and the shooter is expert. My guess is he's shooting from the second floor, though I didn't spot a rifle in a window. Your job is to provide suppressive fire so that I can make a run at the building."

"You're going to run toward the house," Wolf said, sounding incredulous. "You'll be in the open and an easy target."

"Thus your critical role providing suppressive fire," she replied. She took his rifle, inserted a long magazine and cocked it.

"You've got thirty rounds plus two extra mags. I want you to aim at the second floor windows starting from the left and work your way across laying down systematic fire pressing off a round every second. When you reach the last window, start back firing every second. I'm going to pepper the windows first, so that you can stick your head and gun far enough above the hood to do the job. When you're out, slap in another magazine and shoot at the bottom windows and door following the same pattern as the top. Understand?" Wolf nodded and she pointed toward the hood. "Keep your head down until I tell you to start laying down fire."

Using a stick, Colleen hoisted a cap toward the top of the car, her effort rewarded momentarily as a bullet ripped the cap off the stick. Standing up, she issued a rapid-fire series of shots, the bullets smashing through the upper floor windows, followed by her doing likewise to the windows on the ground floor. She got back on her knees, popped out the spent magazine and inserted a fresh one. Rising up she fired a few shots then said,

"Now, Wolf!"

Standing up and using the car's hood for as much cover as he could manage, Wolf aimed and proceeded to systematically rake the top floor windows firing off a shot every second or so. Taking a moment to look for Colleen, he saw she was skirting the edge of the tree line using the trees as cover as she made her way rapidly toward the house.

Wolf raked the bottom windows, then stopped.

"Screw this!" he growled and came from behind the car. He ran diagonally up to the driveway and rushed toward the house, firing as he ran. Before he had gotten half way there, he ran out of bullets. Ejecting the empty magazine, he was reaching for his last one when he heard gunshots ahead. Glancing up he saw Colleen close to the house, firing at the second floor windows. He position the magazine, slipped it in, cocked the firing mechanism and proceeded forward, taking measured shots at the windows, reaching the door moments after Colleen did.

She glared at him. "You didn't follow my orders!"

"Get used to disappointment," he grinned.

"Pistols," she said, her tone icy. "Follow me and try not to shoot me."

Colleen kicked the door open and proceeded to fire in various directions then rushed in, continuing to fire at real or imaginary gunmen hiding around corners. Her technique was apparently effective because there was no return fire. With a quick twist of the wrist, she dropped the nearly spent magazine from her pistol and inserted a fresh one proceeding to move cautiously forward, Wolf following several strides behind.

At the end of the entrance, she stopped at the corner and took a quick peek into the room, the bulk of which was situation to her left.

"Drop the gun or I will drop you!" she cried. "Do it now or I will shoot you!"

Apparently her threat worked because she rounded the corner, Wolf right behind her, his gun raised. Blair Cottier was sitting on the sofa, his hands in the air, a pistol lying on the floor. Serena Cottier was standing some feet further away, clearly shocked, staring at her husband with open mouth.

"What did you do, Blair? What did you do?" she cried. "My God, Blair, what did you do?"

"I'm so sorry honey...so sorry," he replied, looking away.

Colleen kicked the gun toward Wolf. He picked it up, dropped the magazine from the handle, cleared the chamber then stuck the pistol in his belt.

"Cover him," Colleen ordered.

When he aimed his pistol at Blair, Colleen holstered hers. She turned to Serena, instructing her to take a seat next to her husband. As she neared the sofa, a triangular blade appeared in her hand and she slashed at Colleen's neck. As quick as Serena was, fortunately Colleen was faster, her hand striking forward and deflecting Serena's thrust. Then things got real exciting.

Taken by surprise, Wolf allowed himself to be distracted from his task, but only for a second.

"Don't move," he said. Lowering his aim a few inches, he added, "You try anything and I will shoot it off. Got it?"

A clearly shaken Blair must have seen the uncompromising look in Wolf's eye because he nodded several times, peering nervously at the business end of Wolf's pistol. Seeing what appeared to be genuine fear in his face, it dawned on Wolf that the real Syblov was currently engaged in a fight to the death with Colleen.

From the corner of his eye Wolf watched as Colleen grappled with the woman, twisting the knife out of Serena's hand, followed by striking her with an elbow, causing a trickle of blood to issue from her lip. Seemingly unperturbed, Serena stuck, a flurry of fists driving Colleen slowly back followed by a swift kick at Colleen's torso, knocking her into a cushioned chair, falling over backward.

Instead of crashing unceremoniously onto the floor, Colleen performed a backwards summersault landing on her feet. Reaching to a side table, she snatched a magazine, rolled it into a makeshift baton and strode toward Serena, Colleen's baton repeatedly striking her target along her arms, several blows landing on Serena's head.

Colleen's assault came to a sudden halt when Serena lunged forward, her body slamming into Colleens', both combatants tumbling unceremoniously to the floor. A wrestling match ensued, with arms, legs and fists flying hither and dither. Serena managed to grab hold of a nearby electrical cord, which she tried to wrap around Colleen's neck. Her effort caused the lamp to fall next to Colleen who used it as a bludgeon, her blows striking within a hair's breadth of Serena's skull, forcing the woman to abandon her effort to strangle her opponent and scooting out of striking range.

Both women got to their feet, Colleen resuming her magazine baton assault. Falling back, Serena took hold of a floor lamp and using the instrument as a spear, thrust it repeatedly at Colleen who ducked and weaved, managing to avoid being struck. When she appeared to lose her balance for a moment, Serena drove the heavy base of the lamp directly at Colleen's head. Apparently Colleen's stumble had been a calculated feint, because her hand shot out grabbing the pole, jerking it along with Serena toward her. Colleen's free hand delivered a solid blow directly into Serena's face, knocking her down.

"I said, don't move, asshole!" Wolf cried, seeing Blair shift.

But it was too late. He had allowed himself to pay more attention to the fight between the women. Blair kicked the coffee table hard, striking Wolf in the chins and causing him to fall forward. Blair lurched toward an end table to his left, his hand reaching for something. A weapon appeared, which he swung toward Wolf.

A rapid series of gunshots followed.

"You bastard!" Serena screamed, spittle mixed with blood issuing forth, seeing Blair slump and slide off the sofa onto the floor.

Wolf was breathing hard. The fall onto the coffee table had wrenched his left shoulder and neck. But he held on to his pistol and when he saw the gun in Blair's hand, he pulled the trigger again and again.

Blood pouring from her nose, Serena scrambled to her feet, a murderous fury propelling her at Wolf, who aimed his pistol at her. Half way to her target, Colleen slammed the base end of the floor lamp against the side of her head and the feared Syblov killer dropped to the floor with a thud. Colleen readied her bludgeon for another strike, but Serena was out for the count, her face and head a bloody mess.

"Bitch!" Colleen spit, looking very much like she might smash the lamp on her head again for good measure.

Glancing at Wolf, she suddenly drew her pistol and fired twice. He stared dumbfounded at Colleen when it dawned on him what had happened. Turning around, he saw that Blair's body had moved several feet from where it was when he had shot him, a pistol in his hand. Wolf's shots must have only wounded him and gathering what strength remained, Blair almost managed to shoot Wolf in the back until Colleen's quick action ended that.

"Thanks," Wolf said, looking back over his shoulder.

He cautiously approached the prone man and removed the pistol from his lifeless hand, pointing his pistol at him just in case as he backed away.

"What a mess," Colleen said, surveying the room. "You okay?"

Wolf managed a grin. "Have you looked in a mirror?"

She ignored him and proceeded to retrieve a nylon tie from a pouch on her belt and fasten Serena's wrists. Then she walked over to Blair, placing two fingers on his throat. Satisfied that he was indeed a goner, she sat on the sofa.

Wolf sat next to her, using a cloth to gently wipe the blood from her face and head. Colleen did likewise on the cuts and bruises on her hand and arms.

Peering at her for a long moment, Wolf said, "You're one hell of a warrior, Colleen. Remind me to never get in a fight with you."

A wan smile touched her lips. Pointing toward Serena on the floor, she said, "She's had military training and honestly, I'm out of shape for hands-on field work."

"Out of shape?" Wolf said, peering incredulously at her. "Colleen, why did they switch from shooting at us to playing casual weekender mode? I expected to shoot our way in and through the house."

"I'm sure they expected to take us out with sniper fire and failing, decided to play a suburban couple beset by house invaders," Colleen explained. "After all, who riddled their house with bullets and stormed through their front door?"

"But then she tried to slice and dice you," Wolf said. "Why?"

"Because I did such a good job convincing Serena we were on to them, which is why she took that shot at us and why she tried to kill me up close and personal," Colleen replied. "There's a lot of land surrounding the house and a big ocean out there where our bodies could disappear."

"Why didn't you draw your gun and shoot her in the knee or something, instead of hand-to-hand combat?" Wolf asked. "For a second when she knocked you over the chair I thought about shooting her."

She shrugged. "Her little knife trick pissed me off. Also a bit of vanity, I suppose, being able to kick her ass."

"What do we do now? We've got to notify the police," Wolf said, looking at the bodies on the floor.

"We'll do that after we search for evidence which we'll need to support our version of events," Colleen said. "I think we'll find plenty of goodies in their personal computers, hidden compartments and elsewhere. Even so, we're going to have a lot of explaining to do before—and if—we get to walk. Let's get busy..."

Chapter 31

Unexpected

"Fortunately for us, Colleen's car had armored glass which messed up the shot," Wolf said.

Wolf and Colleen were sitting in the Jefferson Conference Room at the Center for Individual Rights recounting the events leading up to tracking Syblov and what followed after calling the Hampton Bays police to the Cottier home. A standing-room only audience was listening raptly to the account of the many twist and turns in the story—stories—since the Syblov killer represented only half the investigation. Wolf had already brought everyone up to speed about Tania Johnson, the computer-hacking killer.

"If the glass is bulletproof, why did the bullet pierce it?" someone asked.

"The glass is sufficient to stop small arms fire," Colleen explained. "Rifle bullets will penetrate, though it will slow and deflect the projectile. Serena didn't count on that, adjusting her sights for normal glass deflection thus missing my head—fortunately for me."

Wolf described their subsequent armed assault against the house followed by an exciting rendition of the fight between Colleen and Serena.

"You and Colleen are lucky they didn't decide to kill you the moment you entered their house when you first arrived," Diana said.

"They needed to find out what we knew first," Colleen answered. "And I didn't walk in there unarmed. I was surprised, however, when Serena shot at us as we were driving away."

"Let me get this straight," RJ said, a skeptical expression lighting up his face. "You shoot up their house, kick in the door, beat up the homeowner and shoot her husband. Then you call the cops and tell them to ignore all the bullet holes, smashed up furniture, the dead dude on the floor and arrest the lady of the house for being a contract killer. How did you manage that feat of magic?"

"We were counting on finding proof of their evil deeds," Wolf said. "Before we called the police we did a thorough search looking for anything to connect them to New World Fund and the killings."

"Fortunately we did find evidence," Colleen said, picking up where Wolf had left off. "A treasure trove, in fact."

"Treasure trove indeed," Wolf said. "Videos, recordings, documents, financial records, names, places, photos and frauds committed. The Cottiers had made sure that if anyone in their circle of crime and corruption even *thought* about trying to double-cross them, they would bring the entire edifice down on everyone's heads. Not to mention that after making information public, they'd go on a killing spree and take them all out."

"They sound seriously psychotic," Brett said.

"You don't know the half of it," Wolf replied, grinning meaningfully.

Looking sarcastically at Wolf, Diana said, "I'm so glad you retired from your dangerous occupation as national muckraker to pursue more mundane interests."

Her comment caused the room to erupt in loud laughter. When the commotion died down, Brett said,

"What did you mean, Wolf, about knowing half? What else besides lies, intimidation and murder were our Mr. and Mrs. Cottier into?"

"How about incest?" Wolf said, allowing his comment to sink in before continuing. "Our lovely Hampton Bays couple where more than husband and wife. They were brother and sister first."

"What do you mean, first?" someone asked.

"I mean Blair and Serena are siblings who married each other," Wolf said. "Obviously they forged a different birth certificate for Serena and then proceeded to get married back in 2002. Their contract killer trade name was Syblov: sibling lovers."

"Like I said, psychotic," Diana remarked.

"Incest and murder, the ties that bind." RJ quipped.

"What did the police do when they showed up?" Brett asked.

"We had taken a seat on the front veranda, our weapons laid out ten feet away," Colleen replied. "Before we called the police, however, we had uploaded everything we collected to my people back in Denver as insurance. There are many powerful individuals crawling around Justin Bellamy's financial golden web and I wanted to be sure nothing was going to go missing between Hampton Bays and the various state and federal authorities. Now it's up to them, but I suspect we are going to see a hundred arrests in the next few weeks, including elected state and federal officials."

"The police held us for over six hours while they reviewed our story and saw some of the evidence that clearly marked the Cottiers as Syblov," Wolf said. "We were allowed to go with the stipulation that neither Colleen or myself were to leave the country."

"That's it? Don't leave the county, pretty please?" RJ said, sardonically.

"You do know who Colleen Silverstone and Grayson Wolf are, yes?" Wolf retorted. "We gave them our word and they took it at face value. Colleen and I are off to India on the next flight out tonight."

He said it with such conviction, the audience stared at him with conflicted expressions. Seeing a smile forming on Colleen's mouth, a cascade of noises swept through the room.

"I have some news to tell about the upcoming fall of the house of New World and associates," Juan Mendez, said, looking quite pleased with himself. "The second I heard about what our dynamic duo had done, I contacted the SEC and FBI about certain components and addendums of the Whistleblower law pointing out how the actions of Colleen and Wolf have brought down a multi-billion dollar fraud."

He paused, allowing the import of his comments to be properly digested by the audience. His reward was not long in coming as a rising wave of exclamations began to sweep through the crowd.

"Holy crap!" RJ cried. "We get a percentage of the total amount of the money recovered!"

"How much are we talking about, Juan?" Annika asked. As CIR treasurer such details were important for everything from meeting payroll to planning for future growth and expenses.

"The range is ten to thirty percent," he replied. "They'll try to lowball us, I'm sure, but I'm going to push for twenty and expect they'll settle for fifteen percent."

"I'll assume ten percent and if you can get more, happy day," Annika replied. "Ten percent of a couple billion will be over two hundred million dollars. That will add a needed financial cushion while you and your legal eagles pick at the thousand colleges we're suing."

"In regards to our class action suits against the universities, the recent college scandal where parents have been cheating to get their kids in colleges such as Yale, will help our efforts, too," Juan said. "Think about it: they're arresting parents for cheating to get kids into name colleges, but when the colleges cheat on their admissions standards, for instance, admitting Black students with low scores and excluding Asian ones with high scores, that's okay? How is that any different in essentials from what parents are trying to do: *differentiating* their admissions standards? Anyway, we're looking at using this scandal as further evidence underscoring our class action complaints."

The meeting having run its natural course, people began to discuss things among themselves while some drifted back to their workstations. Diana pigeonholed Colleen, the women retreating to an open corner while RJ rounded up Wolf, the bosom buddies walking to Wolf's closet-sized office.

"What's the latest with you and Colleen? The two of you finally getting down and dirty?" RJ asked, though it sounded more like a demand.

"A gentleman never gossips about affairs of the heart and the bod," Wolf teased.

"So still no action, huh?" RJ retorted, shaking his head in disgust. "Jeezus, bro, the woman is sleeping in your loft. What are you waiting for? Godot?"

Wolf laughed. RJ wasn't anything if not entertaining.

"You remember what the signs on the back of those big dump trucks warn?" Wolf replied. "Pull, don't push. Colleen is not one to be pushed into anything. I am gently pulling, however."

"You pull any gentler and come summer, the woman will have drifted beyond Hawaii on her way to Japan," RJ retorted. "Sometimes you gotta push or nothing moves."

"Colleen knows I'm interested," Wolf said. "No use pushing or shoving or doing a fertility dance. She'll act when she's ready."

"And if she doesn't? How long will you wait?"

"Then we remain friends and partners in crime busting," Wolf said. "And just so you know, Colleen has invited me to accompany her back to Denver. Maybe she's doing some pulling of her own."

"Or maybe you're just a deluded nincompoop who's being lead around by the nose," RJ countered. "Seriously, bro. Don't let her string you along: you're not getting any younger and the pool of rational, attractive and classy women is shrinking fast."

"Tell you what: I'll let her pull me to Denver but no further."

"I will hold you to that," RJ said, giving Wolf the stink eye.

*   *   *   *

"We will split any award we receive from uncovering one of the greatest financial scandals in history fifty-fifty," Wolf said, as the plane lifted off from Washington-Dulles International Airport.

"Fifty-fifty?" Colleen said, eying him. "I'm thinking more like eighty-twenty."

Peering into her glowing eyes he was tempted to give her anything she wanted. But he wasn't twenty and she couldn't be bought for any price.

"As you wish," Wolf said, nodding agreeably. "We're happy with eighty so long as you're good with twenty percent of the take."

Colleen laughed softly. "Fifty-fifty it is."

He wisely avoided any talk of a personal nature during the flight, focusing the conversation on possible fallout from the shooting in Hampton Bays and other related matters. Colleen felt confident that no charges were forthcoming pursuant to their violent encounter with the Cottiers, especially in light of their having handed over a trove of incriminating material that would bring down a dozen corporations and a hundred individual participants.

"The NYPD has dropped all charges against Barry, too," she said. "Though it remains to be seen if anyone or anything connected with New World Fund winds up pointing at him. After all, Barry was Bellamy's attorney for twenty years and client-attorney privilege goes only so far. Bellamy and friends organized and ran a massive criminal conspiracy to defraud investors, stealing proprietary information via Shred Pro, laundering money using overseas shell companies like

Wossow and, assumingly, hiring an incestuous hit team to ensure the game continued to roll smoothly and profitably along."

"So someone put a hit out on Bellamy just in case he was tempted to make a deal pursuant to him facing a life sentence for rape and murder," Wolf said. "Who do you suspect put the hit out on him which also ensnared poor Maddie Talbot?"

"Could be any of the principals of the cabal," Colleen replied. "We'll know a lot more once the feds dig into that rat den."

"I have to admit that using Shred Pro to secure information about companies, product developments, technical breakthroughs or failure to launch a product was a bold move," Wolf said. "Who'd ever bother to look closely at a document shredding service, especially when anyone could watch the paper being shredded in front of their eyes. Brilliant, really."

"Grayson Wolf did," Colleen said, smiling warmly at him.

Gazing at her beautiful face he felt a rising desire. She was sitting next to him...he had stolen a kiss once before, just prior to storming the Cottier residence. He resisted the temptation, however, thinking the current situation not even remotely a dire one and smiled silently back at her instead.

They landed at Denver shortly after seven p.m. A company car picked them up, Colleen instructing the driver to take her home. Twenty minutes later they arrived at Colleen's building. Wolf wished her a good evening, saying that he'd pick her up for breakfast the next morning.

"You won't need to do that," she replied. "I've canceled your reservation. You kindly let me stay with you and I'm returning the favor."

Once upstairs in her condo, she led Wolf to a bedroom. Entering, he knew immediately it was not the guestroom. He looked questioningly at Colleen who smiled in a very provocative manner.

"You have a problem with staying here?"

Wolf held her eyes. "I don't have a problem being anywhere with you."

"Glad to hear it," Colleen said. Her smile lit up the room as she added, "Take off your clothes and get in bed."

Wolf issued a loud sigh. "A man's work is never done."

The End

ABOUT THE AUTHOR

Hunting the elusive author
From sea to shining sea
Where could he be hidden,
Oh, where could she be?

Many drift amazingly near
The writer extraordinaire,
No crew or entourage, our
Novelist traveling solitaire.

Jack N Kolbë eagerly
Composing fiction aplenty,
Is he or she or they
One or perchance, many?

Made in the USA
Middletown, DE
17 May 2019